What reviewers are saying about the stories in
Luna Ten Chronicles

"With her usual excellent writing skills and sensual imagination, Jacobs has produced another winner. This is a fun, sexy read."
4 1/2 -- Top Pick
--Page Traynor, Romantic Times Magazine

"A wonderful feast for the imagination as you wonder what the world will be like in the future… definitely a keeper."
--Claudia McRay, Romance Junkies

"Ann Jacobs takes her readers back to the sinfully delicious pleasure planet of Obsidion, where your every fetish can be realized… The love scenes sizzle with exquisite detail that left me breathless…"
-- Luisa, Cupid's Library Reviews

"When you put together a man who has lost heart and a woman determined, you get absolute magic."
-- Phillipa Ann, Romance Reviews Today

"If you love sex-bots, and sex scenes that singe your eyebrows, then you will want to read this book. Get your copy today!"
-- Janalee, The Romance Studio

Changeling Press, LLC

www.ChangelingPress.com

Luna Ten Chronicles

Ann Jacobs

ISBN (10) 1-59596-547-5
ISBN (13) 978-1-59596-547-9

Publisher:
Changeling Press LLC
PO Box 1046
Martinsburg WV 25402-1046
www.ChangelingPress.com

Printed in the U.S.A.
Lightning Source, Inc.
1246 Heil Quaker Blvd
La Vergne TN 37086
www.lightningsource.com

Anthology Editor: Margaret Riley
Cover Artist: Bryan Keller

The individual stories in this anthology have been previously
released in E-Book format.

In the beginning...

Earth had once been a paradise, or so said the Old Ones who recalled a time before 2187. That fateful year, the Mutants -- Earthlings possessed of a mutant gene left by alien invaders a generation earlier -- rose up against a mighty army of Earth's Federation and practically destroyed the civilization whose beginnings spanned not centuries but millennia.

In the aftermath of the Mutant Wars, Federation Rulers took bold steps to stem the spread of Mutant genes, establishing a system of planned breeding with harsh penalties for failure to obey the law.

Not all Earthlings accepted Earth's new ways.

Federation Star Commander Brad Gilbreath had chanced upon the little planet and bought it -- not long before his act of defiance cost him his place among Earth's elite and sent him hurtling through space, a hazardous journey in the small transporter in which he had escaped the Federation's repressive rule and found this idyllic colony on this small planet named Luna Ten.

Others followed, each with his and her own reasons for seeking a new Eden...

Luna Ten: Cassiopeia

Ann Jacobs

Prologue

Obsidion. Tourist mecca and more, situated at the farthest reaches of the galaxy. The planet meant for pleasure, for indulging every sense, each desire that back home would earn harsh punishment from the Federation Rulers. A place where nothing was forbidden, where geniuses whose creativity was stifled by Federation law could live and work their magic. Where it was said someday the cyborg makers would create a fully functional living, breathing man from nothing but plastics, electronic circuitry, and microchips -- and no law would stop them.

Since he'd been fated to crash his starship, Guy Stone was damn lucky to have crashed it here, for nowhere else would he have been allowed to survive.

Survival. Guy had been given more than survival. He'd received the gift of sight, of hearing, of the ability to walk and run and hold a woman in his arms... gifts he'd never properly appreciated before fate had taken them away in a moment of searing agony that was forever emblazoned on his mind. Guy recalled the brief, terrible moment that had ended in a void until the miracle workers on Obsidion had begun putting his shattered body back together, replacing the irreparably damaged parts with products from the cyborg maker's workshop.

During the tedious months when Guy had lain healing, he'd done his mourning in a dark and silent world, for lost senses and sensations. Then one day he'd felt his legs again, thought just maybe he might want to stay alive. Later, when the bandages had come off his face and he'd returned to the world of light, heard the rasping voice of the aged cyborg maker, he'd set aside his grief. Guy had been resurrected from the dead, half himself, half cyborg.

Anathema to the Rulers of the Federation. An abomination in a world where only perfection was allowed to survive. He'd known right away that they'd kill him if he ever returned to Earth.

So what if he couldn't go home? So what if he'd never again be allowed to captain a starship hurtling through the galaxy? Guy was fucking alive. Alive and functional in every way, thanks to his saviors' skill.

Chapter One

Milling around with hordes of pleasure-seekers from all over the galaxy now, Guy sucked in a gust of heady Obsidion air. Today, he wanted to find the sort of pleasure he'd denied himself for years while serving in the Federation corps, pleasure he'd been in no shape to seek during the long months of his recuperation.

Neon lights blinked red and green and blue along Obsidion's famed Strip, enticing the milling crowd of Earthling tourists to partake of pleasures not even whispered of back home. Guy Stone leaned on the cane he no longer needed, taking in the sights and sounds of the barkers and sightseers. It all seemed foreign to him now, after the long months he'd spent in Obsidion's only hospital, being snatched back by the doctors and a cyborg maker named Pak Song from whatever eternity awaited him.

Guy had been nearly as broken as his starship. So broken that for a long time he'd welcomed the release of oblivion, surcease from pain. Now, though, he was ready to embrace his new life that had been resurrected from the arms of death. Eager to partake of pleasures too long denied him.

His life as a starship commander charged with curtailing the brisk trade of skypirates in the outer reaches of the galaxy was over. The Rulers of the Federation had invalided him out of the corps, ending his career path toward Starship Corps Commander. Returning to Earth, enhanced as he was now, wasn't an option, either. The Federation had strict rules forbidding what it considered hybridizing man with cybernetics, and not even Guy's powerful father could obtain a dispensation for him -- not that he'd have been likely to try. Too bad for them, because Guy felt great -- fit enough to take on the whole fucking universe. Since Earth wouldn't have him, he'd find a better home, where he'd be welcomed as he was today.

In his travels he'd visited Luna Ten, a small planet that welcomed refugee Earthlings to a utopian life free from Federation strictures and rules. Perhaps he'd go there. Of course he couldn't settle there without a mate, unless he could prove his worth in some other way, and he wasn't at all sure any human breeder would accept him with the modifications that had saved his life. But that was a problem that could wait.

For now Guy wanted to enjoy being alive, to try out his newly healed body and take in the sights and sounds that bombarded him from all angles in the famed Obsidion Strip. Infected with the excitement of the tourists, he visually scanned shops that offered pleasures for every taste.

The roulette wheels and playing cards depicted on the facades of three huge casinos held no appeal, nor did the bubbling neon stem glasses advertising drink and drugs strictly prohibited back on Earth. A blinking blue outline of a naked woman caught his eye. His cock suddenly twitched and swelled within uniform pants that had once fit snugly but practically burst at the seams now, since his muscles had grown to rock-hard, enormous proportions. In some ways his body didn't seem altogether like his own, and if Pak Song hadn't told him differently, he'd have thought they'd enhanced his cock, too, when they'd restored his sight and hearing, and provided him with muscle strength many times more powerful than what he'd lost.

Guy was fucking horny. Hard as a rock and straining at the zipper of his pants. For a woman. An Earthling woman to whom he could give as much pleasure as he took. He didn't want a green-skinned Obsidion whore with surgically enhanced silver-tipped boobs, like the one depicted in a flashing neon sign a couple of doors down the street. And he wasn't interested in fucking a sexbot like the ones Pak Song made in his laboratory. He'd had too many orgasms before his injury that had brought physical release but no real pleasure. Sighing, he strode along the Strip, wanting... fuck, he wasn't certain exactly what it was his newly enhanced body craved.

Yes, he did. Or rather he knew what the man inside the body wanted. He yearned for a soulmate. The soulmate he was unlikely to find working in a pleasure resort.

But then he turned the corner onto the Street of Slaves, and there she was. Obviously a vacationer, not one of the Strip's many female pleasure-givers. Guy imagined tunneling his fingers through her reddish-gold hair that sparkled in the reflected light from a star-shaped shop sign: Earthling Sex Slaves. Concentrating to bring his newly functional eyes into perfect focus, he looked through the modest jumpsuit she wore at her high, firm young breasts, the slightly convex belly and satin-smooth mound that didn't hide the enticing button of her clit. His mouth watered when he imagined burying his face within her silken folds, flicking that impudent nub with his tongue. Damn, his balls had already started to ache.

An Earthling woman, she was one of three. Young. Malleable, Guy imagined. Her eyes twinkled with apparent excitement -- she must have been on her first holiday here. Not yet as jaded as her two companions, who were encouraging her to pick one of the half-dozen naked Earthling men posing on a rotating floor within a curved plate-glass window. He stared at her perky little clit, imagined tonguing it until she screamed for mercy.

"I couldn't. They... they're..."

"Come on, Cassie. For once in your life you've got to fuck a real man. Forget what your mama told you about waiting until it's time for you to breed. These guys have all been fixed. They're no more going to make you pregnant than if they were sexbots. Look, number five is winking at us. Can't you just imagine having his big, hard cock ramming into your pussy?"

So his woman's name was Cassie. Guy tuned out what the other girls were saying. Sometimes it got damn annoying, being able to hear ten times as well as he had before he was enhanced.

When he tuned back in, he heard Cassie say, "You two go on and have your fun with your Earthling slaves. I'll just look around out here, maybe go to that sexbot store in the mall that Yolanda mentioned."

That would be Pak Song's House of Pleasure. Guy had been around long enough to know where the best of everything forbidden could be found here on the galaxy's most famous resort planet. And Pak Song made the best sexbots he'd ever seen. He'd admired the old Earthling's skill with robotics and artificial intelligence long before Pak Song had applied that knowledge to restore Guy's own sight, hearing, and mobility.

For the first time since long before the injury that had nearly killed him, excitement bubbled in his veins. It might be a sexbot that Cassie wanted, but it would be Guy Stone, enhanced Earthling human-slash-cyborg, that she'd get.

Not just for a night's pleasure, either. A picture of the utopian community on Luna Ten flooded his memory, and he imagined Cassie there, his willing mate, ripening with his seed. Maybe... In any case, he was compelled to follow her, fuck her, and explore the paths they might take. Lengthening his stride, he quickly overtook his prey and preceded her into the mall's outer courtyard.

* * *

Omigod! Each storefront boasted another phallic symbol, more erotic toys. Lingerie to inflame dead men. Potions guaranteed to enhance sexual potency. Hairdressers and manicurists and -- omigod again -- there was a hunk who ought to be selling his magnificent body over at the Earthling Sex Slave Emporium where she'd just left Doreen and Nebula. Long shaggy dark-brown hair and beard and his chalky-pale skin hinted he'd been away too long from a civilization where male heads were always shaven, male skin hairless and deeply bronzed by the sun.

Omigod again. Cassiopeia Denton's gaze settled on the man's hard ass -- the most gorgeous male tush she'd ever seen -- and rippling thighs the size of tree trunks, encased in black leather pants like those that Star Commanders wore. Skin-tight pants that matched a likewise skin-tight leather shirt and gleaming knee-high black boots. His cock would be -- *Cassie girl, keep your cool.*

You came here to find a hottie of a sexbot, and that's just what you're gonna do. But she kept staring at the guy's tight ass until he disappeared inside an old-fashioned looking shop with a red-and-white pole that reminded her of a candy cane. Damn, but he had her panting after him and getting warm and damp inside, and she hadn't even seen him up close.

Makeovers by Leander. That was the name of the place where the hunk had gone. But she didn't see him inside when she peered through the plate-glass storefront at a display of grooming products and exotic jewelry backed by a rich burgundy velvet drape. Should she follow him? She wanted to, even had the door pushed open before changing her mind. Chickening out, her friends would have said, and they'd have been right.

Regretfully, Cassie headed for a toy store. If she was getting a sexbot, she should also get some toys to enhance her experience with it. And some exotic fruits to nibble while her sexbot sucked on her. She'd go to the Intragalactic Market next, then to Pak Song's famous House of Pleasure. No, maybe she'd go get her clit pierced first, at that studio she saw that advertised they used the new, self-healing method that didn't hurt. Doreen swore her piercing there made her orgasms ten times stronger...

Suddenly Cassie pictured her doting father -- imagined what he'd say to her, remembered what he'd yelled at Doreen when she'd gotten that piercing a few months back. *Females of the ruling class don't look for thrills. They do their duty, breed new generations of Rulers with the seed of the Chosen males.* He'd sent her here, along with her half-sisters, with strict instructions that they get the wildness out of their systems before she and Doreen would be bred, Nebula neutered because of her defective gene.

Cassie shuddered. Once, just once in her boring life, she'd like sex to grab her up, blow her away to another place in her head. A place her friends all talked about, a place she'd never been. She wanted a real live man, if only she had the nerve. She wanted that hunk with the long silky hair and bulging muscles that she'd almost followed into Leander's. Too bad she hadn't scared up the courage to follow him in there, but she hadn't, so she'd have to make do with a 'bot. Focusing her gaze on a display of multicolored glass dildos beneath a shimmering ball light, she stepped inside the toy store.

* * *

The buzz of Leander's electric clippers rang noisily in Guy's ears. It was fuckin' hard, even with the months of training he'd endured, to shut down his phenomenal gifts of superhuman hearing and sight. The enhanced sensation had replaced total darkness and silence to which he'd almost acclimatized himself before Pak Song had installed the sensors and reopened his world. Guy hadn't tested the strength enhancement yet, but he figured that if he got in a situation where he needed raw physical power, having the super dose of it he'd been given would come in handy. Now, the sharp buzzing sound of the clippers was grating on his senses. It was fucking giving him the sort of throbbing headache no sexbot and not more than a handful of men would ever be bothered with.

The brush of his own severed locks as they slid against the towel the barber had draped over his bare shoulders reminded him how every touch, each breath of air against his body now produced sensation magnified a hundred times by the new, enhanced sensory centers embedded deep within his brain. His balls tightened when he imagined Cassie bombarding those heightened senses with her warm, wet breath, her gentle touch. He damn well might die of pleasure overload when he sank his cock inside her tight, sopping cunt.

Closing his eyes, he tried to turn off his brain to the buzzing of the clippers as they passed over his skull, and concentrate instead on the soft sensations of feminine hands and hot wax. Wax that would rid his body of the rough hair that had been allowed to grow during his hospitalization.

Fuck, concentrating on the waxing was a lousy idea. It hurt like hell when the attendant began ripping away the cloth strips -- and his hair.

Desperate to distract himself from the bombardment of sound and feeling, Guy went on a mental search for Cassie. Yeah.

There she was, buying some nipple clamps -- no, not clamps, but rings. Shiny silver rings connected by a thin gold chain. Three of them. Two for her pert nipples -- he saw they already had holes -- and the third to pierce the impudent little nub that peeked out below her plump, pale mons. He fuckin' loved the way she smiled when the blue midget clerk, obviously a refugee from that colony on Gamma Minor, dropped them into a bag and pointed her toward a display of vibrators and butt plugs. His balls tightened and his cock began to swell when he imagined how those rings would look, dangling from her nipples and glittering in her pretty clit.

Her *oohs* and *ahs* over the biggest of the dildos made him chuckle. Wait until she got a load of her "sexbot's" very real cock and balls. Distracted for a minute by the agonizing pain that followed a jerk of an attendant's hand on hot wax she'd slathered over his groin a minute earlier, he concentrated again, finding Cassie again in time to watch her drop a set of graduated-size anal stimulators into the bag beside the delicate rings and a big, realistic looking glass dong.

"You want big ring, to match this big cock?" The smiling attendant tweaked the tip of his penis.

"Huh?" How the hell did she know he was imagining tweaking those gold rings in Cassie's puckered nipples, catching the one in her clit between his teeth? Then Guy realized the woman was asking if he wanted a ring in his PA piercing, the one he hadn't thought about until now. What the fuck had happened to the thick gold curved barbell he'd worn since his dad had given it to him for graduation? Probably in the safe at the hospital, he guessed, along with his identity papers and the insignia he noticed had been removed from his shirt, most likely as soon as the medical decision was made that he'd have to be enhanced. "Oh. Yeah. And replace the others, too." No self-respecting Earthling would present his unadorned cock to a lady.

"You want wax or shave?" Leander asked, rubbing a hand over Guy's freshly clipped scalp.

"Shave. But get it smooth." It had never bothered Guy to lather up every morning and scrape off the stubble from his skull as well as his face. Besides, the idea of enduring a wax job there, with his enhanced sensitivity, was more than he could bear. On the other hand, he didn't relish listening to Leander's razor cutting through each of the million or so hairs atop his head, or enduring that deafening sound every morning for the foreseeable future.

Apparently Leander realized he was waffling, because he grinned and said, "Wax get it smoother, boss. Like baby's ass. Then tanning lamp. Ten minutes, make you look like you just spent month on Bali beach back home. You not have to have it done again for a week, maybe longer."

Guy laughed. "Okay. If you insist." He gritted his teeth when Leander ripped off the first strip of wax from above his left ear. "Ow, damn it, I heard each and every one of those hairs screaming for mercy."

"Sorry, so sorry. Look, my girl bring pretty baubles to help you impress the ladies. Real gold. Real precious stones brought all the way from Earth and that mining outpost they opened up last year on Mars. Make your cock shine like your scalp will after you try my tanning lamp. Pick what you like. I make you good deal. Real good." Leander laughed, then jerked another strip of hot wax off Guy's throbbing scalp.

What would Cassie like better? Smooth gold or sparkling faceted stones? Guy spotted a simple thick gold cock ring adorned with nothing but a cabochon ruby inset in a good-sized captive bead. He selected it and a dozen matched ruby-studded barbells for the frenum ladder that marched down the underside of his cock and through the four perfectly aligned pairs of piercings in his ball sac. Large ruby studs would fill the holes in his left ear and nostril. As Leander ripped another strip of wax off his stinging head, Guy remembered Cassie's purchase and imagined having her chained to him at chest and groin. "Can you pierce my nipples?" he asked as the girl was putting away her wares.

"Oh, yeah, boss. I love a man with rings in his nipples." She scurried into a back room, only to return with her supplies. "I brought the rings that match this one," she said, tweaking his new PA ring. "Your lady will like them."

Suddenly Guy recalled the pain that had followed the ritual piercings of his cock and balls. Pain he'd suffered before Pak Song enhanced his senses. "I hope you use the new method I've heard people talking about," he muttered, dreading the needle but too proud to back out.

"Don't worry. This pierces and seals the hole, one quick stick and it's over. Won't hurt, I promise." The girl held up what looked like a tiny laser gun.

Although he'd braced himself for agonizing pain, these piercings didn't hurt at all except for an initial light burning sensation. Half an hour later he stood, admiring Leander's handiwork in a full-length mirror, enjoying the bombardment of erotic sensations: the movement of warm air against his newly hairless and deeply tanned skin, the swaying of his cock and nipple rings, and the weight of them and his other body jewelry.

Damn, he was already half-hard and anticipating the pleasure of fucking Cassie. "Good job, my friends. No one would guess by looking at me that I just spent months lying in bed over at the hospital."

His mind zeroed in on Cassie, found her leaving the Intragalactic Market with a basket of fruit, and hurrying toward the entrance to Pak Song's. Fuck, he had to hurry! "You still have that entrance to the back room at Pak Song's?"

"Yes, boss. Right through that curtain. Pak Song still keeps his sexbots there, all lined up waiting for customers. Go through the storeroom, and you'll get to his shop. Wait minute, don't you want your clothes and cane?"

When Guy concentrated, he saw Cassie again, hesitating just a minute before stepping through Pak Song's front door.

"No time." Sexbots didn't wear clothing anyhow. Heedless of his nakedness, for it wouldn't matter now, Guy held out a hand so Leander could scan his thumbprint to get his fee. Retinal scans were out, he guessed, for folks like him who had cyborg eyes. "Thanks," he said on the way out the back door and into Pak Song's storeroom. Listening hard, he was able to make out Cassie's shy request: "I'd like an Earthling sexbot for my pleasure, sir."

"Would that be a male or female, pretty lady?"

"Of course, a male sexbot. After all, I am a woman."

"Oh, yes. That you are. For you, I recommend the giant luxury model." Pak Song clapped his chubby hands, the noise reverberating in Guy's ears. "One night with him, my beauty, and you'll never be without a Pak Song sexbot again. Two hundred fifty Obsidion dinars a day, and a bargain he'd be at twice the price."

"If you think so…" She sounded interested, yet uncertain.

Guy loved her innocence, her shyness. But he had to hurry if he was to pass himself off as that sexbot.

Striding up the line to the first and biggest robot, he concentrated on discerning its mechanism and disabling it with the laser beams implanted in his eyes. He'd never tried using them that way before, except in practice sessions with his therapist. Hurrying now, he stripped off the sexbot's silver collar and leash and strapped it around his own thick neck.

He hesitated a moment when he noticed the wicked chastity device locked on the sexbot's cock and balls, then beamed it open. Wincing, he clamped it over his own burgeoning erection and set the lock. Every place the damn thing touched pinched one of the neural implants beneath his skin.

For a minute Guy hesitated. His equipment obviously worked to a degree, or he wouldn't be rock-hard and throbbing. He worried, though. What if he was more machine than man? What if he stayed like this for hours, unable to get off?

Fuck, he couldn't think about that now. Ignoring the bite of the chastity device, he strode through the door to Pak Song's showroom, praying to all the gods that the cyborg maker was giving Cassie the right key so he wouldn't have to beam it open, blowing his cover before the action even started.

Chapter Two

Oh my. Her sexbot looked almost real. His gleaming, golden skull reflected a fiery glow from Pak Song's red neon lights when he strode through the door behind the counter. Smiling, he bowed before his owner, exchanging a few words in the strange Obsidion tongue. Then he nodded toward her. Smiling, he handed her his leash. His eyes glowed scarlet, as though he could see through her clothes and liked what he saw, and his full, sensual lips curled up at the corners. The ringed, bulbous purple head of his huge, swollen cock jutted from the end of an ornate silver chastity belt. The belt for which his owner had just handed her the key.

So this was the giant deluxe model Pak Song had sold her on. Whew! Cassie's heart beat faster when he moved beside her, his ringed nipples just below her eye level, reminding her of her own piercings and the slim chain that tugged at them and the new, hypersensitive one in her clit, a constant reminder that they were there... and that her flesh was needy but as yet untouched.

"Shall we go now, mistress?" The sexbot's voice was deep and rumbly, like whiskey and honey, when he gestured pointedly toward the door.

Why was it she felt more like a slave than a mistress? It wasn't this sexbot's impressive size as much as the commanding tone of his voice... the heat of his hard flesh beneath her hand when she laid it over his heart and felt the slow, measured simulated breathing for which Pak Song's sexbots were renowned. The rippling of muscle she'd never expected to feel unless she sampled a real, living human male. Her pussy clenched, and her newly pierced clit swelled and tightened with fear -- and anticipation -- when she imagined unlocking the chastity belt and unleashing the luscious beast trapped inside.

"Y-yes. Let's." The key in her hand felt warm, reflecting her heat, her desire. "This way," she said, tugging at his leash when they came to the broad avenue where Yolanda's Resort Hotel lay nestled in a grove of limbless trees.

"You're staying at Yolanda's?" her robot asked as she led him through forbidding looking gates toward a building now painted in storybook tones of yellow and blue and gold. "You know, this place used to be called the Gates of Hell."

"Yes, Yolanda herself told us the story of her enslavement, and of how she came to become mistress here after the evil Mistress Mara met her fate. You are well programmed," she said, sure now Pak Song had truly provided her with a bargain when she'd negotiated for -- "What do I call you?"

"Guy Stone, at your service. Here to fulfill your darkest dreams, unearth the secret passions deep inside you and bring them to the light." His deep voice poured over her like honey, and she had no doubt he'd pleasure her as well or better than any of the human sex slaves who were likely plying their trade now behind Doreen and Nebula's closed bedroom doors.

"Well, Guy Stone, I shall expect you to deliver all you promise." She unlocked the door to her small room, stepped inside, and watched his muscles ripple as he passed through the threshold and filled the small room with his presence. "I'd have you begin now." A shiver went through Cassie, for she had the feeling the sexbot with the rippling muscles and the honeyed voice would deliver all right. That and more than she'd bargained for... more than the shy country girl in her could take.

* * *

The air crackled, appeared charged with the aura of dominance and submission that had been played out here over the resort's long stretch as the Gates of Hell. But Cassie kept the room from seeming small and dark. Guy had no trouble envisioning the walls studded with hooks and eyes... a St. Andrew's cross occupying the space where an inviting bed now stood... oiled whips of various lengths and styles, hung on the neat row of hooks above the single narrow window. It seemed Yolanda's face-lift of the place had stopped with an outside paint job and the planting of a few scraggly flowers around the wrought-iron gates.

For this was a room ideal for a scene of dominance and submission. His dominance. Cassie's willing submission.

He imagined Cassie stretched upon that cross, helpless to resist the attention of his lips, his tongue. Himself taking those anal stimulators she'd bought and stretching her tight ass until she was able to take him there. Ramming his cock up her ass and filling her sopping cunt with that psychedelic pink-and-purple glass dildo. His cock began to swell painfully against the restraint of the chastity device. "Set my cock free, pretty lady, and I'll show you pleasure greater than any you've ever known."

Her eyes wide, as though she just now realized she might have bitten off more sexbot than she could handle, she fumbled in her fanny pack. Trying to recall the names of every god in the universe, Guy sent out silent prayers to every one of them that she'd find the key quickly before he took matters into his own hands -- or eyes, to be more accurate. He let out a long sigh when she dragged it out and knelt where she had a good view of the mechanism on the chastity device.

She also had a good view of his bulging cockhead that was already dripping pre-come around its brand-new ring and glistening almost as much as Cassie's golden hair in the flickering gaslights that lit the room. "Hurry," he croaked before remembering that a sexbot wouldn't care how long it took a client to free its mechanical cock and balls.

"Oooh. You're pierced just like an Earthling." The chastity belt hit the floor with a metallic clank, and Cassie ran an inquisitive finger over his jewel-studded shaft.

"Yeah. I am." It was all Guy could do not to toss her to that bed and show her he was no sexbot but a real, live Earthling male. An Earthling male ready and willing to show her all the pleasures forbidden to them by the governing Federation on their home planet. One who hadn't been made "safe" like the ones at the Earthling Sex Slave Emporium. "Disrobe and we shall get on with the pleasure for which you obtained me," he said, keeping his voice steady, deep, and robot-like.

"I've always wanted to be mastered. Would you like to undress me?"

What he'd like would be to rip off her shimmering pink jumpsuit and sink his cock into her sopping cunt. "If you wish," he said, as though his fingers weren't itching to drag down that zipper and reveal the bounty his enhanced vision had already allowed him to enjoy. "Would you wish your mastery to be physical or emotional?"

She looked at him, smiling. "Why, physical of course. No sexbot has feelings."

"I'm a very special sexbot. If you wish it, I can make you love me."

"Do you think so? Then do. Prove it to me." Her eyes held challenge too great for him to resist. "If you want, you may use the toys I bought. My sexbot back home uses them to heighten my pleasure."

He glanced at the anal stimulators. "You enjoy having your ass fucked?"

"Sometimes." He found the flush on her cheeks endearing.

"Very well. Lie on the bed and spread your arms and legs. Be silent, and do not move unless I order you to. Imagine there are silken bonds holding you open and vulnerable for me." He took the smallest of the butt plugs and rubbed it along her sopping slit. "You'll need stretching more than this to take my cock."

Gently, he spread her satiny butt cheeks and worked the small, glittery plug into her tight little hole. "Easy, relax now." Once the plug was seated inside her, he spread her satiny cunt lips and tongue-fucked her until she rewarded him with a gushing gift of warm, slick fluid. His own cock ached with need to fuck her, but he lapped her clit while tugging gently at the chains that connected its ring to the ones in her hard, reddened nipples.

"Oh, yesss. More. Please." Her throaty purr had his balls so tight he thought they'd burst.

He lifted his head, met her needy gaze. "You're ready to take the larger one now." Slowly, sensually, he removed the small stimulator and replaced it with the medium-sized one, watching her inner muscles strain at the new invasion. "Imagine you kneeling on the bed, your pretty ass in the air. Imagine taking my cock instead of this plug. Think how you'll love it when I fuck your ass and work that big dildo of yours in and out of your swollen cunt. I'll do it, soon enough."

"Now, please --"

"I said be quiet. Feel. Enjoy. I am here to bring you pleasure. To show you the outer limits of all that's erotic. I'm going to taste you and suck you and drink this sweet nectar --" He ran his tongue along her velvet slit, savoring the tart, slightly salty taste of her cunt, the faintly alcoholic overtone from the light perfume she wore. "-- and then I'll fuck your mouth and your cunt and your ass until you've come so many times you can't remember your own name, much less mine." He buried his face between her legs again.

Cassie loved the feel of his full, velvety lips applying the most delicious suction to her clit. More juices gushed from her cunt and wet the tautly stretched tissue around her asshole. Her flesh throbbed around the plug, the sensation not quite painful... perversely pleasurable. The rubies in his ear and nose ring glittered, their color nearly matching his intriguing scarlet eyes. Framed between her pale thighs, his golden-tanned scalp looked almost gilded in the light of the gas lamps, as though he were made of metal, not human male flesh.

Of course he wasn't a real man. But he certainly was a far cry from the sexbot she kept in her room back home. The bulging muscles of his arms rippled against the backs of her thighs, and his fingers rasped against the tender skin of her belly, her breasts. And the wicked things he did with his mouth. The way his tongue worked her clit was magical, and his velvety lips! It was downright sinful, what they did when he pressed them to her pussy and applied just the right amount of suction. By all the gods and goddesses, nothing and no one had ever made her clit swell and harden and her cunt clench with the desire to take in his big, jeweled cock and make it her own.

"Fuck me now. Please."

He looked up, cradling her ass cheeks in his big hands and squeezing them ever so lightly. "We have all night. Longer. Breathe deep. If you can take this last plug, you should be able to accept my cock."

She wanted to. Wanted to take that huge, ringed organ in every orifice, surrender herself to him in every way. She longed for him to let her move so she could pleasure him as well as taking pleasure. "Oooh." The large plug, lubricated with some slick, soothing fluid that eased its path, stretched her sphincter muscle almost unbearably, even though he worked it in slowly... carefully... she'd almost say lovingly if she hadn't known for certain no sexbot could be programmed to give love.

"Easy. Relax for me. You can take it, all of it. When you do, I'm going to fuck your cunt with my cock while I tongue-fuck your pretty mouth. Slow and easy. We're gonna be nipple to nipple, belly to belly. Touching everywhere, inside and out. I'll be you and you'll be me."

What? Her rented sex toy seemed very, very real, as though he had a heart and soul as well as the throbbing cock that now pulsated against her inner thigh. Each pair of beads along the underside and down the center of his sac made its imprint on her flesh, and the ring at its tip nudged at her swollen outer lips, exciting her unbearably. His fingers trembled against her ass when he worked the plug slowly, gently into her, stretching and filling her rear passage while he whispered words of encouragement, erotic words that had her wanting to do his bidding, needing to take everything he offered.

The skin of his huge cock felt velvety soft when he rubbed it between her wet, swollen cunt lips. Its smooth metal ring caressed her, reminded her that beneath its velvet surface, his flesh was rock-hard and throbbing with desire. He drew on the chain that connected her body jewelry, making her squirm and whimper despite his order to be still and quiet.

"You're ready. Ready to be filled, to become my woman in every way." Positioning his cock, he flexed his powerful hips and drove into her.

So tight. So full. Every motion -- even the pulsing of the veins in his huge shaft -- magnified, spread to her womb, her ass. Her clit swelled against its tiny ring, throbbed against his smooth, muscular groin when he sank his cock all the way, made her take more until all he had to offer rested inside her, nudging the opening to her womb. His satiny ball sac nestled in the crack of her ass, keeping the plug vibrating from the outside while the throbbing of his cock within her cunt traveled through the thin wall of tissue between it and her stuffed rear passage. With every thrusting motion, she felt his rock-hard flesh, and each of the jewels that adorned it.

She'd have screamed with the incredible pleasure-pain of it, but he took her mouth, plunging his tongue in and out in time with the pistoning motion of his hips. His nipple rings abraded her breasts, caught momentarily on hers.

Bombarded from all directions, filled as she'd never been filled before, she clamped down on his cock, wanting every nuance of feeling, needing to feel each of the smooth, paired jewels that adorned his monster shaft. Her belly clenched. Her clit throbbed. She sucked hard on his invading tongue as he plunged into her harder, faster, gathering her in his iron-muscled arms when she began to shudder with the hottest, hardest orgasm she'd ever experienced.

And for the first time in her life she felt hot semen bathe her womb in long, staccato bursts that fed her climax and kept it going on forever. Pak Song apparently hadn't been joking when he'd told her she was renting the deluxe, luxury model, she thought as she lay in Guy's arms, for he not only looked human. He functioned like one, too.

Chapter Three

Hours later they lay across her bed, breast to chest. Guy's amazing human-feeling cock nestled snugly in the vee between Cassie's legs when Doreen and Nebula burst through the connecting door. Her amazing sexbot's massive chest even rose and fell as though he were asleep, not merely shut down to recharge his power supply.

"If I'd known they made sexbots like that one, I'd have gone with you instead of picking out a live sex slave." To Cassie's way of thinking, Doreen was paying way too much attention to the naked sexbot's perfect ass. Her half-sister was practically drooling. "The slave I got complained the whole time we were fucking that he needed a day off, and that his boss had been withholding his testosterone shots and overworking him to the point that he could barely get a hard-on. May I borrow *him*?" She shot Guy another lascivious look.

"No." It was absurd, she knew, but Cassie had no desire to share her sexbot, sisters or no. "Go rent one of your own at Pak Song's. I'm going to find out if this one's for sale."

Nebula laughed. "Our Cassie's gone and fallen for a robot. Hey, that's funny."

"He's not just any robot." If only Doreen knew what he'd done to her, how he'd made her feel feminine, helpless -- loved, although Cassie knew that emotion was absurd.

"I can tell." Doreen raked Guy's hard body with a longing gaze. "He's a yummy, yummy sexbot for sure. What's the name of that place again?"

"Pak Song's House of Pleasure. Yolanda mentioned it, but you two were too busy listening to her push the sex slaves. How was yours, by the way?"

Nebula shrugged. "Well, he could get it up. And he did fuck me with more enthusiasm than the guy Doreen chose. Still…"

"It wasn't as good as Yolanda told us it would be." Nebula tossed her chestnut curls. "You'd better not get too attached to that one. Something tells me he wouldn't meet the Federation's standards for an imported sexbot. You know, they can only have so much power. Damn, but that one looks good." She shot Guy a longing look as she and Doreen left for Pak Song's.

Too good to be true. But damn! Cassie wasn't ready to give up her Guy. She wrapped her arms around him, the way he hadn't let her do when they were making love.

Cassie smoothed her hand along the sleek, golden skin of Guy's hard-muscled back. Warm skin, with a light coating of sweat still lingering. By all the gods in the universe, he seemed like he was real. Especially when his cock stirred and began to swell against her swollen pussy... and when he sighed and exerted a very human-feeling pressure on her buttocks with his large, gentle hands, drawing her lower body flush against his own.

"Lie back and let me love you," he whispered, his words no less commanding for the soft tone in which they were delivered.

* * *

Going slowly just might kill him, but Guy had to sample every inch of Cassie's alabaster skin, bathe each damp satiny fold of her pussy with his tongue. He'd nibble her nipples and her clit, and trace the golden chain that joined the delicate rings adorning those delicious nubs. Guy longed to forget the preliminaries and take her now, feel her glove his cock again in her tight, slick cunt.

Another benefit of Guy's improved vision, strong enough to make him forget -- almost -- the scarlet color of his irises that made him look somehow less than human: the clear view of her cunt even now, when it wasn't in his direct line of vision. A delicious sight it was, pouting and swollen within her glistening outer lips, already dripping pale, creamy honey. Being able to see the almost imperceptible tremor in her lush body as she lay there at his command sent a thrill through him, and tiny whimpers he doubted would have been audible to human ears bombarded him, inflamed him more.

Even though Guy had come in her a few short hours ago, his cock felt as though it were about to burst. He had to touch her. Experience her by feel, by taste, by the smell of his musk and hers, mingling to perfume the room. Her reddish-gold hair beckoned him when he stretched out above her, sparing her his weight by bracing himself on his knees and elbows.

When he pulled her hair back, baring the satin skin of her throat and shoulders, the soft strands felt like silk. His nipples tingled with the weight of their new rings, the friction of them brushing against the soft flesh of her lush breasts. The tip of his cock probed her damp, warm folds, his pre-come mingling with her honey. The slickness eased the friction of flesh on flesh, its sound soft, more gentle than the rasp of his cheek against her throat.

Oh, shit. He had to close his eyes. Seeing her expression, full of desperate desire and unslaked need, threatened to shove him over the edge. Laying his cheek on her breast, Guy fought for the sort of self-control that would have come easily to the robot he was supposed to be. His nostrils flared. He felt them distending, as surely as he'd have seen them if he'd been looking in a fucking mirror, when he inhaled the incredibly arousing flowery scent that clung to her skin, wafted around his head.

She trembled, and the whimper that escaped her lips when he took a nipple between his teeth and worried the little gold ring with his tongue sounded more like a scream to his oversensitive ears. Gods, but she was responsive beyond his wildest dreams. He flailed her nipple harder, tugging gently at the chain that joined it and its mate to her pouting clit. The shudder that went through her when he tweaked her swollen clit between his thumb and forefinger told him how strongly his touch affected her.

She came over and over, trembling and whimpering at each touch of his fingers, his tongue, even his ringed nipples against hers. Guy's balls protested, telling him with silent agony that he needed release, too. Still he toyed with her, pleasured her, striving to master her body as she'd conquered his soul at first sight. Before he admitted his deception, he'd have her drugged with satisfaction. She'd be craving him so much it would no longer matter that he was a washed up starship commander no longer welcome at home on Earth, a creature made more of Pak Song's electronic parts than human flesh, in so many ways.

The large glass dildo sparkled in the lamplight, as though daring him to deny his own need, pleasure her more before taking his own release. He closed a fist around it, shivering at the cold, rigid surface that wasn't unlike the cock of the sexbot whose identity he'd borrowed to have this time with Cassie. Rubbing the dildo between her breasts, Guy watched her tremble, then swallowed her little scream when he took her mouth and tangled his tongue with hers.

"Are you my willing slave?" he whispered when he broke the kiss.

Her beautiful, very human eyes opened wide, as though she could see through him as he could see through her. "Yes. I want you to take me, master me. Show me every erotic pleasure I've ever dreamed of... pleasures I will never know again."

Yes, she would. He'd pleasure her like this for the rest of their lives. Rearing back on his haunches, he rubbed the dildo along her wet channel, dipping it into her cunt and then withdrawing it. Her whimper of protest made him bend, tongue her swollen clit and rub cheeks now rough with several hours' growth of beard against the incredible softness of her mound. He'd never realized until now that the rasp of beard against a woman's soft, damp flesh was so arousing... so erotic.

"Roll over now. I'm going to fuck your ass the way I said I would." Reaching into her bag of toys, he found one of the condoms that had been considerately packaged with the anal plugs, and a lush, ripe banana. Quickly, he rolled the heavily lubricated condom over his erection, then peeled the banana and laid it on the bed, within easy reach.

Malleable. Eager. Just as he'd thought when he'd first seen her. Cassie's obvious need to do his bidding made Guy's heart swell with joy. The eager way her rosebud asshole twitched when he rubbed his cockhead over it had him desperate. Desperate to take her, fill her... fulfill her and coax her to take him as he was, go with him wherever he bid.

"Oooh, yesss." Her breathy moans when he sank the long, thick dildo into her swollen cunt had him ready to explode. Slowly, he slid the glass in and out, changing the angle of penetration to enhance her pleasure.

His cock twitched, demanding he glove it within her body now. He tried in vain to counsel restraint and patience. *Pretend you're a sexbot. That you exist only to give Cassie pleasure. Pretend your cock and balls are controlled by those microchips in your brain, just like so many other parts of you.* His cock wasn't listening. He had to speed this up or he'd shoot his load the minute he lodged his cockhead in her tight, hot ass.

He picked up the banana, bent over her upthrust ass, and slid the tip of it between her lips before straightening and aligning their bodies. "Nibble on it. Concentrate on the sweetness of the fruit, the full feeling of the dildo in your cunt. That's my good girl. Relax." Slowly, smoothly, he began to penetrate her tight ass. "You can take it. Gods in the heavens but you're tight. Can you feel me stretching you, filling you?"

"So full. Hurts."

He paused. "Too much?"

"Yesss. No. Oh gods, don't. Don't stop. Please. I'm coming." Her asshole clamped down on his cock, and through the thin wall of tissue he felt every hard contraction of her cunt around the dildo. The erotic smell of banana and woman filled his nostrils, stole the last shreds of his control when she bit on the fruit as though devouring his cock. His balls drew up in their sac, and almost before he had time to anticipate the coming pleasure, his cock began spurting out its load in long, fulfilling bursts until he was dry and she lay trembling beneath him, gasping out words of lust and love and...

"I want to keep you, take you home." A great sob sounded as if it were being wrenched from Cassie's very soul. "But I know I can't."

Chapter Four

"But you can, my darling slave." Guy couldn't have asked for a better opening than Cassie had just given him. He lifted her, cradling her lush body in his arms before laying her on the bed and propping her golden head on a stack of scarlet satin pillows. Stretching out beside her, he met her gaze. "I have a confession to make."

"What?" A single tear made its way down her cheek, and he leaned over to catch the salty droplet on his tongue.

"I'm no sexbot, but a man. An Earthling like you."

"Bu… but your eyes… and your hard, hard body…" Cassie stroked his arm, tracing his biceps upward to where they joined with pecs that had never been so prominent before his injury.

He covered her hand, holding it in place above his heart. "I've been enhanced."

"B-but that's against the Federation's laws."

"I know. The doctors had no choice other than to let me die. Some months ago I crashed my starship into Obsidion while trying to land in a storm. When the medics dragged me from the wreckage, I was barely alive, or so I've been told. Blind and deaf and paralyzed.

"To save my life, the doctors summoned Pak Song. He implanted electronic cyber-eyes and internal ears, the kinds he uses to make his robots. When I'd begun to heal from my other injuries, he embedded microprocessors in my brain that make them work. As for the hard muscles, they are a result of other modifications Pak Song made that allow me to function as if my spinal cord hadn't been severed."

Cassie's mouth dropped open, and she stared at him, wide-eyed. "You can never go back home, can you?"

"No." His confirmation sent tears streaming down her cheeks, and she bit her lower lip as though to keep from crying out loud. "But you can stay with me."

"Here?" she croaked.

"No, baby. Not here. Obsidion is for adventurers and opportunists and tourists looking for forbidden thrills. It's a great place to visit, but not the sort of place where I want to make my home. Cassie, you're my soulmate. I want you with me. Not just now, but forever. I sense you want that, too."

Damn it, she was fighting him, and he didn't like it. He hated having her look at him with love in her eyes -- and terror that was so transparent it hung in every molecule of air that was still redolent with the scents of banana and their own animal musk. "I know a place -- a small planet with a colony of Earthlings. Not too far from here. We'd be welcomed."

"But... I'd miss my sisters. I'd never see my father again. My job." She paused, as if gathering her thoughts. "What about your job? You can't defect and keep on working for the Federation."

"I got a generous settlement. When Star Command discovered how I'd been kept alive, they rewarded me richly for my years of service -- at almost the same time as they relieved me of my command. I could support us both if I never worked again, but I plan to start a shuttle service and take supplies from planet to planet in this part of the galaxy. Trust me, little one. I'll take good care of you."

Omigod, this was too hard to process all at once. Cassie's head spun, trying to make sense out of what she'd gotten into. Guy. He said she was his soulmate, and she was certain he was hers. A soulmate she'd found and believed was a sexbot, only to learn he really was a man. No, not a man but a cyborg forever exiled from their home planet.

"Why?" she asked, her heart breaking as she tried to withdraw her hand from his chest. "Why did you make me fall in love with you when I can never have you in my life?"

"But you can." Guy clasped her hand firmly, pressing it against his chest so hard she felt the imprint of his nipple ring on her palm. "You'll have to give up some things, that's true. But think of what you'll gain. No breeding farm where your mate is chosen for you, then sent away, but a home where your children will know both of their parents' love. Freedom to serve me and only me as Master. Freedom to let me pleasure my only, beloved slave." As though desperate to prove a point, Guy laid his other hand between her legs, his fingers finding the still-wet folds of her cunt lips, stroking the still-swollen flesh, coaxing out more honey even though she'd thought the well quite dry.

"What do you say, Cassie? I know what sort of life awaits you back on Earth. Breeding, then having your children given to their father if he wants them. Getting your only sex from a mindless 'bot. Living under the thumbs of the Federation's rulers, having to abide by all their rules. I'll give you more. Much more." He dipped a finger into her cunt, stroking gently against the wet, hot walls that so recently had convulsed wildly with the multiple orgasms he'd coaxed from her. Reminding her of the pleasure -- pleasure she wanted to go on enjoying forever. But gods, she was afraid to leave all she knew, follow this compelling cyborg into a new and frightening world where...

"You promised children. Are you..."

"Pak Song and the doctors assured me my reproductive parts were unscathed, and are in perfect working order. My seed may be growing inside you even now. Would you like that?" Withdrawing his hand from her sex, he laid it on her belly, his touch gentle, almost reverent. "I'd like it very much. I never visited the breeding farms when my starship docked on Earth. Never wanted to sire children I'd never see, or to lose my balls once I'd sired the requisite number of sons. I made do with sexbots, as you most likely have until now. I want to love you, live with you, have children with you and watch them grow up free... in a place where such relationships are not forbidden."

He tempted her. Made her want to toss away all she'd ever known, follow him to the ends of the galaxy. But... she needed time. "I've got to think. Omigod, I came to Obsidion for an adventure, but I never expected..."

"To fall in love? I never expected it either, when I took a walk along the Strip to check out my new freedom. But then I saw you, your hair all reddish-gold, your eyes wide with wonder as you stared at those altered, overworked Earthling sex slaves and argued with your sisters. I knew at that moment I'd found my soulmate... lover, companion, best friend."

Cassie felt that way, too, but she was torn. Part of her was still the dutiful daughter committed to meet the expectations of her father and follow the social mores of the Federation community where she'd grown up. To do what everyone had expected of her as long as she could remember. Another part -- the perverse part that reveled in a cyborg's touch -- listened with rapt attention while Guy described this amazing colony where Earthlings lived as the Old Ones had in centuries past. Where men and women mated for life, let their emotions soar, and accepted the miracle of electronic rebirth and enhancement as a blessing, not the abomination for which it was seen back home.

A loud knock at the door dragged her back to the present. Embarrassed for her sisters to see her in this intimate position, now that she knew she lay with a man -- apparently a complete, functioning human male, not the sexbot she'd thought she'd rented -- she moved to raise the covers. But Guy stayed her hand.

"Let them see us like this. Tell them who I am, what I ask of you. I believe you'll be surprised at their response. Come in," he said, his deep voice full of confidence. Of command.

Doreen burst in, with Nebula hard on her heels. "You're gonna have to pay late charges if you don't get that 'bot of yours back to the rental place. That old Chinaman swore he's one of a kind, and that he didn't have another for me to rent, so I put down money to reserve him next."

Nebula laughed. "What makes you think Cassie's gonna let him go? Looks to me like they're still goin' at it. I told you not to waste your money. If you didn't like the sex slave you got, you should have just taken him back and picked out another one. I rather liked mine. Cassie, are you gonna let that hunky robot recharge his batteries and go with us to the casino?"

"Sit down, ladies. Cassie has something to tell you." Guy's voice resounded off the thick, dark walls, and it didn't surprise Cassie at all when Doreen and Nebula plopped on the edge of a fainting couch by the window and shot her a pair of expectant, quizzical looks.

"Guy's an Earthling, not a sexbot. A whole male." Cassie paused, watching her sisters register disbelief. And horror, or was it wonder?

Nebula found her voice first. "Gods above, Cassiopeia, what are you thinking of, fucking with a man who hasn't been fixed? You could --"

"Get pregnant. Yes, I know. I may be, already. If I am, I'm glad. I always dreamed I'd be allowed to get to know the fathers of my children." Then she dropped the bombshell. "Guy was enhanced following an accident that nearly killed him."

"Then he can't go back to Earth. Not that you'd be allowed to pick your own mate anyway, even if he could," Doreen pointed out.

Cassie's abdominal muscles clenched so hard, she almost doubled over, but Guy's warm hands held her fast, easing that pain if not the tearing sensation in her heart and head. "He wants me to stay with him, go live on this planet called Luna Ten."

Nebula shot a dubious look at Guy. "If it weren't for those eyes, he could pass..."

"The Federation Star Command is aware of how I was injured -- and what was done to keep me alive and functioning. Besides, I want to take Cassie to a better place." Guy paused, then smiled. "Turn on that entertainment center and have it beam in on Luna Ten. I'll show you what she'll be missing if she chooses to go home. What we've all been missing by following the New World Order."

Eden. The commentator said Luna Ten had been given that informal name by Lady Aurora, the ethereal looking woman he'd just shown frolicking with three young children in a shady glade. Shot after shot of verdant meadows and glades sheltered from the sun by lush trees and shrubs with brilliant pink and purple flowers took Cassie's breath away, but what impressed her most was the freedom -- the obvious happiness -- of Luna Ten's naked, uninhibited inhabitants. And the cleanliness. A few pristine shelters -- one for each of the twenty families, all refugees from planet Earth, the announcer said -- seemed to blend into the pastoral setting of lush vegetation and sparkling streams.

The scene shifted to the far side of the planet, a picture-postcard view of snow-capped evergreens and a lodge with a roaring fire. A couple, unashamedly naked, lay on a fur rug before the fireplace, limbs entangled as she cradled his head to her swollen breast. Watching them, like this, Cassie's arousal grew, blossomed. Suddenly it didn't matter that she and Guy weren't alone. All that mattered was the insistent nudge of his rigid cock against her thigh, the need to feel it throbbing within her needy cunt. She couldn't let him go. She couldn't. "I want to make you feel as good as you make me feel."

He chuckled, but drew her closer, parting her legs and sliding his cock between her damp, swollen folds. "Now I know something new about you. You get hot, just watching others fucking. I love it. Love you. Do you like what you see of your new home?"

"From what I see, the place must be like heaven."

"Yes, love, Luna Ten is all you see there and more. Come live with me there. I still have friends in the Star Command who could get word to people who'd worry when you don't return." Guy turned to Doreen and Nebula. "You both would be welcome, too. You could live with us until you meet your Masters. I understand there are several unattached males, actively looking for mates."

Doreen laughed. "No man will ever master me. I could be quite happy with a sexbot, and even happier without the threat of indiscriminate breeding hanging over my head. What do you say, Nebula? Shall we cast our lots with the sexy cyborg who's so easily won the heart of our sibling?"

"We could..." Nebula's voice trailed off, and from her troubled expression Cassie gathered that she was remembering, dreading the fate that awaited her when she returned. And why. "...but from what the announcer said, they want women who can be bred. I cannot."

That -- Nebula being diagnosed as a carrier of the dreaded mutant gene that had forced the Federation to set stringent rules for breeding -- was why they'd made this trip. To give her one last chance to enjoy living before she presented herself to be transformed into a sexless drone. Cassie wrapped her arms around Guy, aligning them breast to chest, taking his cockhead just inside her weeping cunt. "Will you take Nebula, too? You know what they'll do to her back home."

"You're asking too much. Unless..." A tear slid down Nebula's cheek. "...unless I could be sterilized here first. Then maybe I could be a servant, help take care of the babies, cook and clean for you."

Guy held up a hand, then rolled Cassie to her back and impaled her completely on his hard, throbbing cock. "You need not be a servant, Nebula, just because you can't help grow Luna Ten's population. I know Brad Gilbreath, who founded the colony. I'm sure he'll welcome you, even though you must not reproduce. I saw several eunuch males when I was there -- they seemed well enough accepted."

Cassie heard the sound of bubbling water, the voice of the announcer inviting guests and future colonists to check out Luna Ten. Guy's magnificent body blocked her view, even as it put a golden cast on his satiny, bronzed skin. With each smooth stroke of his cock into her welcoming body, she became more certain he was her destiny... her future. The master she'd dreamed of but never hoped to find.

"I will go with you, my Master. Whatever Doreen and Nebula decide to do."

"Doreen, let's leave them now," Nebula said. "Will you come with me to help me see to what I must do?"

"Sure." Doreen cast one last, longing look at Guy. "Too bad you're not a fuckin' sexbot. If you were, I'd try to talk Cassie into sharing you. Maybe I'll make another stop at Pak Song's and see if he has any other cyborgs he could point in my direction. Have fun. And don't worry, Cassie. I'll make sure they take good care of Nebula."

"If you want to join us, be at the private transporter dock station tomorrow at fifteen hundred hours," Guy called out as Doreen hurried after Nebula.

He bent, brushing his lips over hers. "I hope they do. I'd have you happy and content. Never lonely." Then, with loving deliberation, he threaded a gossamer golden chain through her nipple rings and his and fastened the clasp, so the sensitive nubs brushed each other with every plunge of his cock deep within her cunt, each erotic tug of the other chain on her throbbing clit. When he took her mouth, she tasted her own honey on his lips.

His enhanced muscles contracted with each thrust, as though he fought to maintain control. When she reached between their bodies and caressed his balls as they lay in their sac within her damp and swollen labia, he lost it. His big body shuddered. His come bathed her womb in fiery bursts, over and over. The familiar, delicious congestion built in her cunt. Her clit, too, and in nipples being tugged both up and down as he sucked her tongue deep in her mouth, swallowing her whimpers of need -- and her screams of perfect pleasure.

The following morning they packed their belongings on a small, sleek transporter Guy had bought, then purchased a few luxuries Guy said they needn't do without: a collar of gold and diamonds with matching gold-link leash, matching gold tongue studs that were the traditional gifts exchanged by brides and grooms, several lengths of fine gold chain, and a ready-made flogger with a burnished leather handle.

"For your discipline, my darling."

"Then you don't want one made of my hair?" Cassie had seen a slave being readied for her Master yesterday in one of the shops along the Strip and found the process of weaving severed lengths of the woman's hair into the ends of one skinny braid, then stiffened, intriguing. She'd gotten wet, just thinking of kneeling before Guy and sucking his cock while he shaved off the flogger made of her own hair to use for her discipline, leaving her scalp as smooth as his.

"I want your golden hair left on your head." While flattered, Cassie couldn't help feeling disappointed that she wouldn't be able to give him that very obvious symbol of her submission. "I want to run my hands through it. Feel it slide along my thighs when you suck my cock. Grasp it when I fuck you from behind. Never doubt you'll be as submissive as if I had your head shaved bald and flogged you with your own hair. I have just one more thing I need to buy."

Abruptly, he drew her into a craftsman's shop where he purchased a sleek St. Andrew's cross, complete with padded restraints. Cassie creamed her panties even more when she imagined Guy strapping her to that cross, administering loving torture until he took pity and filled her empty, aching cunt.

Epilogue

One month later, on Luna Ten, at the altar where commitment is made in the way of the ancients of the galaxy, Guy and Cassie stand before her friends, newly arrived from Obsidion... and the twenty-some-odd families who live in peace together on this idyllic planet. Cassie has agreed to a lifetime as Guy's slave... and he has insisted upon going through the ancient rites, knowing that as he does he will suffer excruciating pain because of his enhanced sensation. He wants to do it for her... and to give thanks that because of his enhancements, he is alive to love her. To be her beloved Master.

Guy stood in the mossy glade called Eden, his tongue outstretched to accept the tongue stud society demanded be worn by all Masters and all beloved slaves. He tried hard not to wince when Luna Ten's ritual celebrant clamped his tongue and drove a large bore needle through it to re-open the hole that had closed during his convalescence. The pain was excruciating, more so for him than for Cassie because of his enhanced senses -- yet somehow cleansing. He loved her for understanding how every sensation affected him ten times more than it did a human without modifications, for suggesting that they forego this ritual, but he'd refused. He absorbed the agony, welcomed each test of inner strength because enduring symbolized victory. His life, snatched back by modern cyber-technology from certain death. Snatched into the arms of his beautiful, perfectly submissive soulmate.

The matched studs also gave visible evidence to all of the promises they'd made -- of her vow to be a loving and obedient slave, his to be a loving and protective Master who'd ensure her pleasure and safety. Guy forced himself to ignore the nausea that rose in his gut as the gold post was threaded through his tongue and screwed in place.

Once the celebrant had sprayed on some salty substance that miraculously eased the pain, Guy rubbed the upper bead over his own lips, imagining how Cassie's pert nipples would bead when he ran his tongue over their sensitive tips, catching the golden ball in her small nipple rings, tugging with it on the delicate chain that joined them and the identical adornment in her clit. His own ringed nipples throbbed when he pictured her tonguing them, and his cock, already at full attention, dribbled glistening lubrication from its ringed tip when he thought of how her pierced tongue would feel when she licked and sucked him there.

"You are now Master and slave. Sir, you may place your collar on your slave."

Glad he'd foregone the custom of taking her silken hair to make the flogger tradition decreed that all Masters have, Guy caught up the golden mass and gathered it into a high ponytail. After securing it in a gold barrette, he took the jeweled collar and locked it securely about her slender neck. As a good slave should, Cassie lowered her gaze when the celebrant -- a eunuch or Guy would have nixed this part of the ritual, too -- knelt behind her and worked a long, thick stimulator into her anus until its flat base lay flush within the satiny folds of her outer labia. Guy tongue-fucked her mouth, the recent pain of his piercing forgotten in the erotic haze of this ancient rite of submission.

Gods but he loved her. "Kneel and pay me homage," he told her when he broke the kiss, exerting enough pressure on her leash to bring her to her knees. Her hands cupping his balls, she lapped the underside of his cock.

Holding back was agony. Every velvety swipe of her tongue, the erotic tinkling of her tongue ring against the jewels in Guy's cock, the heat of her hands and the soft whoosh of her breath against his hairless groin, the tug of her tongue on each jeweled barbell that marched up the underside of his cock, and finally the wet slick heat of her mouth when she took him in her mouth and sucked his cockhead, had his semen bubbling, demanding release.

The celebrant's bell struck three times. Guy had to last through two more torturous minutes, lest ill luck befall him and his slave for all eternity. Oh gods in the universe, the delicious sensations of her stabbing her tongue into his slit and lapping his pre-come was almost too much to bear. Why did she have to suck him so voraciously? He gritted his teeth, trying to ignore the way she worked his PA ring around until its bead rested in his slit.

The celebrant knelt behind Cassie, working the plug in and out of her ass. Her whimpers resonated against his cock. Each second of holding out was pure torture. As the last bell tolled, Cassie deep-throated Guy, accepting each burst of his semen and swallowing it as though starved. Then, with him still in her mouth, she wrapped her ponytail around the base of his cock, symbolizing that her hair was his to do with as he would.

Compared with this, the rest would be easy. Guy drew Cassie to her feet, leaving the butt plug in place, and licked away the drops of semen that had gathered on her swollen lips. Gently he lifted her, draping her face down across a moss-covered altar made from sacred stone, watching with wonder as the fragrant flowered vines that grew around it captured her, confined her much like the ropes he'd been taught to use for bondage as a young star commander eager to begin the road toward sexual dominance. Her breasts jutted forward, inviting his mouth. Between tightly bound, widespread legs, her swollen satin lips pouted and glistened. Her cunt wept, as though begging for his mouth… his cock.

Let her see the instrument of her enslavement. Though no one had spoken, Guy heard the male voice clearly. The voice of his trainer. Stepping up to where his cock aligned with her face, he fed it to her, endured the incredible pleasure of her licking and sucking until he could take no more. "Do you want me to fuck you now?"

"Oh yes, Master. Please fuck me. If it pleases you."

It pleased him, all right. He stood between her bound, outstretched legs and worked his cock into her cunt, made incredibly tight by the presence of the large, ceremonial plug that lay embedded in her pretty ass. With slow, measured strokes, Guy fucked her from behind, gritting his teeth against the need to come, determined to give her the release she deserved.

With every thrust, each gentle tug of his fingers on her clit, every slap of his balls against her pussy lips, Cassie felt his need more than her own. The slick sheen of sweat on his glowing skin, the scarlet heat in his eyes and bulging, straining muscles in his neck and chest gave evidence of what it cost him to hold back.

Helpless to ease his suffering, bound as she was, she did as she'd promised an hour earlier, when the celebration of their joining had first begun. *I will love you, obey you, submit to your desires. You are my Master, I am your slave, for now and forever. I give you my heart, my soul, my body, trusting you to treasure them always and keep me from harm.*

An incredible pressure built in her cunt and ass, stronger than anything she'd experienced before. "Master, may I come?" she whispered, almost beyond speaking as searing feelings spread along nerve endings already stimulated by her bindings... the collar that proclaimed her his... the stimulator that felt so much like his huge, hard cock. She clenched her inner muscles around his cock, feeling bursts of pleasure at each point where his lush jewelry made contact with her cunt that already had begun convulsing... "Please, Master."

"Come, slave. I order you to come now." He groaned, a tortured animal sound that came from somewhere deep in his belly.

The first shooting, fiery blasts of his come triggered feelings so incredible they defied description, delicious feelings that swept Cassie away, beyond slavery, beyond ritual, to her own Eden. Her own dream of loving submission come true. When she raised her gaze, she saw Doreen and Nebula smiling, apparently finding joy in her contentment, hope for their own taste of Eden on Luna Ten.

Luna Ten: Shedir

Ann Jacobs

Prologue

Earth, 2226

Shedir loved his home, a small-scale replica of the villa on the Arabian Sea where his ancestors had lived for centuries before the Fall of the Old Civilization on Earth. His job gave him everything he'd ever dreamed of -- command of a starship to patrol the skies, protecting Earth from the Federation's off-planet enemies. On his journeys, he'd found opportunities to visit faraway places and do things most Earthlings never did. The gods of the Federation willing -- for the Allah of his forefathers was a term never spoken in the New Order -- he would soon be gifted with a son.

The only thing he wanted that he couldn't have here was a woman.

His cock and balls ached from the rough milking they'd endured an hour earlier at the hands of a sperm-collecting machine at the breeding farm. The pain reminded him pointedly of that lack, for which he was compensated in small part by a harem full of nameless, faceless, sexless drones like the two who always stood by at his bath -- and a sexbot who wasn't anywhere near as enticing as the whole, flesh-and-blood females he'd fucked in the brothels on forbidden pleasure planets like Obsidion.

Shedir, newly named leader of the Eastern Galaxy Wing of the Federation Star Command, stripped off his uniform and climbed into the bubbling marble hot tub. He lay back on the lounger, fixed his gaze on the Vid-panel on the wall large-screen monitor to watch his email, and let the built-in water jets do their thing, pummeling his backside like a thousand tiny fingers of sensation. One drone massaged his waxed skull while another knelt in the water rubbing away the soreness from feet ensconced too long in knee-high uniform boots.

Nothing but spam in the email. What the fuck did he need with another hot tub, or another sexbot? Any fool should know a man could only use one of them at the time. "Delete," he snapped for the twentieth time.

Then the face of his old squadron mate, Guy Stone, appeared onscreen. Guy's glowing electronic eyes still shocked Shedir. Otherwise, Guy looked much the same as he had before the near-fatal crash that had resulted in him becoming a cyborg. "Greetings from Luna Ten," Guy said. "I hear you'll be coming by this way on your next assignment."

"Yes." The 'bots on his starship had loaded an intriguing looking wooden bondage wheel this morning, along with various less interesting supplies bound for Guy's new home.

"I hope you'll be able to stay a few days. This is Cassie, my bonded slave." The camera panned out from Guy's face to reveal a glade lush with grass that looked soft enough to use as a bed. A woman knelt before Guy, wearing nothing but the red-gold hair currently gathered tightly in his fist. A ring and chain dangled from her clit, and a jewel-encrusted plug winked from her tempting little ass while she sucked Guy's cock.

Shedir's own cock twitched. Envy, pure and simple.

The scene shifted to another woman, a gorgeous blonde with a hungry, sex-starved look about her. He salivated at the sight of her full, ripe breasts with nipples the color of the roses in the Rulers' Garden. Although the screen cut her off at the waist, Shedir had no trouble imagining what the rest of her would look like. A satiny ivory mound, rosy clit peeking from between the damp, inviting folds of her pussy, just asking to be tongued. He pictured her in his harem, sucking his cock the way Guy's Cassie was sucking his. Shedir's sore cock turned as hard as the marble tub.

Guy's voice intruded. "And this is Cassie's sister Doreen. Doreen needs a man. She's just fucked another deluxe model sexbot to death, and Luna Ten is plain and simply out of males that haven't been neutered and aren't already mated." Guy gritted his teeth, then let out a tortured growl. "Don't stop now, baby. I'm coming."

Torture me, will you? It might have been okay to get a blowjob where Guy was, but it was against every rule on Earth and Guy damn well knew it. Why the fuck couldn't he have had a little tact? Shedir killed the picture and wrapped his fist around his hard-on, then let go and willed it to go away. When he regained a measure of control, he flipped the Vid-panel back on and dictated a terse reply.

"Expect me on Friday. I will test out the equipment I'm delivering with that piece you already have. I've a possible match in mind, but I'd test it first." One could never be sure when or if the Rulers were listening, and Shedir wasn't taking chances. He'd worked too hard, given too much to risk losing it all -- but Luna Ten should be far enough away from prying eyes for him to indulge himself with impunity.

For a moment he allowed himself to wonder why the Rulers didn't modify the New Order, let males be Masters as nature had intended, pleasure their women as Masters did on faraway planets like Luna Ten where a few rebellious Earthlings had settled to live life in the manner of their ancestors. Although he'd been taught since childhood that the Federation laws were necessary to prevent more of the genetic mutations that had nearly destroyed Earth a hundred years earlier, Shedir sometimes doubted the necessity of turning those deemed unfit for breeding into drones like the ones now standing by to serve his needs in a purely asexual way. After all, ensuring that only the pure bred children hadn't required more than a laser directed toward the right body parts, since well before the Fall.

Even the ancients had gelded their slaves without obliterating all outward signs of their personalities. They'd left them with their humanity, neutered them the way the Rulers fixed their "favored" non-breeders now. Shedir couldn't help shuddering when he imagined living out his life without the pleasure of sexual release, as a good friend and former colleague had been sentenced to do once one of his half-sisters had delivered a child possessing the mutant gene.

He rose from the tub, standing still while two drones used soft Turkish towels to blot the water from his skin. When they finished he murmured thanks and patted each featureless head. While they had no will, they'd once been human. Shedir imagined that on some level they registered and appreciated the small acts of kindness that cost him little, considering the services they silently rendered.

Anticipating blast-off in the morning -- and forbidden pleasures soon to come -- he stretched out on his sleeping couch and dreamed of how it must have been before the Fall.

Chapter One

Luna Ten, a few days earlier

Ecstatic moans and whimpers from Luna Ten's mated couples mingled with the chirping of the birds. The wind rustled gently through the branches of fruit trees laden with ripening peaches, pears, and apples. The heady scent of purple flowering vines that bound the slaves for their Masters lent a sweet, spicy fragrance to the breeze.

What a perfect day for fucking in the glade, for savoring erotic perfection and sharing sexual pleasures without the repression of Federation laws! Doreen Kelly strolled across the soft grass carpet of the fucking glade, enjoying the gentle tug of the breeze on the gold ring that pierced her clit, the brush of her long unbound hair against her back and shoulders.

Doreen couldn't help watching Guy fuck Cassie, envying each thrust of his rock-hard cock into her cunt, each delighted exclamation that came from her sister's mouth. Her cunt clenched when she imagined a real cock was reaming her instead. Guy's cyborg eyes burned red, signaling the lust that fueled every deep, deliberate thrust, each light tug of one big hand on the chain that connected Cassie's nipples and her clit. Guy had his other hand fisted at the base of Cassie's braid, tugging it every time he pulled his glistening cock back to plumb her cunt once more. Gods but she wanted that kind of fucking, too. She wanted to feel a man spurt hot semen into her, to contract her muscles around a rock-hard, jeweled fucking tool.

Doreen inched closer, drawn inexorably by the sights and sounds of impending sexual gratification. Guy sank to his satiny smooth balls in Cassie one last time and bellowed. His powerful ass muscles contracted as he shot his load. His balls and her labia glistened with the slick juices of sex. Doreen's cunt clenched rhythmically, as though it were trying to milk the semen Guy was spurting into Cassie's deliciously helpless body.

Good trick if you could do it, Doreen. Her nipples tingled, fiery hot with lust even though the cool breeze swirled around them. Her sister and the big, gorgeous cyborg were mated. Promised to each other and each other alone for life.

Doreen couldn't stand more watching and wanting. She looked to the other side of the glade, only to see the colony leader fucking his mate's ass with a strap-on while gently probing her cunt with his own impressive tool. What would it feel like for a Master to lick her own slick, smooth scalp the way Brad was doing to Aurora? How would it feel when her own Master rubbed his pierced tongue over the taut skin of her distended belly that would soon expel his son or daughter?

Damn it, Doreen wanted no Master, a good thing since Guy had been mistaken in his assumption there would be unattached male Earthlings on Luna Ten. Her sexbot and the twin eunuch houseboys who'd become her friends in the two months since she'd settled on Luna Ten could satisfy her. They'd better satisfy her. Now. Her nipples tingled in anticipation of Aloysius and Argus's attentive suckling. Her clit twitched, setting the small gold ring to swinging. Gods but her cunt was on fire.

By the time she sprinted the two hundred yards or so to her shelter beneath a graceful native tree much like the towering oaks on Earth, she was wet, hot, and more than ready for release. She eyed her sexbot, reclining in readiness on her sleeping couch. Good thing she didn't have to find *him*, too.

"Aloysius! Argus!" She impaled herself on the sexbot's ten inch cock and programmed it to start fucking.

"Yes, mistress?" they asked in unison, their white robes flapping and the bells on the ends of their rope belts tinkling. Before Doreen could order them to service her, they'd prostrated themselves beside the couch, the fronts of their turbans cushioning their foreheads from the hard pink tile flooring. She'd yet to figure why eunuchs -- both male and female ones -- covered their bodies from head to toe, while all the other inhabitants of Luna Ten went naked, weather permitting.

"Come on, boys. I thought we were beyond all this bowing and scraping. Busy yourselves pleasuring me," she told them with as much patience as she could muster. It felt strange but good when Aloysius knelt at one side of her and Argus at the other, each suckling on the hard nub of a nipple and kneading one of her breasts while she rode the 'bot.

The exotic, erotic smell of the purple flowers in the fucking glade lingered in her hair, still warm from the rays of the scarlet suns of Luna Ten. Something magical, highly arousing, emanated from those vines that only trapped and confined bound slaves of the Masters. Her cunt clenched around the sexbot's cock, but she wanted more.

Her swollen clit ached for attention. She shifted position slightly, brought the hard nub in contact with the 'bot. It wasn't enough. "Go faster, damn you. Fuck me harder. Now. Fuck me, sexbot. Hard and fast and deep, and don't stop until I come."

"Your... wish... is... my... command... my... mistress."

The 'bot's deliberate monotone annoyed Doreen.

The 'bot creaked a bit, slid its cock deep into her cunt with a little more force, increased the rhythm of its thrusts. Mechanically. As though it were a child's toy programmed to make one motion at one of three speeds. If it hadn't come with ten inches of thick, realistic feeling equipment between its legs, she'd have sent it back to the mail order house where she got it and commissioned Pak Song, the master robot maker on Obsidion, to make her a replacement.

"Argus. Keep sucking my nipples. I like how you do that. Aloysius, fuck my ass. Use your fingers. Gods above, I'm so hot I'm in agony, and the 'bot's just not doing the job." Doreen squirmed, trying to change angles, take the cock deeper inside her swollen cunt. "Fuck me faster, damn you!"

The 'bot sped up, slamming hard and fast into her. She met its movements, enhancing the sensation that had her ready to explode. Argus sucked first one nipple and then the other, licking and lightly biting the sensitive tips while he massaged her breasts with big, gentle hands. "Oh, yesss. That feels delicious."

Aloysius probed her anus with one finger, then two, then three, stretching the tissue there while the sexbot fucked her. Oh, yeah. It felt good. So good. "Faster. I'm almost ready. Help me, damn it."

The sexbot responded almost as though it were human, accelerating its motion way beyond its tested top speed. Doreen gasped. The pressure built inside her. She was ready... gods above, she was about to come. She loved her 'bot when it moved like this. "Don't stop. Fuck me. Harder."

"I... am... arghhh..." As the 'bot began to make ominous groaning noises, it slowed practically to a crawl.

"Fuck me, you miserable machine. If you stop now I'll toss you in the trash dump. I'll... I'll shoot you into space and watch you orbit Luna Ten."

"Mistress... I... am... burning..." Suddenly the sexbot came to a complete halt and slumped, its head half off the chaise lounge. A strange, acrid odor rose from it, permeated the air.

Aloysius paused in his sensual massage of her ass, snatched the 'bot from beneath Doreen, and slammed it to the ground. "Beg pardon, Mistress, but the sexbot is on fire."

So was Doreen. "Make me come. Both of you." Aloysius obliged, probing her ass again as deeply as he could while Argus tongued her clit. He used his fingers, too, to fuck her cunt, but she needed more. "By the gods, I knew I ought to have bought strap-ons for you two when the supply ship stopped here last week."

Her release, when it came, was a poor imitation of the ecstasy Doreen had witnessed Cassie and Aurora enjoying in the glade. To add insult to injury, she had to watch while the sexbot she'd been so proud of disintegrated on the floor in a haze of flame and black smoke. Her nostrils stung from the increasingly putrid smell, while Argus and Aloysius kept dumping pitcher after pitcher of water on it to put out the fire.

Doreen eyed the smoldering carcass of the sexbot, then glanced at her houseboys, who seemed not at all perturbed to have missed out on the casual caresses she usually bestowed after they brought her pleasure. Suddenly it hit her. Her touch meant nothing to them, other than probably to remind them they no longer had the capacity to enjoy the sexual pleasure she took as her due. When they stimulated her, they got none of the pleasure she demanded they give her.

The strap-ons she'd threatened to buy them wouldn't do a thing toward giving Aloysius or Argus pleasure, any more than reaming her with its mechanical cock had gotten the unfortunate sexbot off before its demise.

Doreen was taking pleasure from them all, without giving any in return. And that was what kept her constantly unsatisfied, seeking...

At that moment she made her decision. Fuck independence. If she was to be completely satisfied, she needed a Master after all. By giving him pleasure, she'd find the ultimate sexual ecstasy she'd been missing for so long.

* * *

A whole man. "Don't even talk to me about a new sexbot," Doreen told Nebula and Cassie as her sisters stared at the still sizzling carnage a couple of hours later. "Not even one of Pak Song's deluxe models can do what I want."

"So you fucked your new sexbot to death." Doreen would have loved to wipe the smirk off her brother-in-law's handsome face, especially when he slid his hand down Cassie's shoulder until it covered her breast and bent his head to nip her earlobe. "Cassie, don't you feel lucky that you don't have to rely on technology?"

"Yes, Master." From the way Cassie squirmed, Doreen figured Guy was jiggling that chain that connected the rings in her nipples with the one in her clit. Seeing her sister flush with arousal was getting her hot -- again. It was purely disgusting, yet incredibly arousing, the way Cassie bent her head and lowered her gaze in a gesture of pure submission.

Doreen managed to focus on Guy's face, not what he was doing to her sister. "Technology? Just what do you think *you're* made of, Guy Stone?"

Guy laughed. "If Cassie and I weren't mated, I'd show you. Since we are, you'll have to take her word that I can't be fucked to death. What can we do to help?"

Nebula stood in her pale-blue robe, her hands folded, her veiled head held erect. Though she'd taken to wearing the garb of a eunuch since her sterilization last month, at least *she* didn't bow and scrape to any Master the way Cassie did. Unlike Doreen, she seemed serene, at peace with herself and her life here on Luna Ten. "Let me know if you need help later, cleaning up this mess. I'm going to find Argus and Aloysius and make sure they aren't hurt."

"They're okay. And they should be able to manage disposing of the body. After all, it's only one burned-out sexbot. Fortunately it didn't catch the whole house on fire." Nebula couldn't help with what Doreen needed. Guy might be able to, though. Doreen looked the big cyborg in the eye. "You -- you talked us into coming here. Now I think you owe it to me to help me find my own Master."

"But Doreen, you said you'd never be a man's slave." Cassie leaned into Guy's hand, her breathing growing ragged when he increased the tension of his thumb on the chain. "Although I can't imagine why --"

"On your knees. Now." Guy shifted his hand, caught the golden leash on Cassie's wide gold collar, and tugged it gently. Cassie knelt and began to lick the jeweled length of his cock while she raked his hard-muscled inner thighs with light touches of her pale pink nails. "More." It took nothing more than Guy's murmured command for Cassie to sink fully onto his shaft, tilting her head so she could take the thick, bulbous head of his cock down her throat and swallow.

Doreen tried not to stare. After all, on Luna Ten having sex was as natural as breathing. Guy ordering Cassie to suck his huge, satiny cock while he spoke with her sister was no breach of etiquette. Not at all. So why was Doreen's mouth watering, and why were the muscles of her pussy contracting furiously? It wasn't she who was giving head, or whose ass held a long, thick plug most of the time it wasn't being occupied by her Master's cock. A plug like the one whose ruby-headed base now glittered between Cassie's round ass cheeks.

More was the pity. "Guy, I've decided I want a man. A whole man." She wasn't about to defer to hers the way Cassie did -- except when it came to sex -- but she was tired of getting off with a 'bot and a couple of eunuchs who didn't even care if she gave them affection in return.

She was even more tired of feeling guilty for taking pleasure she couldn't give back in kind. What she wanted was a companion who'd treat her as an equal, who'd demand as much as he was eager to give. A mate who'd make her his sex slave, force her to the limits of pleasure as she'd never had done before. A man she could bring to climax, one with whom she could share body and soul. It surprised the hell out of her because she'd always valued her independence, but she wanted more than a fucking machine.

She wanted a Master she could stand with before a celebrant. The weight of his collar when he locked it around her neck would remind her he belonged to her, as much as she belonged to him. Her butt tightened at the thought of the plug the celebrant would insert there. As she watched Cassie pleasure Guy, Doreen decided she wouldn't even mind enduring the pain of having her tongue pierced with the symbol of their mating, since his tongue would be pierced, too. Her cunt clenched when she imagined her Master's steel-studded tongue lapping her most sensitive flesh. Or making him moan with pleasure when she licked his shaft and sucked his ball sac on his command.

"Oooh, baby, that feels good." Guy groaned, shoving his hips forward to force the satiny root of his big tool hard against Cassie's open lips. When he glanced at Doreen, he wore a surprised expression. "You want a Master?"

"Well..." Doreen hated the thought of placing her entire life in the hands of somebody else, but she'd begun to see the benefits. On Luna Ten -- Earth, too, for that matter, since long before her birth -- all whole men were Masters, their mates slaves. "... yes. I do. I want a man. Or -- if you know any guys like you -- cyborgs -- one of them might work."

"I don't know -- Cassie, baby, oh gods, I'm gonna come..." Guy let out a deep sigh of satisfaction, then stood, his big body trembling while Cassie licked his cock clean. "That was good." He caught her ponytail, brought her to her feet. "Ride me."

When he had Cassie perched on his cock, her legs locked around his waist and her hands on his shoulders, he leaned against the wall. He began tweaking her nipples and tugging at the gold rings that adorned them. Giving as good as she'd just given him. Maybe better, Doreen decided when she saw Cassie's eyes glaze over, heard her whimper the way she always did when Guy made her come.

Guy paused and eyed Doreen. "I'll do my best to find you a mate. I have a buddy coming in a few days to drop off some supplies. He may know a breeder male on Earth who's run afoul of the Federation Rulers." Each word came out slowly, punctuated by a hard thrust of his hips, a downward pull on Cassie's nipples, and Cassie's breathy whimpers as her climax neared. "If you show him a good time, he might be willing to scout you out a Master. I know he's going back to Earth after he stops here."

"Master. Please, Master. Please let me come. Oh, yesss." Cassie's voice was ragged, her buttocks straining. The rubies in her butt plug and those that decorated Guy's big, satiny ball sac twinkled in a sea of glistening lubrication. Doreen's mouth went dry. Their climaxes must have come together, the way Doreen wanted her Master's orgasms to trigger her own.

It was times like these that Doreen wished Luna Ten had rules -- no fucking in plain view of non-participants. Even from her vantage spot across the room, she got a painfully arousing, envy-eliciting view of every orgasmic twitch of her sister's straining body, each hard thrust of Guy's massive cock.

"Argghhh." Guy slammed Cassie onto his cock and took her squeal of pleasure-pain in his mouth as he let go again.

The second time in what? Five minutes? Doreen knew then she'd made the right decision. She'd fucked her last sexbot to death. "You two keep on having your fun. I'm going to find Argus and Aloysius and set them to cleaning up this mess."

"Eight o'clock on Friday. Dungeon. Be there if you want to meet Shedir." Though Guy was panting so hard he could barely speak now, Doreen had no doubt he and Cassie would be fucking and sucking again before long. If the gods were listening, they'd go home instead of staying here and setting her on fire with unrelieved lust.

More than they already had, that is.

Chapter Two

When in Rome...

In his stateroom aboard the starship, Shedir stripped off his uniform and began to oil his skin from head to toe. Good thing he'd visited the barber three days earlier, since wearing clothing on Luna Ten was apparently frowned upon as much as nudity would be back home. He ran his fingers over his scalp and groin. Good. No sign of re-growth from the waxing he'd endured. The thick titanium ring through the head of his cock caught the light, as did the matching ladder of barbells that pierced his shaft and scrotum. Signs of pride. Of graduating from Federation Flight School and being marked a breeder.

A breeder. A Master who, if he ever settled on Luna Ten, would be seeking a mate. Since he still had things to do, honors to receive on Earth, Shedir would seek pleasure only for the short time he had on this tiny planet some called Eden. Pleasure from a willing sub, not a slave. Doreen, Guy's sister-by-marriage, who apparently had recently tested the stamina of her sexbot and found it wanting. A hot beauty, if the image on the screen had done her justice.

Shrugging at his reflection, he lifted the heavy gold chain that held the insignia of a Federation star commander -- a Celtic cross sparkling with tiny diamonds and emeralds -- and laid it on his sleeping couch. A symbol of his station, one the Rulers had decreed must never leave his person. Of course they'd also forbidden him to take his pleasure with anything but the sexbot they'd issued him -- the cold machine now staring at him from its place in the corner of the stateroom. Still he hesitated to break too many rules, so he picked the chain up and hung it back around his neck.

His heartbeat quickened when he imagined taking Doreen, fastening her to the bondage wheel the starship's robots had just unloaded for Luna Ten's impressive dungeon. Shedir anticipated bringing her to climax with his hands and mouth before claiming her cunt or ass.

Though he loved flying, loved his position in the Star Command, patrolling the skies had its downside. It had been too long... too long indeed since he'd lingered on one of the pleasure planets, slaking the lust he could relieve on Earth or his starship only with mechanical sperm-collecting sexbots. Too long since he'd indulged in pleasures so forbidden that, if they were discovered by his superiors, would cost him his cock and balls if not his life.

Picking up the bag of sensual toys he'd assembled, Shedir left the ship and strode across the landing strip to the open-air dungeon where pleasure awaited him.

His first sight when he entered the dungeon was the wheel, standing in solitary splendor across from a beautifully crafted St. Andrew's cross. His testicles drew up at the sight of Guy's mate, Cassie, buckled to the cross with wide leather restraints. Guy drew his face away from Cassie's glistening cunt long enough to call out a greeting.

Then he saw her. Doreen, Cassie's sister. From the look of her, a sub in dire need of a Dom. She stood in the center of the dungeon, bathed in starlight, beautifully naked but for a sparkling gold ring swinging from her swollen clit. Her long blonde hair hung down her back, leaving her full, ripe breasts uncloaked from his hungry gaze. Damn. Her eyes looked equally voracious. He watched her gaze shift to his swollen cock, enjoying his growing arousal when her pink tongue darted out between rosy, generous lips, inviting him...

She made him want to forget the niceties, toss her across one of the fucking benches and take her now, without preliminaries. But he wanted to please her, too. Her pink-tipped breasts invited his hands, his mouth. Her impudent little clit called louder, summoning him to explore further between her satiny cunt lips.

Unlike a proper slave, Doreen spoke first, her expression frankly appraising -- and apparently, from the way she licked her full, red lips, she liked what she saw. "You must be Shedir. What can I do to make your visit with us more pleasurable?"

You can try your best to fuck me to death, the way Guy mentioned you did to your sexbot.

Shedir gestured toward the wheel. "I'm certain we'll think of something. Come here, and I'll show you what it's like to mate with a man instead of a 'bot."

She looked at him, her gaze scorching his flesh. "Gladly." With a sassy swing of her slim hips, she closed the distance between them, following where he led. When he reached the wheel, he set his bag of playthings on a conveniently placed bench. "Back up against the wheel and raise your arms."

Carefully, he strapped the padded leather belt in the center of the wheel around her narrow waist and bound her arms to opposing spokes. When he tilted the wheel to raise her feet off the floor, she spread her legs -- before he could order her to do so. His nostrils flared at the heady scent of her -- something that reminded him of the flowers on the little planet's famous fucking vines, mingled with her own female musk.

He bound Doreen's firm, shapely legs to the wheel at ankle, knee, and thigh. Her slick, swollen cunt beckoned, spread wide open as it was to serve his pleasure. When he leaned over and licked the dew from her satiny outer lips, more blood engorged his already rock-hard cock.

"You distract me with your sweet, juicy cunt." He blew on her clit, then circled her two enticing holes as he pulled away. "I got ahead of myself. Wait. I've got just the thing to make you feel very, very full." First stroking her anus and cunt with the tip of one finger, he then reached in his bag and withdrew two sparkling acrylic dildos. "You're one hot woman. As hot as though you were waiting especially for me, not the Master you say you want me to help you find." The head of the larger dildo slid easily along her slick slit before he slid it up her hot, dripping cunt.

She wiggled her ass, as though trying to take more of the toy, and whimpered.

"Are you so happy to see me?"

"Mmmm." Doreen squirmed, lifting her hips as far off the wheel as the restraining belts allowed. Gods but she wanted the hot-blooded star commander to get on with it, ram his huge cock in her and make her come. She wanted to milk his seed, feel him spurting inside her spasming cunt. "Fuck me. Don't make me wait."

"All in good time. *My* time." Shedir bent over her bound body, giving her a good enough look at his glowing scalp that she could tell his hair, if he let it grow, would be black as a midnight sky, as black as his compelling eyes. Her cunt clenched when she got a whiff of the aromatic oil that burnished his swarthy, golden skin. His pecs rippled when he shifted. When he straightened, she got a good look at his magnificent cock, the shaft pale, the corona dark and thick, his scrotum round and full and darker than his shaft. The heavy, thick ring and barbells that indicated his status in the Federation looked richly elegant in their simplicity.

"Don't worry," he said, flashing brilliant white teeth when he smiled. "You'll get to pleasure me soon enough."

Now wouldn't be soon enough, but Shedir had Doreen deliciously helpless. Her cunt clenched, and her nipples hardened and tingled with anticipation when he opened a vial and coated the fingers of one hand with some slick, gel-like substance. "What..."

"To enhance your pleasure. And stretch your pretty ass to take my cock." When he worked first one finger, then two, up her rear passage, she gasped. A painful stretching sensation gave way to the burning of arousal, an arousal heightened when he withdrew his fingers and seated the smaller dildo deep into her ass. The tongue-like projection of the large dildo in her cunt put delicious pressure on her clit.

He secured the bases of the dildos to a narrow shelf he slid out from the wheel spoke beneath her ass. When it began to vibrate, the dildos mimicked the motion of the shelf, reminding her he'd stuffed all her orifices but one. A painful pressure built in her belly. Her nipples throbbed. She panted as the first waves of pleasure overtook her. Her mouth fell open as the wheel turned, around and up, positioning her upside down, her mouth level with Shedir's rock-hard cock.

Lubrication oozed around the thick ring that protruded from his slit, tempting her. He stepped closer, his hand on his shaft, positioning the thick, ruddy corona between her waiting lips. When she tongued him, sampling the salty slick fluid, pressure began to build again. She wanted...

His cock. All of it. He fed it to her inch by inch, until she had to tilt her head backward so she could swallow its head. She'd never felt so full. So taken.

Shedir groaned, a deep, purring sound as he laid his palms on her upper thighs, adding the brushing of his thumbs on her labia to the pulsating rhythm of the dildos. Doreen wished then she could wrap her arms around him -- an emotion she'd never experienced with her 'bots or the sex slaves she'd rented on Obsidion a few months earlier. His cock throbbed, its blunt head pulsating with life in her mouth, its taste uniquely arousing.

Gods help her, she was coming. Waves of pleasure undulated through her bound body, over and over, and when he came, the staccato bursts of his hot, salty come in the back of her throat set off another, stronger orgasm that left her limp, drained.

Aftershocks of the most intense climax Doreen had ever had surged through her body, overwhelming her. She barely noticed when Shedir rotated the wheel, retrieved the dildos, and set her free.

He wasn't finished, though. Scooping her up as though she weighed no more than a small child, he laid her over his shoulder and strode out of the dungeon. "I've always wanted to try out Luna Ten's famous fucking glade, and I can't imagine finding a more delightful partner with whom to do it."

* * *

The vines let out their intoxicating fragrance, and for the first time since Doreen had been on Luna Ten they curled around her like undulating fingers, teasing her wrung-out body back to life while Shedir knelt and tongued her cunt. Incredibly, arousal curled around her, surrounded her, made her forget the satiated state of lethargy that had claimed her moments earlier.

"You're wet. Swollen. Just as I knew you'd be." Standing, he rubbed his cock along her slit, nudging her ass a bit before sliding forward and claiming her cunt from behind. "So tight. Gods but you feel good." He moved in her slowly, stretching her with his huge, throbbing sex.

The vines twined around her breasts and back, rendering her deliciously helpless to his sensual assault. He sought and found her nipples, tugged and squeezed them as the vines tightened their hold. His hot breath singed the bare flesh at her nape, and that got her hotter -- frantic. "Fuck me harder. Gods I want to come again."

"Demanding, aren't you?"

"Please. Oh, please." Doreen was desperate now, desperate to relieve the intense pressure in her cunt, her ass, her nipples.

Shedir chuckled. "That's better, my hot little sub." Standing and bracing himself behind her, he slammed into her cunt over and over, one hand on her clit, jiggling the ring there. With his other hand he spread her ass wide, inserted first one, then two fingers into her rear passage.

He thrust harder, faster. The vines caught her nipples, twisted and tugged them as he'd done with his fingers. She gasped at the feelings that began in her cunt and spread, fiery ribbons of pleasure that came in waves... over and over, until she heard him shout out his release, felt him withdraw and spurt out his seed on the tender skin of her back.

By the time Doreen regained consciousness, Shedir had unraveled the vines and carried her to her shelter. He lay beside her, his handsome face relaxed in sleep, his magnificent cock resting now against her belly.

* * *

A day and two nights of the hottest sex he'd ever had, hours of getting to know and like Doreen's sassy mouth had spoiled him. Much longer, he imagined, and he'd be thinking about tossing away his promising future on Earth and defecting to Luna Ten, as Guy and Brad had done.

Because of Guy's illegal enhancements and Brad's imminent castration if he'd stayed on Earth, they'd had good reasons for opting to live life here. Shedir did not. No woman, not even Doreen, was worth giving up the power and prestige that awaited him back home once he'd put in his time as a star commander, performed a few more feats of daring and valor, fought off the challenge of a few more determined sky pirates and rogues.

Shedir looked down at Doreen and watched her incredibly long eyelashes cast shadows across her skin as she slept. Damn, he hated to do what Guy had asked, take her surreptitiously to Earth and find her a likely mate -- a Federation breeder willing for whatever reason to give up his privileged life there and come settle on Luna Ten.

He knew just the man. Conan, his former captain, who'd recently run afoul of the Federation and had made up his mind to leave Earth rather than pay the price for having been caught breaking the rules.

When he imagined Conan fucking Doreen as he'd been doing, Shedir cursed softly. He ran his fingers through her golden hair, imagined her shorn, those tresses woven into a lash and offered to her Master for her discipline as Aurora's had been. If he stayed, he'd be the one doing the shearing, wielding the whip Doreen would give him to bring her pleasure. He'd find all the places on her scalp that gave him so much pleasure when she caressed his own cleanly shaven head, sharing the arousal it brought with her.

She shifted onto her side, the gentle curve of her breasts attracting his gaze. He loved sucking those rosy, responsive nipples, nipples her Master would most likely pierce as signs of his possession. Nipples he would have left as they were made, unadorned by anything but the rasp of his late-day beard, the light marks he'd make with his teeth, or the clamps he'd use on them from time to time.

Tomorrow they'd leave for Earth. No doubt he would get over this crazy infatuation that had him wishing he could take Doreen for his own. Stroking her satin skin, tracing the shadows from the starlight, he memorized the lines of her arresting face, the way her hips flared from a waist he could span with both his hands. He'd find her a Master as Guy had bade him do, probably Conan, who'd be easy to entice away from a newly unfriendly Earth. After he did, Doreen would become a pleasant memory -- a memory that would fade in time.

Chapter Three

Once he set a course for Earth, Shedir would have little to do, Doreen imagined. Unlike the passenger transporter she'd taken to Obsidion, and Guy's small sports model that had brought her to Luna Ten, this starship had every imaginable convenience. Specialized 'bots performed all the routine functions of flight, including takeoff and landing. Maybe...

"Yes, my insatiable beauty, I'll take care of you once the ship is programmed. Remove your robe and veil. I'd have you naked until we break through Earth's atmosphere." Shedir dragged his gaze to the console and punched in a series of orders. "Perhaps I will let you share me with my sexbot. I understand that in centuries past, my ancestors kept harems of women to pleasure them."

"Father taught us we must never allude to our ancestry, that the only heritage we possessed was that of the Federation."

"Your father was right. Mine, however, held a different view, that the few of us who'd survived the conflagration unscathed by that aberrant gene should pass along the histories of our past." Shedir flashed a smile, then ran a hand down the front of Doreen's now naked body. "Since I've been flagrantly -- and very pleasantly -- violating the Federation's laws about citizens enjoying sex with Earthling women, I thought I'd share another secret with you. Gods above, but I will miss this." He slipped a finger along her slit, made her gush moisture onto his hand that he brought to her lips for her to lick away. "I'll miss *you*. You would have been quite the prize in my ancestors' harems."

Doreen's heart beat faster at that admission. Damn. She didn't want the Earthling stranger Guy had sent her with Shedir to find. She wanted Shedir. Not just as a sex object but as a Master. And from the hot look in his eyes, she guessed he wanted that, too. "Why miss me? Why not chuck all this --" she gestured at the gleaming console, the 'bots doing Shedir's bidding "-- and come be my Master on Luna Ten?"

"I cannot abandon what I've worked so hard to attain." Shedir looked away into the starry red-blue sky framed in the window of the starship. With the fingers she'd just licked clean, he lifted the jeweled insignia of the Federation Star Command that never left its place around his thick, muscular neck and stared at it, as though its glittering jewels would fortify his resolve. "We can enjoy this time together, but once we get to Earth, I will do as I promised Guy and find you a potential Master. I assure you, any unaltered male Earthling can satisfy you much the same as I do. Come now, let's enjoy the here and now, not worry about the future. My cock's already hard, ready to experience what you and my 'bot can do to ease it."

* * *

Shedir's sexbot, like his piercings, smacked of simple, basic functionality. A titanium frame visible beneath its transparent covering that felt amazingly like human skin and flesh would be damn hard to break, Doreen decided when she faced her competition for the first time. Shedir stripped efficiently and lay on his sleeping couch, and before she could bend to pay proper respect to her lover's sex, the 'bot had straddled him and taken his rigid cock into its pussy.

"Come here. The 'bot has only a single function. It's all I need to gain release, so I saw no point in paying for a more elaborate model. While it does its job, I'd show you another kind of pleasure. Come sit on my face. I wish to taste your very human delights."

Her heart beat faster, harder as she straddled him. When her clit ring brushed his lips, he caught it between his teeth, gently dragging her lower as he spread her outer lips with his fingers and closed his lips around that most sensitive flesh. He flailed her clit with his tongue until it felt as though it would burst, all the while stroking her ass, her thighs.

Then he lengthened his strokes, dipping into her swollen cunt, licking its spasming walls while he worked one finger into her ass, then two, and began to slide in and out of her ass and stab her cunt in slow, incredibly stimulating motion. Gods in the heavens, this felt delicious, nothing like when in her own desperation, the eunuchs had serviced her to climax.

It was coming, that buildup of pressure that led to blessed release. Coming. Doreen suppressed a scream, rode the waves of delight while Shedir tended her. His hips rocked, as though he were fucking her, but he never missed a stroke until she collapsed beside him, spent yet still unsatisfied. She watched the transparent robot ride him, wishing it were her impaled on his cock, cushioning his velvety sac between her own smooth outer lips.

"Like watching? I bet you never saw that before."

No. Doreen hadn't. Though she knew how a hard cock felt inside her cunt -- she'd certainly never watched a cock in action, seen the throbbing veins, the flush of blood in the shaft, the darkening that began in Shedir's thick, rounded corona and spread downward as his climax neared. "I'd like that inside my cunt," she said, feeling ridiculously jealous of the 'bot.

"After the 'bot drains me, I'll oblige you. Arggh! I'm coming now."

Spurt after spurt of creamy come spewed from his cock, collected inside a womblike reservoir. Doreen imagined feeling that hot, slippery come spurting inside her, wished...

No, that wasn't possible. Shedir had made it clear mating with her was not in his future. He was only doing her a favor, and sharing some pleasure in the process. Her cunt twitched with the aftershocks of her orgasm, as though asking for the impossible. For the man it had chosen to be her mate.

"Lie here. I will return." When he opened a hidden flap on the robot's belly, retrieved the bladder of semen, and replaced the bladder, she remembered a story Guy had told, and then she knew. He had to deliver the requisite amount of frozen semen when he returned to Earth, or pay the consequences. This was the Federation's way, it thought, of assuring the chastity of its starship captains while they were out in the galaxy on their assigned duty.

When Shedir returned, he claimed her conventionally, the way the Old Ones spoke of making love. Mouth to mouth, breast to chest, belly to belly, legs entwined. A gentle mating, more of the minds and emotions than of the body, though his big cock filled her cunt exquisitely as they moved in slow, sensuous rhythm while the starship hurtled through space and time.

"Gods in the heavens, woman, I wish I dared come in you," he said when he pulled out and came over her belly. As though he wanted to mark her his, he rubbed his slick, hot come into her skin until it practically disappeared. "But I do not."

A bell rang, shrill and piercing in Doreen's ears. "We approach Earth now," Shedir told her. "I must see to the landing."

* * *

After experiencing the beauty and peacefulness of Luna Ten, Earth seemed to Shedir like a wasteland. Particularly this part of Earth where he'd landed to meet his former captain, Conan. "Where are we?" Doreen asked, her expression one of shock when she stepped off the starship onto burned-out land destroyed in the conflagration more than a hundred years ago. "I thought you said we were on Earth?"

"We are. The man I believe will make you an excellent mate will meet us here. I dared not bring you where the Federation Rulers might witness this meeting."

"Afraid of losing your job?" Her tone was brittle, her step tentative as she descended the stairs from the starship.

Shedir had trouble believing her naiveté. What he'd heard must have been true -- Rulers shielded their daughters from learning the extent of brutal enforcement that kept the masses under control. "I have no wish to lose my manhood, which would be the least of my punishment were I caught assisting an Earthling fugitive in his escape."

"This man you want to mate me with is a fugitive?" Doreen stopped, turned, and looked Shedir in the eye. "What are you and Guy trying to do to me?"

"Conan is a good man. He fell into disfavor with the Star Command because he helped his brother stow away on his starship. The brother had been scheduled to be imprisoned and turned into a drone."

"Where is the brother now?"

"On Obsidion. Working in one of the pleasure palaces."

Doreen's mouth dropped open. "Not the one Nebula and I visited, I hope."

"I doubt it. There must be at least a dozen places there where a woman can rent an Earthling eunuch." Shedir looked toward the sound of a mighty roar. "There. Conan should be on that transporter. Good thing this side of Earth has plenty of room to land."

"I suppose." She didn't sound convinced this was a good thing.

Shedir squeezed her hand. He'd thought their conversation on the starship had convinced her when she begged him to take her for himself that any Earthling male who hadn't been neutered could satisfy her as well as he. Though she'd pouted, she'd eventually conceded that this new man might please her -- even more than Shedir.

Her attitude now seemed to say the opposite, but she did perk up when Conan stepped into the light. His former captain was a good-looking devil, with twinkling eyes and a few days' dark growth on his head and cheeks. Though dirty and unkempt in tattered remnants of his uniform, and missing his right hand, Conan still was an impressive figure -- almost as impressive as he'd been before they'd stripped him of his insignia and drummed him out of the Star Command.

When Doreen would have gone to him, Shedir held her back, unable to fight back the jealousy that suddenly overwhelmed him. "Get back on the ship," he spat out. "He is not for you."

Confident the 'bot steward would follow his quietly transmitted order, Shedir approached Conan as the battered transporter lifted off. "Come quickly. I'll take you to Obsidion," he told the other man. "I was mistaken about having a woman for you on Luna Ten."

* * *

As soon as she stepped onto the starship, the 'bot steward grabbed Doreen. She struggled, but she was no match for it. It hefted her over its shoulder and delivered her into Shedir's sleeping couch, tying her arms with the tethers he'd used the night before. Her robe hiked up when the 'bot jerked her legs apart and secured them to the lower supports for the mattress.

Just wait! I'll have Shedir destroy this insolent 'bot. Then Doreen began to laugh. The damn 'bots on the ship did nothing except on their master's order. The roar of the other starship's engines told her it -- and Conan -- were gone.

She wanted to shout for joy. Shedir had chosen her over his precious starship command. He'd sent Conan away. She'd have the Master she wanted -- the one she'd loved from the moment he'd secured her to the wheel and made her swallow his cock. Good. They were on their way out of this desolate place. Back to Luna Ten. The shudder and creak of the big ship's outer shell and the deafening sound of the rocket boosters were music to her ears.

When she licked her lips she could almost taste him there. The arousing smell of clean male musk clung to the bed linens, had her nipples puckering with anticipation, her cunt creaming, readying itself for a Master's invasion. She lifted her hips when she heard him coming, offering herself for his pleasure.

"I've decided to take you for my concubine. You'll travel with me when that's possible, and wait for me on Luna Ten when it is not."

His concubine? Not his mate? His slave? Doreen choked back the protest that came to her lips. She wanted Shedir any way she could get him, especially when he stood there, every inch the Master, stripping off his boots and skin-tight uniform pants, tempting her with his huge, hard sex and golden, muscular thighs. Her mouth watered, and her nipples hardened in the cool, still air of the starship. But a voice inside her head told her this was not enough, not by a long shot. "Your concubine?"

"Yes. I've set a course for Obsidion. We need to drop Conan off there. You will not talk with him. You are mine." Gloriously naked now except for that damn glittering insignia he never removed, Shedir sat on the edge of the bed, his dark eyes glowing with desire as he cupped her breasts and rubbed the thumbs over her hardening nipples. "I do not share what's mine." He slid one hand down her body and slid it over her exposed crotch. "I will have you fitted for a chastity belt while we're there. And a collar."

"You'd deny me my eunuchs and my sexbot when you are away?"

"You fucked your sexbot to death, remember?" He slid a finger into her damp cunt and wiggled it around. "Since I understand all the eunuchs on Luna Ten have been relieved of their cocks as well as their balls, I'll have the belt designed so the eunuchs may pleasure you like this, or with their tongues. I am not a cruel man. These, though, belong to me alone." With his thumb and forefinger, he tugged on one nipple, rolling it until shivers of desire had her trembling in her bonds.

So she'd wear the symbols of concubines back on Earth -- a chastity belt and nipple shields. Her nipples hardened under Shedir's scrutiny. Her cunt grew wet and swollen. Then she remembered his sexbot and the bladders of semen he stored in the starship's freezer.

"What about *that*?" She turned her head toward the sexbot that sat, idle, in the corner of the stateroom. "Will you still give it all your seed?" The idea that some faceless breeder on Earth might even now be swelling with his child infuriated Doreen.

He grinned. "Jealous? If you wish to bear my child, I will oblige you. I imagine I'll still be able to provide the necessary proof of my chastity to the Federation officials when I go back to Earth. They expect a twice weekly deposit, and with you I know I can get it up for much, much more."

"Have you any children?"

"I don't know. Members of the Star Command are not informed whether their seed is used, the thought being that knowing one has children on Earth might deter some of us from doing our jobs with the necessary enthusiasm." He bent, took her clit ring between his teeth and tugged it lightly before looking up and meeting her gaze. "I'll buy a gold chain to hook to this, and lead you about by it.

"Meanwhile, I want to fuck you. Fill you as I did on the wheel I brought to Luna Ten." He reached in a drawer, pulled out a butt plug and a tube of lubricant, and worked it past her anal sphincter. Then he knelt between her outstretched legs and filled her hot, wet cunt. "The plug will grow as it absorbs your body heat. Stretch you. Ready you to take me up your ass."

"Ooh." He took her mouth, his tongue rubbing the seam of her lips, demanding entrance. She couldn't resist him, couldn't deny the sensations of being filled -- completed. When she tightened her inner muscles around his cock as he pulled back, she absorbed his groan in her mouth. Though tied hand and foot, she felt a surge of feminine power. Shedir was obviously not immune to her efforts at seduction.

And she was certainly not immune to his. She raised her hips, inviting him deeper, enjoyed the slap of his testicles against her flesh, the increasing fullness as the plug expanded. Oh, if she could only wrench herself free so she might wrap her legs and arms around her lover, bind him to her as he'd bound her for his pleasure.

The waves of ecstasy that began as a small stirring in her womb and radiated to every cell in her body crippled her, left her trembling beneath Shedir while he bombarded her with a new sensation. For the first time in her life she felt a man's hot spurts of life deep within her body. And she came again, the contractions of her cunt drawing out his seed until he had no more to give.

* * *

Hours later Shedir rose and freed Doreen from her bonds, memorizing the gentle curve of her lips as she slept, the way her hand curled to support her chin and her legs bent in a graceful arc as soon as she was free. In a few short days she'd come to mean far more to him than release, even more than the exhilarating, forbidden fucks he'd sneaked in the pleasure planets of the galaxy. He enjoyed her quick wit, her frank enjoyment of his body -- neither of which he'd find in a sexbot, even a deluxe model from

Obsidion's famed Pak Song. He'd never found it, either, in any of the women whose favors he'd bought.

Never before had he wanted to take a mate, share his life with another human being. Now he did. If it weren't for his plans, his dreams...

But no. Shedir had set a course, and he wasn't about to waver. Even in the face of the greatest temptation he'd ever encountered. Covering that sexy, sensual temptation with a light blanket, he dressed and strode to the bridge. Perhaps there, surrounded by the tools of his trade, bombarded by a panoramic view of the heavens, he'd get a grip on his ambition, his goals in life. Perhaps his brain would overrule his cock -- and, he feared, his heart -- and allow him to do as he should, and let his woman go.

As though drawn by what no longer was his world, Conan emerged from his stateroom and gravitated toward the control console. Bathed and freshly shaven, he might have been a second pilot flying check on Shedir -- not a fugitive from Federation justice, stowed away on one of its starships as Shedir would claim he was, if his superiors should learn of his undocumented passenger.

"Do you miss it?" Shedir met the solemn gaze of the man who once had been his mentor.

"The ship? The feeling I'm commanding the heavens? Of course. I always will. The Rulers? No. I'm grateful to have escaped their clutches, for I did nothing any decent man would not have done to try to save his brother. Love isn't wrong. It's a necessity. Lose the ability to love, and you lose your humanity." Conan stretched his legs out before him and gazed out the window at an exceptionally brilliant sky. "I fear that loss will eventually mean the end of the Federation, though I'm certain I'd be dead now if I'd said so before my Tribunal."

Shedir had no doubt that was true. "So you made it out unscathed other than for losing your command and your right hand?"

"Hardly. If it were just this --" Conan held up his stump -- "I'd have bought an intelligent prosthesis and made do with it. I wouldn't have risked stowing away on your ship, taking a chance on getting us caught if you're boarded for inspection, not just to get Pak Song to do his illegal magic with *this*."

"Oh." Fury bubbled up from Shedir's gut, too fierce to tamp down with even the strongest of ambition. The Rulers took too much, demanded more than any man should have to pay.

"Yeah. My lawyer had to do a lot of talking to keep 'em from having me turned into a drone. Unless and until Pak Song can do even more of his magic for me than he did for Guy, I'm useless to the woman you're so protective of. Completely useless. I'll go back into hiding now, in case the Star Command decides to place you and your ship under surveillance. Wouldn't want you to pay for helping me as I'm paying for having helped my brother. As soon as we land on Obsidion I'll change to my 'official' robe and make my way to Pak Song. Perhaps someday we'll meet again."

Official robe? Of course. The Tribunal had ordered Conan made a eunuch, which meant he must wear the white or blue robe that indicated his altered state. A chill permeated Shedir's own recently satiated cock, and it was all he could do to keep from hunching over, protecting his precious sex. As though that would matter if the Rulers caught him flaunting their orders.

Hopefully Pak Song would be able to restore Conan's manhood as handily as he'd restored Guy's sight and hearing... as easily as he created bionic limbs to replace those lost or made useless in battle. Shedir shuddered when he imagined the processes involved -- the mental and physical agony of losing part of oneself, the undoubtedly painful process of having the doctors and Pak Song replace the missing parts with robotics. Looking at Guy, knowing his eyes and ears were not his own but electronic substitutes, realizing he moved with ease only because of Pak Song's electronic genius, still gave Shedir pause, for he had been the one to bring in Guy's broken body.

A bell rang, signaling their approach to Obsidion. Needing distraction, Shedir took the controls from the pilot 'bot and guided the starship into the planet's atmosphere, downward onto its assigned pad. While there, he'd see to purchasing the trappings of concubinage for Doreen, for he'd never willingly let her go.

* * *

"Why did your friend not join us?" Doreen asked later as they walked along Obsidion's famed strip.

"It would be dangerous for me to be seen with Conan. If any of the other starship captains docked here see you, they'll think I've rented myself a woman. An unusually beautiful, desirable one who must be robed and veiled lest she inspire the lust of those who have not paid." Shedir paused, slipped his hand between the folds of her veil and stroked the satin column of her throat. "Since most of them do the same when business brings them here, they'll not report me. They would, however, if they saw I'd transported a fugitive off Earth."

"Oh." Her eyes widened. "After going naked for so long, it feels strange to be swathed from head to foot like this. Must I always wear the veil?"

"Only when I take you with me, away from Luna Ten. And only then, where other men may see you. I find myself not that much different from my ancestors in that I want you for myself alone. I want to hide you from other men's lascivious gazes." In the window of a fine jeweler, Shedir spied the collar he wanted to clasp around Doreen's neck. "Come."

"I wish to see the collar in the window, sir," he told the old man who hobbled to greet them.

"Yes, sir." When he looked at Doreen, the man flashed a yellow-toothed grin before scurrying to the display window, keycard in hand. Even robed and veiled with only her compelling dark eyes visible, it seemed to Shedir that Doreen drew broad smiles from every man they passed. In the case of the wizened shop owner, however, he allowed that perhaps the Martian's happiness emanated from the prospect of starting his day off with a large, profitable sale.

Shedir watched, impatient, while the man made a show of laying a deep-green velvet cloth on the counter, then arranging the beautifully crafted collar on it so each of the tiny diamonds and emeralds embedded in the smooth, gold finish caught the light just so. "You have good taste, Captain," he said as though he found it common for star commanders who passed through his shop to have concubines in tow. "This collar comes with other accouterments," he said, shooting Shedir a sly glance.

Moments later they headed to Leander's grooming salon, Shedir's bank balance considerably shrunken. Justifiably so, he decided when he pictured Doreen adorned only with the collar, matching wrist and ankle cuffs, and the glittering diamond studs he'd impulsively bought for her ears and nostril. Marks of his possession. His dominance.

At the old-fashioned barber pole above Leander's shop, Doreen paused. Shedir turned. Her eyes focused on the image in the window, of a Master shearing away the flogger fashioned from his slave's hair. "I'd give you that," she said, her voice small as though it pained her to speak.

"By the time I come to you to stay, the handle of your flogger will have grown to an impressive length. And the rest of your hair will have grown enough to lengthen the flogger to a full-size whip. I have no desire to hurt you, only to enhance your pleasure with pain."

"Yes, Master." Eyes downcast, Doreen fell in step behind him as they entered Leander's shop, but it was clear she wanted to flaunt the symbols of submission. Of being his loving and beloved slave.

Shedir couldn't tell her no. By her every act of submission she commanded him to do her bidding. To please her as much as she pleased him. No harm would come from allowing her what, to her, must seem the ultimate symbol of commitment. "I'd have you weld the collar and cuffs on my submissive, and prepare her for a ritual mating," he told the pretty young attendant. "You may also pierce her ears and nostril to accommodate my other gifts. Meanwhile, I will let Leander tend to my grooming."

Chapter Four

Two hours later, Doreen stood before Shedir in the starship, now set on a straight course for Luna Ten. Her gaze locked with his, she shed her robe and veil. Her skin glowed like his own from the head-to-toe waxing Leander had administered, making Shedir's fingers itch to stroke every satiny surface of her body.

"I like that our jewelry matches," she said, her gaze on the insignia he wore on a chain around his neck.

"So do I." His collar and cuffs sparkled around her throat, her wrists, and her slender ankles, their clasps welded shut, marking her as his concubine. Her skull, pale, ivory, and bare like his, but for the flogger at her crown, beckoned his fingers, his tongue. At their mating he'd take that, too. If there were going to be a mating, which there was not. Trying to put all this into perspective, Shedir opened his fly and released his sex. "Kneel, woman," he told Doreen, "and pay me homage."

When she began to stroke his cock and balls with gentle fingers, he fastened the three diamond studs into her ears and nostril. "Suck me," he ordered softly, pleased when she immediately took the head of his cock in her mouth and ran her slick, velvety tongue along the sensitive tip, catching the ring and rotating it through his flesh. If they'd mated, her tongue would have felt like velvet and steel, its round metal stud pressing into his flesh, tugging at his cock jewelry and enhancing his pleasure. His tongue would have been studded, too, to bring her greater pleasure when he licked her nipples, her cunt. He knew now that he wanted, or needed, that. He longed to possess her fully and know she possessed him, too.

He pictured them kneeling in the glade on Luna Ten, repeating the ritual of centuries long past, pledging themselves to each other and each other alone, Master and slave. He'd take his razor-sharp scimitar and detach the flogger that now bobbed atop her shining head, accept her gift and make it his own. At that thought, his balls tightened painfully beneath her seeking fingers.

Shedir closed his fist around the flogger and raised Doreen's shapely head. "Rise. If you pay me much more homage, I'll spill my seed where it cannot take root." The slight risk of being detected by his superiors seemed less important than wasting his seed. Though he wasn't ready yet to say the words, he doubted he'd ever be able to leave Doreen long enough to continue his ascendancy with the Star Command.

Seeing Conan, knowing they'd mutilated him in spite of his years of faithful service to the Federation, had Shedir reassessing his goals. Though he'd thought fleetingly before of injustices he witnessed every day on Earth, he now found himself questioning the rules, believing many of them were born more of cruelty than the need to preserve humankind as the Rulers insisted.

"Do you not enjoy me, Master?"

He'd have time for solitary consideration later, after he left her to patrol the Eastern District. Shedir let go the braided topknot of Doreen's hair. He pressed his fingers against her satiny scalp, finding and caressing the zones he found erotic on his own head, along her delicate occipital bone and on the seams where the plates of her skull had grown together. Her sighs of pleasure and the increased vigor with which she caressed him told him she too found his touch on her shaven scalp arousing. "I loved your long hair, but I love you more without it."

"I'm glad. Please, tie me up and fuck me. Fuck me hard. Take the flogger and use it to stripe my ass."

"All in good time." Shedir caught her wrists, hooked a chain through the loops on each one, dragged them toward the floor, and secured them to a sturdy hook on the lower console -- a hook meant for hanging navigational aids but perfectly positioned for his purposes. "Kneel and present your pretty ass for my pleasure." Taking up a long, slender cord, he looped it through the hasp of one ankle bracelet, threaded it through her collar and around to the other ankle, tethering her to her own collar.

"Don't move. I'd not hurt your pretty throat." Shedir knelt between Doreen's widespread legs, bending to run his tongue over her incredibly silky buttocks. Her little whimpers told him she liked that. A lot. Pausing, he raised his head. Gods but she had him hard as steel. He rubbed his cock along her swollen, glistening slit, debating with himself for a moment whether to take her cunt or her inviting, incredibly tight ass.

She decided for him, luring his cock, sucking it in, caressing it within the slick, hot walls of her cunt. Taking him completely. He slid his hands beneath her body, finding her breasts, tugging at the hard nubs of her nipples as he bent over her, nipping and sucking her newly bared scalp, toying with the diamonds in her earlobes. Despite her bonds, she lifted her hips to his thrusts, clamping down on his cock head as her orgasm began deep within her cunt.

He held out as long as he could, fucking her hard, then gentler, rolling her nipples between his thumbs and forefingers, sucking her earlobes, her scalp, biting the juncture of her head and neck, above the collar that marked her his. She'd come more times than he'd counted when he could last no more. He came in short, staccato bursts, flooding her womb with his essence, letting her milk him until she'd taken all he had to give.

There was no way in this lifetime that Shedir was going to let Doreen go.

* * *

The glade at Luna Ten was even more beautiful than she remembered. Fragrant, peaceful, and incredibly erotic. Plump peaches were starting to ripen on the trees in the adjacent orchard. Doreen stood in the glade facing Shedir, loving that he'd consented to be her mate. Loving him. Understanding she'd have to share him with the Star Command, at least for now. She smiled at Aloysius and Argus, glad she'd asked her friends to preside over the sacred mating ritual Shedir had wanted to take place now, before he left Luna Ten on a patrol that would take him temporarily back to Earth.

Her stiffened braid swung in a gentle breeze, tickling her naked back, reminding her it would soon be Shedir's to do with as he chose. Her nipples tightened when he looked down at them, his tongue darting out from the corner of his sensual mouth as if he could hardly wait to lick and suck her there. Gods but she hoped he'd have time before he left to fuck her properly, stroke her with steel and velvet the way she'd be stroking him.

"Are you ready, Master?" Aloysius asked, bowing before Shedir while Argus worked the ceremonial double dildo into Doreen's cunt and ass.

Shedir nodded, his gaze locked with hers. "Kneel, slave, before your Master." When she did, he also dropped to his knees. "As I will always bow to the needs of my beloved slave." He took Doreen's hands and held them, his grip strong and sure.

Doreen welcomed the sharp sting when Aloysius plunged a needle through her tongue and inserted the evidence of bonding. Shedir's hands shook, but he held on while Argus pierced him and inserted an identical titanium tongue ring. An icy-feeling spray worked wonders to ease the pain of the old-fashioned tongue piercing.

When her Master rose, Doreen took his cock in her mouth. He lifted the flogger. Cold steel grazed her scalp, its razor-sharp blade severing the symbol of her willing servitude. Slowly, as if he took one strand at a time. Gently, though his blade of choice was a wicked looking scimitar his ancestors might have used to lop the heads off those who displeased them. She licked him, memorizing his taste for the time, coming soon now, when he'd be gone. The heat of the stars bombarded skin now bared that had never been bare before. Her head suddenly felt lighter, freer, unburdened by the weight of her hair.

His hair now, with which to discipline his beloved slave. "What was yours is now mine, as you are mine. I will rule you with love. Protect you with my life. These are my promises." Simple words. Straightforward sentiments. Like Shedir.

He lifted her, draped her face down upon the mating altar, and laid a few strokes of the flogger she'd given him onto her ass cheeks, following each stroke with a soothing kiss, a tender tracing of each welt with his newly pierced tongue. Tendrils of the purple-flowered fucking vines embraced Doreen, held her, opened her for her Master's pleasure.

Colorful birds chirped in the nearby orchard, their song symbolic of this solemn bonding. Anticipation built in her when she felt the dildos being slid from her cunt and ass, leaving her open for her Master. The heat of his rigid cock seared her ass. His fullness stretched her, painfully, for she'd never taken him there before.

"Easy, relax." His tone hypnotic, masterful, Shedir coaxed her to open, accept him in this way as she had in all others. Her crisis loomed, more quickly than ever before, and when he bent over her and tongued an incredibly sensitive spot at the base of her skull, ripples of pleasure overtook her, leaving her limp and spent on the altar of submission.

She felt him withdraw, knew their houseboys cleansed him as they were cleansing her with cool water from the stream that ran through the glade. With a gentleness she hadn't realized until now that he possessed, he untangled the vines from her body, lifted her, and carried her to the shelter where several weeks ago she'd lain unsatisfied while her sexbot smoldered on the cool tile floor.

"I want you to myself, now, before I leave," he whispered, licking and nibbling her breasts as he laid her on their sleeping couch. "My lover, my mate."

Kneeling between her legs, he joined their bodies, dipping his head to suckle at her breasts before bracing his weight on his elbows and tangling their tongues. It was a slow, thorough fuck, a hello and farewell, a promise of forever that Doreen embraced as her climax neared. Like a well-orchestrated ballet, they moved together, every motion a pledge of love, of possession and being possessed. When they came together, it seemed the stars sparkled more brightly in the sky, lighting the universe in celebration.

An hour later, Shedir was gone, off to do the bidding of his Earthly masters. Doreen stood at the edge of the landing pad, watching the bright-red bursts of rocket fire as his starship rose into the heavens. Her clit ring tinkled against the bright gold of his chastity belt, and a warm wind swirled about her, enveloping her in a sensation of loss while the twinkling stars offered silent assurance that her Master would soon return.

Soon, she prayed to every deity she'd ever believed in... every one she'd heard spoken of by the Old Ones on Earth, the pleasure seekers on Obsidion. Soon Shedir would come home to stay.

* * *

Though his mate had never been here in the villa he'd called home for many years, the place felt cold and empty without Doreen. The promise of prestige and power that had driven Shedir so long loomed a lot less important in his mind than the prospect of a simple life with his loving slave on Luna Ten.

How could it be that the way of life he'd taken for granted for so long was suddenly coming across as unnecessarily regimented? Downright cruel? He pictured Conan, mutilated for having rescued his blood brother before the Rulers made him into a drone. Hell, any decent man would have done what Conan had.

Two drones stood, watching Shedir, mindlessly waiting for him to voice the smallest command. Just looking at them made him feel guilty, as much as if he'd been the one to order the obliteration of their humanity. Had these creatures been transformed as children, before they'd known more than the need for food and rest?

The wholesale mutilations made no sense. Mutant gene or not, its victims could have been sterilized and left to experience the joy and pain of living. The Rulers hadn't needed to steal their minds and hearts. If they'd wanted to destroy the males' ability to dominate and master their female counterparts, they could simply have made them eunuchs but let them retain their humanity. Ironically, Shedir's own ancestors had been shunned as barbarians for using castrated male slaves to guard their harems.

The Rulers had nothing against sterilizing females to use for their own pleasure. Not long ago Shedir had looked forward to the day he'd be granted his own harem full of concubines modified to give only pleasure to their Master. Now, all he wanted was to escape, return to Luna Ten, find each erogenous spot on Doreen's velvety, sensitive skull while she knelt and sucked his cock. He'd fuck her tight little ass, then free her creamy cunt from his jeweled chastity belt and fill her with his hot seed while suckling her firm, pink nipples.

By now her nipples would be swollen in preparation for nourishing their child. A child who'd grow up whole... free from the constant threat of mutilation or destruction. Damn it. Shedir didn't want to visit the breeding pens as he'd been ordered to do. He lusted only for Doreen, had longed to hear her little whimpers of pleasure for months now while he'd patrolled the galaxy, fought sky pirates. He'd barely been able to focus on business this morning while he'd given the requisite report of his exploits to his superior officer.

He'd come here thinking of Earth as home. It wasn't. No longer. Home was with Doreen. Stripping off his uniform, he stood naked before the drones. In slow motion he lifted the heavy pendant of the sky command over his head and set it down. No more. Wrapping his naked body in the robe of a Federation sperm donor, he strode from the villa, past the breeding pens he'd been ordered to visit.

Nodding to the occasional passer-by, Shedir made his way to the landing pads, sparing a fleeting glance at the starship he'd commanded for so long. As he fired up the engines in a small transporter he'd bought for off-duty play, he realized he no longer needed the pride, the ambition that a Federation starship had always represented.

Shedir was going home. Home to Luna Ten, this time to stay.

Epilogue

One fine day six months after Shedir's departure, Doreen held a ladder in the orchard while Nebula picked sweet, succulent grapes to make Luna Ten's ceremonial wine. They'd need more for the celebration Doreen planned for her Master's triumphant return.

Her cunt ached with anticipation, for it had been six months since he'd mated with her and gone away. Only his son, kicking merrily in her belly, had kept her from going mad with loneliness, need.

"Do you hear that?" Nebula asked.

"What?" Then Doreen heard it, the roar of a ship breaking into the atmosphere of Luna Ten. "Shedir!" she yelled, dropping her basket of grapes and sprinting to the landing pad. "My Master is home. That's him climbing out of the blue transporter."

Sprinting from the small, sporty space vehicle, Shedir scooped Doreen up, laying sweet, gentle kisses over her swollen breasts and belly as he strode with her to the fucking glade. "By the god of my forefathers, how I've missed this. Missed you." Once inside, he laid her on the velvety grass beneath the magic vines and lifted a thin gold chain from around his neck. A chain that held the key to the chastity belt and nipple shields.

His clean male musk and the fragrance of the purple flowers above them swirled around her. Her clit swelled, and her cunt creamed with anticipation when he unlocked her jeweled restraints and swept them away.

"I have missed you, too, Master." Greedy for the feel of his hands, his mouth, his hot cock, she spread her legs. "Will you take your pleasure now?"

With both hands, he cupped her swollen belly. "I'd not hurt you or our child."

"You will not. I beg you, Master, take me."

Very gently, her Master lay between her legs, using his pierced tongue to trace a heated path along her wet slit. "I love your cream," he said, laying his cheek briefly against the mound that was their child before resuming his sensual assault on her swollen sex. "I love you."

When he plucked and twisted her distended nipples, she whimpered with pleasure. It had been so long. Too long. She welcomed the rasp of his facial hair against the tender skin of her cunt. She stroked his gleaming skull, remembering when he let out a groan of pure ecstasy how good it felt when he fondled the erogenous areas on her own cleanly shaven head.

For hours he petted her, giving of himself with hands and tongue while taking little in return. She'd come until she thought she could take no more when finally he shifted, positioned his throbbing cock, and filled her as she'd longed to be filled for six long, lonely months. "Oh, yesss. Master, you feel so good. So hot. Fuck me hard."

Doreen had never felt so wanted. So cherished. So complete when he sank into her so deeply that his heavy testicles slapped against her ass. Braced as he was on his forearms, sparing her his weight, he gave her an incredibly erotic view of each careful thrust. She loved his power, so obvious in the hard bulge of his biceps, the rippling motion of his sculpted abdominal muscles.

It was the soft look in Shedir's dark eyes, though, that warmed Doreen's heart, told her she was more than a warm body to provide his pleasure. And the gentleness of his full, soft lips, still glistening with her juices when he bent to take her mouth. She grew impossibly wetter, more swollen... wanting... "Please, Master, may I come?"

"Come. Come with me. Oh gods, I can't hold out much longer." He threw back his head, came in her in hot, staccato bursts that triggered feelings so intense she trembled beneath him. Bursts of sensation lifted her onto another plane where there was no thought -- just the sensation of his seed searing her cunt, her inner muscles gripping him as though she could hold him inside her forever.

When Doreen began to recover, she felt his large hands cupping her head, saw him leaning over her, a look of wonder on his handsome face. "I'm home to stay," he murmured, punctuating each word with kisses along her temples.

Doreen could hardly believe her ears. Her Master was giving up the power and prestige on Earth that meant everything to him. Giving it up for her -- for the sake of freedom on Luna Ten. "You mean it?"

His dark gaze met hers, and he smiled. Then he bent over her belly and lapped her distended navel. "What can I give you for giving me this child?"

Doreen met his soft, loving gaze. "I want you to help me find a mate for Nebula."

"Anything." Shedir gathered her in his arms, dropping kisses on her head, her throat, her swollen, aching breasts. "My precious slave, your wish is my command."

Luna Ten: Nebula

Ann Jacobs

Prologue

No need to disembark from his starship. He'd be leaving again at daybreak. Conan's superiors had annoyed the hell out of him by ordering him back to base in the middle of a patrol of the Delta quadrant, and for no better reason than to make up for a shortage in his required sperm deposits last month. Damn them anyway. By the time he could get back into the fray, the sky pirates they'd been fighting might well be taking out the unprotected flanks of the Federation defense.

The more he thought about it, the more asinine the Federation's laws on breeding seemed. It made no sense to Conan for designated breeder males to have to provide enough sperm to impregnate a thousand faceless women, yet never fuck a one, and never be father to any of the unknown number of children their seed might help produce.

Complaining would do no good. The law was the law. Shutting down his mental processes so he could do his duty, Conan loosened his uniform pants and stepped up to the sexbot that stood ready to accept his semen. He'd leave a deposit as required by Federation law, and then he'd get back to his real business of combating space terrorists. This detour had cost him two weeks. Spiriting his scapegrace half-brother to safety had taken him away from his duties for less than two days.

Fuck, the rulers must consider his seed as valuable as the platinum the Federation was trying to mine on Mars. Otherwise, why would they have quibbled because his deposit was a few ounces short of quota last month? Lucky they got any at all, as furious as he'd been when he learned they'd ordered Brendan turned into a drone because he'd sneaked into a breeding farm and tried to impregnate several of the women the old-fashioned way. Feeling distinctly unmotivated to do his duty to the Federation, Conan grasped his cock and inserted it in the sexbot's well-lubricated cunt.

The familiar whirring noise of the motor, the 'bot's tight, cool cunt jacking his cock, and the stimulation of his prostate by its rigid metal finger felt cold. Mechanical. Conan's cock swelled within the false cunt, and his balls drew up close to his body as it raced toward the expected, precisely timed release. He thought back on the human sex slaves he'd fucked when off planet, recalling the silken touch of their bodies on his, the incredible feeling of spilling his seed in another human being instead of in this sterile sperm depository.

A safe sex slave. That's what Brendan had decided to become once Conan had delivered him to the pleasure planet Obsidion. Good thing for him Conan had managed to intervene before the surgeons had finished carrying out his brother's sentence and made him into a mindless, totally sexless drone. Although Conan had held higher hopes for his younger sibling than for him to service sex-starved space travelers, at least Brendan still possessed his mind, his humanity -- and his cock though not his balls.

Conan was almost there, though the process of draining his seed was singularly devoid of emotion. He stood, his legs braced, knees slightly bent, anticipating the rush of sensation he knew would be coming in a few seconds. Coming now.

A clash of metal, and three burly men stormed through the cabin door. "Enjoy it, traitor, for it will be your last time." The harsh voice penetrated Conan's fuzzy mind as his climax washed over him. "Here's what happens to those who thwart the rulers' will."

A flash of silver caught his eye, just before mind-stealing agony overwhelmed him. He hadn't been sent home to make a sperm deposit. Some bastard had turned him in for saving Brendan, Conan realized before he blessedly lost consciousness.

* * *

"Where... what?" Conan blinked, then glanced around... a

tent?

"The rulers have ordered you into exile. We're in the Wastelands, waiting to rendezvous with Shedir. He will take you somewhere safe."

"Miles?" Exile? Wastelands? Why was he here with Miles, his copilot, somewhere on the deserted half of Earth that had been destroyed generations ago in the wars with the mutants? "Why?" It hurt to move, even his lips. Conan struggled to stay awake. Mind was fuzzy. He hurt. He remembered. The flash of that knife... He lifted his right arm, nearly cried out when he saw the tightly bandaged stump that ended just below his elbow.

"The Security Enforcement Corps. They cut you the old-fashioned way, instead of using a laser gun. The rulers ordered it, to make an example for any who might consider aiding another fugitive in his escape from justice."

"My..." Conan tried to sit up, but he fell back against the primitive excuse for a cot.

Miles diverted his gaze. "They took that, too. All of it."

A one-armed eunuch. Why the fuck hadn't they killed him outright? "Where will Shedir take me?"

"He's booked on a mission to Obsidion. He has spoken to Pak Song, the cyborg maker there, who assures us he can make you a new hand. Maybe a new cock too." Miles laughed, as though trying to make light of Conan's situation. Then he sobered. "The Star Command takes care of its own."

* * *

Two weeks later, Conan donned the white robe of a complete eunuch and hobbled on shaky legs to Shedir's sleek space fighter. Not his own starship. Not now, not ever again.

Fuck, he'd been the Federation's best. He'd given his best years to patrolling the galaxy, keeping Earth safe from would-be invaders. He stared back toward his old starship. He'd miss commanding a squadron, fighting forces of evil in the name of the Federation. He wouldn't miss the motherfuckers who'd mutilated him because he'd put blood loyalty over the Federation's laws. He'd do the same today.

Life as he'd known it was over. Briefly he considered using his remaining hand to finish what the SEC operatives had begun, but his gods would protest if he ended his miserable life. He tried to persuade himself Pak Song might be able to restore him.

By the end of the following week, Shedir had delivered Conan to Obsidion, to the man in whom Conan had placed all his hopes.

"I fix arm. No problem. About cock, not so sure. Never tried to put bionic cock on human. Making it work will take some doing," the robot maker said, his wizened face wrinkled and thoughtful looking. "We see what I come up with."

Chapter One

"You want arm stay on all the time, or you take off, make adjustments whenever you want?" Pak Song looked up from the scarred stump where Conan's right arm had been.

Conan didn't want to become a cyborg at all, since Pak Song hadn't seemed at all sure he could restore amputated genitals. Still, if Conan was to earn his keep on some planet where its rulers would accept his modifications, he needed the use of two strong arms. "What type of adjustments are you talking about?"

"Arm complex mechanism. Many electronic components to making hand work. Many parts to wear out, malfunction. Thought since you are engineer you might like to make minor repairs."

When the wizened genius showed him a schematic of a robotic hand, Conan saw what he meant. "Let's make it removable." After all, there was no chance -- no chance at all -- that there might someday be a female in his life to object that he could remove an appendage at will.

Not now. He was as impotent as any drone back on Earth. A eunuch. He'd almost become accustomed to thinking of himself as one, but he hadn't yet dredged up the courage to say the word out loud. Conan cringed with shame at the thought of his empty crotch -- a shame broadcasted to one and all by the hooded white robe decreed by custom throughout the galaxy as standard apparel for creatures altered as he had been. Fury overcame him, as it had every time since he'd awakened and learned what they'd done to him. He clenched his fist until the nails dug into his palm, welcoming the pain there and in the hand that was no longer there. Welcoming the dull ache between his legs where they'd hacked away his manhood.

Conan hated the bitterness in himself, almost as much as he hated the bastards who'd mutilated him. "I can see where being able to adjust the mechanism in the hand might come in handy," he said, trying for a smile.

"Okay. Think I figured out how to give you new cock. May as well implant it while I got you in surgery to implant bionics for arm. Will save you second operation."

"You figured out how to make one that works? Good."

Pak Song grinned. "I make cocks for sexbots every day. No reason won't work for you." He waved an arm toward a long row of dildos on a nearby shelf. "Any of those models work well in my deluxe sexbots. Have testimonials from many happy ladies. Pick one you like best."

Conan visually scanned the colorful false cocks that ranged from almost natural looking to outrageous. "The one at the end, with the flashing green neon color in the veins, looks interesting." It sure as hell didn't look *real*. "While you're at it, why not make me a new set of balls too?"

Pak Song gestured toward Conan's robe. "I wish I could. Also wish I could promise cock would work like real one. Like I said, never tried this before, but will do best I can." Then he paused. "I consult with urologist. He can help me connect what remains of your urethra to artificial extension so new cock will function correctly for elimination. No reason I cannot implant a bionic cock that will work at least as good as sexbot. Would love to try. Never had chance before." The old cyborg maker let out a sigh. "Most times, Earthling eunuchs like you -- ones that have lost it all -- get sent to the mines on Mars. Or made into drones."

"I've already put myself into your hands. If you think you can make me a new cock, go right ahead."

"Okay." The cyborg maker lifted the neon cock off the shelf. "You sure this is what yours looked like?"

"Don't they all look pretty much the same?" Conan liked the hefty size of the glowing dildo, and who the fuck cared if it provided a beacon in the dark?

"Up to you, Captain. Next week you get new arm." Pak Song shifted the artificial cock from one hand to the other, his eyes twinkling with amusement. "And new cock."

Conan hoped so. He'd still be a eunuch, but if he had a cock he wouldn't be quite as much a subject for pity and disdain. When Pak Song shuffled out of his hospital room, Conan stripped off the hated symbol of his unmanning and lay on the narrow bed to await his date with destiny.

His eyes closed, Conan imagined himself whole, his cock proudly rigid against his belly, his balls tight against his groin. As he approached his sexbot, it morphed into a voluptuous female... an Earthling woman whose sensuous movements tempted him beyond resistance. He moved closer, until they stood mere inches apart, his cock head brushing the slightly convex satin of her belly.

Forbidden. Her rich woman-scent filled his nostrils, made his mouth water to taste her mouth, her throat, her satiny cunt lips. His fingers itched to pluck ripe nipples the color of cherries. Her auburn hair called out to be stroked, caressed. Claimed in the way his ancestors had marked their mates for centuries before the Fall.

She knelt at his feet, as he expected a well-trained slave to do. Her mouth felt hot and wet, like nectar of the gods on his smoothly shaven balls, his rampant cock. His juices bubbled, stimulated by her hands and mouth and the sight of her there, subservient to his desire. She'd drink his come, then beg him to give her more of the same where it might take root.

Pressure built in his balls. He strained to find release. When it didn't come, Conan reached for his lover. Had to have her take more of his cock down her agile throat. "Suck me, damn it. I'm..." He felt not the woman's silken hair but his own empty groin. "... fucking dreaming."

Chapter Two

"Ouch." It felt to Conan as though Pak Song were ripping away his skin along with the pressure bandages that had covered his crotch for what seemed like at least the last six months.

"Look." The old man beamed down at his handiwork. "I make you cock."

Conan stared at the mirror suspended above his bed -- at the biggest penis he'd ever seen, complete with a catheter protruding from the slit at its tip. It sprang from his hairless groin the way his own cock once had, and curved against his thigh as though a permanent part of his anatomy.

Apparently it was.

When it twitched and began to thicken when the robot maker lifted and examined it, Pak Song cackled. "I told you. I make you cock that works."

Gods in the universe, he had a cock again. A hot-pink cock with a glowing purple head and neon green veins that blinked up at him as the flesh hardened beneath his gaze... "It doesn't look -- real."

"Cock looks exactly like the model you picked, except I made it bigger. You big guy. Bigger than sexbot I designed that one for."

Shit. Conan hadn't exactly envisioned having a cock that looked exactly like the one he'd selected. Or one quite so fucking huge. "All it needs is a ring or two," he commented, imagining some sparkling stones winking from the head and shaft of the monster appendage.

The wrinkles on Pak Song's forehead deepened, as though he were deep in thought. Finally he looked up at Conan's face. "Once you've healed, piercing it should be okay as long as you get acrylic ring. Metal would short out electrodes."

It was all Conan could do not to break out laughing. "When

can that be done?"

"Another week, maybe. After catheter comes out."

Conan lifted the monster cock -- the thing felt real enough -- and slid his fingers lower. "No balls?"

"I work on prototype. Maybe have one ready by time you wear out this cock."

"Wear it out?"

"Sure. Ladies love this model. Told you so. Still, if color too much for you, next time try for more natural look. Had to give it electrical energy to get you aroused, so you can come. Neon fiber-optic sensors transmit impulses through cock to surface, like nerve endings. Lights get brighter as sensation gets stronger. You like light show when you come. Maybe next time I tune it up, I make sac with fake balls too. Hate making things that don't work right." The corners of Pak Song's mouth lifted, and he held his palms apart. "Is twelve inches when erect. Like this. Two inches diameter. Deluxe sexbot sized. Don't believe in doing things halfway. Made you most popular sexbot model."

Conan wondered if he'd be able to get his man-made, neon cock up at will or whether he'd have to pump it as he understood women had to do with most sexbots, but he wasn't inclined to ask just now. Now that he'd recovered from the first look at the outrageous cock -- he was actually rather intrigued by it -- he turned his attention to his arm. He could feel it, or maybe he was just feeling the arm that wasn't there anymore, because while it looked absolutely real, Conan hadn't been able to control the movement of the wrist or fingers, no matter how hard he tried.

"It doesn't work," he said as the arm came off in Pak Song's hands.

"It will." The cyborg maker set the realistic looking forearm and hand on Conan's stomach, then lifted the stump of his arm to the light. "Ah. Just as I thought. Loose connection here. Not making contact." Pak Song folded back a flap of skin-like material, revealing a grid of complex circuits that passed nerve impulses from Conan's stump to the bionic arm. Pak Song looked up and grinned. "I made flap this way so you not scare people when you not wearing your arm. You like?"

Pak Song's skill amazed Conan. His meticulous attention to detail in hiding the high-tech circuits that connected his own severed muscles and nerves to the ones in his prosthesis seemed unimportant now that the prosthesis acted as an extension of Conan's own body. "I doubt anyone will have occasion to see."

When he had on the prosthesis, the only visible evidence of his severed hand and lower arm would be the barely discernable line where flesh met the bionic replacement -- unlike his colorful cock, which was now a permanent part of his anatomy. If he ever disrobed, that new addition couldn't possibly escape notice. Of course the empty crotch it had replaced would have grabbed attention of a different kind.

"Oh, yeah, Captain. Some pretty lady will see. You gonna work better than sexbot, even best ones I make." The robot maker grinned. "Just wait. You be horny devil once this hormone starts working. Get back sex drive." Pak Song slapped a small square patch onto Conan's left hip. Testosterone, forbidden on Earth, was apparently easy to come by on Obsidion. "You try out new cock in one of the pleasure palaces, once catheter comes out and Leander gets cock pierced to please the ladies. Better yet, I lend you one of my best sexbots to practice on. Now sit up and pay attention. I show you how we make this arm work good as the one you lost."

* * *

The following week, freed from his bed at last, Conan made his first stop the barber and piercer next door to Pak Song's Sexbot Emporium. He felt naked without a ring in his cock -- almost as naked as he'd felt when he'd had no cock at all.

"Pak Song says use this," Leander said, grinning as he held up a thick, clear circle. "I never put a fiber-optic cock ring on a man before. Just on Pak Song's deluxe sexbots. Changes color, tells your lover you're in the mood." He lost no time once Conan had stripped, climbed onto the piercing table, and positioned his legs in the stirrups. "This shouldn't hurt. Pak Song says cock only has feeling when it's hard, except for sensors that let you know when you need to pee. This piercing won't interfere with them."

He laughed. "Good thing, in case you get into fight. No pain when opponent knees you in groin." Quickly, Leander marked and pierced the head of the glowing hot-pink cock with its psychedelic green veining. As he'd promised, the large gauge needle went through without causing the slightest twinge, and Leander threaded the transparent ring through the hole.

Once he'd closed the ring with a purple captive bead, he glanced up at the five weeks' growth of hair on Conan's shaggy head. "You need shave. Or wax. Head, not body. No hair on body. And you should get new nipple rings to match cock."

Conan glanced down at the simple gold barbells that adorned his nipples. It seemed they'd already grown slightly larger and softer since his castration. Perhaps Leander was right. "Do you have acrylic rings? Thinner ones?" He couldn't imagine having rings as thick as the one now swinging from his cock head dangling from his nipples.

"Yes, boss." Reaching into a drawer, Leander brought forth a pair of rings and laid them in Conan's hand. "These one inch diameter. Perfect to make your nipples stand up for attention."

"Thanks. I guess that will be all."

"What about shave?"

"I have no body hair to worry about. Pak Song permanently removed it. Said it would have interfered with the electronics inside me. I think I'll keep the hair on my head. It covers the scars where Pak Song inserted his electrodes. Go ahead, though, and clip it back to about a quarter-inch or so." Once Conan would have cringed at the idea of anybody seeing him with hair sprouting out of his skull, but no more. He no longer cared that he didn't look the same as every other Earthling male. Hell, he was no longer welcome on Earth, and no longer male, strictly speaking, a fact that had to have been obvious to the barber who'd just finished inserting a fiber-optic ring through his prosthetic penis. There wasn't much point in keeping his head shaved now.

Once Leander cut his hair, Conan ran the fingers of his bionic hand through the short stubble. It felt good. Soft, yet prickly. Different, after a lifetime of keeping his scalp cleanly shaven in accord with Federation regulations.

"Thanks, Leander. I'm sure we'll meet again." Conan stepped through the connecting door from the barbershop to Pak Song's workroom and switched on the sexbot the robot maker had provided for him to test his cock.

"Here. Try this. Helps eunuchs to find pleasure," Pak Song said, handing Conan a slender silver plug that reminded him of the finger on his Federation-issued sexbot. "Let it massage prostate while you have sex."

"Thanks." Untying his robe, Conan bent and worked the plug up his ass, then stepped up to let the sexbot do its thing.

It worked. His fuckin' cock worked, and not just to pass urine. It got hard when the 'bot jacked it in its soft, feminine hand. When he began to fuck the 'bot, it milked him in its tight little cunt. Damn, but he felt each contraction of synthetic flesh on his own man-made cock. An almost-forgotten sensation of fierce arousal claimed his mind and his body -- followed by a climax of sorts, thought not exactly the same spurting, tension-releasing feelings he recalled, but still a climax. A sense of satiation, satisfaction.

Conan missed the buildup of pressure in his balls, the feeling of them drawing up close to his body, filling his cock with the hot, slick semen he'd never again spew into a 'bot's sterile depository, even if Pak Song should come up with balls that worked before his next tune-up. But damn it, he could fuck and he could come, if not in quite the same way as before. He could fuck a real woman and not only bring her to pleasure, but also find a good measure of gratification for himself. He wanted to grab the old cyborg maker and hug him until he begged for mercy.

Dismounting from the sexbot, he noticed his old friends Shedir and Guy talking with Pak Song, and he hurried to the showroom to join them.

* * *

"We've found you a master. A mate. His name is Conan, and he was an Earthling Star Commander before the Federation exiled him. As a matter of fact, he once was Shedir's boss."

"You didn't." Nebula looked first to Guy, who'd just made that incredible pronouncement, then at Shedir, whose attention was focused at the moment not on the conversation but on the blowjob Doreen was putting on his cock. They both must have been desperate for release since they'd just returned to Luna Ten from a week-long journey to Obsidion.

Self-conscious in her blue robe when everyone else in the room was gloriously naked, Nebula asked, "What will this Conan think when he finds out I'm sterile?"

"He knows. He's been fixed too. Think of him as a sexbot with a brain." Guy laughed as he shot a look at Doreen. "A 'bot who can't be fucked to death."

Doreen lifted her head off Shedir's throbbing cock, and the look she sent Guy's way could easily have killed. "Shut up, cyborg, or my master will make you pay."

"Your master will make you pay if you take your pretty lips off his cock again before he comes." Shedir grasped Doreen's head, caressing her bare skull as he pushed her face back down to his groin. "Suck me, my beautiful slave." He moaned when she deep-throated him, a sound that conveyed impending ecstasy, then turned to Nebula. "Conan's a good sort. Used to turn all the breeder women's heads when he'd drop by the breeding farm to leave a sample."

Shedir closed his eyes, thrust his hips forward, and groaned, louder this time. "Oh, yeah, baby, I'm coming. Gods, but you suck cock better than any 'bot I ever had."

Nebula's mouth watered. She imagined herself on her knees as both her sisters were, giving pleasure to a master she'd never dreamed she might be allowed to serve that way. Though she couldn't visualize a real man wanting her the way she was, she trusted that her brothers-in-law wouldn't have come back home with this shocking news if it weren't true. "You mean he's a cyborg? Like you?" she asked Guy.

"Not exactly." Guy had the decency to blush as he gestured toward Cassie's busy mouth -- and his own impressive package. "We're both cyborgs, but we've had different body parts replaced.

My cock's all natural. Conan's isn't."

"But can he..." She didn't quite know how to ask. Males were so... so hung up about their sexual prowess. Argus and Aloysius, Doreen and Shedir's twin eunuch houseboys, seemed to have lost all vestiges of their maleness along with the equipment that long ago had hung between their legs.

"Absolutely. When we visited him, Conan was testing his bionic cock out on one of Pak Song's female 'bots. Looked to me as though it worked just fine. Big, too." Shedir bent and ran his pierced tongue over the crown of Doreen's gleaming scalp while he cupped his big hands around her very pregnant belly.

There'd be no babies for Nebula. She'd asked the doctors on Obsidion to destroy her ovaries to keep her from passing on the aberrant gene everyone feared so much. Maybe, since he'd been so badly injured himself, Conan might be willing to accept her, imperfect as she was. Still... "How did he --"

"A Federation Tribunal ordered his mutilation. They considered it fit punishment because he'd rescued his half-brother and spirited him off Earth before the rulers could turn him into a drone." His handsome face contorted with rage, Shedir lifted his hands from Doreen's belly, clenched them into tight fists. Since he'd given up his dreams of becoming a member of the Ruling Council and made Luna Ten his home, he'd become more and more openly critical of Federation policy.

Pity. Nebula believed the former captain of the Federation Star Command would have made a good ruler. A fair one. "This Conan is on Obsidion now?"

"Yes. Pak Song has a few more adjustments to make. The man's a genius, but he's incredibly picky when it comes to his bionics. When Conan is ready, he'll contact us, and either Guy or I will fly to Obsidion and bring him here."

"When you do, I'd like to go with you." Nebula refused to let herself become too eager, too soon. Bionic or not, this Conan was an Earthling, and the last Earthling male she'd offered herself to had said he'd rather fuck a sexbot than spill his seed in a live female who'd been neutered.

Chapter Three

A mate. A companion to love and care for, to serve as Doreen and Cassie served Shedir and Guy. As women served their men on Luna Ten. Nebula wanted that, so much she ached with need. But she didn't dare hope this Conan would be any different from the Earthling privateer who not too long ago had driven home the fact that love -- companionship -- was not for her.

In the fucking glade where lovers mated, she slipped off her blue robe, let the sunshine warm her naked skin. The sweet smell of flowering fruit trees filled her nostrils, and birds chirped overhead. They didn't care that she'd been altered... that she'd been marked since childhood for a life of loneliness. Of servitude to those who'd not been cursed with the mutant gene.

She'd been naked then as she was now, and the exiled Earthling had caught her unaware. He'd not had Guy's awesome presence or Shedir's commanding looks. In fact, the man had looked quite ordinary. Unremarkable. Nebula had been sunning herself, drying off the water from the stream in which she'd bathed... combing tangles from the long, wavy hair that had veiled her body, hidden her shame.

He'd smiled at her, the smile of one who felt desire. Her nipples had tingled with the heat of his gaze. His cock had risen in silent salute. For the first time in her life Nebula had felt whole.

"Let me." He'd taken the comb from her, run it through her hair, bent and sucked first one nipple and then the other. "You are beautiful. You're mine."

"No." A warning rang somewhere deep in Nebula's head, but the pleasure of another human's touch had muted her protest. Her would-be lover had laid her over the fucking stone, as though to mate with her...

Could he? Could he want her, imperfect as she was? It seemed he did. His cock prodded her from behind, seeking her ass to claim her.

She couldn't let him… not until he knew. "I welcome you as my mate, but you must first know, I'm a eunuch. Altered to prevent the spread of the mutant gene."

He'd jerked away as though she'd burned him, rolled her onto her back. His gaze hung on the tattoo, her mark of shame. "Mate with the likes of you? I'd rather die. And I'd sooner fuck a sexbot than spill my seed in you. Eunuch." He spat out the word as though it were a curse, then walked away.

Come to think of it, it was. A curse Nebula would have to live with all her life.

* * *

"Can one of these do for a woman what it does for me?" Conan gestured toward the patch on his hip while Pak Song was making a final check of his handiwork before pronouncing him fully recovered -- he hoped.

"That one can't. Females need different hormone." The elderly cyborg maker bent his head to the task of adjusting a tiny electronic control implanted below the skin of Conan's thigh. "Different patch for women. Patches look almost like yours. Have to be replaced monthly. Outlawed practically everywhere in the galaxy. Why? You have a neutered female friend?"

"Possibly. Do you recall my two friends who visited the day I was in your shop, trying my new cock out on your sexbot?"

"Guy Stone. My first successful attempt at creating a bionic human. And your mutual friend Shedir. They both now live on Luna Ten, yes?"

"Yes. I have been invited to resettle there, and offered a mate. An Earthling female, sister of Shedir and Guy's wives."

"A eunuch?"

Hearing the word, whether applied to himself or the female he'd been offered as his mate, rankled, though if she'd not been one herself, it would have been unthinkable to offer her to a -- one like him. "Yes. She had herself neutered because she carries the mutant gene."

"You worry she will not pleasure you?"

"I worry that I will not be able to give *her* pleasure. That she will find no joy in serving my sexual needs." Conan recalled crude jests made in locker rooms and barrooms back on earth about neutered females being of less use for sex than 'bots.

The old man smiled. "I will get you what you need. Have secret family recipe to keep females horny. Not fair I make you cock if it can't give your mate pleasure. You tell no one, though. Pak Song could lose head for dispensing it, even here on Obsidion."

* * *

Maybe... Conan had avoided the sex brokers, not wanting to encounter Brendan and make his brother feel guilty for what had happened to him. Still, he soon would leave Obsidion. Deciding he could conceal the worst of his punishment, thanks to Pak Song, Conan headed to the Street of Pleasure.

At the third of the sex slave emporiums, he spotted Brendan posing in the window, his body tanned and oiled, a large heart-shaped patch on his left hip. Testosterone, Conan guessed, although his own patches were square and skin-colored. As all the slaves did when a passerby stopped to look, Brendan lifted his flaccid penis, confirming his "safe" state while inclining his shaved head and flashing an encouraging smile. He didn't seem to mind the jeweled platinum collar fastened around his neck... or the tug of the chain attached to it when the man who apparently had purchased his services came and led him away.

Brendan had a new life. One he seemed satisfied with. He hadn't even seemed to recognize Conan. His brother had rented himself out as a sex slave, a common path for handsome eunuchs. He now sold sex to all comers -- mostly males, from the flow of customers Conan had seen go in and out of that pleasure palace. Conan had the feeling Brendan wouldn't want to be seen as he was now -- especially not by someone he'd revered in his former life on Earth.

A life where only women had been slaves. Here, in a land with few rules, male eunuchs serviced whole males and female adventurers alike. From what Conan had observed, sex slavery was one of the few career paths open to those who'd been altered for whatever reason.

It wouldn't be Conan's path, though. He'd soon have a mate. He'd be a master. From what Shedir had told him, Luna Ten was a utopian sort of place, where women were willing slaves, men their masters. Conan couldn't imagine himself taking part in the group sexfests that Shedir had explained took place nearly every day -- or going about naked with his glowing bionic cock standing tall for everyone to see.

Perhaps he could. Stopping before a pleasure palace displaying beautiful females -- guaranteed neutered, according to the sign in the window -- he imagined himself leading one of the beauties away by the light chain around her slender neck, taking her in a fucking chair. Pounding his cock into her cunt while he pressed her against a wall. One lady's full red mouth caught his eye. His cock swelled within his robe. Gods, but he'd love to have her give him head. He'd love to go down on her.

She looked at him. No, she didn't. She looked through him, as if because of his blue robe he were beneath her notice. An eager looking space privateer, from the look of his uniform, stepped up from behind Conan, went inside, and came back out, leading the woman of Conan's fantasy.

Fuck the damn robe. He might be a cyborg, but he was no damn eunuch sex slave. Conan headed from the Street of Pleasure. He'd seen a clothing store somewhere not far from Leander's. Surely he could find a uniform -- not like the ones he used to wear, but one that would do justice to the civil engineer he was to become on Luna Ten.

He was right. Clothes did, as old legend said, make the man. Glancing at his reflection an hour later, Conan admired the snug black boots, tight breeches, and bright-blue tunic he'd chosen, then turned his thoughts to Nebula. She'd be his mate. Together they would face his brave new world.

* * *

An hour later Conan settled in at Yolanda's Resort. It had been a long time since he'd stayed here -- long before his mutilation and exile, even before he'd decided to risk himself and save his brother. Then the imposing hotel had been a pleasure palace known as the Gates of Hell. He saw from the brochure on a nightstand that Yolanda had retained the main dungeon where he'd once tortured and fucked most of the nubile submissives who'd worked there. She'd also created new, smaller dungeons that apparently catered to every perversion known on Earth -- and a few that weren't.

Then he'd pleasured a bevy of willing subs. Now he only had to please his future mate. Nebula. Pretty name. Conan looked at himself in the mirror.

Damn, he'd forgotten about his hair. As much as he preferred the uniform over the damn blue robe, he slipped it on and adjusted the hood. Wouldn't do to shock her immediately. Maybe he should have stopped by Leander's and had his head waxed one more time.

Shedir had told him he and Guy would be arriving at twelve hundred hours with their mates. And his. The plan was for them all to take a short holiday, have Pak Song recheck Guy's bionics, and avail themselves of exotic wares in Obsidion's shops, considered the most exclusive in the galaxy. And enjoy their mates in the arousing atmosphere of the hotel's renowned dungeons before returning home to Luna Ten for the mating ceremony.

The farce. There'd be no fertility rites, not for them. Just a public mating. An acknowledgment of their physical limitations before the entire population of Luna Ten, to be repeated, admittedly with less pomp, every day they returned to the fucking glade and joined the others in a sex ritual as old as time. A holdover from the Old Order on Earth, before the Fall. Before the Federation with its ironclad rules and swift punishment for the least infraction.

Restless, Conan strode to the window, discovered it overlooked the hotel entrance. What time was it? Lifting his bionic hand, he checked his chronometer. They should be coming soon. There they were, coming toward the main entrance to the resort.

Shedir, he'd have known anywhere from his swarthy skin, the fine sheen of his freshly shaven, well-oiled skull -- but mostly from the swagger that said louder than words that he was a man. An Earthling ruler, even though he now wore the red jumpsuit of a space privateer, not the awe-inspiring black uniform of the Federation Star Command. Guy looked different than Conan remembered him. He'd known there would be changes, expected them. Still, seeing his old colleague's glowing scarlet eyes, set off by large faceted rubies in his nostril and one ear, unnerved him.

Until Conan remembered he, too, was not as he'd been before. His glowing neon cock certainly attracted its share of stares when he had occasion to bare it to prying eyes. His unshaved head would have attracted even more astonished comments if he ever went out and about without concealing it within the hood. He tightened his anal sphincter muscles on the titanium plug he wore at Pak Song's suggestion that it would enhance a eunuch's sexual performance, although in truth he doubted the plug had as much to do with his newly recovered libido as the one-inch square testosterone patch stuck to his left ass cheek.

Three women trailed behind the two tall men: a delicate looking blonde, a striking pregnant goddess whose cleanly shaved head reflected the noonday sun, and another -- his mate, he guessed from the pale blue robe that hugged her curves and framed a perfect oval face. As befit an unbred Earthling -- or a female eunuch -- she cast her gaze modestly toward the ground. Gods, but she was beautiful, a shy goddess dropped onto Obsidion for his personal pleasure.

Conan's cock rose in salute. He checked the drape of his robe over his newly purchased uniform, adjusted the hood once more, and hurried downstairs to meet his mate. His Nebula. The woman with whom he hoped to find not only pleasure but -- if the gods willed it -- companionship, friendship, and maybe even love.

* * *

Conan. Nebula murmured his name. He'd meet her soon. Her heart pounded in her chest. What if... "What if he doesn't want me?"

"Hush, little sister. He'll want you, all right," Doreen said. Cassie squeezed her hand, offering silent support.

"You're sure?" Gods, if he rejected her, she'd die.

Doreen shook her head. "He's known. He's known from the beginning about the gene. He doesn't care."

Please let that be true. Nebula doubted she could take another rejection like the one she recalled so vividly.

When Shedir opened the door to the resort hotel where they were staying, Nebula spied a tall man hurrying toward them. His blue robe proclaimed his altered status but did little to mitigate the aura of masculine power that surrounded him.

Conan. She repeated the name in her mind, envisioned herself serving her master's needs, whatever they might be. When he came close and paused as though for her obeisance, Nebula sank to her knees. As she'd been taught a slave must do, she lowered her head to the cool tile floor of the hotel lobby, then raised his flowing blue robe enough so she could kiss his feet, only to encounter gleaming leather boots instead of a eunuch's sandals.

"We'll leave you to your own devices, old friend. Our mates are weary from their journey." Shedir dragged Doreen away, and Guy scooped Cassie into his arms and bounded down the corridor toward the dungeons. A tremor went through Nebula's body at the thought of being alone with Conan, but she managed to hide it -- staying starkly still, her forehead anchored to the cold tile floor.

"Rise, Nebula. I'd see your face, not the back of a hood with which I'm growing quite familiar." Unlike other neutered males Nebula had met, Conan possessed a booming voice resounding with masculine command. It sent a practically forgotten twinge of something -- desire? -- from her cunt and through her body. "Shedir tells me you've been on Obsidion before. Is there anything in particular you'd like to visit while we're here?"

Nebula smiled. "Well, perhaps I'd enjoy shopping a bit if that pleases you. Finding a few items to enhance your enjoyment of me."

"You please me, just as you are. Come, I'm sure that like your sisters and brothers-in-law, you're weary from your journey." When Conan took her hand, that twinge deep in Nebula's belly began to grow, warming her blood as it flowed through her body. "I'd see you naked, and I'd let you see me. Privately, not in the public dungeon for all to witness. We may dispense with these robes once we reach my rooms."

She rose, as gracefully as one could rise from her kneeling position. "As you wish, Master." Though she half-feared looking upon him and was more than half afraid for him to see her without the concealing robe, Nebula looked forward to having his big, rough hands on her. She longed to feel the heat of another human body on her, in her. For a moment she mourned the loss of her libido, but she quickly squelched her sadness. After all, her own pleasure was immaterial, so long as she was able to please her mate. She should be -- she was -- grateful he was rescuing her from a life of drudgery, of nonentity. Hopefully, he'd bring her the friendship and emotional closeness she'd thought forever beyond her reach.

She would do whatever she must to please this big eunuch with the booming voice, to serve and service him as was his pleasure. Anything to keep him.

Chapter Four

Conan must have pleased the gods to have been given so beautiful a mate. Auburn hair, long and silky and hanging halfway down her back, contrasted with satiny skin the color of rich cream. Except for her cheeks. They flushed prettily when she shed the robe and stood before him, her eyes downcast.

Her firm, ripe breasts would fill his hands, and the rosy tips of them beckoned his mouth. When his gaze moved lower, his cock rose to full attention. She had the prettiest belly, slightly convex... a plump mound. His mouth went dry at the sight of her little clit poking impudently out from between her satin-smooth labia. Gods save him, he could barely wait to feel those long, sexy legs wrapped around his waist... his neck.

"You please me, slave." If only he'd please her as much. Taking a deep breath, then steeling himself for a less-than-happy reaction, he tossed back the hood of his own robe and loosened the ties that held it closed.

"You -- you have hair," she stammered, her sober gaze fixed on the short crop of dark hair he'd insisted be left to grow on his scalp. "I -- I never --"

"You never saw a man with hair growing on his head? I doubt you've ever seen one with a glowing, neon-veined cock and no balls, either. Or one who could take one of his arms off and put it back on again." After shrugging out of the robe, he unbuttoned the row of shining fasteners on his tunic and shed it.

Gods, but he had massive shoulders and a smooth, tanned chest that tapered to a trim, narrow waist. She couldn't help watching the unusual looking twin rings swing from his taut brownish nipples. Then she remembered, and she turned her attention to his hard-muscled arms. What did he mean, he could take his arm off? His arms both looked normal enough until he grasped his right wrist, twisted it, and separated it from a point just below his elbow. She gasped.

"Bother you?"

For a moment she looked at the stump... the circuits connecting man and device... and the prosthesis itself. "No, it doesn't bother me. Seeing it for the first time was a bit of a shock, though. How does it work?"

"It's bionic. Sensors in the stump translate my mind's commands to the prosthesis. Occasionally the mechanism requires adjustment, so Pak Song made it detachable. As for how I lost the original parts, they were hacked from my body by order of the Federation rulers."

"Why?"

"I helped my half-brother escape from Earth before the rulers had time to turn him into a drone. Nothing I wouldn't do over again." Conan reversed the procedure, checking the connections first before reattaching the artificial extension onto his arm. "If you think the arm's shocking, brace yourself for a real surprise. You haven't seen anything yet," he muttered as his hands went to his belt.

His lower abdomen was ridged with muscle. Nebula had to restrain herself from reaching out, touching the smooth, golden skin, exploring the neat indentation of his navel and sliding her hand lower to explore the impressive bulge beneath the fabric of his tight pants.

He sighed, then shucked the rest of his clothes and straightened, his gaze defiant. "Go ahead. Say whatever it is you're thinking."

Nebula was speechless. Her voice caught in her throat. Her gaze wouldn't waver from the biggest, brightest cock she'd ever seen. "It -- it glows," she stammered when she finally found her voice. "And it's... huge."

It was growing bigger and harder before her eyes. "Oh, no. It's -- bright pink. No. Red. The veins are glowing. What --"

"Fiber optics. When I get hot, they let off energy." He grinned, but then his expression sobered when she reached out as if to touch him, then hesitated.

"I -- it's huge."

"The better to fuck you with."

Nebula looked dubious. "Does it feel like a real cock?"

"Yes, it feels like the real thing." With only a second's hesitation, he took her hand and wrapped it around the glowing appendage.

"Mmmm. Yes, it does. It's warm, and it feels alive." She slid her palm along his shaft, making him wish she'd pay equal attention to his tingling cock head.

"You look surprised," he said, teasing her. "Did you imagine it would be shrunken and useless?"

"Well, not exactly... but I didn't realize... that is, I didn't realize it would, er, work so well." Her cheeks, already rosy, turned an even deeper pink as she stared at his colorful erection.

"My sweet, you have no idea yet how well it works. But you will." *Soon.* Conan focused on her lips, full and ruby-red like the succulent meat of papayas sold in Obsidion's open-air produce markets. "I'm getting incredibly hot, imagining how your sweet, hot lips will feel surrounding it."

She reached out with her other hand and hesitantly stroked his cock head, which cooperatively grew hotter and harder. Its color deepened, the tip now glowing a darker reddish purple. Soon, he knew from his previous encounters, a clear drop of lubrication would well up around the ring she was now rotating gently through his flesh. Pak Song's answer to pre-cum, injected weekly into a reservoir behind his slit. Gods, but it felt so fucking good to have her caressing him.

"It feels so real." Wonder in her expression, she looked up and met his gaze.

"And how many cocks have you had occasion to play with?" Though he tried to sound stern, the question came out sounding playful, teasing.

"Very few, Master." The gentle curve of her spine caught Conan's eye. That and the distinctive tattoo on her mound. The small yet telling mark Earth's Federation placed on females deemed unfit for breeding. A mark that would have given him pause not too many months ago.

It didn't now. When she knelt before him, he parted his legs slightly, took his cock in hand, and held it to her lips. "You may taste me." His flesh tingled at the warm, damp kiss of her breath when she bent and took his glowing tool between her soft, red lips.

She lifted her face, met his gaze. "Can you feel..."

"Oh, yes, my pretty slave. When I'm hard like this, I feel every wet, warm swipe of your tongue. Every breath you take tickles my shaft. When you take me in your mouth, I'll feel that too. Suck me now."

"Yes, Master." When she bent over his aroused flesh, her hair formed a shimmering mahogany curtain that flowed over his thighs, obscured her face. He imagined the way her flushed cheeks would hollow out when she applied the gentle suction that had him straining to make her take his cock deeper down her throat. He wished he could see her. But it didn't matter. With the delicious sensations that bombarded him from her touch alone, he didn't need the visual stimulation.

Gods, but she gave great head. She sucked him as though she wouldn't stop until she'd drained him of every ounce of seed... seed he no longer possessed. She caught his cock ring with her tongue and rotated it.

She hesitated, as though afraid he'd protest. "Keep doing what you're doing," he said. "Oh, yeah. Like that, don't stop."

He tunneled his fingers through the rich silk fall of her hair, catching it up at her crown in his bionic hand, tugging the thick mass to coax her to move faster. Take more. Make him come.

Pressure seeped into his thighs, his belly. His nipples tingled when a breeze crossed them from an open window. With every draw of her throat against his cock head, his sphincter muscles contracted around the plug in his ass, pressed it against his prostate. Waves of pleasure began there, spread to his cock... flowed throughout his body. "Oh, yes, my sweet slave," he muttered, holding her head to his crotch. "Gods, it feels so good."

* * *

"But you didn't come," Nebula said later as they lay in bed. What had she done wrong?

Conan lifted his head, propped it up on his bionic hand. "I came. You gave me great pleasure. Never doubt it."

"But... I should have felt you coming, drunk of your..."

Conan laughed. "My seed? I have none, my sweet. Why do you think I wear the garb of a eunuch? Trust me. You provided me with pleasure. Pleasure that now takes more the form of yours."

"Oh." Nebula knew not whether to believe Conan. He seemed to have all the attributes of a whole man -- but for his amazing false cock, now resting, its color a pale, glowing rose-pink as it lay against his taut abdomen. "I wish to serve your needs," she said, leaning over to bathe the tiny nubs of his nipples with the tip of her tongue.

"And I yours."

If only Nebula still possessed sexual needs! "I await your attention then," she murmured, thankful that a female need not come to please a mate. The doctors had assured her of that.

He bent, took her mouth, his tongue warm and wet along the seam of her lips until she opened and welcomed it inside. Catching her at the waist, he dragged her atop his muscular body. "Straddle me," he ordered.

His tongue plumbed her mouth. His chest abraded her nipples, and his cock rubbed along the length of her dry slit when he moved beneath her. A year ago she'd have been wet for him. Swollen and ready. Ripe. In the silence she savored the closeness, mourned for the loss of involuntary, animal awareness that had been so much a part of that long-ago adventure in this very hotel... with a nameless eunuch sex slave who hadn't possessed half the appeal of Conan -- her designated mate.

She tried to stop it, but a sob escaped her throat.

"What is it, little one?" Conan's expression hinted at his concern.

"I cannot be a mate to you. I feel nothing. Nothing of what a woman should feel when her lover caresses her." Suddenly it struck her how accusatory that must have sounded. "It's not you, Master, but me. When they fixed me, they stole my youth. I'm as dried-up as an elder long past her breeding years."

Conan smiled, as though relieved. He grabbed her hand, laid it on his exposed ass cheek. "Here. Feel this."

A little square, barely noticeable to the touch. "What?"

"Testosterone. The hormone that drives a man's desire. If I didn't have it, I'd have very little interest in fucking. My muscles would atrophy, and I'd grow soft as a woman. Before Pak Song prescribed it, my nipples had already begun to soften and enlarge."

Nebula rubbed her finger over the little bit of magic. "A miracle then."

"A miracle I will make for you too, but you must keep it secret. What I wear has been outlawed on Earth -- distributing its equivalent for female eunuchs is an offense punishable by castration or death in nearly every jurisdiction in the galaxy." He stroked her belly, his touch gentle, soothing. "I care not. Much of my pleasure comes from pleasuring my partner. I'd have you able to enjoy my lovemaking fully."

"How?"

"We'll begin with an injection, to reverse what nature has already done. It will make you frantically aroused for a short time. Afterward, you will wear a patch as I do. Over this," he said, cupping her mound where the hated tattoo proclaimed she bore the mutant gene. "It seems a fitting place."

"Yes, Master." Gods. It was as though he knew her mind, understood the emotional pain she'd carried since she'd been marked as defective. It was as if he knew just what to do and say to wipe away the years of humiliation and give her back her pride.

"Good. It is time then. Come, I have booked a dungeon to ensure your pleasure... and engaged a eunuch sex slave to help me provide it. First, though, I will inject you with desire."

Chapter Five

Nebula lay helpless, her hands bound above her head on a table covered in butter-soft leather. Her legs lay spread apart in stirrups, letting cool air flow around her exposed, dampening cunt. A full feeling warmed her outer thigh, where Conan had injected the miracle hormone he said would restore her sexual desire.

"I want you to watch, slave." Still wearing his blue robe, without the uniform he'd had on beneath it -- he'd stripped her naked again as soon as they'd arrived in this small dungeon -- Conan lifted her and stuffed a soft bolster pillow beneath her head and shoulders. "The slave you see is Ulric. His purpose here is to join us in our quest for pleasure. Ulric, remove your robe. There is no place here for shame... or reticence."

With that, Conan stepped into Nebula's field of vision and removed his own garment. Her cunt clenched at the sight of him, magnificently aroused, his cock glowing, a kaleidoscope of colors. He stood by Ulric, whose natural cock paled by comparison, although he wore an impressive array of jewels along its slender six-inch length. The slave lifted his flaccid cock, demonstrating that, like all pleasure partners on Obsidion, he had only an empty seed sac. Evidence of his castration -- his safety as a sex partner beyond the medical certification form she'd seen him hand to Conan before taking off his robe.

Conan stepped away a moment, returning with a vial of something fragrant. Something exotic smelling, surprisingly arousing. He dribbled a small amount onto Nebula's nipples, her belly, her mound. As though they'd orchestrated this in advance, Ulric began to rub the oil into her skin, heating her. Arousing her as she hadn't been aroused in... almost forever.

Conan's tongue wet her slit, stabbed at her cunt, ringed her asshole, then made its way back until he took her throbbing clit between his teeth and sucked it like a tiny cock. His big hands warmed her inner thighs as he used his thumbs to spread her outer lips.

"Come for me, baby," Conan growled against her flesh.

Ulric's fingers plucked her nipples into tight, hard points. He kneaded her breasts and belly. His tongue claimed her mouth. Gods, but she wanted to do as her master ordered and experience the joys again that now lived only in her fading memories.

She lay there, wanting… on the brink. That moment of release still wouldn't happen for her, though, no matter how hard she tried. "I can't," she cried when the sex slave released her mouth.

Conan blew on her clit, sending small waves of sensation through her. It was as though her cells remembered, yet they couldn't replicate the overwhelming need, the pressure she remembered from… before. So close, yet -- nothing more than a twinge of remembered ecstasy. "Perhaps the hormone will not work for me. It doesn't matter. So long as I can give you pleasure."

Conan groaned, but lifted his head and smeared some glistening lubricant first on his own cock, then on Ulric's. At Conan's command, Ulric raised Nebula's platform to a vertical position, then moved behind her. Kneeling, he positioned his cock at the entrance to her anus. Conan joined him, but facing her. The heat from his glowing cock seared her where it nestled, poised to fill her cunt. Ulric slid his arms around her and began to tug at her nipples, rhythmically, a three-pronged assault on her slowly awakening senses.

"Open to us." Conan sank his oiled cock in her cunt until his pelvis rested against her slit. Then he spread her ass cheeks and inserted first one lubricated finger, then two, into her resistant ass. A sensation of heat, of excitement began slowly, grew stronger with each gentle probing. "You can take a cock here too."

Nebula fought the urge to tighten up when she felt Conan pressing the blunt head of Ulric's shaft against her, demanding she let him in.

Conan's cock throbbed in her cunt. Ulric's stretched her ass. Conan kneaded her ass cheeks, his touch firm yet gentle... an arousing reminder that only her mouth stayed free. Empty. She licked her lips, whether in invitation or to ease a sudden dryness she couldn't say.

Her lovers thrust and withdrew in tandem, setting up a delicious friction. Her skin burned. Sensations assailed her as though suddenly a dam had burst inside her, setting all those suppressed desires free. "Oh, gods, fuck me harder." Tears ran down her cheeks as the first wave of ecstasy attacked her.

She wanted to swallow up the pulsating flesh within her. She wanted to grasp Conan's well-muscled ass, feel his anal sphincter constrict around her fingers. She wanted -- gods of the universe, she was coming. Coming. Coming as she'd never done since before her alteration. As she'd never dared to dream she'd do again.

When her trembling slowed and she lay against the fucking bench, drained for the moment, Conan withdrew, his huge cock still glowing. Still purplish red. "You haven't come," she said when he came up beside her and adjusted the bench so she reclined.

"I will. Soon you'll want this again... I will keep it in readiness. You may watch while Ulric eases his desire in me. I've heard it said that it arouses women to watch males fuck one another. Of course," he added, a slightly embarrassed look on his handsome face, "I'd never have done such a thing... back on Earth."

When he was whole. Nebula heard the words Conan did not say. Her heart ached for his loss, more even than it had ached when she'd given up her womanhood in the cause of protecting future generations. Her cunt wept for his stolen seed that would never take root in a fertile woman's womb.

* * *

Ulric knelt at Conan's feet, his large hands skimming Conan's calves, his thighs. Conan sighed, parting his legs, slowly, as though he wanted to close them, conceal the evidence of his unmanning. When Ulric caught the ring in Conan's cock between his teeth and sucked it in, Nebula gasped. She wanted that cock. Wanted the touch of a lover's tongue on her clit, in her cunt.

The graceful line of Ulric's neck and shoulders, the glow of candlelight on his gleaming skull, the vulnerability of his smooth asshole stretched around a silver plug made Nebula's skin grow warm. If it were only she, paying Conan homage! Conan's abdominal muscles rippled, though he remained motionless, and a sheen of sweat formed on his brow, his powerful chest and arms.

Her own asshole twitched when Ulric reached around toward Conan's rear entrance. The slave moved as though he'd choreographed this scene -- first the caresses, the arousal, inexorably moving toward a crescendo. Nebula imagined their eventual joining, cock to ass. The pressure building. The explosion, when one or both of the beautiful eunuchs before her would achieve nirvana.

Who would fuck whom? Nebula's sex wept at the thought of Conan's big cock filling her there. Her ass ached from the slave's earlier invasion. Her nipples puckered, and her belly muscles convulsed when Ulric rose, kissed Conan full on the mouth, and whispered something she couldn't hear.

"No." Conan spoke sharply, grasped Ulric, and positioned his cock at the sex slave's anus.

Nebula couldn't help crying out. She wanted Conan's huge cock in her, not up the ass of a hired sex surrogate.

As though Conan had divined her thoughts, he glanced up at her, then stood. "I've changed my mind. You fuck me. I need to see to my woman's pleasure."

Conan presented Ulric his back, his rounded, muscular ass cheeks spread by his own hand. Nebula noticed that Conan, too, wore a plug in his asshole -- a eunuch's toy, perhaps. Ulric began to slide it in and out -- slowly, sensuously, not unlike the way he'd worked his own cock in and out of her asshole moments earlier. She wanted Conan's cock... his tongue... his big hands invading every orifice in her body.

"Gods in the heavens, I die for wanting you." Nebula clamped down her lips, determined to say no more.

Too late. Conan looked up, met her needy gaze. "Let us indulge my future mate," he said, striding to the head of the table and rotating it so all Nebula needed was to open her mouth and take in his engorged, brightly glowing phallus while he attended her throbbing cunt with his tongue.

When Ulric sank his cock in Conan's ass, pumped slowly, deeply, Conan worked the vibrating ends of a double dildo up Nebula's cunt and rear passage, then resumed licking and sucking her cunt. While Conan ran his hands over her breasts, her belly, her mound, Ulric pinched and pulled at Conan's own distended nipples.

Incredible. Sensation crackled through them, arousing and enticing. Overwhelming. Conan's huge cock throbbed in her mouth. She wanted to take it deeper, consume him as he was consuming her. Her clit swelled against his tongue while he worked the dildo in and out of her cunt and ass. Ulric pounded his cock into Conan as they all strained toward nirvana.

She felt the ecstasy pouring from Conan, as surely as if she were drinking his essence. It crackled, like electricity flowing from body to body, ass to cock to her own thrumming clit. An aura of contentment, of pure pleasure, wrapped them in a cocoon of sensation. Joy.

Joy she'd never expected to experience again.

Chapter Six

Later, while he sat beside her on the bed in his room, Conan rubbed soothing salve into the chafe marks the restraints had put on Nebula's tender skin. He shouldn't have marked her. Didn't feel the need to establish his dominance, no matter what society demanded.

Yet they would live on Luna Ten. A utopian refuge for Earthlings... where, according to what Shedir had told Conan, females were eager slaves, males their loving masters. He visualized the communal dungeon, the fucking glade where mates gave and took their pleasure.

Conan reasoned that he must have lost much of his natural male aggressiveness with his balls, because he didn't want to exert his dominance over Nebula, but rather to love her. He felt no particular urgency to mark her as his own in the traditional ways, even though the mating gifts he'd chosen awaited her at Leander's.

"You look so serious. Is something wrong?" Nebula rolled onto her side, then sat up and met his gaze.

"I hurt you."

"No. You didn't. I'm sorry I bruise so easily. Pay those little marks no mind. I'd have suffered far worse to experience the joy you gave me." Shyly, she stroked his side, his hip. "I'd thought only to be given the pleasure of servicing your needs."

"Much of a man's satisfaction -- a eunuch's too, apparently -- comes from pleasing his partner. Does your pleasure increase when you're confined?" He circled the reddened spot on her wrist, wishing --

"Only if it pleases you, Master. I'm your willing slave."

Only if it pleases me. Well, it displeased him to see her skin marred. And, despite the hype he'd been fed all his life, he doubted the aspect of her bondage had enhanced the sexual experience for either of them. Oh, yeah. She'd come. He had the feeling, though, that was the result of refreshing her body with the hormones she'd been deprived of -- and sexual stimulation from him and the sex slave who'd come with the weekend pleasure package the resort had sold him. "Does pain enhance your pleasure, my sweet?"

"No... I mean, only if it pleases you." As though afraid she'd overstepped herself, Nebula lifted her face, met his gaze with troubled eyes.

"Never be less than honest, with me or with yourself. Do you wish to join your sisters and their mates in the communal dungeon?"

She looked away, settling her hand over the tattoo on her mound. "I do not look forward to flaunting my shame."

"You have nothing to be ashamed of. Nothing at all. Still, I understand how you feel. As grateful as I am that it seems to work almost as well as the real thing, I'm not anxious to show this off to one and all." He lifted his cock, now at rest, and shot her a grin. "I will hide this puny mark with the patch you will wear."

She felt so warm, so silky -- so alive. Conan stroked down the curve of her gorgeous body. "You know, not even Pak Song can create skin as soft as yours, and I've tried out the very best of his sexbots." When he reached the tattoo on her mound, he traced it with a curious finger. "This feels no different from the rest of you. I should be grateful you have it, for otherwise you'd never have consented to settle for me."

"I find you immensely attractive. And I should be thanking the gods you're as you are, for if you weren't you'd not have looked at me either." She rubbed his cock, then slid her fingers past the scar where they'd cut away his balls and found the base of the plug in his ass. "Why do you wear this when we fuck?"

"To stimulate my prostate. It helps a eunuch to achieve a kind of climax."

"Like the sex slave's cock did in the dungeon?" Gently, she jiggled the plug and smiled when his cock began to lengthen and harden. "Yes, I see it does. Do you like for me to stimulate you here?"

"I want you to touch me in ways that give you pleasure." He loved the way her cheeks flushed when he slid his bionic hand between her legs and found her wet and swollen. "Want me to summon Ulric, or shall we do it solo this time?"

"Solo. Please. If you don't mind."

"I don't. Want to climb on and ride my neon toy?"

"Oh, yes." Her eagerness got him incredibly hot -- especially when she picked up an anal probe and inserted it in her own ass. "I like the feel of this too."

Conan cupped Nebula's beautiful breasts when she straddled him, then raised his head and took one pert nipple between his teeth. His cock rose, and she sank onto him. Gods. No 'bot could ever duplicate the moist heat of her cunt.

He was a lucky man. Make that a lucky eunuch. She moved, slowly at first, then faster, harder. She bent, took his mouth. She tasted of exotic fruit and sex -- hot, sweaty sex. Her cunt gripped his cock as if she'd never let it go.

Pressure built in him, almost as though he hadn't been neutered. Felt good. So good. She squeezed him harder, dug her nails into his shoulders, screamed out his name. He trembled as sensations carried him over the edge... to a place he'd never thought to go again.

* * *

"You look well-fucked, little sister," Doreen commented. She and Cassie had joined Nebula for a late lunch in the resort dining room. "I bet you can hardly wait to get back to Luna Ten and have Conan take you in the fucking glade. We missed you in the dungeon last night."

"Doreen, he's -- well, I wouldn't be surprised if he was shy about showing off his bionic parts before half the civilized world." Cassie smiled. "I have to assume that Guy and Shedir didn't lie -- that the cock Pak Song made for him works just as well as the real thing."

"It does." Part of Nebula wanted to share every detail with her sisters. Another part wanted it all -- the sex, the instant connection their respective losses had helped them form -- to belong to her. Her and Conan, not to be shared. "I don't believe we'll have a formal mating ceremony."

"Come on. Tell us. What does he look like? What does *it* look like?" Doreen tilted her head, set her large dangling earrings into gentle motion against the gleaming oiled backdrop of her skull. "All we could tell, with him wearing that damn eunuch's robe, was that he's tall."

"He's got *hair*."

"No! Where?" Cassie's eyes widened. "Don't tell me he doesn't bother to keep himself groomed. Not that he could be blamed, of course, considering what he's been through."

"No. The hair is only on his head. And it's cut short. I like tunneling my fingers through it. It's soft, dark-brown. Prickly down around the hairline."

"Oh." Doreen stroked her own clean-shaven scalp, as though wondering what it might feel like if she let the hair grow back. "Are you going to make us drag every bit of information out of you? Come on. *Talk.*"

"He's muscular. Strong. And he has kind eyes. He didn't sneer when he saw my tattoo. He acted as though he saw altered females every day." Nebula's cunt twitched when she recalled Conan taking off his bionic arm, holding it in one hand while he let her look her fill at his stump -- and the huge, glowing hot-pink cock whose pulsating veins changed color from light to glowing chartreuse as it grew rigid before her eyes. "His cock is... well, you'll see it soon enough."

"Big? Can he get it up?" Cassie asked.

"Yes. To both questions." Nebula looked around, saw no one, but lowered her voice anyway. "He got the female hormone for me. And a sex slave, to help him coax out a climax as soon as the injection began working. I love him."

Doreen laid her arms across her bulging belly and asked, "What about the arm?"

"He put it right back on. When it's on, it seems to work just like a real hand would."

Cassie smiled. "It would. Guy's bionic parts are all permanently attached to him. That's why he had to make this trip, to have some adjustments made -- and the rest of us decided to tag along and meet your Conan before the mating ceremony. Come, let's take care of our own shopping while our mates visit with Pak Song. I want to find some nipple rings that are a little thicker than the ones I have. And a heavier chain to connect them with the one in my clit."

"Maybe I'll get my nipples and clit pierced too," Nebula said. She never had, because body piercing was forbidden to any female marked for neutering. But then, using the hormone that made her feel like a woman again was forbidden too. Delightfully, deliciously forbidden. By all the gods, she'd do it. Maybe she'd even pierce her nostril. Her navel. Have a dozen jewels pierced into each ear. "And buy a tongue ring to give to Conan. Can't let him avoid all the traditions of a mating, can I?"

* * *

"You should be good for another year or more, my friend," Pak Song told Guy as he stood and put away the instruments he'd used to adjust Guy's bionic eyes and ears. "I should have made your parts removable like Conan's arm."

Guy laughed. "Fat lot of good it would do for me to be able to take my eyes out, because then I couldn't see to adjust them."

"True. Conan, you'll be able to tell when your cock needs adjusting. Colors will fade, and it will slowly stop glowing. Should be okay for at least a year. I think. Never made a cock before. By then maybe I figure out how to make you some balls too. And to make it" -- he laughed -- "not quite so colorful."

Conan glanced down at his cock, now concealed by his snug uniform pants. "I think I like it like it is. I know Nebula does. After all, it's not as though it's so bright it shows through my clothes."

"No clothes on Luna Ten," Shedir reminded Conan.

"We'll see about that." All Conan wanted now was to be on his way, to settle in and start building permanent shelters and service buildings on Luna Ten. He'd recruited a handful of workers -- mostly displaced Earthlings like himself -- to augment the small group of laborers Guy and Shedir had said would be put under his command. Of course, he thought about Nebula too. She'd felt so warm and soft this morning, cuddled up around his back, one arm resting on his lower abdomen -- near the cock Pak Song couldn't seem to forget about. "Don't worry, I'll take excellent care of your creation."

"You do that. Take care of your new mate too. Excuse me, I must care for this customer." Always anxious to provide yet another customer with one of his deluxe sexbots, the old robot maker hurried to the showroom as Conan followed Guy and Shedir into Leander's shop.

"You sure, no shave?" the barber asked when he handed Conan the mating gifts he'd ordered.

"I'm sure. Unless there's some rule on Luna Ten..."

Shedir shook his head. "Only the rules we imported from Earth, which thank the gods we can ignore if we want to. Maybe I should let my hair grow. Only thing is, I'd miss the incredible sensations when Doreen nibbles and licks me. When she rolls her tongue ring over the sensitive spot here" -- he reached up and ran his finger over a spot at the back of his tanned, oiled scalp -- "it nearly makes me come."

"Everything makes you come, my friend. Conan, I follow the Federation rules out of habit. So do Brad and the rest of us on Luna Ten. Because we want to. If you want to let your hair grow, do it." Guy grinned from his spot in the barber chair where Leander was preparing to wax away the stubble from his bald dome.

Conan considered taking a seat in that other chair, giving in to tradition. He could shave his head. Shave Nebula's as well, since that was part of the time-honored ritual of mating.

He'd leave the traditional mating braid attached to her head, loosening it once they found their bed, wrapping the silken strands around his fist. And he'd keep his own hair too. After all, he was a eunuch and so was she. Traditions need not apply to them.

While they waited for Guy to finish with his grooming, Conan and Shedir talked. "What would you think if I chose to forego the mating ritual altogether, say the vows and take Nebula somewhere private?" he asked when his friend began describing the very public mating ritual in the glade.

Shedir smiled, but then his expression turned serious. "You don't want to stake your claim for everyone on Luna Ten to see?"

"I don't want Nebula embarrassed. She's sensitive about her tattoo -- and I'm sure about the glowing cock Pak Song gave me, though she hasn't said anything. I know men dominate... and that females are supposed to come only when they're mastered, made to feel helpless against their own desires. It's just..."

"Just that you feel less than a man?"

"Not less. But different. I want the kind of devotion from Nebula that you have from Doreen -- the kind I sense that Guy has from Cassie. She's wounded, only now beginning to believe she can have any more than a sterile existence. So am I. We need the time alone, to learn to love ourselves as well as each other -- before we join in the public rituals of the mated couples on Luna Ten."

"That makes sense. By the gods, man, they shouldn't have done this to you. Or forced Nebula or any other woman who carries the mutant gene to destroy her femininity. Leave it to me. And Doreen. We'll see that you aren't subjected to the scrutiny of all Luna Ten when you're mated."

Epilogue

A beautiful day dawned on Luna Ten when, two months later, Conan strode naked to the fucking glade, his glowing cock a beacon to any who might chance to intrude on his private mating with Nebula. Nebula lay tied across the sacred stone, face down, her cunt glistening with the pale, slick fluid of desire. A priest, also exiled from Earth, murmured the words he never would have dared to say back home even before the Fall -- words that joined the bodies and souls of two eunuchs. Lovers whose joining could never produce a child, whose pleasure would forever be missing the element of continuity... of bubbling, overflowing life.

Suddenly Conan knew. He couldn't take Nebula as a master, only as a friend and lover. An equal. His step firm, he moved to the stone and cut her bonds. "I'd have you come to me of your own volition. Share with you, not take from you. As you'd be my slave, so would I be yours."

Nebula's smile when she stood and faced him lit his heart. She held out both hands, a gesture of commitment more profound than she'd made earlier when she'd let the priest bind her to the fucking stone for Conan's pleasure. "I want no slave, only you. Come, let us seal our vows here, in the glade. I care not if the others see us."

Conan turned, sat on the stone, and drew his lifemate onto his lap. When he stroked her satin slit and found her ready, he lifted her... impaled her on his bionic cock... kneaded her ripe, firm breasts as she moved on him.

She milked him with her cunt, and the pressure built in his belly, his ass. He saw colors brighter than the glow of his cock when she tightened around him in the throes of her climax. As they came together in the glade, the others joined them.

Shedir, his newborn son cradled in the crook of one arm while he held Doreen with the other, Guy and Cassie, Brad and

Aurora, the planet's benign rulers, and the others -- eunuchs like him, saved from a lifetime in the mines of Mars by Brad's timely intervention.

Together they had begun building a new and kinder world. As he looked into the peaceful, sleeping face of Luna Ten's newest citizen, Conan sensed an even greater mission awaited them. A mission of mercy, not revenge. It wouldn't be soon... and it might not be his generation but the baby's that would reclaim the planet of his birth and wrest it from the evil hands of its rulers.

Obsidion: Star of the East

Ann Jacobs

Chapter One

A pearl without price, she glittered in his memory, called him beyond all thought, beyond all reason.

Federation Starfighter Giles Oberon wasn't going to give in to his obsession. He wasn't. He'd opted to wait out this Winter Solstice on Obsidion because his superiors had ordered him to have his ship serviced... not because he lusted after the notorious Star of the East.

Barkers hawked their wares on this, the Street of Pleasure. Giles tried to focus on the twinkling lights and bustling crowds of holiday revelers, the sex slave emporiums where visitors might purchase a pleasure partner for an hour or a night. The titanium heels of his black leather boots clattered against the surface of an agate sidewalk. A ribbon of temptation that ended at the Gates of Hell.

Where the Star of the East would be plying her shameful trade.

If only he'd never met her that fateful night two years earlier while he'd toasted the Solstice season with fellow Starfighters furloughing on Obsidion. If only he'd never succumbed to her lure. He should have resisted rather than eagerly submitting himself to her will, allowing himself to be bound for her to work her shameful magic. Earth men were milked with sexbots, saving their seed to service the Federation's chosen breeders. To do otherwise was to risk mutilation... exile. Even when allowed to take female companions, Earth men applied the shackles, forced their partners to pleasure rather than vice versa.

No one must ever learn how Giles had shamed himself, and he must never do it again.

Yet he picked up his pace, lengthened his stride, lured beyond all reason toward what he knew could be the instrument of his destruction. His cock swelled and lengthened, pressing hard against the fly of his skintight uniform pants, obviously eager to participate in its master's destruction.

* * *

Brendan set down the communication device and resumed oiling Star's naked body. "Just as I predicted, Mistress, the Earthling Starfighter Oberon returns. He has asked for you."

Star should have learned by now not to doubt Brendan. The handsome Earthling eunuch she'd bought to assist her in her pleasure-giving had an uncanny knack for foretelling the appearance of one of his fellow Earthlings. "Ready the dungeon for his pleasure."

Pleasure. And pain. Not physical pain, for she'd never inflict real harm on a client. No. The Earthling's pain would be no less intense, however, for apparently in his culture, males were the masters, females their slaves. For it to be otherwise, according to Brendan, caused the men great shame along with incredible pleasure.

Strange creatures, Earthlings. She'd have thought, since nearly everyone on her home planet of Eastphalia had migrated from Earth generations earlier, their cultures would have been similar. But apparently they weren't. No matter. Star laced herself into a shimmering silver leather bustier and applied cherry-flavored rouge to her exposed areolas.

They tingled with anticipation. Anticipation for the bite of the Earthling's straight, white teeth, the brush of his rigid cock over the swollen nipples. Her body ached for him to give her more than his submission... much more. As she had since their first fruitful encounter two winter solstices ago, she wanted his domination.

It wouldn't happen, though. She stared in the mirror at her mound, at the colorful tattoo she'd been so proud of when her mother had commissioned it. Exotic tropical flowers and vines, much like the lush gardens that had once flourished on Eastphalia, perfectly framed the stark, black numerals 46945 -- her intergalactic license as a Mistress of Pleasure. Idly she tweaked the silver ring in her clit, working the sensitive flesh until the nub hardened and throbbed.

"Mistress, he is prepared to serve your pleasure. I warmed the anal probe for you." Brendan strode to her, his soft cock swinging between his legs as he moved.

"You don't want one?"

Brendan glanced down at his limp phallus and shrugged. "I inserted one a few minutes ago. It doesn't have the effect it used to."

"It's all right." Since Brendan had developed an allergy to the testosterone patches that had kept his libido alive, he was no longer able to fuck her clients, but he seemed happier now, she thought, sucking cock or being fucked by those with a taste for some male/male action.

"Come, we mustn't keep our client waiting. Put my probe in." Bending, she spread her ass cheeks so he could insert and inflate it.

* * *

He was at her mercy, this powerful Earthling warrior who'd haunted her dreams, made her wish for something more... for sex that meant more than release. Something she could never have, for she'd chosen her path as a pleasure-giver.

Not that Star regretted her decision. What she earned in her trade kept her small family in comfort back home, provided sustenance for a score of her countrymen. Star strode into the dungeon, her attention now focused on Giles Oberon.

For although he'd taken her without the protection she usually insisted upon and sired her daughter during their prior encounter two winter solstices ago, a client was all he could ever be.

Brendan had prepared Giles well, securing him in the sturdy padded fucking frame that supported his body comfortably, yet kept him immobile and open for their pleasure. Laid out face down, magnificently naked and totally denuded of hair according to Earthlings' strange custom, Giles was oiled from the top of his head to the tips of his toes. His satiny skin glistened, reflecting multicolored light from strobe lights suspended from the dungeon ceiling. Star's cunt contracted at the sight of his massive cock with its heavy gold ring, the snug black leather straps that confined both his long, thick shaft and his smooth, round ball sac. Her mouth watered to taste him, suck his big balls, swallow his cock, and taste his essence. She desperately wanted him in her, fucking her, spurting his hot, creamy release into her weeping cunt.

But that would have to wait until they played out the scene she and Brendan had devised for their clients' pleasure in submission. She had to play the role she'd chosen when she'd exchanged her personal freedom for her people's means of survival. When she picked up a long, fat butt plug and lubricated it heavily with a fragrant aphrodisiac from Mars, Brendan moved beneath the frame, took Giles's cock in his mouth, and began to suck it as was the eunuch's role in this sexual vignette.

"Welcome, and Happy Solstice to you. It's a pity I have but one eunuch for you today," she murmured silkily, breaking into the familiar script as Giles bucked helplessly under Brendan's and her dual assault. "Open for me."

"No," he spat out. His buttocks tightened as though to keep out the plug when she began to work it around the crinkled opening to his anus.

She slapped his ass smartly with one hand, using more pressure on the plug to nudge him to let her in. "Yes. You must experience the pleasure of being fucked by another male. Since there are none here, and since my eunuch's tool is limp and useless... Relax. Realize you're helpless to prevent me from taking your ass." After setting the plug aside, she massaged his tense glutes slowly, sensually, until she felt them give way. She slipped a finger up Giles's ass, then two, while Brendan methodically sucked his cock.

Giles moaned, as though resigned to this particular intrusion of his body that had long been forbidden on Earth. All her clients gave in -- some more readily than others. "There, now. Enjoy. Think about how delightful Brendan's mouth feels on your cock. Sucking. Licking. Feel the bite of my leather on your balls and anticipate the fullness of my dildo up your ass. You'll want to come, but the cock ring will prevent that. Maybe if you're very, very good..."

She slid her fingers out, missing the tight heat of his flesh on them, and inserted the lubricated butt plug instead. When it was seated fully, she secured its base in a mechanical arm that moved the plug in and out as she silently directed by means of the remote control device seated in her own ass.

He shuddered as she moved to the head of the frame and adjusted its height so his face was level with her dripping pussy.

* * *

Star. She was gilded golden from head to toe, but for the long black braid that flowed from her crown to brush her rounded ass cheeks, eyes the color of the midnight sky back home, and rouged nipples fully exposed above the tightly laced silver basque that was her only garment. As much as Giles wished to remain aloof, he could not prevent the sudden and painful swelling of his cock and balls against the leather restraints that bit cruelly into the sensitive flesh.

Her musk enflamed him. A unique, arousing scent, it robbed him of the will to resist, to hold onto a shred of his dignity, preserve his manhood. Giles fought his bonds to no avail as his nemesis stood before him, the ring that decorated her tempting rouged clit poking impudently from a tattooed flower garden that adorned her plump mound. Temptation. Like the legendary Garden of Eden. And its serpent, he thought, staring at the neat numerals that proclaimed her a licensed pleasure-giver. A whore. Back on Earth, she wouldn't have lasted one trick before being arrested and turned into a drone.

The eunuch's tongue tickled Giles's slit, then slid down his shaft to ring the base of his cock where the leather and metal constrained it. The plug in his ass vibrated as it slowly moved in and out, reaming him, stimulating his prostate while the eunuch sucked and swallowed his swollen cock.

Giles had to come. No. He couldn't. Wouldn't. He'd come here to experience the thrill -- the ultimate pleasure -- of finding release in the receptive body of a living female. The female who'd haunted his dreams since their first forbidden encounter two years earlier. He gritted his teeth against the incredible stimulation of the eunuch's mouth on his tightly restrained cock, the slow, steady motion of the large dildo fucking his ass. Perhaps if he closed his eyes to the delectable and forbidden prize not a foot from his hungry lips...

She stepped forward, tilting her hips forward, offering her honey for his delectation. "Pleasure me, Earthling. Make me come with just your mouth and tongue. Please me, and perhaps I'll provide you your release. You'd like that, wouldn't you?" she purred, her warm breath tickling his scalp when she bent over and blew on him there.

"No." He tilted his head back. Gods but he wanted to be free, to ravage her as a man should take a woman. He feasted his eyes for a moment on her rouged nipples, imagining how they'd taste, the texture of the hard nubs against his tongue. Then he met her violet gaze. His balls ached, and his entire body throbbed from the dual stimulation he was helpless to control. "Yes," he muttered when she slapped him smartly on the cheek.

"Yes, *Mistress*. And keep your eyes averted unless I give you permission to look."

Chastened, he focused on her garden of pleasure, on the rosy ringed nub of flesh that protruded, tempting him. "Yes, *Mistress*." With his tongue, he caught her clit ring and drew her to him. In this position he was spared looking at those numbers... the evidence of her profession, of the scores of men she'd pleasured and would pleasure again.

She tilted her hips toward him, demanding he take her prize. With both hands she took his head, brought his mouth to her clit. "Suck me. I like feeling your hot wet tongue lapping up my honey."

Gods but he liked it too. A lot. There was something about her flesh... the hot, damp smoothness of her rigid clit with its dangling ring, the heady smell of her sex mingling with curls of arousing smoke from the incense that smoldered near the door. His balls tightened, the pain when the leather bit into his sensitive flesh reminding him his pleasure was at her command. When her eunuch sucked harder on his throbbing cock, he opened his lips, caught her jewel between his teeth and flailed it with his tongue.

"That feels -- incredible." She widened her stance, offering him more. "Tongue-fuck me now."

Her moan when he penetrated her tight hole and licked her honey was like music to his ears. She caressed all the erogenous places on his skull, stroked the sensitive flesh of his earlobes, then used them to tug his face to her cunt as though to drag him into her... to absorb him into her until he was no more than the inanimate plug now reaming his ass or the eunuch slave who was sucking him off. But Star was not immune to the pleasure he could give, even bound and helpless as he was now.

He could tell by the increased cadence of her breathing, the flow of her hot juices over his chin... from the way her clit swelled and hardened against his upper lip. The tremor in her widespread legs and in her soft, practiced fingers revealed her own arousal as she pressed herself close, ever closer.

His fingers itched to stroke her taut, silky skin, pluck the reddened tips of those full, creamy orbs that bobbed invitingly above the neckline of her tight, shimmering costume. He wanted to break his bonds, snatch his cock from the well-trained mouth of her eunuch, mount her, and fuck her until he made her scream his name.

His name. Not some meaningless endearment. He wanted her to beg for *his* cock in her cunt, her ass, her mouth. *His* hands on her body, kneading and pinching her delightful breasts, tangling in the ebony fall of her hair.

He wanted to fuck her the way he recalled from a similar night two years ago. It had been just the two of them, with her punishing him with a knotted silk flogger when he didn't fuck her fast enough or hard enough. No eunuch had knelt beneath him as he lay helpless on a fucking frame, his cock and balls stimulated beyond belief. No ass plug had reamed him from above, its accelerating rhythm apparently dictated by the motion of his tongue as it fucked her cunt. Though she'd dominated him, she'd allowed him a certain degree of freedom. Freedom he yearned for now, even if that freedom meant only the freedom to enjoy the bite of that flogger.

The pressure built in his balls, almost unbearable, yet the cock restraints prevented him from coming. He redoubled his efforts, tongue-fucking her cunt faster, harder, rubbing his upper lip softly on the sensitive tip of her clit, then grinding his flesh to hers. Desperate now, he strained against his bonds.

They held. Clearly he was in her power until she chose to set him free.

"Oh, gods, don't stop!" She ground her cunt into his face, tugged at his earlobes with both hands. Her honey flooded his throat, his chin.

Gods indeed! The plug in his ass fucked him harder, faster. The eunuch's tongue probed his slit, lapped up the pre-cum that oozed from him despite the constricting ring.

"Gilesssss. I'm coming. Make me come for you."

Giles held back the explosion that bubbled in his balls, absorbed Star's climax in his mouth. The way she screamed his name made him wonder...

Chapter Two

"Be still while we release your bonds." Star sounded not like a dominatrix but more like he imagined an ordinary woman would when she'd just enjoyed an explosive orgasm and wanted more. Giles felt her tremble as she loosened the straps that held his arms and chest to the frame. "Careful, Brendan," she cautioned when the eunuch began to unstrap the rings that restrained his genitals.

Relief. Blood slammed into Giles's cock, making him even harder than before. His asshole ached. Sexual tension sizzled through every cell of his body as they set him free.

"You've pleased me well, Earthling. Very well. You may now please yourself..." Star indicated three doors that led from the dungeon. "Choose one."

At the entrance to the first lay a whip and chains. The center door bore a carving of a male being pleasured by a trio of buxom females. The third was unadorned, but Giles recalled it was from that door that Star had emerged. The first would afford him safety. The second would feed the ultimate male fantasy. The third represented danger -- the risk he took by ignoring his Federation's rules, choosing pleasure over duty. Giles took a step forward, uncertain of what his choice would be until he laid a hand on the third doorway.

The wanting overwhelmed the fear -- and the revulsion at himself for wanting not just an orgasm, not just any female bowing to his command... but Star herself. Giles turned, met the gaze of his obsession, and smiled. "Leave the eunuch behind and come with me."

* * *

Determined now to provide Giles the pleasure he'd just accorded her, Star went on her knees before him, her cunt still thrumming with the aftershocks of her climax. Soft music filled her ears, the strains of ancient Earthling melodies of the season surrounding them, soothing yet hauntingly erotic. When she looked up at him, she saw it -- the golden halo around his gleaming skull, formed by reflection of the candlelight with which she lit her private haven.

What had made her offer this place where no other client had ever gone, her place of rest and refuge?

He was different... he'd touched emotions she'd long reserved for family and countrymen. When he'd invaded her body that first Solstice night, he'd left part of himself. Tonight she'd forget her job, join him in his pleasure, and pretend there had been more to his seeking her out than lust that demanded release.

"You may suck my cock."

He hadn't come. He should be bursting now, yet he maintained control when she took him in her mouth and sucked the plum-like head of his big cock. At his sigh of delight, she took his ball sac in both hands and stroked it.

Suddenly he lifted her off him and laid her across the bed. "Spread your legs. Wide." He slid his hand between them, his callused fingertips abrading her needy flesh. "You're wet. So wet. Tell me you want my cock in your cunt."

"I do."

"Say it." He rubbed the broad head of his phallus over her clit, catching her tiny ring in his thick PA and setting up a delicious vibration that had her cunt clenching, aching.

"I want your cock in my cunt. Please."

That was all Giles needed to hear. He reared back, then sank into her wet heat. Gods but she was tight. Exquisitely so. She milked his cock with her inner muscles, so much sweeter than the efforts of his Federation-issued sexbot, authorized and certified though it was to relieve his sexual tension. Soft, yet firm, slick with her honey and his pre-cum, Star gripped him with every stroke, almost as though she wanted to hold him there, never let him go. The way he'd dreamed about her doing many times until reality had intruded.

He bent, nipping first one and then the other of her painted nipples, tasting the familiar Martian aphrodisiac with its sweet, cherry flavor. They seemed larger than he remembered. No less responsive, though, for they beaded under his tongue. The lush flesh of her breasts pillowed his head.

His balls tightened painfully. She clamped down on his cock as he pounded into her cunt harder, faster, desperate now to release the pressure, spurt out his seed.

"Come. Give me your seed. You know you want to." She held his head to her breasts, moaning softly when he sucked hard on a distended nipple.

He felt it then. The plug in her ass, expanding, tightening her grip on his cock even more as he fucked her. "Oh gods!" The first hot burst of semen exploded into her. He buried his cock to the balls, spurting his life into her womb, suckling her breasts. Devouring her. Doing to her what his people had taught must only be done to a seed-harvesting sexbot.

A long time later he lay spent, his body cradled in the arms of his forbidden lover. His nemesis.

* * *

"Want Mommy!"

Oh no. Star glanced at the communicator screen, saw Giles's gaze locked there, too, on the toddler she doubted he'd ever believe was his own daughter.

He turned to her. "What the hell?"

"Let me talk to her." Wrapping herself in the blanket, Star moved close to the screen. She'd try to placate Giles later -- now her concern was for her little girl. "It's past your bedtime, angel."

"Want Mommy."

"Gillian, Mommy will be home very soon." Within light-days if she could catch a transporter. "I bought you a new toy to celebrate the Solstice."

"Solstice?" The word came out funny -- at just fifteen months, Gillian hadn't mastered the letter "S".

"Yes. To get it, though, you must go sleep now. G'night."

No sooner had Gillian's image faded from the communicator than Giles turned to Star, disgust plain on his handsome face. "You leave your child with others so you can ply your trade?"

"With my mother."

His sensual lips curved in what Star could only call a sneer, and his gaze settled on the numbers tattooed on her mound. "The woman who brought you up to become such a paragon of virtue?"

The paragon of virtue who's shown the sanctimonious Earthling ecstasy beyond his wildest imaginings, not once but twice. Star squelched the urge to grab that flogger and use it to give pain, not pleasure. "The giving of pleasure is an honored profession among my people. One I proudly embrace and one, I note, that you seem to enjoy utilizing whenever your business brings you to Obsidion. Men like you, to whom I give sexual favors forbidden them back home, provide me with the means to care for my family... my daughter."

Magnificently naked, Giles strode to the communicator, recalled the child's image. "How old is she?"

"Fifteen months." The intent way he was studying Gillian's face unnerved Star.

Finally he blanked out the screen and strode back to her. "She could be mine." He didn't sound pleased.

"She is mine."

He laid his hands on her shoulders, so hard she felt the imprint of each large finger on her tender flesh. "Am I her father? Or do you even know?" He paused, his jaw tight when he stared down at her. "Of course you wouldn't know, would you? How many men did you fuck that Winter Solstice two years ago?"

"None but you, at least not in a way that would produce a child. Almost every male in the galaxy finds pleasure in being fucked, not fucking a woman. Only Earthlings seem obsessed with dipping their cocks into female cunts... and you were the only Earthling I pleasured during the time when she was conceived.

But why should you care? According to Brendan, Earthling breeders father countless children without ever knowing them."

"I have no idea whether I've fathered children on Earth, or if so how many. But I've never before seen a face so much like my own." Giles glanced at the screen again, then looked back at Star. "I want to meet her."

"Why?" Did he intend to take her daughter from her?

His grip on her shoulders loosened somewhat, as though he realized he was hurting her. "Because... I need to see her. Come, gather whatever you were planning to take back to Eastphalia. I have use of a small transporter, and I will take you there." As though he sensed the terror that had suddenly gripped her, he lifted her chin and looked down into her eyes. "You need not be afraid. I won't try to take her from you. I just need to know she's being cared for, and she has all she needs."

Though he'd eased her worry, Star had no doubt Giles had issued not an invitation but an order.

* * *

An hour later, Giles performed a preflight checklist on the sleek privateer his friend Shedir had loaned him for the trip, while Star and her slave loaded armloads of gaily wrapped packages into the luggage compartment. He should have bought gifts of his own, he supposed. But he wouldn't have had a clue about which of the sparkly goodies the merchants peddled might make a small child smile.

Of course, he could have purchased some small trinket for Star. Pleasure Mistress or not, she was no sexbot. She had human emotions. If what she'd said was true, she was the mother of his child -- the only child he'd sired that he'd ever have the opportunity to know.

Covered head to toe in fuzzy red cold-weather gear, with her face framed in a white fur hood, Star looked like a holiday present wrapped for Giles's delectation. His cock stirred again at the thought of her -- at the prospect of idling away long hours during the journey through space, sampling her charms. Putting a smile on her gorgeous face by giving her some shiny trinket to mark the Winter Solstice.

Did they have stores on Eastphalia?

Damn it, what was coming over him? What did he care whether or not he pleased her? If he paid her, she'd fuck him. She'd fuck anybody who had her price in gold or silver, or the legal tender of whatever planet where she was plying her trade. Giles focused on that. It helped him tamp down the growing emotions that welled up in him when he thought of her choosing to bear his daughter, giving her the feminine version of his name... submitting to him, however momentarily, rather than forcing him to submit to her and her ever-present eunuch slave.

But not enough. "Brendan, I have a chore for you before we take off," he told the slave when he stuck his head out of the transporter hatch. Handing over a fistful of Obsidion's octagonal silver credits to the blue-robed eunuch, he said, "Go find gifts for me to give the child -- and Star. Hurry back, for we're taking off in less than an hour."

Brendan grinned. "What would you like me to get?"

Giles found it discomfiting, encountering the sex slave who'd so recently sucked his cock, outside the Pleasure Dungeon where the debauchery had taken place. "Whatever you think they'd like."

Chapter Three

"Where did Brendan go?" Star asked when Giles stepped back into the transporter and began fiddling with settings on the control panel.

She loved the way Giles looked in his body-hugging black uniform -- strong, invincible, able to protect her from any sort of harm, yet somehow more vulnerable clothed than he'd been stark naked. She had to fight an urge to hug him, kiss the worried expression off his handsome face.

"I sent him on an errand. He should be back any moment now."

"Is this ship like the one you fly when you're working?" she asked, her mind full of images -- Giles performing all sorts of daring feats, routing sky pirates. Stories from her childhood -- told by exiled Earthlings who'd revered the prime manhood of their planet, the chosen ones who'd flown for the legendary Star Command -- rattled in her brain. Wanting to tease him, she slid her hand down the front of his uniform, rubbing it suggestively over the impressive bulge of his sex.

He laid his hand over hers as though to still her, and shook his head. "I command a starfighter. It's smaller, faster, and better armed than this transporter. It's being serviced here on Obsidion during the Solstice holiday. The bad guys celebrate too -- so the galaxy should be fairly safe to travel. By my calculations we should land on Eastphalia tomorrow about seventeen hundred hours."

"Would you like me to pleasure you?" When Star perched on the edge of the control console, the tiny bells attached to her nipples tinkled, sending tiny shock waves to her cunt.

Giles glanced toward the sound of the bells, smiled. "Later. As soon as the slave returns, we will be on our way. Takeoff will require my full attention." He reached out, caught one bell and gently tugged at it. "You didn't have nipple rings before."

"I take them off when I'm working."

"You just offered to go back to work, didn't you?"

It took a second for that bit of sarcasm to reach her. "No. I offered to share some pleasures with you. Because it pleases me to do so, not because I expect payment. I'm on holiday, off to celebrate the season with my daughter... and her father."

He looked -- shocked. As if it had registered for the first time that they'd had a child together. Then his expression softened and he patted his thigh. "Come here."

When she obeyed and moved onto his lap, he cupped her breasts, making the bells jingle and her cunt go wet. She felt his strength -- the hard muscles of his thighs beneath her own and the insistent pulsating of his cock against her ass... the slow, steady beating of his heart against her back as he fondled her. His touch seemed different -- tender as well as carnal -- as if somehow he'd accepted that she was his lover now and not his whore. She couldn't help wanting him -- her baby's father, not just for a holiday night but forever.

A daydream. Star knew it, accepted that forever would end with this holiday season. The mere idea of a Federation Star Commander giving up his exalted position to mate with a Pleasure Mistress like her was so ridiculous as to be laughable. Banishing that painful thought, Star snuggled back against Giles's muscular chest.

She'd enjoy what time they had... and not ask for the impossible.

* * *

The transporter hurtled through the blackness of space toward Eastphalia, its course programmed as fully as Giles's life had been since he'd been tapped as a teenager for the Star Command. He checked the control panel one last time before unbuckling his seat belt and heading -- by force of habit -- for the crew's sleeping quarters.

His cock twitched. This time there would be no sexbot, but Star -- and, he guessed, the eunuch who had joined her once he'd returned with the gifts Giles had asked him to select. Perhaps when they returned to Obsidion, he'd visit Pak Song and upgrade his sexbot, though something told him the old sexbot maker's finest would never hold a candle to Star. He opened the hatch to the small sleeping room, eager not for sleep but for more of the incredible, forbidden sensations.

More of Star.

When he saw her laid out on the sleeping couch, Giles gasped. Her body glistened, all gold and glitter and silver bells dangling from reddened, glistening nipples. The robed and hooded eunuch knelt at the edge of the narrow cot, her legs draped over his shoulders as he applied more of the arousing red stuff to her cunt lips while she moaned with apparent delight.

"Want Giles," she murmured.

The eunuch rose, bowed. "She is ready for you, Master. May I make you ready for her?"

Giles needed no further stimulation than seeing her, smelling her sweet musk, hearing her call out for him. His cock was hard as stone, and his balls ached with the need to come. "I need nothing but the sight of your mistress," he said as he tore off his garments and sank to his knees where the eunuch had been.

She tasted like honey and sex, and Giles drank his fill. Her little clit hardened, swelling against his tongue. She whimpered when he slid his hands along her slick, satiny skin and clutched her full, firm breasts. Gods but she had the most beautiful body he'd ever seen, a body that for the moment belonged to him. Tugging gently at her nipple rings, he made her bells ring, their sounds unmuffled now by her clothing. His own nipples tingled, the flesh hardening against the small rings that pierced them.

As hard as he tried, he couldn't banish the tender emotions that welled up inside him, couldn't bury them in the heat of his passion... and hers. He had to, though. Couldn't let himself be seduced into throwing away all he'd worked for, lived for. Desperate, he tongued her harder, digging his fingers into her lush flesh until her cunt convulsed and she whimpered with ecstasy. Ecstasy he'd brought her.

Maybe if he fucked her he'd drive away these unwelcome, alien feelings. Rising, he tossed her onto the sleeping couch, positioned his cock head at the hot, wet entrance to her cunt, and plunged inside.

She gripped him with tight inner muscles, as though she didn't want to let him go. Her little whimpers told him she liked it hard and fast, liked the feel of him in her, on her, plunging his cock into her cunt and his tongue deep down her throat. His back stung from the bite of her nails -- the bite of passion, not the practiced technique of a Pleasure Mistress.

Gods help him, he wanted to make this last. It wasn't going to happen. His balls tightened. When she screamed and her cunt convulsed wildly around his cock, he began to spurt his hot, wet semen.

Not into a sterile depository but into a living, breathing woman. Not a Pleasure Mistress but just a woman. A woman who'd taken his seed, nurtured it, and borne his child.

When he was spent, he did what no self-respecting Starfighter would do. Rolling off Star to spare her his weight, he gathered her in his arms and held her. He breathed in the heady fragrance of her perfume and rested his head on the soft pillow of her breasts... and as he drifted off to sleep, he imagined a life with her -- a life adrift in a universe that would no more accept him than it did her. A life that would by necessity include their child -- and the Earthling eunuch who was her sex slave.

When he lay in her arms the prospect didn't seem all that terrible.

Chapter Four

"Why did you buy the eunuch?" Giles asked Star when she joined him at the command center of the small transporter in preparation for their landing on Eastphalia. "Does he provide you pleasure?"

That sounded suspiciously like jealousy -- an emotion distinctly rare in clients of a Pleasure Mistress. "No. I bought Brendan to help me pleasure my clients. He'd been working in the Sex Emporium too long, and he didn't react well to the patches they made him wear."

"So he's..."

"Yes. Although he's no longer interested in sex, I believe his giving pleasure to others -- male or female -- provides him with a measure of satisfaction. Did you not enjoy his attention?"

Giles snorted. "I enjoy yours more."

"Yes. I could tell." Typical macho reaction of an Earthling Starfighter, Star thought, trying to squelch a grin. "Will you tell Gillian she's your daughter?"

"I want to. Looking at her on the communicator... Seeing her did something to me. Seeing myself in her eyes, her light hair... it was a heady experience. Somehow I'd never considered until I saw her that there might be hundreds of children at the breeding farms back home. Children I'll never know. How do you --"

"You may tell her. On Eastphalia, there's no shame in what I do -- no stigma on children born to Pleasure Mistresses. There's also no prejudice against Earthlings since we are descended from Earthlings who left Earth years ago to colonize Eastphalia. Gillian will be taught to be proud her father is a member of the Federation Star Command."

"Thank you."

"It is I who thank you. You gave me great pleasure, and you gave me a child."

Giles cleared his throat. "Fasten your seat belt. We're about to land." He pressed a button and advised Brendan, who had stayed in the sleeping quarters, to prepare himself.

* * *

Home. Lights twinkled from every barren branch, in the windows of nearly every home and business. Happy lights, red and blue, green and gold, white and every shade of the rainbow, Star recalled her mother saying when she was not a lot older than Gillian.

"Happy Solstice," she murmured to Giles and Brendan as they trudged through a light dusting of snow on the tarmac toward the spaceship terminal, their arms laden with wrapped packages. A fat snowflake landed on her lip, and she captured it with her tongue. Her bells jingled, seemingly in tune with the holiday tune coming from loudspeakers inside the terminal. "It's good to be home."

As soon as they stepped inside, Star saw Gillian break away from her grandmother, a huge smile on her baby face. The little girl began to toddle toward them on unsteady legs. When she stopped at his feet and looked up at him, Giles sighed. "Gods in the heavens," he murmured, his gaze glued to his daughter's tiny face. "She's beautiful."

Star smiled up at him. "She looks like you. Gillian, give your father a hug."

Hesitantly, as though he wasn't quite sure what to do with such a tiny human, Giles knelt and held out his arms. When the baby went into them, all childlike trust, Star felt tears spilling down her cheeks. "Come. Let's go home."

Giles lifted Gillian, laughing with her when he perched her on one broad shoulder. "Yes. Let's."

Hope blossomed in Star's heart at the sight of them, father and daughter, together. She motioned for her mother to join them, but the older woman smiled and shook her head. Mother was right. Star and Giles needed this time alone with their baby... and with each other.

Star took Giles's hand and showed him the way, and her heart raced when he squeezed it and smiled down at her.

Maybe... just maybe her Solstice wish would be fulfilled.

* * *

Later, after they'd put their daughter to bed, Giles looked down with wonder at Gillian. The toddler snuggled under a puffy pale blue coverlet that reminded him of the clouds surrounding Earth and Mars. Gods! She looked beautiful, clutching the old-fashioned baby doll Brendan had picked out as though it were the greatest gift she'd ever received.

Having a child -- and celebrating the Solstice here on this barren planet where nothing of value existed but love -- felt good. Better than elaborate celebrations back on Earth. More honest, more real. Giles reached over the crib and took Star's hand. "Thank you."

"It is I who should thank you." She bent, kissed Gillian's chubby cheek. "Sweet dreams, my angel," she said, love evident in the softness of her expression.

Suddenly Giles wanted Star to look at him that way, not just with lust in her eyes but with true affection. He needed her to treat him not as an attractive customer who'd happened to sire her daughter when he'd fucked her, but a friend -- like her eunuch, Brendan -- a part of her life she valued beyond all else.

It no longer mattered to him that she'd fucked a thousand men, Earthling and alien. Giles felt the love in every room of the home she'd made for Gillian. At that moment he recalled her saying the only thing of value she and her fellow Eastphalians had to trade for gold was their beautiful women -- the Pleasure Mistresses Earthlings decried as whores even as they took forbidden pleasures from them at every opportunity.

Surely Eastphalia possessed some other source of sustenance for its people. If it hadn't, the original colonists would never have stayed. Giles gave a mental shrug. He'd consider that later. Now the important thing was that he believed Star had done what she'd had to do. What she'd never have to do again if she'd accept his protection.

A crackling fire in the main room of her cozy home banishing the chill. Giles sank onto the plush stack of cushions where he'd played earlier with his daughter and pulled Star down beside him.

"Do you want me to call Brendan?" she asked.

"Not tonight." Giles held no illusions that she'd cast out the slave. He didn't even want her to, for her compassion toward Brendan was one of the qualities that made him love her. "Another time you may have him help you pleasure me. Tonight I want you to myself. Lie back against the cushions and let me love you."

"Love me?"

"Yes. I do, you know." He tried to summon up distress for that impending loss -- and for the fact that when he placed love over duty he could never go home again -- but it no longer made a difference that he'd be throwing away all he'd worked for since he joined Star Command. All that mattered now was Star, their child... and their love.

Her skin felt like satin beneath his fingers when he unwrapped her from the bright red jumpsuit. When the material brushed her nipples and made the bells ring, she smiled, and he couldn't resist nuzzling her naked breasts with his nose, making them chime again. "Happy Solstice, sweetheart."

"To you, too."

Gently, more gently than he'd ever touched a woman before, Giles traced the reflected firelight along Star's jaw, her throat, down her voluptuous body to the tattooed garden on her mound. He fingered the numbers at its center. "I will have these removed," he said, bending to kiss the proof of her profession. "You will be only mine."

"Yes."

He rose over her, locking their hands together as he slid his cock into her warm, welcoming heat. Slowly, for he wanted to experience every nuance of sensation, he fucked her. Her midnight gaze locked with his as they moved, a carnal dance made more intense by the emotions that passed between them.

He was coming. He couldn't hold back. Not now. "Come for me," he ground out, holding out from spilling his seed by sheer power of will. When her cunt convulsed around his cock, he let go, coming in short, steaming bursts deep into her womb.

"Happy Solstice, my darling Earthling," Star whispered.

"Now and always." He wished he had a gift for her -- a ring to seal their mating. Not wanting her to sense his discomfort, he glanced at the fire.

When he noticed the distinctive blue-purple glow emanating from one of the logs, it came to him. Unless he was mistaken he was looking at a source of great riches for Eastphalia. "Where did that wood come from?" he asked, sitting upright and staring at phosphorescent sparks as they sparkled and sputtered.

"The dead forest. For a time the forests thrived, but eventually everything the terraformers planted started dying off. Once the last of the trees is consumed we will have to import our fuel too," Star said, her expression desolate. "Then our only asset will truly be our women, trained as Pleasure Mistresses. I'll never be able to belong just to you..."

"Yes. I think you will. I believe that bitter smell and the blue glints in the fire are from cesium, a propellant we use in the ion engines on our spacecraft. The terraformers must have unearthed veins that reacted with the water from the rainfall. In order to produce enough alkali to kill an entire forest, Eastphalia must be rich in cesium. If I'm right we can stay here, with your family and friends, and make a handsome living, once we start mining and selling off the mineral."

Giles paused long enough to gather Star in his arms and cradle her against his chest. "If your people agree, I can arrange for Shedir's privateers to transport cesium around the galaxy. I'll gladly trade my starfighter for a merchant ship and transport it myself, if it means I can have you as my mate. You, Brendan, and our little girl."

"Oh, yes. If only..." She seemed as if this was too much for her to believe, too good to be true.

He held her close and lowered his head to whisper in her ear. "Believe me. What I say is true. This holiday I should be lavishing jewels on you, marking you mine in the manner prescribed throughout the galaxy. Instead, I give you freedom. Freedom for yourself and for your people."

Star turned to Giles, tears glistening in her gorgeous violet eyes. "Freedom," she murmured. "Freedom to love you, and I do. You've just given me the best present I can imagine, and I wish I had half as wonderful a gift for you."

"You do, my beautiful Star. Yourself and our little girl, now and forever a family."

Obsidion: Diamond in the Rough

Prologue

His girls were priceless. More precious than the most costly jewels in his inventory. Eli of Obsidion, jeweler to kings and rulers throughout the galaxy, had just made matches for each of his three beloved daughters. All in all, the matchmaker's choices pleased him.

For Pearl, his youngest, who craved sensual satisfaction above all else, they'd settled on the cyborg-maker's son, with the wedding to take place two years hence on Pearl's twenty-fifth birthday. Garnet, his middle child, would have found her lust for gold well satisfied by then, for in less than a year she would mate with the alien but fabulously wealthy purveyor of sex slaves and the pleasure they provided.

And Emerald, his willful eldest whose perfection she'd always insisted could only be properly appreciated by a prince, would take the greatest prize of all. It had cost Eli a king's ransom in dowry, but he'd bought this favored child a real, living prince -- the reclusive heir to Obsidion's throne, recently brought home and elevated upon his elder brother's death. He looked forward to Emerald's mating next week -- an event that would make his daughter a royal princess.

Eli knew nothing of his daughter's future master but that his name was Arik and he would rule Obsidion upon the death of his father. The matchmaker had assured Eli she'd seen Arik, though it had been several years ago. She'd smiled and pronounced the prince a fit mate for Emerald -- a diamond in the rough. Eli had no problem accepting the word of the wizened, highly respected matchmaker who'd brought him together with his own late, beloved wife. He felt certain the girls would find the same sort of happiness he'd enjoyed with Sadie for nearly thirty years before her death earlier this year.

Chapter One

"You've arranged a mating for *me* with one of Eli's famed jewels? I'd sooner take a whore from one of the sex slave markets of Obsidion." Arik, newly named Crown Prince of Obsidion, clenched the fist on his remaining hand and shoved his right arm with its vicious looking hook before his father's eyes. "A sexbot would be an even better choice."

"You cannot mean that, my son."

"At least the whore would close her eyes, give me my money's worth... and I'd walk away satisfied, with no obligation to provide her pleasure in return. A 'bot would care naught about anything... even *this*." Arik lifted his hand and touched the empty eye socket and a mass of scars that crisscrossed that side of his face and neck.

The old man's eyes dimmed when he glanced up Arik's body, his gaze settling on the hideously scarred surface of his son's cheek. "The one named Emerald will not dare reject you."

Arik curled his lip in disgust. "So you've bought me a princess with Obsidion's gold. Do you think also to buy forgiveness for having sent your minions to destroy me?"

"There can be but one heir to the Diamond Throne. Tradition dictated that heir be my eldest, son of my consort." The king's expression softened. "I ordered your death to prevent the battle that would have been inevitable between you and Tabor had you both lived at the moment of my death. The gods must have known Tabor would fall in battle, to have looked over you and nursed you back from near death. I am grateful I still have a son of my body to continue Obsidion's rule."

"A son for whom you must *buy* a consort since you barely failed to destroy me." The translucent robe that indicated his station flapped against his legs. Arik pondered the irony of it all as he limped across his tower chamber. "Had you left me to live my life in peace rather than hiring that trio of my fellow mercenaries to kill me, you would not now find yourself with an heir no woman would willingly take to her couch."

The king followed, then reached out to lay a hand on Arik's damaged shoulder. His gaze fastened now on the scarred arm and the hook Arik had become accustomed to using after losing his arm on Eastphalia, where more modern prostheses weren't available. He realized that while the device functioned adequately, it looked more beastly than human -- and it gave him a perverse sense of satisfaction that seeing the thing unnerved his father.

His expression stoic, he met Arik's gaze. "I did not buy a woman for you, though I'd have gladly done so had it been necessary. Meredith the matchmaker brought me much gold from Eli, whose spoiled eldest daughter apparently has insisted she must have a prince for her mate."

"I take it I was the only prince in Meredith's inventory of possible mates for Obsidion's sheltered beauties."

"It is of no import, for you'll mate with Emerald tomorrow." The king met Arik's gaze but looked away quickly, as though it pained him to see the son his would-be assassins had turned into a monster before losing their own lives.

Arik relished knowing the old man suffered every time he looked upon the damages he'd orchestrated. Perhaps someday that satisfaction might multiply enough to compensate him for all he'd lost. But not yet.

"Your bride has been certified fertile, and I cannot doubt her beauty will stir your loins. I expect she will produce you an heir some ten moons hence."

Arik wished he were as certain as his father that his bride would do her duty, not run screaming at the sight of him in the all-concealing garments he wore whenever he had to venture from these rooms. He'd chance that, though, over the certainty that seeing him naked would set her to screaming in horror. As forbidding as he looked in head-to-toe black leather, it beat revealing the ravagement of his flesh. Drawing his robe around him to ward off the evening chill, he strode to the window of his tower as soon as his father left and stared out at what would one day be his domain.

Obsidion. The pleasure planet. His home. Even now the galaxy-renowned sex slave parlors and shops twinkled with many-colored lights, though night had not yet cloaked the sky in darkness. Arik stood, fingering the rough surface of his ruined cheek and idly rubbing a painful spot in his empty eye socket as he watched dusk fall on his last day as a free man.

He could not, would not, submit to the restorative surgeries Pak Song, renowned cyborg-maker of Obsidion, had sworn would restore his former appearance. Pak Song had been summoned to the palace soon after Arik's return from exile. He saw his ugliness as a source of well-deserved pain to his father, a reminder to all of the cruel fate that befell younger sons of kings who had refused to bow to Obsidion's laws and submit to a gelder's laser knife before they grew to manhood.

His cock swelled against the sheer golden silk of his robe, as though in silent thanks to him for having spared it by fleeing the palace rather than becoming a royal eunuch along with his four half-cousins -- sons of the old king, half-brother to Arik's own father. They'd also been at or approaching puberty that summer ten years ago.

If only his princess would look past the scars that marred his body and see him for the man he was, not the monster who greeted him in the mirror each morning... and not the king he would someday become. Arik fixed his gaze on a glittering star -- Nebula, he thought -- and made the wish, though he knew it was futile.

No. He'd not leave his chamber without the mask and body suit that hid his ugliness, and he'd never invite his mate to join him here. Better that she fear what she did not know than run in horror from the monster he'd become.

* * *

"There. That one must be your bridegroom, framed in the highest window of the tower. Those who say a monster lies beneath the leather hood and suit he wears must have lost their minds. The man is gorgeous. What a face! What hair! What a body." When Pearl handed over the hand-held telescope, Emerald noticed the lascivious look in her sister's eyes. "I've never seen such a magnificent cock. If only I were the eldest," Pearl commented, her tone wistful.

"Or I. When Arik becomes king, he will have more wealth than Croesus, or so people say." Garnet moistened her deep-red lips. "Still, I look forward to a life with my man of gold. What think you of your prince, Emerald?"

Emerald focused the eyepiece, then took in the man who tomorrow would become her mate -- her master. She stifled a sigh, for her sisters already were envious of her, and she'd not spoil the pleasure of her royal mating by having them scrap over what her father had already decided -- that the crown prince of Obsidion would be hers and hers alone. Garnet and Pearl must not only wait for their own matings but also satisfy themselves with the lesser males Meredith the matchmaker had chosen for them.

In profile, backlit by the bright lights in what she imagined must be his bedchamber, Prince Arik looked gorgeous. His shimmering robe let light through, enhancing the look of his impressive body in an aura of pale gold that contrasted with his jet-black hair and skin that reminded her of caramel and cream. She liked the way he kept his long hair pulled back in a queue.

Emerald could hardly wait to loosen that hair and thread her fingers through the silky fall. He had a rugged look about him, a nose not quite straight, yet regal, high cheekbones, and a strong, clean-shaven jaw. A look of blatant masculine command.

A huge man, he gave the appearance of fluid motion even while standing still. His massive thighs reminded her of tree trunks. She shivered when she focused on his cock, so big it sent a wave of anticipation from her cunt to her pierced nipples. It looked fearsome, a somnolent beast resting in its nest of dark pubic curls against a pair of large, round balls.

A sudden frisson of fear made her look away for a moment when she considered how his mighty weapon would feel, penetrating her virgin flesh for the first time and making her his own. Perhaps that was why some called him monster. She'd take that monster cock any day, along with the rest of the gorgeous man who'd soon be her mate.

Emerald had her prince, and from what she saw he was the embodiment of all her girlish dreams. In less than twelve hours now, they'd be mated, and her fantasies would all come true.

* * *

Fantasies. Emerald had barely slept, rising eagerly as soon as a pink and purple dawn sky began to emerge from darkness. Today she'd become a princess, the pampered consort of her royal master. The most handsome man she'd ever seen, with perfection of face and form that matched her own.

Excited, she bathed and dressed, taking special care to drape a silken robe artistically around her naked body -- a robe not unlike the one she'd seen her prince wearing in his chamber the night before.

She could hardly wait.

"You will ready yourself, my daughter," Eli told her a few moments later. "The king has sent a litter for you. He has decreed the ceremony will be private."

"But..." Emerald clamped her lips together, stifling the complaint her father's stern look let her know would be futile. She'd so much wanted all of Obsidion to witness her triumph -- to see that she, Emerald, had captured the planet's finest prize. The perfect mate... the perfect master. She'd feign compliance, pretend submission, then use her wiles to twist her prince into doing her bidding. "Yes, Father," she said, making no complaint when he assisted her into a litter and motioned for its bearers to rise and take her to their master.

Sweet incense swirled about in the inside of the jeweled litter, cloaking Emerald in a sensual haze, hiding her thinly robed flesh from those who'd glimpse their prince's bride on her journey through Obsidion's streets to the castle -- to the man who'd be her master.

The arousing scent of precious oils she'd rubbed into her naked body mingled with the incense, set her nipples to tingling and her cunt to clenching with anticipation. She could hardly wait for her prince to claim her... take her. She longed for the moment she would feel the cold, heavy weight of his collar closing about her neck -- a moment her father had assured her would take place as soon as the crown prince penetrated her cunt with his mighty cock, as was traditional at the royal matings that occurred but rarely on Obsidion.

In less than an hour I'll be a princess. Mate to the handsome prince of all my fantasies.

Emerald ran her fingers through her waist-length auburn curls, suddenly eager to feel them being cut off, as always happened during mating ceremonies for members of Obsidion's upper classes. She welcomed that, and the collar, and all the symbols of submission she'd wear to show the world she belonged to her prince.

For she'd engage his lust and capture his heart, and he would belong to her, too.

Arik. Over and over she repeated his name in her mind as six matched Martian slaves bore her through the streets on the golden litter, and later in the castle's great hall while three of the four royal eunuchs she'd heard about lovingly prepared her to be presented to their lord and master.

The eunuchs fascinated her, for each of them wore the precious stones allowed only to Obsidion's royal family -- diamonds set in red gold from Mars. Huge studs in their ears, smaller ones in their right nostrils -- and elaborate, diamond-studded shields centered over smooth hairless flesh where she imagined a laser beam had cut away all evidence of their maleness.

What puzzled her more was that they went about their chores with gentle precision, exquisite care, and a total lack of the admiration she'd come to expect from all males -- even the eunuchs who served in her father's household.

Chapter Two

The fourth of the royal eunuchs attended his master, preparing him to greet his mate. When Arik waved away the royal robes Hikaru tried to set on his leather-clad shoulders, the eunuch protested. "My lord, you must look the part of a prince."

Indeed. There'd be no mistaking his position, as he'd be the only whole male participating in the mating. Already his cock had stiffened, whether from anticipation or the loving attention Hikaru had shown it while freeing it from the confines of his leather body suit and arranging the opening around its base, Arik couldn't say. "I will dispense with the royal trappings. It is not as though my bride is likely to object to their lack -- after all, I look less fearsome in leather than in my princely robes."

Momentarily he imagined himself whole, naked but for his translucent robes, presenting himself for her inspection and admiration. Shoving that fantasy aside, he reached behind his neck and checked the tightness of the lacings that secured his hood. "We go now."

"As you say, my lord." When Hikaru bowed, the diamond studs in his ears and left nostril twinkled.

The bridegroom cometh. It is of no consequence that he looks less adorned than the royal eunuchs who serve him. Arik had refused the diamond-studded cock ring his father had offered the night before and wore only a single diamond stud in his left earlobe to mark his status. A stud hidden beneath the leather hood that hugged his face, concealing his ravaged side from view.

Arik's footsteps resounded against the marble staircase, strong yet muted by the soft kidskin boots that encased his feet. One step sure, the next halting, each footfall brought him closer -- closer to the point from which there could be no return. The point he'd crossed, in truth, when he'd finally obeyed his father's orders and returned to Obsidion to take his place as heir to the Diamond Throne.

He'd become immune to courtiers' stares, and to the sympathetic murmurs that drifted to his ears whenever he ventured from his chambers. The black leather body suit he wore outside the privacy of his own rooms served to distance him -- to provide a mask that shielded his emotions as well as his ravaged body from their view. Today, in honor of his imminent mating, he'd left off the codpiece in which he usually encased his sex.

There she was. His bride. Laid out on the dais in the great hall below, her ivory skin glowed with the sensual oil he'd chosen earlier from the selection the royal eunuchs had offered. The smell of her female musk, accentuated by the aphrodisiac in the oil, made Arik's nostrils flare behind the mask.

His cock swelled with anticipation. This delectable morsel belonged to him, as certainly as his princely robes of gold and purple and the cask of jewels he kept secure in his chamber where no one could plunder them. His balls tightened when he watched her squirming with obvious pleasure at the attention she was getting from the two royal eunuchs who stirred her passions with their practiced hands and mouths while a third one harvested her fiery curls, leaving her with the soft looking pelt he ached to touch with his naked hand but knew he must not.

The short, springy curls only her master could look upon once the vows were said.

If they were said.

He'd not take her against her will. And he couldn't believe she'd accept him willingly once she saw what he'd become. He should disrobe, show her the monster behind the leather... give her the choice of walking away.

Arik paused, his gaze steady on Emerald's perfect face as his head filled with the smell of woman -- his woman. His balls tightened against the skin-tight leather of his body suit, weakening his resolve to reveal himself. His cock, the only part of him beside his eye that he had not encased in the concealing garment, reared up against his belly, rock-hard and throbbing now at the prospect of burying itself in the fragrant cunt of his mate. Ignoring the voice of his conscience that screamed for him to show his true colors, he stilled the hand that had moved behind his head to unlace his hood and continued his deliberate journey toward destiny.

"Come, my lord, your bride awaits you." As always when he spoke, Hikaru dropped to his knees before Arik, touching his bald head to the floor in obeisance.

"Rise." Seeing Hikaru and his three brothers prostrated before him, realizing each time they did it that they no longer were royal princes but merely the royal eunuchs, always unnerved Arik. But for a quirk of fate and a sense of preservation he'd developed early on, he would have been bowing today before his prince or his king, forever denied his royal birthright because he'd chosen life in the comfort of the castle over exile with his manhood intact. Hikaru had made that choice before he'd had the chance to understand what pleasures he had sacrificed... he'd been only nine years old to Arik's seventeen when the king had decreed that excess males of the royal family's next generation were to be gelded or exiled.

Arik sighed, then growled the traditional order Hikaru obviously expected to hear. "Go to my bride and make her ready to accept my cock."

"Yes, my lord. Would you have the lady Emerald restrained for your pleasure?"

If only Arik could count on her accepting him willingly... but no. He dared not risk her bolting before his father and the court, as she might well do anyway when she got a look at him decked out head to toe in black leather. Unmasked and unclothed, though, he would surely frighten her more. "Yes. Bind her well. Take care, though, not to cause her pain." Slowly, painstakingly, for he wanted no one to realize the extent of damage his attackers had caused to his leg and hip, Arik followed Hikaru to the dais where Emerald lay, a pagan sacrifice to his father's desire to perpetuate their line -- and to his own raging lust.

Her striking green eyes widened when he stepped into her line of vision. She strained against silken bonds even as she raised her hips to give Hikaru better access to her glistening cunt when he bent to tongue her tiny jewel. Hikaru's brothers stepped aside and prostrated themselves, giving Arik an arousing view of his bride's hardened nipples with the emerald-studded gold chain connecting them to another emerald that winked in her navel.

Emerald stifled a cry. *This* was her master? This fearsome creature stood a head taller than the next tallest man in the hall. The skin-tight black leather suit encased him from head to toe but for his rampant arousal and one glittering dark eye. It clung lovingly to massive, rippling muscles. The gleaming leather caught light from a thousand flickering candles held in sconces around her and along the expanse of pink marble walls.

Certainly this monster could not be the same man as the perfect prince she'd glimpsed last night. Yet he had to be. The royal eunuchs who'd prepared her fell back and knelt at his approach, touching the tops of their shaved heads to the marble floor in a sensually choreographed act of pure obeisance -- the kind of total submission these proud royals would offer only to their prince or king. Courtiers who'd been conversing quietly turned silent and bowed their heads as the giant passed them by.

Yes, the man behind the fearsome mask had to be her prince. Her master.

She stared at his cock, a huge purple-headed beast that stood straight up against his belly, the milky drop of pre-cum on its tip a stark contrast with the supple black leather that framed it. Her cunt clenched with anticipation despite her fear, and when she looked up she saw the heat in that one dark eye when he raked her naked, well-primed body with a look of pure lust -- pure possession. He made her squirm, made her cunt cream and her heart pound in her chest.

Impatient now, she strained against her bonds. Despite herself, despite her fears, she needed to caress that huge, swollen shaft, pay it homage with her mouth and tongue.

Take me, I beg you. Impale me on your huge, beautiful cock. Give me your seed.

She dared not speak for he'd not granted her permission, yet when she saw his cock grow impossibly longer, thicker, harder before her eyes, she knew he'd somehow heard her silent entreaty.

He met her gaze, held it, spoke in a deep, gravelly voice muted ominously by the all-concealing hood. "I claim you as my mate. My slave. Future mother to my sons and princess to the people of Obsidion."

The eunuch who had crawled silently between her legs licked Emerald's slit, stoking her flames for their master's possession. Moisture gushed from her cunt when he tongued her there, intensifying when he inserted a finger into her tight rear passage and began to slide it gently back and forth. He began to suck her clit as he finger-fucked her ass, flailing it with his tongue until she thought she'd scream with frustration.

Pressure built in her belly, bringing heat that radiated, blossomed, came into full bloom when her master reached out with a gloved hand and tugged the chain that connected her nipple rings. "You have permission to speak. To accept or refuse me."

"Oh, yes, please take me," she begged, straining at her bonds. By the gods, she needed her mate. Her cunt had never been hotter, wetter. She needed his huge pulsating cock to fill her now, more than she feared what manner of creature he was to hide behind the mask.

"You accept me as your master?"

"Yessss." When he bent and touched first one nipple and then the other, the heat of his mouth scalded her through the leather barrier. "I would feel your flesh, see the magnificent body I now can only feel."

"Perhaps someday. For now be grateful that I cover myself."

She sensed regret in his muffled voice, but her cunt contracted painfully. Lust overwhelmed her. The eunuch's intimate invasion of her ass stoked her desire but did nothing to assuage it. She had to feel her master's monster cock stretching her... filling her.

Now.

"Fuck me, my prince. Please."

"Your pleasure is my own." As though they'd orchestrated this move a thousand times -- perhaps they had -- the eunuch rose, making way for his master. The heat of the prince's huge cock seared Emerald's wet cunt when he stepped between her widespread legs and rubbed the blunt, thick head of it along her slit. "So wet. So ready." He positioned himself and sank into her cunt slowly, his heart-shaped cock head stretching her, making way for his full possession. "So mine," he said, his voice full of wonder when he'd finally breached her virgin barrier. On his signal, three of the eunuchs rose, two taking her tingling nipples between their teeth and suckling her while a third one -- the one who'd accompanied her master, she thought -- tunneled his fingers into the shorn curls on her head.

"I want you to see." At the prince's terse command the eunuch lifted her head, cradling it between his hands. "Look at us, my princess. Watch my cock slide in and out of your wet, hot cunt. Watch me while I fuck you."

Focusing on the look and feel of his possession, seeing his hips flex as he slid his cock out of her body then slammed back in harder and faster than before, aroused Emerald almost beyond endurance. The slapping, sucking sounds of flesh on flesh and leather punctuated each stroke of his giant cock.

Did he feel it, too, this searing heat? Was his skin flushing like hers beneath the mask, prickling with the need to come, to break the pressure and find the nirvana of release? Could he smell the musk of sex that filled her nostrils, and did it stimulate him the same way it aroused her?

"Gods above, I'm coming," he growled, slamming into her cunt once more. Hot spurts of his seed filled her womb, triggering a series of contractions that wracked her body, left her panting and drained yet wanting still more. More of this masked man who held her future in his hands.

When she opened her eyes, her prince stood over her, his one-eyed gaze on the collar one of his eunuchs had just locked around her neck. She licked her lips, anticipating that he'd let her taste his renewed erection, now jutting proudly toward her hungry lips. "Your hungry look tells me you want to suck my cock. Do you?"

"Yes, master."

"Your wish is my command. Open your mouth." Straddling her, he fed her his cock head. He tasted... indescribable. His cum and hers mingled on her lips when she took him in her mouth and licked all around his plump corona. His collar, heavy platinum encrusted with the diamonds reserved for Obsidion's royalty, rested easily against her throat, supporting her head as she serviced him.

Someone's warm breath tickled her thighs, and soft hands spread her outer lips. A moist tongue tickled her clit while another lapped the length of her slit from cunt to ass. A warm, wet object pressed against her asshole, coaxing her to open and take it in. A cock? No, the only cock allowed her was her master's, and she had it firmly in her mouth. Emerald sucked harder, swallowed reflexively as she took more of his hot flesh down her throat.

He groaned. "That's it. Relax. Let Hikaru fuck your pretty ass with the dildo. You can take it. Soon you'll be ready to take my cock there, too. Meanwhile there are many ways the royal eunuchs can give you pleasure -- some ways that I cannot because I wear the mask. They may take your ass, your mouth, caress and suck your pretty nipples and..." His words trailed off as though it pained him to forego the sexual foreplay the mask prevented. "Remember, though, my princess, your cunt belongs to me. It's mine... and mine alone, now and for all time. Gods but that feels good," he growled when she relaxed her throat muscles and swallowed his cock head.

The eunuch sucked her clit harder, flailed the delicate bud with his tongue. Emerald wanted more, wanted to feel her master's tongue and hands and naked flesh on her, in her. She swallowed reflexively against her master's rigid cock, and he rewarded her with a groan that sounded as if he was in exquisite agony.

"... *give you pleasure... in ways I cannot because I wear the mask.*" Why wouldn't he take off the mask? Why did he insist on covering his magnificent body in the leather that felt warm, alive against her hands? She didn't mind, but instinct told her his own smooth hot skin would feel even better.

Emerald recalled the glimpse she'd had of him last night, the perfect beauty he now hid from his father's subjects -- and from her. She was his mate now, not some sex slave from the emporiums or a sexbot from Pak Song's extensive collection. She'd persuade him to remove it later. At the moment she had a better use for her mouth. And the royal eunuch had a magical tongue that had her on the edge of yet another climax.

Her pussy clenched and contracted wildly as she sucked her master's big, beautiful cock dry and swallowed his hot thick cream. She barely missed the lack of that cock stretching her spasming cunt -- but then how could she miss it, when one royal eunuch nibbled her clit while another reamed her ass with a dildo that felt remarkably like a smaller, cooler version of her master's magnificent cock.

Chapter Three

He'd come three times during the ritual mating, yet his cock was still rock hard and ready for more when he lifted his princess from the dais and carried her to his tower. Arik laid Emerald on his bed, atop the velvet coverlet. She slept on, her surprisingly dark eyelashes forming a pattern against the creamy skin beneath her closed eyes, her full lips slack.

His gaze fell on the icy brilliance of her collar, and he noted the stark contrast between the white diamonds and platinum, and her fiery pelt of closely cropped curls. Light and bright. Hard and soft. He longed to strip away the leather that was his personal prison and feel with his hands and body that which he would only allow himself to touch with his cock.

He wouldn't do it because he intended to keep her. Wanted her to take him willingly, as she'd done earlier. Gods but he hated the idea of having to restrain his lover. He'd done it too many times in the pleasure palaces. He'd even hooded his partners so he wouldn't have to see the revulsion in their eyes. It was his fate to hide behind the leather, his prize that the concealment seemed not to repulse his princess.

At least he could feel the creamy heat of her cunt surrounding his naked cock, hear her cries of pleasure when she came. Standing over her now, watching the slow rise and fall of her breasts, Arik sent silent thanks to the gods that he'd not been totally blinded, that he could stroke her visually, imagining in the deepest confines of his mind how her ivory skin would feel -- warm and incredibly soft against his naked flesh. His nostrils flared at the scent of her that permeated the chamber -- the scent of woman and arousal and fulfillment.

His cock rose again against his belly. He had to feel her warmth. Experience her woman's softness. With his good hand he reached down, slid his fingers through those fiery shorn curls.

Perhaps... perhaps he could free his hand from the leather glove, learn by touch if the short springy curls felt as soft as they looked.

Without thinking, he reached behind his head for the lacings. Then he remembered. He'd insisted that the leather garments be fashioned in such a way that once Hikaru had laced one onto him, it was there to stay until the eunuch appeared in his chamber each evening to remove it for the night. Its only opening that he could control was a small zippered slit at the crotch through which he could empty his bowels when the need arose -- and the removable leather cock-sleeves he could wear or not as the occasion dictated.

No way had he wanted to flaunt the scars that had sent strong men running for the latrines... scars that brought tears to his father's eyes and satisfaction to Arik for having revisited a small portion of the pain he'd suffered at the king's order. Neither had he felt any desire to look upon himself, compare his undamaged left side with the devastated flesh on the right.

He lifted a gloved hand to the right side of his face, feeling the sunken hole where his eye had been as a reminder of the ugliness that lurked behind the mask. The sight of it, he knew from experience, terrified children and sent grown men running for cover. Not even for the tactile pleasure of running his fingers through his mate's inviting curls, of stroking the ivory expanse of her belly, of dipping between her thighs to feel the warmth and wetness there, would he risk sickening her by exposing to her what he bore stoically as evidence of his father's shame.

"Shall I rouse her for you, my lord?" Hikaru asked. "Or would you have me ease you?"

If he roused her, Arik feared he'd give in to the compulsion to indulge his sense of touch for the first time since he'd wakened in an Eastphalian clinic, more dead than alive, to see pity on the faces of those who tended him -- and a glimmer of hope in their eyes months later when they told him his father, the man who'd decreed that he be destroyed, had now ordered him to come home to Obsidion and take his rightful place as heir to the Diamond Throne.

"No. She needs her sleep. Carry her to her chamber, go cleanse yourself, and return to me. I'd pass the night outside my leather prison -- and I'd make use of your ass to ease my lust." It was the least Arik could do to provide the only sexual pleasure left to this royal cousin who served him with unfailing devotion -- especially on this night.

Hikaru bowed low, his forehead brushing the plush carpet before he laid a kiss on one of Arik's booted feet. "Yes, my lord. I will be forever grateful. You may trust me to care for your princess as I care for you -- and to hasten with my preparations and return quickly to you."

Once Hikaru left, Arik grasped his cock, felt it pulsating with life beneath his leather glove. What did seeing him swell with lust at the sight of his mate do to the royal eunuchs whose bodies were forever denied arousal and release? How did they feel to know they were so sexless their uncle the king deemed them completely trustworthy to prepare and arouse the Crown Princess of Obsidion for her prince's pleasure?

Arik imagined it must pain them to realize that while they licked and stroked his princess and plumbed her tight ass with their false cocks, they could never experience the lust that had been so evident in her eyes, in the creaming of her cunt -- and the swelling of his own eager cock.

Over and over during the long day's mating ritual, the royal eunuchs had witnessed Arik fucking Emerald. They'd had to watch while she brought him to climax with her mouth. They'd been forced to stand by, experiencing vicariously the sort of sexual pleasure they'd been denied forever with one quick slice of a gelder's laser scalpel.

Yes, Hikaru deserved whatever puny release Arik could give him. No doubt his three brothers would even now be massaging each other's prostate glands, ass-fucking each other with dildos as they'd done to Emerald earlier.

Arik reached into the drawer beside his bed and drew out a condom and a tube of lubricant he'd brought back from one of his rare trips outside the palace -- to the Sex Slave Emporium where he rented the occasional willing female to ease his lust.

One thing about being less than whole -- he had to plan safe sex well in advance. Opening up a condom with a hand and a hook while wearing gloves, even ones of supple leather like the ones built into the arms of his bodysuit, wasn't something he'd be able to manage through a haze of lust, especially when he couldn't use his teeth. He barely got the job done and laid the condom beside the lubricant before he heard Hikaru's footsteps in the hall.

* * *

Clearly, Hikaru had hurried. Water still glistened on his hairless skin, beaded on his prominent nipples while he unlaced Arik's hood first, then loosened the laces that snaked down each side of the garment from his hands to his feet. Cool air made his skin tingle as Hikaru exposed it inch by inch. His queued hair tickled his back. He tried not to wince when the hood fell away, but the slightest pressure on his crushed facial bones still sent shards of agony darting through the damaged nerves.

His body, seen only by his father and Hikaru since he'd returned, reveled in the freedom from confinement. From the first, he'd exposed himself deliberately to his father, an act of well-thought-out revenge, for it obviously unnerved the old king each time he saw the devastation he'd wrought on his only remaining heir. At first Arik had refused to leave this chamber, declined to receive anyone but the king, not even the royal eunuchs.

One day Hikaru had stationed himself outside Arik's locked chamber door and shouted out for all to hear. *My lord. You've lost your beauty and your eye, you've got a hook for a hand, and you don't move about as gracefully as you once did. So what? We've all lost our cocks and balls -- and our freedom. Open the door and let me in. My brothers have chosen me to be your body slave.*

If Arik had possessed the strength when Hikaru had uttered those hurtful words, he'd have snatched up the mouthy slave and heaved him through the tower window. He hadn't, though, so he'd merely sat and nursed his fury -- until he'd realized the truth of what Hikaru had said. Then he'd opened the door to a soft-skinned hairless creature who apparently took pleasure in flaunting his status as royal eunuch by using a large diamond-studded crest of the House of Obsidion not only to cover the indentation where they'd cut his cock and balls away, but also to secure a thin flexible acrylic tube through which he apparently passed his urine. The creature was, yet was not, the carefree young cousin with whom Arik had spent much of his childhood.

Since that day they'd bonded -- the royal eunuch and the crown prince, slave and master as custom decreed -- yet more. Hikaru became Arik's only friend. The only soul other than the king he'd allow to see the bitterness he wasn't yet ready to relinquish. Arik smiled down at Hikaru as the slave undid the last of the laces and worked the tight leather garment down and off.

Arik stood, balancing on his good left leg while Hikaru kissed his feet. He sighed when the eunuch began to stroke his scarred calf and thigh, imagining it was Emerald's slender hands on his flesh, soothing away the pain that never completely subsided. "Ahhhh, you have magic hands. Do not stop."

Hikaru didn't, but tonight he did something he'd never done before. Arik held back a moan when he felt a warm, wet tongue bathing his ball sac, then sliding along his half-hard cock, licking and nibbling much like Emerald had done earlier. Hikaru's hands slid upward, found Arik's nipples and began to pinch the sensitive nubs.

It felt good. Too good. Arik reached down and caught Hikaru's smooth skull between his hand and his hook. He pictured his princess's short cap of curls, imagining how they'd feel against his fingers if he dared caress her this way.

Gods but he was about to come. And this was supposed to be for Hikaru. "Cease, slave. I want to fuck you now." When Hikaru stood, Arik positioned him over the bed on all fours, butt in the air, then reached on the table and put on the condom he'd opened earlier. "Spread your ass cheeks for me."

Arik smeared lubricant on his sheathed cock and worked a large glob of it into Hikaru's asshole, still cool and damp from the thorough internal cleansing he must have performed. When Arik rubbed his cock around the rim of Hikaru's ass, the flesh gave way easily and sucked his cock head past the tight sphincter muscle. Fuck but it felt good, sliding in and out of the tight hole, his naked balls slapping Hikaru's soft crotch while he clutched the eunuch's ass cheeks.

Naked flesh on naked flesh. Arik's cock swelled further as he imagined kneading Emerald's plump breasts while he pumped in and out of her cunt... or her ass. She'd be tight... so tight there. Soft and womanly. Caught up in his fantasy, he slid his damaged arm higher, catching one of Hikaru's prominent nipples carefully between the prongs of his hook and giving it a playful tug, the way he'd love to do to her.

Harder. Faster. Hikaru reared back and took Arik's cock to the balls into his slippery ass. "Oh, my lord, thank you," Hikaru said when Arik found and prodded his prostate, his tone one of wonder and gratitude.

Knowing he'd made the eunuch come made Arik so hot he lost control. Mindless now, he concentrated on the building sensations that bombarded his cock and balls. Couldn't hold back. Had to come. Now.

"Don't move." Grasping Hikaru's hips, Arik slammed into his ass once, twice. With the third powerful thrust his cock spasmed and began to spurt hot semen, bathing his own sheathed flesh with creamy heat.

Chapter Four

Emerald blinked at the blinding light of the morning sun, then looked around again at the unfamiliar surroundings. Her first impression had been right. This wasn't the chamber where she'd fallen asleep in her master's leather-clad arms last night, the one with a west-facing window that overlooked her father's house. The window that had framed her prince in all his perfection the night before their mating.

She was a princess now. And this room was obviously part of her prince's tower. A lady's chamber, like those she'd read about in ancient tomes? Perhaps royalty did things differently than commoners who fucked together and slept together...

Well, that was about to change. She'd submitted her cunt to her royal master -- loved every minute of it, too -- but that didn't mean she'd suddenly become another royal slave.

She pressed a button on the bedside console, stretching and reflecting on the delicious soreness between her legs until Prince Arik's personal eunuch stepped through the door and laid himself face-down on the floor beside her sleeping couch.

"Up with you. Where is Prince Arik?" All this subservience got annoying pretty quickly.

"In his chamber across the hall, my lady."

"Then I will join him there." Swinging her legs over the side of the brocaded sleeping couch, Emerald started to get up but hesitated when the eunuch hesitantly cleared his throat.

"I would not, my lady. My lord does not receive visitors so early."

"Visitors? I am not a visitor. I am his royal highness's mate. Who are you to tell me I cannot go about this palace as I see fit?"

The eunuch cast his gaze downward, studying the toes of his bare feet with apparent fascination, but when he spoke his voice held the ring of command she'd have expected only from those of the royal blood. "I am Hikaru, royal eunuch and personal slave to Prince Arik. He has charged me with dressing you before you descend with him into the great hall. And it is on his order that I must prevent you from joining him unless he has need for you."

That pronouncement made Emerald seethe, but she rose and forced what she imagined was a regal smile. "We must begin, then. I'll assume you're as talented a lady's maid as you are a personal pleasure slave."

Hikaru shrugged his broad shoulders, then shot her a mischievous smile. "We shall see, my lady. Take a seat here by the window and we'll get started."

She'd never felt quite so pampered. Beginning with her toes and moving up the outsides of her calves and thighs, the slave massaged warm oil from the sweet olive trees on Mars into every square inch of her skin. Unlike her maid at home, he had long, strong fingers and a sure touch that was more stimulating than relaxing, especially when he spread her legs and worked his magic along her inner thighs and the outer petals of her sex.

A handsome creature, he seemed oblivious to her feminine charm. Of course he was. He was a possession, different from herself only in the fact he was neither male nor female -- a sexless servant who could arouse but not become aroused himself.

A pity. Emerald's juices were flowing. She wanted release... had to have it before she faced the courtiers. She reached down and stroked his cleanly shaved scalp, his ear with its diamond stud. "Service me now," she ordered, and when he dipped his head between her legs and tongued her clit she pressed his hands hard against her breasts, needing to feel their weight... to feel the tug of the nipple rings and the chain between them.

So wet. So hot. She wanted her master's cock in her cunt, her mouth, her ass. When she moaned, Hikaru began to tongue-fuck her, his warm mouth and methodical stabbings more soothing than arousing. He plucked at her ringed nipples until they swelled and hardened. She'd never been so aware -- aware that she needed the man in the room across the hall. Her master, who in one short day had spoiled her with his monster cock… taught her there could be no substitute for it, not now. Not ever.

Emerald no longer wanted to come. Not like this. Not without him. She wanted him to be the one to stroke and pet her, to arouse her with his tongue. "Stop!"

Hikaru sat back on his haunches, his head bowed. "I know what you need, my lady, and I wish I had it to give. Come now, and I will dress you to meet the king's faithful subjects."

Shame washed over Emerald. "I am sorry." Surely it must pain this beautiful eunuch who was once a royal prince to look at himself and see winking diamonds instead of a functioning cock and balls.

"Don't be. They cut me when I was nine years old. Yesterday was the first time in my life I got an idea of what I lost." He fell silent as he picked up a pair of clippers from the dresser. "Don't worry. I'm only going to even it up. Prince Arik insisted that you be clipped closely, not shaved."

"I don't mind bald. Your head feels… incredibly soft. Still, I'd rather have some hair, even if no man but my master will ever get to see it." Emerald loved the feel of the tightly curled, short pelt, the incredibly light feel of her shorn head, the coolness of the breeze when it tugged the short strands and swirled over her scalp.

"It's traditional for the royal eunuchs to remove their hair. By now it seems as natural as brushing my teeth to lather up each day and shave my own head clean. Stroking it with the razor feels almost as good as stimulating my prostate with a dildo." Hikaru set down the comb and clippers and tunneled a finger into the hair at the crown of Emerald's head. "There. I think you're finished here. Are you ready for your wig?"

"Yes." She didn't relish wearing the heavy jeweled headgear, but she figured she had to put up with a little discomfort for the prestige of being consort to her country's reclusive Crown Prince Arik.

"Close your eyes, my lady." When Hikaru clapped his hands, the door flew open. She felt a surprisingly light weight settle on her head, heard the eunuch dismiss whoever had come in. Something soft and silky fell over her shoulders, kissing her belly, her arms and legs.

"You may look now."

Yesterday a submissive bride, today a princess. The short, curly-haired wig, not much different from the pelt Hikaru had just trimmed, had been strewn with diamonds set on fine wire mesh. Her robes were not gold or silver but a shimmering combination of both colors, so sheer she could have spotted the smallest blemish if one had dared pop up on her royal person. "I would see my master now," she said, imagining him similarly attired, his muscles rippling beneath his own princely robe.

"In but a few moments, my lady. I must go now and ready him now that he has broken his fast."

* * *

This morning he'd even hidden his big cock behind black leather. He had to be roasting, for Obsidion's sun beat down on them as they strolled through the palace gardens. Emerald bit back a sarcastic comment when she smiled up at Prince Arik -- or rather at the single deep-brown eye she could see. "How do you eat?" she blurted before she could call back the words.

"The same way you do, I imagine." His tone implied amusement, but it infuriated her, having to converse with a mate she'd fucked and sucked yet never seen up close. "I take my meals in my chamber."

Away from everybody, including me. "Why?"

"Because I cannot eat while I wear this --" He lifted his left hand and touched the spot where she guessed his mouth must be. "-- and trust me. You do not want me to remove it."

Did he hide some horrible disfigurement? Emerald couldn't imagine he did. Still he seemed quite sane -- not the sort of man who'd adopt his fearsome mode of attire for no better reason than to intimidate his father's subjects. "Were you in your chamber the night before we mated? Standing in the window overlooking town?"

"Yes. I find it clears my mind, looking down at the Street of Pleasure, imagining myself there like other men."

"I saw you. You are beautiful. Perfect. I wondered then as I wonder now why you choose to hide behind all this." When she reached out and touched the leather stretched over his right upper arm, he winced.

"I don't know what you thought you saw, or what kind of trick telescope you were using. I'm not beautiful. I am scarred, so scarred I'd terrify children and give their mothers nightmares." He spoke slowly, as though he thought her a simple-minded child. "The scars are reminders of injuries I suffered in a dogfight off Eastphalia with three other mercenary captains. My father sent them to kill me, in case you want to know."

She'd attributed his halting gait to the tight leather body suit, but maybe... "Were your legs injured?" That was the only possible infirmity she'd noticed.

"One leg. One arm. One side of my body and face." He sounded weary, resigned. "If you saw me in the window and didn't notice, it must have been my uninjured side you were ogling. Come. You have already taken my seed into your luscious body. Since you are obviously fascinated about seeing what I hide from the rest of my father's subjects, I will show you."

* * *

In his chamber, he punched a button on the intercom. "Contain yourself, my princess. The unveiling will necessarily have to wait until my body slave arrives. Meanwhile, you may disrobe. I will enjoy watching you -- and watching him restrain you."

"I need no restraining. I am your willing mate." Her steady gaze as she slipped off her royal robes and stood before him naked but for her wig very nearly persuaded him she spoke the truth -- that she possessed the fortitude necessary to withstand looking at the devastation that nearly made him puke every time he saw himself.

She might even think she could take it, but he knew better. "You forgot to take off your wig. When we're alone, I want to see you in all your naked glory."

"I have no shame, not before my master." She lifted off the diamond-strewn confection of auburn curls, moved in front of the window, and shook her head. She must have known that would make the sun's rays bounce off her closely clipped hair, must have sensed how much he longed to discover with his own hand the feel of that bright, curly pelt.

He'd soon indulge that longing. And stroke her silken skin, and lick the cream from her plump cunt lips the way Hikaru and the other royal eunuchs had done in his stead during the mating ceremony. He wet his lips behind the hood.

Where was Hikaru? His cock had swollen painfully within its leather sheath. He couldn't free it, either, not while his hand and hook were trapped inside the bodysuit. But Emerald could. "Come, then, if you have no shame, for looking at you has me seriously aroused. Free my cock and pleasure me while we wait for Hikaru."

"Yes, my lord." When she fondled him through the leather, searching for the fastenings that held the cock sheath to the body of the suit, he couldn't stifle a groan. "I love this... love the feel of it in my cunt."

The sheath came off, and she tossed it aside, slipping one hand down inside the suit to cup his sac. "I want to suck these, too. I want to feel them bouncing against my warm, wet slit. And I want to feel every inch of you caressing me."

Gods help him. She was offering him the sort of fucking he'd accepted was forever beyond his reach -- an offer he knew she'd rescind as soon as she saw him as he was -- as he would stay for the rest of his life.

Emerald drew up a cushion and knelt on it, taking his cock head in her mouth, encompassing it within that hot, wet cavern, licking around the corona and lapping the slippery pre-cum that oozed from its tip. Her lips tightened around his shaft while she gently squeezed his balls. Fuck, he was about to come, and he didn't want it to be like this.

"Stop."

She lifted her head and looked up at him but kept caressing his balls and the base of his cock with gentle hands. "Why, my lord?"

Because... because he couldn't bear to have her show him heaven only to snatch it away. And she would. No woman could possibly stand looking at the monster he'd become, yet no woman could tempt him to change his path -- to give in to lust and toss away the righteous vengeance he enjoyed each time he saw pain and guilt in his father's eyes.

"I do not want you to see me. If you do, you will run, as others have, and I want very much for you to stay."

"We mated before the entire court of Obsidion. I am your princess, and I intend to remain your princess for the rest of my life."

As certain as Emerald sounded now, Arik wouldn't let himself hope her determination would survive the shock she was about to receive. But he was impatient, no longer willing to wait for Hikaru. "We shall see. Take off my hood."

"How?" She reached up and stroked his cheeks, a puzzled look on her beautiful face.

He managed to hold back an oath when she ran the back of her hand over the ravaged side of his cheek, sending shards of pain down his neck and arm. "Not there. The seam around my neck unzips all the way around. Once the hood comes apart from the bodysuit, you can loosen the laces at the back of my head and lift it off."

Cool air surrounded Arik's throat as the hood separated from the suit, biting like a noose into his skin. A hiss erupted from Emerald when she slid her fingers into the opening. "I told you I'm scarred," he said. "You said you wanted to see."

"I do." She didn't sound as certain now that she'd felt part of the thick raised scar that took a jagged path from the stump of his right arm over mutilated flesh and bone, until it disappeared into his hairline above where his right eye had been.

"Zip the hood back on, and satisfy yourself with knowing only as much of me as I show to my father's subjects."

"No." As though she knew her touch would steal his resolve, she wedged one hand into the hood and tunneled her fingers into his hair. "Your hair is as soft as I imagined," she told him. "Move in front of the stool so I can stand on it and reach the laces. First, though, call off your royal eunuch. I wish to serve my mate... in every possible way."

Her touch was warm, soothing, yet incredibly arousing, her suggestion mesmerizing... hypnotic. He spoke into the communicator by the bed. "Hikaru, wherever you are, I no longer require your service. I will summon you after --"

" -- after he services his mate -- properly this time." Her husky promise made Arik's cock twitch to life, though it had shriveled at the sound of her distress a moment earlier.

He moved in front of the stool, sighed, and awaited the horrified reaction that always accompanied anyone's first sight of him. No words could adequately prepare her for what she was about to see -- but he had to try. "Be careful of the right side. I've lost an eye. And some of the scar tissue around the socket is still sensitive."

"You aren't going to scare me off, so you may as well save your breath. I wanted a prince for a mate, and now that I've got you I intend to keep you. Have you any idea how jealous it made my sisters when Meredith matched me up with you?" Emerald's banter eased Arik's fears, but the feel of each lace giving way to her gentle fingers fed them. Damn it, he could barely breathe.

By the gods, he wanted her to accept him. He'd never before met a woman willing to defy a prince's order -- or one so determined to impose her own will on her master. When he'd told his father he'd sooner fuck whores from the Street of Pleasure than take a mate chosen by a matchmaker, he'd been wrong. In one day the beautiful redhead who now had his hood loose and was about to lift it off his head had captured more than his animal lust -- she'd engaged his emotions.

He'd never been so scared, not even when three mercenary craft had circled him off the small planet called Eastphalia, shooting their lasers with deadly precision -- determined to take his small transporter down. Or when he'd come to in a primitive clinic on that planet, in a haze of pain that almost but not quite dulled the revulsion he felt, looking for the first time at the charred stump of his right arm, realizing that was only a small part of what had happened when he'd crashed his burning ship.

He'd give all of Obsidion's wealth to keep Emerald from seeing it now. "Wait," he told her, lifting his hand and trying to grasp the loosened leather but succeeding only in putting pressure on the tortured flesh beneath it.

"It will be no easier later. Let's do it now."

He couldn't watch. Couldn't bear to see the horror in her eyes. But he couldn't deny her right to see the man she'd mated with, the father of the child who even now might be growing in her belly. Defeated, he closed his eye, then lowered his head and steeled himself to hear her scream.

All he heard as the concealing leather fell away was her swift intake of breath... and a thud when her body hit the ground.

Chapter Five

No! Fate couldn't have played such a cruel trick. Half-conscious now, Emerald lay not on the floor but on Arik's bed. He'd lifted her and put her here -- clumsily but ever so gently. Softly, so softly, he'd spoken to her as though she'd been a frightened child. How long had she been lying here? She had no idea. Could have been mere moments -- or hours.

Though his words hadn't lingered, she'd never forget the tear that fell from his solitary eye and lingered on her cheek, a warm, wet kiss from her master. A kiss that held regret... resignation... and disappointment. One that made her want him more than ever -- even more than she wanted to experience a repeat of the delicious climaxes he'd brought her yesterday.

Shame washed over her, for she sensed she'd hurt him as badly as the injuries that had mutilated him.

You shouldn't have insisted he bare himself. Should have kept your curiosity under wraps. Curiosity, nothing, it was you wanting all of him, needing him to bring you pleasure not just with his cock but with all of him. Couldn't be satisfied with him fucking you, and his royal eunuchs doing what he would not, could you?

She heard voices, Arik's... and Hikaru, she thought. And felt someone tying silky-feeling scarves around her wrists and ankles. *I told you I wouldn't run away. That you didn't need to tie me to your bed.* Although she wanted to speak, her voice wouldn't work, and her eyelids felt too heavy when she tried to open them.

"I believe she's waking up, my lord."

"Then release her bonds and go. I will call when I need you to get me back into the leathers."

Footsteps, too light to be her master's, padded along the marble floor. The door opened and closed. Tentatively she moved her arms and legs, found them untethered. When she raised her hand to her cheek, she found the spot that still was damp from the prince's tear. "Master?"

"Yes, it's me. Open your eyes and take a good look. Hikaru finished the job you started. At least this time when you faint, you'll already be on the bed."

Emerald forced her eyes to open, the edges of her mouth to lift. "I never faint," she said, but her words sounded hollow to her own ears. She looked up, steeling herself not to wince or scream. There he was, in profile, his uninjured side to her, as magnificent now as he'd seemed when she'd seen him in the window -- and she spied a tear on his cheek, sparkling like a diamond.

A diamond in the rough, as courtiers often whispered about the man who'd one day sit on the Diamond Throne. "I want to see all of you."

Slowly, he turned, showing her his back. Broad shoulders tapered to narrow hips and massive thighs as thick as tree trunks. On the left side he was perfection, his skin reminding her of satin-smooth caramel and cream. On the right lay crisscrossed scar tissue that extended the length of his body, its devastation most evident in the hideously mangled stump of his arm. "When you wear the bodysuit, it looks as though your arm is there. Oh gods, I'm sorry. Forgive me. I shouldn't --"

"Why? You'd have to be blind not to have noticed. I usually use a primitive sort of hook prosthesis, and the bodysuits are built to accommodate it."

Beneath the gruff, almost defiant façade, Emerald sensed he must be hurting. Though she still shuddered, recalling her shock at the sight of his ruined face and the gaping hole where his eye had been, the emotion that overwhelmed her now was not pity but anger. Anger with him for thinking her so shallow she'd reject him because he was less than princely perfection.

He wasn't. He still had his mind... his emotions. Again she recalled the tear he'd shed when he thought he had repulsed her. She'd show him he didn't, much as he'd shown her yesterday that they'd been destined to mate -- that he only needed that lustful eye and his magnificent cock to make her cunt explode.

She rose and faced him, her expression as stern as she could manage while trembling like a leaf in Obsidion's hot summer wind. "Forget you're my master and lie down on the bed. Face up. I want to look at every inch of you, caress you, show you the kind of pleasure I can give you with my hands and mouth."

For a moment she thought he'd refuse. His mixed emotions showed in his solitary eye, in the set of his mouth, in the way he clenched his fist before sitting on the edge of the bed and meeting her gaze. "You don't have to do this."

"But you do." Smiling, she moved to the foot of the bed and looped the silk scarves Hikaru had used to confine her around his ankles, then bound his left wrist to the ornately carved headboard. "I guess we'll just have to pretend I've tied down this arm, too." Settling cross-legged by his ravaged side, Emerald reached down and stroked the worst of the scars from where it seemed to have begun above his right ankle. "You must have taken quite a hit," she commented as she traced the jagged reddened mass up his leg and body. "All this came from just one blow, didn't it?"

"So the surgeon told me." He flinched when she stroked the mangled stump of his arm but looked at her and said, "Don't stop."

She'd been right. Her master was literally starving to be touched, treated as though someone still found him worthy -- desirable. Bending, she touched her lips to his stump. Nuzzling his warm flesh as she moved inward, she found his right nipple buried in his dark chest hair and laved it with her tongue. "Mmmm," she said, lightly tracing along the web of scars on his upper arm with a finger, "this must have been terribly painful."

"Feels good when you touch it like that."

She straightened, then rose and straddled his torso. His cock felt good -- incredibly good, warm and rigid yet velvety soft where it nudged her swollen cunt lips. "Touch me, too," she said, watching his expression change to one of wonder -- of lust -- when he looked up and finally met her gaze. "And let me fuck you."

"Untie me and I will."

Emerald slipped the silk scarf down over his large hand. "I believe I'll leave your legs tied up so I can have my way with you."

Arik's balls tightened. His cock throbbed. Once his hand was free he wasted not one moment before impaling his mate -- his beautiful Emerald whose wet, swollen cunt told him better than words how much she wanted him.

Wanted him as he was now, not as he'd once been before his father had commanded his death. And he wanted her. His only regret as he stroked her satin skin and took her nipples between his teeth was that he couldn't turn back time, be the perfect lover for his perfect love.

But he could. Somehow it no longer seemed important that Arik continue making his father pay on a daily basis for having tried to kill him. He'd seek out Pak Song, let the cyborg-maker remake him...

Later. Blood slammed into his groin when Emerald leaned over and laid soft kisses on his ravaged cheek. Her plump ass cheek filled his hand, firm but woman-soft. Steadying her with his stump while she fucked his cock, he slipped two fingers of his good hand into her ass and gently fucked her there. When she took his mouth and sucked his tongue between her lips, her tight, wet cunt contracted around his cock.

He swallowed her little scream, answering with one of his own when his own climax slammed into him. Gods but he loved her. He even loved his father for having contracted the match between them. Without thinking, he cradled her to his body with his naked stump -- an act he'd never imagined he would do again.

Epilogue

At the sound of footsteps on the tower stair, Emerald handed their eleven-week-old son to his nanny and shooed them both from the room. Yesterday she and Arik had celebrated the anniversary of their mating with the king and members of the royal court. Today she intended to have her own private celebration with the prince who'd made almost all her fantasies come true.

The matchmaker had done right by them -- for since that day Emerald had never doubted they were soul mates, not since Arik had offered to go to Pak Song and have himself turned into a cyborg so he could appear as he had before -- the perfect prince for his perfect princess.

Emerald hadn't let him do it, for she'd learned she loved her mate for what lay within him -- no matter how the gods had wrecked the outer wrapper. She was glad she'd persuaded him to compromise, keep his own body parts but let the surgeons repair the damaged facial nerves that kept him in constant pain. His only concession to his appearance was to let Pak Song fit him with a prosthetic eye and cheekbone to cover the ruined side of his face -- not a bionic eye, for as long as he could see well with his left eye, he wouldn't trade it, not even for the flawless X-ray vision he could have with bilateral bionic replacements. Not for her, because she encouraged him to take it off when they were alone together, but so he could appear in public without the hood, without evoking screams and fainting. That had become important these past few months, since the king had ceded most of his royal duties to Arik.

He'd let the cyborg-maker fit him with an "intelligent" prosthetic hand and forearm, but Arik had become used to the primitive hook he'd learned to use soon after his injury. The new device collected dust on a shelf in their dressing room -- which bothered Emerald not at all. He sent marvelously arousing sensations through her when he caught the hook in her nipple rings and gave them gentle tugs. Maybe tonight... The thought of what he'd do had her positively lightheaded.

Fainting had become almost their only subject of contention, for Arik seemed determined never to let her forget she'd passed dead away the first time she'd seen his face. But she had him now. Every time he mentioned her squeamishness, she reminded him how he'd collapsed in a heap on the birthing room floor when little Arik made his entrance into the world.

A light tap on the door brought her out of her reverie. Hikaru stepped inside when she opened it, his arms loaded with the supplies she'd ordered. As always when he entered the royal bedchambers, he set down his load and prostrated himself at her feet. That still irritated her, but she'd learned to expect it -- after all, Hikaru had spent eleven years now since his fate as a royal eunuch slave had been sealed, and she realized habits that old were hard to break.

"Rise, slave," she said as sternly as she'd heard Arik do so many times. "I'd have you ready me for our master."

Hikaru scrambled to his feet and ran a pick through her short auburn curls that Arik so loved touching, then accompanied her to the bidet and administered the most thorough cleansing she'd ever had. While her cunt tingled and her asshole puckered from its unfamiliar dousing, she watched him hurry to rig a gleaming black-leather and chrome fucking swing from sturdy hooks secured in the high ceiling for just that purpose.

Emerald's cunt creamed when she imagined Arik stepping up behind that swing, lubricating her ass, and finally doing what he'd promised to since the day they'd mated but reneged on when he thought it might hurt her. That had been the only downside of learning his seed had taken root the first time they'd mated. He'd often tortured her while they waited by fingering her rear hole, whispering about how he intended to deflower it. Now! She was finally going to find out what she'd been missing.

"The swing is secured, my lady." As if to prove it, Hikaru gave the seat a hard jerk.

Her pulse raced. Her prince's halting footsteps echoed from the base of the tower staircase, urging her to hurry and position herself face-down, ass in the air. She'd persuaded Arik to buy the toy on one of their shopping trips to the Street of Pleasure, but they'd never tried it. "Help me. Secure my arms and legs so I don't fall out of this thing."

She'd never felt more open, more vulnerable. Her body was suspended on two leather straps, her legs spread wide and secured with padded cuffs to braided leather ropes. When she moved her ankles, pulleys on the ropes raised them, opening her even more. His touch impersonal, Hikaru brought her arms behind her back, cuffed her wrists, and tied her at the elbows. Gods help her, she was now completely and deliciously helpless.

"I see you're at your master's mercy." Emerald recognized the gravelly timbre of Arik's voice, knew without looking that he'd donned the full bodysuit and hood he'd worn the day of their first mating -- the one he often put on when he invited one of the royal eunuchs to join their games. Warm cream dripped from her cunt, slid over her swollen clit. "Hikaru, blindfold her now."

"Yes, my lord prince." The eunuch knelt before her and secured a satin-lined leather blindfold over her eyes, tying the soft streamers at the back of her closely cropped head.

Darkness isolated her, but she had no fear. Her master would bring her exquisite pleasure, never pain. His gloved hands -- she'd become used to thinking of the hook as an extension of his body -- cupped her breasts, caught the rings in her nipples and tugged them gently. "Oh, yesss," she hissed, loving the contrast of his big gentle hand on one breast, the smaller gloved hook on the other, its clawlike talon tugging at a nipple ring, tangling in the chains of diamonds and emeralds that joined them. "Fuck me, master, please."

His sharp intake of breath told her it would not be long. As always, though, he'd move at his own pace. He'd taunt her until she burned for release, provide it, then arouse her to orgasm again and again before giving her what she wanted above all else.

His perfect cock. In her cunt. In her mouth. In the last place it could go to seal his full possession.

Soft lips nibbled her clit. Hikaru's. The rasp of a zipper broke the silence in the room, and suddenly she felt the head of her master's huge cock sliding along her dripping slit. "I can't resist fucking your delightfully wet cunt first, my princess." At the same time Arik sank into her cunt, Hikaru found her asshole and slid in the large lubricated plug she'd barely been able to insert immediately after he'd cleansed her. Her muscles protested, but soon clenched both monster invaders with pleasure, not pain.

Her slippery cunt sucked Arik's huge cock noisily when he withdrew. When he pushed back in, his balls made slapping sounds against her clit. Deprived of sight, all her other senses seemed enhanced. The smells of sex -- clean, slightly salty, a little bit musky -- intensified with every stroke of his cock in her spasming cunt. She became more aware of how things felt -- the velvety hardness of his rigid cock as he fucked her, the brush of his leather garment against her nipples and thighs and of the tougher leather straps that supported the weight of her torso. The contrast of feeling between his hand and the hook. Warm breath and soft hands -- Hikaru's -- stroked her ass cheeks, moving now and then to keep her aware of the lubricated plug as it stretched her to take Arik's cock.

"Yesss. Don't stop." Sensations bombarded her. The hot spurts of her master's cum set off another climax, left her panting yet wanting more. Much more. When he withdrew his still-swollen cock, she felt empty, but only for a moment until Hikaru worked something cold and hard into her still-spasming cunt and set it to vibrating... slowly.

She felt the plug come out of her ass, heard the pop her body made. Cold, slippery lubricant made her asshole contract, but when she felt her master's huge, well-lubricated cock pressing into that narrow opening she squirmed with anticipation. Her mouth opened, as though she could take him there as well.

Hikaru must have been waiting for the opportunity, because he slid a penis shaped gag into her mouth and secured it. Arik's whispered words, repeated many times as she lay in his arms in the dark of night, echoed in her ears. *I'm going to fuck your cunt, and your mouth, and your pretty ass, and if the gods will give me a way to do it, I'll fuck all three at the same time.*

He'd found a way. Fresh, intense arousal warmed Emerald's belly, curled through her body. She relaxed as he'd said she must, and took intense pleasure in his final conquering of her body, her soul. When he entered her fully and began to move, she saw stars -- no, diamonds.

Later they lay together on the bed, legs tangled, his fingers ruffling her hair while he whispered to her of love... of sex. "I hurt for Hikaru and the others," she said, the eunuch's stoic look as he'd untied her and washed the smells and dampness of sex from her body and Arik's. "You'd never let them do that to our sons, would you?"

Arik turned her to face him, his expression fierce. "Once I'm king I will outlaw the making of eunuchs on Obsidion. Not just royal sons. I'll not be responsible for any man being unable to fully enjoy his lovers' bodies. I vow that on my life. On our love."

The matchmaker had truly found Emerald a diamond in the rough. Some still whispered that the reclusive prince was a monster, but she would love him now and for all time.

Obsidion: Garnet's Fantasy

Ann Jacobs

Prologue

It was with boundless pride that Eli of Obsidion, jeweler to kings all over the galaxy, opened his home today to Obsidion's elite. Fragrant incense swirled in the air. Musicians played on ageless instruments, haunting melodies Eli recalled from his youth. Servants scurried about, preparing the altar where his spirited Garnet would soon become one with the Aurelonian purveyor of sex slaves whom Meredith had chosen to become her mate.

Meredith the matchmaker had done well, even though at first Eli had wondered at her choice of the horribly disfigured Crown Prince Arik for his eldest daughter. He'd been wrong, for he had never seen Emerald happier than she was with her prince as they anticipated the birth of their first child.

A little over a year ago, he'd made matches for his three precious daughters, the second of which would soon be consummated here, in his own house where he'd lived thirty years in love with his own Sadie. The sounds of his daughters' voices as they prepared Garnet to meet her mate warmed the old man's heart.

Today he would give Garnet to Romulus of Aurelion. Alien though he was, Romulus would bring his middle child the fabulous wealth she'd coveted as long as Eli could remember. His eyes still ached from looking upon the tiara Romulus had sent as a bride-gift, for never had he seen such perfect stones, such gleaming gold. Garnet's pleasure at the gift had been Eli's own, for he wanted nothing more than to assure his daughters' happiness.

Tomorrow only one precious child would remain with Eli -- Pearl, his youngest, whose betrothed had just arrived for the ceremony with his revered father, Pak Song the cyborg-maker. Eli would have time later to reminisce, and to reflect on the wisdom of the matchmaker's choices. Now he must play host, for the mating ceremony was soon to begin.

Chapter One

"Come, Garnet, you've no time for daydreaming. Your bridegroom awaits you." Pearl let go the hangings that hid them from the guests assembled in their father's receiving hall. "He is…"

"… magnificent." Emerald, the eldest of the sisters, turned to Garnet, a lascivious smile on her face. "The man is gold. Pure gold. Wait 'til he takes you with that long, thick cock. You will be a happy bride, that's certain." She arranged Garnet's translucent veil and secured it to her head with an elaborate jeweled tiara her future mate had provided. "There. Go quickly now, and lay yourself down before your master on the altar of submission."

Emerald, the very pregnant crown princess of Obsidion, obviously loved the sex part of being mated with her fearsome looking prince. And Pearl, soon to wed with the sexbot-maker's eldest son, seemed to think of nothing but having her cunt invaded by a hot male cock or cocks, for she often said she'd not only take her mate but all his high-tech 'bots as well.

Garnet wanted more. Though she'd willingly accommodate her mate's carnal desires, what she wanted was access to his wealth. A constant shower of jewels and furs, the houseful of treasures and servants that awaited her…

Oh gods! Those servants would include the pleasure-givers who worked in his famed emporiums. Would her mate expect her to welcome them to their bed along with him? Surely not. She doubted even Emerald, who whispered of the incredible ecstasy to be had from her mate and the palace eunuchs, would approve of that. After all, well brought up women on Obsidion did not consort with the sex slaves who plied their trade in the Streets of Pleasure.

Oh, well.

Garnet smiled from behind the translucent veil that pretended to hide her nakedness from the revelers and from her bridegroom. No way would she show fear or nervousness. Mating was a ritual to be anticipated, not feared.

A handover of a woman's life, her identity, to her life mate, her father had said when he'd spoken with her last night about her sacred duties as a wife.

Tradition be damned. Garnet had no intention of giving up her own identity or of sharing the master of Obsidion's sex slave emporiums with anyone, be they male, female, or neuter. The silken bonds her attendants placed about her arms and legs once she'd lain down on the altar were merely symbols of subservience. She had no intention of living a life of servitude, however pleasurable some women apparently believed such a life might be.

No, Garnet would rule her own house. She'd use her considerable charms to woo her fabulously wealthy mate, to tie him to her and her alone. Romulus could use his sex slaves to make them yet more money -- Garnet had no problem with that -- but his cock would belong to her alone.

* * *

"What will become of me?" Remus asked, his expression glum as he attended Romulus at his bath in preparation for his mating ceremony.

"For the sake of the gods, quit whining." Occasionally Romulus thought the physician who'd cloned him had done a faulty job, especially at times like this, when Remus's brain seemed to function as a totally independent entity from his own. "Just because I'm taking a mate does not mean I intend to dispense with you."

Romulus and Remus had grown up together, shared every milestone, every dream, ever since Remus had been created from a strand of DNA taken from Romulus's body.

It had always puzzled Romulus that in his adopted homeland the practice of cloning was forbidden, while the rulers made eunuchs of their younger sons to secure the succession for the elder ones, and businessmen like himself were encouraged to make their fortunes dealing in altered sex slaves, even altering them especially to meet the needs of their customers.

Other than the difference in their ages, he and Remus were physically identical in every way but one. Only Romulus could pass along his genes to the next generation. Only he could procreate in the way of the Obsidion people -- male to female, in the ways the Old Ones on Aurelion had employed before advancing science to the point that having sex with one's mate was unnecessary for the continuation of the species.

At least it was superfluous on Aurelion, not to mention forbidden. Here on Obsidion, Romulus had to take a mate. Fortunately he had found Meredith, the wizened matchmaker who supposedly had never made an unsuccessful match, who had assured him when she took his money and presented him with the jeweler's second daughter that she'd found him the best life mate his substantial wealth could buy. In a little while he'd have to go to Garnet -- the matchmaker had mentioned that was her name -- and take part in the strange ritual of an Obsidion mating.

The downside to mating this way was that Romulus would have to actually mate with his bride in person. He'd have to fuck her cunt the way he fucked his clone's tight ass. Worse, because of the damnable customs on Obsidion, he'd have to do it before her father and a room full of witnesses. Afterward, he'd be expected to take her home and let her share his bedchamber. Not to mention that he'd have to fuck her every day until she started to swell with his son.

He could do it. He had to. Romulus had made his fortune on Obsidion, and he had no desire to abandon his business. Besides, he could fuck a woman. He'd proven that to himself two nights ago, when he'd summoned one of the sex slaves from his finest emporium, just to be sure -- a buxom redhead newly arrived from the Federation of Earth.

She'd been soft... and willing enough to do her employer's bidding. Her mouth had clamped onto his cock and sucked out his seed as well as Remus's did. She'd spread her legs and offered him her cunt. Warm, wet, inviting, her flesh had milked his, brought him pleasure, if not quite the degree of ecstasy he enjoyed when he buried his cock in his clone's receptive ass.

Since he'd lived here on Obsidion, Romulus had judiciously hidden the existence of Remus from those with whom he lived and did business. He'd not dared to risk incurring the wrath of this planet's rulers by flaunting the law that forbade the making and keeping of sentient clones. At one time he'd considered passing his clone off as a younger brother, but if he'd done that he'd have risked having to explain how it was that Remus shared his bed.

It struck him as ironic that he'd made his fortune catering to the varied sexual desires of those from the far reaches of the galaxy but could not publicly indulge his own preference in bed partners -- a preference perfectly acceptable on his home planet but strictly forbidden on Obsidion. He'd come to the Pleasure Planet and made it his own. Now he had to leave behind the traditions that had been part of his life until he fled Aurelion.

He needed an heir to carry on once his own life ended. A son. Romulus closed his eyes, imagining his eventual return to Aurelion, the joy he'd see on that as yet unborn boy's face when he received his own clone -- a playmate and lover created in his own image, subservient to his every wish.

Pity he couldn't have done as he would have if he'd stayed on Aurelion, where men of class confined their mates to breeding farms and impregnated them by artificial insemination, while they took their pleasure with their clones. If the Aurelonian men were of sufficiently high birth, Romulus reminded himself, they fucked bed eunuchs who'd been chosen and castrated for their perfection of form, to serve the pleasure of the planet's ruling family.

"Why must you wed? Do I not satisfy you?"

Remus's petulant expression and whining tone dragged Romulus forcibly back to the present. Although he managed for the moment to keep his cool, he doubted his calm demeanor would survive for long. Though he loved Remus -- not surprising since the clone had been created in his own image when he'd been just five years old -- Remus had a way of getting on his nerves when his mind moved out of synch with Romulus's own. "Stop your complaining. You remind me of a sniveling girl."

"Your new mate will *be* a sniveling girl."

Why must Remus have picked this particular time to grow possessive? "Of course you please me. How could you not? Still, we now live on Obsidion, and custom demands I -- we -- take a female mate. We will still be of one mind, one body. Garnet will merely be a new toy for us to enjoy."

"I am not certain..."

Romulus slammed a fist onto the table beside his bed. "Enough already. Shut up and finish with my grooming. This is our home now. I must marry to get heirs and cement my place here among the elite of planet Obsidion. I doubt the jeweler's daughter will supplant you in my affection. After all, in a manner of speaking, you *are* me."

"And you prefer my tight asshole to a female cunt. Admit it."

"Enough! I don't want to be late to my mating." Truth be told, Romulus did favor his clone's asshole. Still his cock twitched at the thought of taking his mate for the first time. Garnet would doubtless be less used than the pleasure giver he'd sampled the other night. Nonetheless, she was a female, and thus to his Aurelonian way of thinking inferior.

"If not for me, master, we'd both have been altered to serve in the bedchambers of your cousin, the king," Remus reminded him, his tone petulant.

"I hardly need reminding of that." Romulus shuddered, even now after so many years had passed, every time he thought about their narrow escape from the royal gelder's knife.

Remus had overheard their king commanding their castration and hastened to tell Romulus of their impending fate. Together they'd led their pursuers on a frantic chase before managing to stow away on a transporter bound for Obsidion, leaving their childhood home behind forever.

Remus gestured about the opulent chamber where Romulus would soon be bringing his mate. "My life since then has been within these four walls, with no one but you." Remus closed his fingers around Romulus's cock, his hand shaking slightly as though he could barely control his emotions.

Romulus couldn't help his reaction, or control the swelling of his flesh at his clone's arousing touch. But now was hardly an appropriate occasion to slake his lust. "Stop that. We've no time. Change the cock ring and be done with it. It would insult my mate and her family if I were not to appear at the appointed hour."

Remus pouted, but he stopped his teasing and efficiently removed the thick platinum ring from his master's cock and the matching barbells that decorated his frenum ladder. "Puny jewels, these," he said as he inserted the bride-gifts, gleaming pure gold with cabochon garnets. The dozen barbells marched down the underside of Romulus's cock and along the center of his ball sac. "One would think she'd have known the gold would not show up well against an Aurelonian's golden skin…"

"One would think a clone would have learned his place after so many years. Stow your comments and get a move on. I don't intend to be late for my mating."

Romulus stood, determined to do what he had to do. He would take the jeweler's daughter in the manner of the Obsidion people. He knew the woman would be wedding him for his wealth. After their initial mating he'd introduce her to Remus, the unseen third party to their mating vows. She'd find wealth, all right. A wealth of Aurelonian mates as well as the gold and possessions for which she lusted.

Romulus chuckled as he pictured their first threesome, though he wasn't all that certain his bride would take calmly to the ménage he had in mind. From the whispers he'd heard since their betrothal was announced, he gathered that Garnet thought to rule him, not be ruled.

* * *

By the gods, her Aurelonian took her breath away when he strode into the mating chamber. Naked, he looked like a living statue hewn from pure gold. Garnet gasped at the sight of his hard, muscular body, his perfection of form. Her cunt clenched when she imagined his cock invading her there, filling her with his seed.

His *golden* cock. Long and thick, its blunt tip glistened like a rare, succulent apricot from the orchards of the Federation. The rings she'd sent to him glowed, paler than his golden flesh. Alien but beautiful, like the rest of him, the blatant symbol of his maleness drew her gaze as he approached the altar through a haze of smoldering incense.

He'd worn all the gifts she'd chosen. Had he needed to visit Leander the barber and have his cock and balls pierced to accommodate them? Or had he already worn the types of jewelry Daddy had told her were customary for the men from Aurelion as well as most males from Earth's Federation? Fine garnets, her namesake gemstones, glowed in the bright light, contrasting with the warm gold hue of the settings and the deeper gold of his flesh. The jewels were the perfect foil for his big, jutting cock and low-hanging balls.

His cleanly shaven golden head glistened as though he'd just polished it, and his muscular body glowed. Yes, Meredith the matchmaker had found Garnet a fit mate. Romulus, lately of the planet Aurelion. What mattered to her was that he was now the richest man on Obsidion from his business as purveyor of sex slaves for sale and rent. He was the ideal mate to provide Garnet with all the riches her heart desired.

His close scrutiny heated her skin, made her cunt clench with anticipation for the mating.

"May we prepare this woman to be your life mate?" the priest asked.

"Yes. I am ready." Apparently her future mate was a man of few words. His deep, mellow voice, however, seduced her despite her determination to maintain her self-control.

The haze from incense that surrounded the altar must have been laced with some aphrodisiac, because Garnet noticed how her nipples tingled and her cunt grew wetter by the second, preparing for its first penetration. The new, arousing sensations kept intensifying, practically robbing her of the ability to think, to the point that she barely noticed when her attendants swept away the diaphanous veil that covered her and began to prepare her to serve her master's pleasure.

Fragrant oil dripped from jeweled ewers onto Garnet's throat, her breasts, her thighs. A dozen hands spread it, massaging it into her naked skin, heating her with their touch and making her swollen cunt grow wetter, hotter.

Although she fought hard to retain control, she could not. "Oh gods help me," she moaned when the chief celebrant lifted her head and began clipping off her hair. The sound of the shears, the feeling of lightness as her long hair fell away, excited her more. The rasp of the razor that followed, transforming her from maiden to life mate, rang in her ears, floating on sensual sounds of music that filled the room. Her nipples turned to rigid points of sensation, and her clit stood at attention, even before the priest finished polishing her shorn scalp and stepped between her legs to insert the ceremonial plug in her virgin ass.

She'd expected the rush of sexual excitement at that first invasion of her body, but not the fierce arousal that had accompanied the shearing of her long dark hair and the rasp of the golden razor against her scalp. Even the sharp twin stings when the priest pierced her nipples -- thankfully with a laser instead of the old-fashioned needles they still occasionally used -- and inserted her marriage rings heightened her anticipation.

Soon Romulus, her new master, would plunge that golden cock deep in her cunt, claiming her as his own. When he did, Garnet vowed she'd be well on the way toward enslaving him.

* * *

Prime. Romulus regarded his bride as he might a potential sex slave for his emporium. Pert breasts tipped with rosy nipples were now adorned by gold rings, the marks of his possession. Lower, he eyed a flat belly, hips wide enough to bear his sons. Her perfectly shaped skull gleamed pearly white, shadowed by dark roots plainly visible beneath the newly denuded skin.

He especially liked her mouth -- deep red and wide enough to take a man's cock between gleaming white teeth. Her pale satiny cunt was already swollen and wet, as though anticipating its penetration. His gaze dropped to her pink, puckered asshole, already stretched by the dildo he'd watched the priest insert there moments earlier.

As he'd observed was the custom on Obsidion, Romulus paused at the foot of the altar and visually inspected the slick, swollen flesh he soon must penetrate. When he spread her damp cunt lips and inserted two fingers, his nostrils flared. Gods but she smelled good -- female mingled with the sweet musk of the ceremonial incense. He wished he dared remove the plug and fuck her ass.

He'd do that later. His cock reared up against his belly in silent salute. "I take the lady Garnet as my mate," he said, mouthing the words that made them one before bending and placing the traditional kiss on her throbbing clit. "I will fuck her now."

His cock already leaked milky pre-cum when he slid it along her wet, hot slit. Her cry when he penetrated her virgin cunt made his balls draw up and his cock swell more within her tight, silky flesh. He wanted to take his pleasure and plant his seed, but for the first time in his nearly thirty years of life he wanted desperately to fuck a woman -- to hear her cry out with pleasure when he brought her to orgasm.

Slowly, taking care not to hurt her further, Romulus withdrew, then sank into her satin sheath once more. Gods but her sopping cunt gloved his cock to perfection. She surrounded him with her virgin heat, made him crazy with the need to come.

When he skimmed his hands over her soft, full breasts, she moaned. "You like that, don't you?"

"Oh, yes. Please don't stop."

"Yes, what?"

"Yes, master. Oh gods, please don't stop fucking me now."

"I won't." Nearly bursting now with lust, he rammed into her harder, faster. He scissored her rigid nipples between his thumbs and forefingers until they became as rigid as the precious jewels that adorned them. For the first time in his life he wished society's rules would let him cover his bride completely with his body, fuck her tempting mouth with his tongue while he fucked her cunt with his cock. He wanted to caress her satiny scalp with his fingers, find the erogenous zones there that would trigger her orgasm.

"Gods yesss," she cried out, straining toward him against her bonds, tilting her pelvis up to suck him deeper inside her convulsing flesh. She clenched him, milked him, drew out the climax he'd been holding back. Spent, he withdrew, breathing hard.

Already he wanted more of the Obsidion woman who was now his mate.

Romulus's ears barely registered the raucous sounds of cheering surrounding them when he freed Garnet from her silken bonds and drew her to her feet. But for the first time in his life he felt a need to cover a woman from prying eyes... to keep her for himself alone. This feeling of possession -- make that damn near obsession -- was new. And it scared the shit out of him.

Chapter Two

The next morning Garnet stretched, enjoying the sensation of tenderness in her cunt and ass, the satiny kiss of her master's fine bed linens on her totally hairless body every time she made the slightest move. Her scalp tingled at the remembered rasp of the priest's razor, and her nipples swelled and turned rock-hard when she shifted on the bed, making the marriage rings sway against her sensitive flesh.

"So, you're finally awake."

Surprised at first to hear a male voice in her private chamber, she rolled over. "Romulus?" The male Aurelonian looked exactly like her mate, but there was something -- something about him that set him apart.

"I am Remus. Like you, I am our master's bed companion. He will join us soon. Rise and I will prepare you for him."

Bed companion? Garnet barely managed to suppress a scream of rage. No one would share her master's bed but her. "What is this, some perverse alien custom? I share my bed with no one but my lord and master Romulus."

"You will share my bed with whomever I choose." Garnet's bridegroom strode into the room, a scowl marring his handsome golden face. "I command now that you share it with me and my life companion. In a manner of speaking, you will be sharing it with me, for Remus is my clone." Romulus paused to place a kiss on the right nipple of his double -- the one she noticed for the first time bore a ring similar to the ones that dangled from the tips of her own breasts -- and identical to the one that pierced her mate's left nipple.

He's only supposed to kiss me that way, damn it. "Make me." Garnet snatched up the coverlet and wrapped it around her body.

"As you wish." With a smooth, casual motion Romulus snatched away the covers and pinned her to the bed. "Remus, I believe our bride needs to be taught a lesson. Prepare the fucking platform, and then join us on the bed."

"Our bride?" Garnet struggled to buck Romulus off her, but to no avail. Romulus's muscular chest pressed hard against her nipples, and his hard cock nudged her cunt. Gods but he took her breath away when he sandwiched her head between his large palms and splayed long fingers over the taut skin of her scalp. "I belong to you and you alone."

"It isn't your choice, but mine. You wanted wealth. I give it to you now. I am not one man but two, and I am about to show you even greater pleasure than before -- the ecstasy a woman can attain when two lovers fuck her at once."

"But -- do you not want to be certain any child I may have is yours?" Despite her shock, the idea of taking both men had Garnet's sopping cunt clenching... and her virgin asshole twitching against the plug her mate had yet to remove.

"I will be supremely certain of that, my sweet, because the only whole man to ever fuck you will be me. As I told you, Remus is my clone. My *sterile* clone, created from a strand of my DNA to provide me pleasure. Be happy that I now allow him to pleasure you as well as me. Consider the two of us as part of the bounty I brought you at our mating, an abundance of capacity for giving and receiving pleasure."

A smile on his full, sensuous lips, Romulus took her mouth, licking and nipping and fucking it with his long, agile tongue. His hot cock throbbed against her thigh, raising her anticipation. When he freed her lips and took a throbbing nipple into his mouth instead, she couldn't suppress a groan of pleasure.

By the gods, her mate knew how to arouse a woman. Despite herself, Garnet wanted all he promised. Each muted sound of wood on wood as his clone prepared the fucking platform reminded her he -- they -- would soon have her helpless. Bound for his pleasure, and the pleasure of his Aurelonian clone whom she apparently would have to welcome as a second bed companion. She glanced at the clone, then returned her gaze to Romulus.

The only whole man to fuck you will be me. "What did you mean?" she asked, for the man adjusting a polished wooden device in front of a shuttered window looked whole as far as she could tell, from the top of his polished skull to the tips of his long narrow toes. Remus's cock jutted forward, as though eager to penetrate her cunt... or her ass. Unlike the eunuchs in her father's household, he had testicles, the twin orbs plump and firm within an impressive sac between his legs.

"Remus is an Aurelonian clone, created in my image for the sole purpose of giving me pleasure. Unlike the barbarians other places in the galaxy who alter men to serve in the pleasure palaces, we create clones for young boys so their sexual needs may be satisfied. The only eunuchs created on Aurelion serve in the royal family's own bedchambers." Romulus dragged her hand down his body, to his own bulging ball sac. "Clones like Remus are not eunuchs. They are exact duplicates of their masters, but for the lack of ability to pass on their genes and a submissive nature that complements their masters' dominance. They are ideal companions for the males from whom they were cloned -- and I imagine for any woman chosen by their masters."

"The platform is ready." Remus strode to the bed, his cock bobbing.

The bed companion certainly looked whole. Desirable, too. Garnet's cunt clenched when she found herself sandwiched between her mate and the beautiful slave who apparently was his genetic double.

As though they'd practiced this move a thousand times, Romulus and Remus raised their golden heads, leaning across her until their lips met. Garnet sensed the heat, the passion that flowed between them. She longed for that heat to enter her body, to take her and make her part of their desire...

They broke the kiss, each moving to suckle one of her ringed nipples, their glowing skulls identical against the alabaster paleness of her breasts. Their cocks throbbed against her thighs, beckoning her hands. One cock was ringed, hard as stone. The other felt firm yet unadorned. When she stroked their ball sacs, she felt the base of a butt plug in Remus's ass -- a plug not unlike the one she'd worn since her mating ceremony the night before.

Four hands stroked her, caressing her in all her tenderest places. Twenty strong fingers applied the lightest of pressure to erogenous zones on her skull and throat, her earlobes, her aching nipples. Those fingers tugged gently on her nipple rings while she played with the marriage ring in her mate's hot cock and ran her fingers along the unadorned shaft that belonged to his clone.

Their pre-cum dampened her fingers, made her aware of her own wetness, her own heat. "Take me, please," she said, her words little more than a pitiful whimper.

"In our own good time." Romulus's voice poured over her, dark and molten in its intensity. The heat of two magnificent male bodies seared her, made her impatient to drag Romulus over her, take his thick, long cock in her aching cunt. "You must learn patience. Imagine yourself suspended on the fucking platform, with me fucking your cunt or ass while Remus fucks your mouth. We'll both be moving in you with perfect rhythm, using our hands and mouths to stimulate you as you've never been aroused before."

"Oh, yesss."

"But first... oh gods yes, you learn quickly how to please me." Apparently he liked it when she gave his ball sac a gentle caress, so she did it again. He rewarded her with a groan that came from deep in his muscular chest. "First, though, we will all pleasure each other, learn the joys to be found by touching, tasting..."

"... by joining us in sharing all the sensual pleasures granted to a man and his clone." Remus reached across Garnet's belly and closed his fist over her hand on Romulus's swollen cock. "You know, if I'd been given a choice, I'd much rather have kept my master to myself."

"Remus has not yet discovered the joy of joining with a female," Romulus said, leaning across Garnet and stroking his double's cheek. "Relax, my reluctantly submissive clone. You'll always come first in my affection."

We'll just see about that. Garnet rolled onto her side and rubbed her body against Romulus, grasping his tight ass and drawing him closer. Surely he couldn't prefer fucking this clone to having sex with her. She wouldn't allow it. Neither would she permit the two of them to seduce her into abandoning her plan. Though it might be more difficult than she'd thought, she'd eventually enslave her mate. If she had to, she'd entice the clone, too.

"I'll be an active partner in this ménage if you don't mind," Garnet said, raising her head off the pillow and insinuating herself between her mate and his alter ego.

Romulus's deep roar of laughter at Garnet's sudden burst of assertiveness rang in Remus's ears and made him terribly afraid -- afraid his master had already become enchanted by this pale, incredibly soft-skinned Obsidion woman. Remus watched with horror as Romulus began to stroke her quivering breasts, her slick cunt, all the while murmuring words of admiration... of desire.

Remus's cock grew harder. The unfamiliar scent of a female in heat mingled with the more familiar smells of aroused male. He felt hot, so hot, his senses aroused by the taste and feel of his master... and of the woman, too. His breath came in hard bursts, and blood pounded at his temples.

"Fuck her for me," Romulus ordered, "while I fuck you."

An hour ago Remus would have told his master that was impossible, but now his cock throbbed with anticipation. Sliding beneath Romulus, between the widely spread satiny smooth legs of his rival, Remus slid his cock head along her wet slit, searching... fitting hot flesh to hot flesh, his cock to her slippery cunt.

"Oh, yesss. Please fuck me." She liked it. Liked this invasion. Apparently she enjoyed it as much as Remus liked having his master ram his cock deep into his own ass. Remus moved, experimentally, and found the friction made her flesh swell around him, glove his in tight, sopping heat.

A strange sensation, but an arousing one.

"Move in her. Feel how soft she is, how giving." Romulus's own body heat bathed Remus's back, and large fingers ringed the base of his cock. "Slowly. Gently. Fuck her with love, the way I fuck you."

Remus felt empty when the butt plug popped out of his ass, until Romulus replaced it with his own hot, hard cock. The dual stimulation was... unlike anything the clone had ever experienced. They moved in tandem, Remus fucking Garnet while Romulus fucked him.

"Yesss. Fuck me harder now." Garnet clutched his head, drew his lips to hers. Gods but she tasted sweet. And the soft, tight cavern gloved his cock with undulating heat... heat that radiated through his balls and flooded his body with incredible sensation. Remus understood for the first time why so many clients who flocked to the emporiums chose women rather than the more popular eunuch sex slaves to slake their lust.

Pressure built in him with each stroke of Romulus's cock that pounded his ass, every foray of his own tool into Garnet's wet, slick cunt. Remus took her mouth, fucked it with his tongue the way Romulus sometimes tongue-fucked him.

How would it feel to have a woman's satin lips on his cock, his balls, her tongue wetting his most sensitive flesh?

Romulus slammed into Remus's ass, and Remus slammed into Garnet. His balls tightened. His sweat-slickened body clung to hers. His nipple ring caught on one of hers, tugging at his flesh and sending him into sensual overload.

The salty taste of her skin and his own, the smells and slapping sounds of fucking and being fucked, the feel of skin on skin at his back and front were more than Remus could bear. He thrust his tongue down her throat, rammed his cock up her sopping cunt. And he came. Wave after wave of ecstasy sapped his energy, left him breathless by the time his cock stopped shooting hot spurts of cum.

When Romulus grasped his clone's butt and flooded his asshole with staccato bursts of slick heat, a new wave of fulfillment practically took Remus's breath away.

Chapter Three

Romulus woke slowly the next morning, his head pillowed on the soft breast -- Soft breast? He cracked open one eye. Yes, it was a breast. Plump, pale *female* flesh tipped by a rosy nipple pierced with a ring.

His ring, one of the two that had pierced Garnet's flesh just yesterday at the strange Obsidion mating ceremony. Her chest rose and fell slowly, as though she slept in perfect contentment. Perhaps she did, and perhaps she dreamed she was nourishing their child, because she rested her hand on his head, as though she were holding an infant to her breast.

His cock swelled once more, as though he hadn't come hours earlier in the tight asshole of his clone while Remus had filled this woman with his own sterile essence.

Had Garnet come for his clone the way she'd come for him at their mating? Had she liked feeling Remus's lips on hers, his tongue fucking her mouth while his fingers found the erogenous spots on her perfect, gleaming skull? A wave of unfamiliar possessiveness rose in Romulus. Garnet belonged to him.

Of course Remus *was* him, in a manner of speaking. That didn't keep Romulus from clenching his fists when he spied the clone sleeping peacefully at Garnet's other side. He drew her closer still, until her flat belly lay flush with his own.

Her rounded ass cheeks cushioned his own fingers -- and Remus's half-hard cock. The resilient baby-soft skin fascinated Romulus. Judging from his clone's hard-on, her asshole apparently beckoned Remus's cock much the way it did his own, and that disturbed and confused him. Always submissive when they fucked, Remus had never even hinted that he'd like to use Romulus's own ass the way Romulus regularly used his.

Romulus had to demonstrate his dominance... his possession of the woman he'd taken as his mate. Still, he had no wish to hurt his clone, who seemed in the past days to have developed a mind of his own. Maybe he needed to buy a sexbot for Remus. Or provide him with a sex slave from one of the emporiums.

But not now. Now Garnet's delicious body lured him. Romulus slid from the bed, lifted Garnet in his arms, and carried her to the fucking platform Remus had erected near the window. It seemed appropriate that the platform overlooked a courtyard rampant with blooms from all over the galaxy, for he realized his mate was one of the finest flowers of all. Romulus counted himself a lucky man.

"Remus!" he called once he had Garnet positioned the way he wanted her -- face-down on the platform, her legs spread in stirrups and her delectable ass at the proper angle to take his cock.

The clone rolled over, a surprised look on his face, then scrambled out of bed and onto shaky feet. "Yes, master."

"Come here. I want you to pleasure my mate." On his order, Remus approached and slid submissively onto the lower level of the platform.

At least he hadn't forgotten who was master and who was slave. Romulus watched the clone slide into position, squelching a protest when Remus seemed to rub his chest deliberately against Garnet's full breasts. After all, that was what Romulus had ordered. "Touch her," he said, not happy about the unfamiliar waves of possessiveness that assailed him now.

"How?"

"Caress her the way you touch me. Stroke her head. Kiss her. Use your tongue to fuck her mouth." He had no reason to be jealous. None at all. After all, what Remus did, he did at Romulus's own order.

"May I fuck her again, Master?"

Remus sounded eager. Too damn eager. "No." From henceforward, the only cock to fill his mate's sweet cunt would be his. Romulus didn't know when he'd decided that, but he had. "You may use the dildos to pleasure Garnet. Her cunt is mine, and so is her ass -- at least until I've sampled it for myself."

If Garnet hadn't been on sensual overload, she'd have laughed out loud at her mate's sudden wave of possessiveness. Not a half-day earlier, Romulus had been willing -- no, eager was the word -- to share her with his identical clone. Though the idea of it had horrified her, the reality had proven incredibly pleasurable. Now it seemed her mate only intended to share parts of her -- the parts he apparently considered were not as personal as the wet, swollen channel between her legs.

Oh gods. He was tonguing her there, flailing her clit until it was nothing but a rigid ball of nerves. His warm breath tickled her mound while he used his fingers to work the ceremonial plug from her ass. Her cunt contracted, anticipating...

"I'm going to fuck your pretty, tight little ass," Romulus promised, the dark words reverberating against her flesh and making her hot -- hotter even than she'd been before. His clone's warm flesh caressed her belly, chafed her sensitized breasts as he slid upward, and when his hard, hot cock nudged her lips, she couldn't help but take the ruby knob of it inside and swirl her tongue over the sensitive tip.

"Suck in my clone's cock the way your ass will soon suck in mine," Romulus ordered.

When he moved away from her clit, Garnet would have protested if her mouth hadn't been full of Remus's unadorned male flesh. Her nipples tingled when he rotated the rings through them, tugging gently... sensually. She sensed rather than saw Romulus step back between her legs, then felt him sliding something wet and cold into her cunt. Oh gods. It was a vibrator, buzzing gently now, its motion so arousing it made her squirm. Gods but she wanted Romulus's hot mouth sucking her clit, his cock invading her wet, slick cunt the way the vibrator was doing now.

"Mmpf." No way could she talk while Remus had his cock rammed halfway down her throat, and trying only lodged him deeper. Desperately aroused, she sucked and wiggled as much as she could within her bonds, but that only made the vibrations grow stronger.

"Relax. Gods but you're tight. A virgin here, I'll wager." Her mate inserted first one lubricated finger, then two, past her anal sphincter, moving slowly in and out, stretching her more than the plug he'd removed moments earlier. His movements pressed the vibrator against the mouth of her womb. More fluid gushed from her cunt, trickling down to bathe her clit in hot, slick wetness.

When Garnet sucked harder on Remus's cock, it swelled and hardened more. He groaned. Pre-cum oozed down her throat. Did Romulus do this to him, too? Did her mate like to suck his clone, taste the salty, slightly bitter pre-cum and swallow his ejaculation down his throat? Garnet found the picture horrifying -- yet terribly arousing.

"Relax." Romulus's terse order came along with intense pressure against her tightly closed rear opening -- the sensation vaguely painful yet incredibly arousing. He used both hands to spread her ass cheeks while his ringed cock head pressed gently, then harder against her anal sphincter, until it opened and he seated himself inside her.

Full. She'd never felt so terribly full. Her heart beat faster. Sweat slickened her body and Remus's beneath her. While she sucked Remus's hard cock, she felt Romulus's sliding in and out of her ass. The vibrator hummed in her cunt. For a few short moments she savored the sensation of fullness before it burst, sending wave after wave of ecstasy through her nerves... into her lovers' bodies. When they came, as if in unison, they triggered her climax anew.

* * *

In his office the following day, Romulus considered how best to deal with his newly discovered possessive streak, his unnaturally nonsubmissive mate -- and Remus, whose submissiveness seemed to be going the way of Garnet's. By late afternoon when his assistant delivered the edict that had just arrived from Crown Prince Arik, Romulus had already worked himself into a fit of ill temper.

No more making or importing eunuch sex slaves? Having to offer the existing ones their freedom? What the fuck was Arik thinking about? How did the prince think Obsidion could keep its reputation as the premier pleasure planet of the galaxy if its rulers were going to restrict the supply of merchandise?

Then Romulus remembered. The badly disfigured prince was now his brother-by-marriage. By all reports, Arik doted on his pregnant mate, Garnet's own sister. Perhaps not all was lost.

* * *

"You want me to do what?" Garnet sounded as though she'd been asked to commit murder that night as they shared an evening meal in their suite.

Romulus lifted her hand to his lips, spoke softly. "Talk to your sister. Have her help make Prince Arik realize this insane new rule of his will kill business. If it's allowed to take effect, fewer people will flock to Obsidion to take their pleasure. More particularly, tourists won't keep flocking in droves to my emporiums -- the ones you're counting on to keep you in jewels and rare treats like the ones you're eating now."

Garnet glanced down at the lobster on her golden plate, a rare and succulent delicacy Romulus had ordered imported from Earth's Federation -- the only place in the galaxy where the crustaceans seemed able to grow. "I will do what I can -- but only if you will do something for me."

Romulus bit back a reminder that he was Garnet's master as well as her mate, by the laws of her own planet. "You know, my pet, your wish is my command."

Remus chuckled. The gods only knew what Romulus was to do with his suddenly assertive clone. He started to bark out an anatomically impossible command, but held back the words. "Remus, you may leave us."

"Gladly, master, but where am I to go?"

Remus had a point. Because Romulus had kept Remus in his quarters at his constant beck and call, Remus undoubtedly had no idea what he might do once he walked through the door. Romulus was in no mood to begin educating him now. "You cannot leave. Go in the sitting room and do not return until I call for you."

As the clone left, Garnet looked up from her nearly empty plate. If looks could have killed, Romulus would just now have breathed his last. "You've kept your clone confined for how long?" she asked, her tone venomous.

"Since we've lived here, where cloning is not allowed. Almost eight years. It is not your concern." Hoping to disarm her, Romulus took Garnet's hand and brought it to his lips. "Did you not say you wished not to share me?"

"That was before..." Her words trailed off, and a dreamy look came into her large, long-lashed eyes. "... before I realized what a wealth of sensation you offered me when you brought Remus to our bed."

"Humpf." This wasn't going at all the way Romulus had planned. "You need only me. Come, let's bathe each other." After dragging her into the marble shower stall and soaping them both with sweet-smelling body wash, he slid to his knees and spread Garnet's legs. Gods but she was already hot. Her rigid little clit seemed to strain toward his teeth and tongue the moment he lowered his head and began to taste her honey.

Slick. Clean, yet wet with anticipation. He loved the way her inner muscles contracted around his fingers when he inserted his fingers into her wet heat. Sex with Remus had never been quite so incredible, he thought as blood slammed into his cock.

Romulus realized now that Garnet could easily control him. He also knew that if he valued peace in his household, he could never let her know the power she held in her small, soft hands. He rose, rejecting the sense of urgency to fuck her now... accepting that to control her, he first must control himself.

"We will continue this discussion in bed," he said, pulling Garnet from the shower, wrapping her in a towel, and scooping her into his arms. Once he'd placed her spread-eagled across the ruby-red coverlet he guessed she must have used to replace the black one he'd had on the bed before, he followed her down, straddling her face and feeding her his eager cock.

Gods but her mouth felt good. Too good for him to let her use it on any cock but his own. When he bent over her firm, shapely body to taste her honey again, he realized he'd just slammed the door on Remus. Surprisingly, he didn't care. His people were wrong -- dead wrong -- to believe sex only felt good when shared by a man and his clone. When Romulus sipped the lush slick honey from Garnet's cunt, he knew he'd found the real nectar of sensual delight.

After she'd sucked him dry and he'd done the same for her, Romulus held her, cradling her beautiful head against his chest. He'd never felt so complete after coming in his clone. Even the knowledge that Garnet had mated with him for his wealth did little to weaken the bond forming between them.

Wealth. Implementing Prince Arik's new law would do nothing to enhance Romulus's financial position, especially when word spread around the galaxy that Obsidion no longer possessed the finest of eunuch sex slaves to pleasure men and women alike.

Romulus sat up abruptly, dragging Garnet with him, holding her so close that their nipple rings brushed against each other. "What the fuck are the eunuchs who're already here to do if the rulers take away their way of making a living?" What was Remus to do now that Romulus had no further need of his sexual services? "Remus, come to me now."

Garnet raised her head and looked at him, a puzzled look on her gorgeous face.

Before Romulus could respond to her unasked question, Remus burst into the room. "I am here, as you commanded, master. What would you have me do?"

Romulus stared at his clone, amazed as always that Remus appeared to be his own mirror image. "You're not a eunuch, but your tastes run more to me than to my mate. Right?"

"Yes, Master, but I must say the lady Garnet stirs me as I never believed a woman could."

"Would you like me to get you a sexbot?"

Remus laughed. "I'd prefer being fucked by one of the pretty eunuchs you sell in the emporiums, if you're telling me your need for me is finished. I truly do prefer a passive role, so I doubt I'd get much pleasure from a sexbot." He shot a wistful look at Garnet's rounded ass. "She is a beauty. She has possessed you, as I feared she would."

Garnet stretched, her motion so seductive Romulus's cock stood at attention even though he'd come mere moments earlier. "Have I possessed you, master?"

"I fear you have. Now be silent while I attend to business."

She clutched his forearms, as though to let him know she intended to be heard. "Tell me, what is this about this new law that has you so upset, and what could it possibly have to do with you losing your livelihood?"

"Ask your brother-by-marriage, Prince Arik. He has issued an edict that stands to ruin all of us who make our living in the Streets of Pleasure." Romulus got up and grabbed the document that was causing him so much distress, and tossed it Garnet's way. "Here, read it for yourself. Now I must think of something more immediately pressing. What do I do about Remus, now that you've stolen the lust I once felt only for him?"

"Why not give him his choice of the sex slaves you possess? It seems unfair that you've kept him locked away for all these years, serving your needs without regard to his own." Garnet glanced at the royal edict, but without the degree of obvious concern Romulus had expected her to display.

Actually, her suggestion made sense. "My mate is right. Tonight I will take you to the emporium and introduce you as my younger brother, newly arrived from Aurelion. You may amuse yourself by managing the daily slave auctions, and you may choose the eunuch of your choice and reserve him for yourself. Choose quickly, for if this new law takes effect there will be no more eunuchs made or imported. There may even be a mass exodus of the ones now working as sex slaves, since their owners must offer them their freedom -- unless I'm able to persuade Prince Arik of his folly in establishing this new law."

"But --"

Romulus raised his hand, cutting off Remus's protest. "I'll hear no argument from you. Take another suite within the house, and assign servants to take care of these rooms and belongings.

Tomorrow I will go with Garnet to plead my case before her sister and our ruler, her mate. Tonight I wish for you to choose a mate of your own."

Chapter Four

Had Remus found a soulmate?

Romulus had left early to take care of some details at one of his emporiums. Garnet lay fiddling with the bedcovers, recalling with a little regret the brief interlude she'd shared with Romulus and his clone -- or rather his brother, she must remember to say in public.

Part of her wished they could have continued the ménage, while her heart told her it was only Romulus with whom she wanted to share her life. She stretched out on the bed, pleasantly sore from the attention he'd bestowed on her earlier, along with a magnificent cask of jewels and a dozen fine silk robes for her to wear when she ventured outside their quarters.

How many times she'd dreamed of wallowing in precious gems, flaunting her mate's wealth before friends and strangers, basking in their envy. Now, those things didn't matter much, for the real treasure she'd gained was Romulus himself and not the beautiful gifts he might bestow on her.

Soon she must dress, and so must he. Garnet rose and rummaged through his closet, shaking her head at the few garments possessed by one so rich. Not having much choice, she selected a black velvet cloak lined with gold silk.

"That will go well with the black gown I chose for you."

Garnet whirled around at the sound of her mate's deep voice. He held an elaborate jeweled headdress. "I thought this might make up for the loss of your hair," he said, a smile on his sensual lips.

"Oh, master, I love it." The headdress was gorgeous -- exquisitely crafted of gold filigree studded with sparkling diamonds, rubies, and emeralds. Then she sobered. "You shouldn't have, though, not when you know your business soon may begin to suffer."

Romulus set down the exquisite piece and bent to kiss her naked scalp. "I love *you*. When we come back I'll show you how much. Now we need to hurry, for it won't do to keep a crown prince waiting."

As though he were her servant, Romulus draped her in the jewels he'd provided -- nipple shields, elaborate navel ring, and a diamond encrusted hoop he dangled from her new clit piercing. He adjusted the headdress on her head, then inserted a large diamond stud in the piercing in her nose. She loved the jewels... but she loved more the fact he said he loved *her*.

The stones winked merrily from settings of glittering gold, plainly visible through a black silk robe so sheer each jewel shone through. Garnet fingered the elaborate ornaments that dangled from the filigreed gold cap that hugged her naked scalp and wondered why the proof of her mate's great wealth didn't excite her the way she'd thought it would.

"When we are alone again, I intend to taste every inch of flesh those jewels hide," Romulus said, his red-gold eyes hot with lust as he draped the black cloak over his golden, naked body. "Now we must go if we are to reach the royal palace in time for our audience."

Before her mating, Garnet had anticipated riding along the Streets of Pleasure in Romulus's solid-gold ground transporter, basking in the envy of everyone who saw her. Today, though, she found her pleasure coming more from being with him -- from the press of his muscular thigh against her barely covered leg, the warmth of his fingers caressing the bare skin between her jeweled collar and her headdress. Hot with anticipation for yet another mating, she reached between his legs and stroked his deliciously rigid cock as they approached the entrance to the royal palace.

"Not now." Gently Romulus took her hand and moved it to his thigh. "I need to keep my wits about me, and I can't think when you're touching me that way."

Yes. He did need to concentrate on the business at hand, as did Garnet. It hadn't been easy, persuading Emerald to include them on the list of petitioners Prince Arik would see today. They would have to use all their powers of persuasion if they were to succeed in getting Arik to lift his edict and ensure the continued success of Romulus's business.

* * *

Unlike many petitioners, Romulus refused to cower before the prince who hid what were whispered to be horrendous scars behind an all-concealing mask. Garnet prostrated herself before Prince Arik, her jeweled headdress glittering in the sunlight, while Romulus bowed over the soft, small hand of the very pregnant Princess Emerald.

"I assume you're here to argue against the decree I circulated yesterday," Arik said as he helped Garnet to rise. As always, his voice was muffled by the leather that covered him head to toe but for one eye. "Come to my quarters since you are family now, and we will discuss it. It has been a tedious day, and I feel certain my mate is weary."

When they entered Arik and Emerald's private tower, Romulus gasped at the sight that greeted him. He'd seen the four royal eunuchs before -- but not when they were unclothed. "They're..."

"... nullified. They were completely desexed, for no reason other than that they were younger sons of my father's brother. I believe it is wrong to mutilate boys and men whose only wrongdoing was an accident of birth or circumstance."

Romulus tore his gaze from the eunuchs and looked at Arik. "You were a younger son, as well, were you not?"

"For someone not born and raised on Obsidion, you seem to know our history well. Yes, I was a younger son, exiled and hunted because unlike my cousins, I refused to consent to the removal of my cock and balls.

"For that, I was very nearly killed, though I was left whole sexually, for which I am grateful. The only reason I am here now as my father's heir to the diamond throne, covering my scars so my subjects don't run from me in horror, is because my brother had the misfortune of picking the wrong fight and losing his life." Arik gestured toward the mask that obscured his head, then turned to his cousins as though to end that thread of conversation. "You may leave now."

Her touch gentle and loving, Emerald rubbed a hand along the prince's leather-encased cheek as he watched his cousins leave. "You do not owe your subjects explanation for your edict, not even a subject who is mated with my sister. What you have ordered is right."

"But has your mate considered what abiding by that order will do to Romulus's and others' business in the sex slave trade? Not to mention what is to become of homeless, unemployed eunuchs who decide they no longer wish to ply their trade on the Streets of Pleasure. Has Prince Arik considered what harm his order will cause to the tourist trade on Obsidion?" Garnet grasped Romulus's forearm so hard he had to fight not to wince from the pain -- and not to become aroused from the simple fact of her nearness and the heat of her body touching his.

Arik stood, a fearsome figure in his leather garb. "I considered it. Some loss of business may take place, that's true. Not enough, I believe, to justify continuing the barbaric practice that has become ingrained in Obsidion's society."

"What of those like your royal cousins, who have already been altered? Would you have surgeons attempt to make them whole?" Romulus asked.

"I doubt that is possible. My intent is to see that no more boys are mutilated on this planet, and that none who have been mutilated elsewhere are brought here to service customers in sex slave parlors like yours."

Romulus stepped forward, determined to meet his ruler without showing the slightest fear. "But, your highness, the edict says eunuchs may no longer be kept as sex slaves in the emporiums. What is to become of the ones already in my employ, and in the service of other purveyors in the Streets of Pleasure?"

Arik strode to the window, as though considering his response. "Tell me, Romulus, for I'm sure you know. Can your eunuchs perform as men?"

"Do you mean, can they fuck a woman? Of course, as long as they were allowed to mature fully before being cut... and as long as they take the hormones they are prescribed. Some don't. As with all sentient beings, some eunuchs want to dominate their partners sexually, while others prefer to play a submissive role. Submissive eunuchs play well with male customers whose societies forbid them from having sex with females. Dominant ones are obviously more suited to meeting the needs of female customers."

"I see." Arik turned back to Romulus, his single eye compelling Romulus to maintain contact. "Then, if the eunuchs no longer worked in the sex trade, they might live normal lives outside the Streets of Pleasure?"

Romulus felt the heat of Garnet's hand on his thigh. "I suppose they might. Still, they are popular with tourists, particularly Earthling females and males from planets like Aurelion where same-sex sex is the norm. I shudder to think of the losses you'll suffer in tax revenues if you go ahead with this and outlaw eunuchs from working in the emporiums."

"You are Aurelonian, are you not?" Emerald asked.

"Yes."

Arik stroked his leather-encased chin. "Would your countrymen pass on having sex with a woman or a whole man if they were not given the choice of taking a eunuch?"

"Except for members of the royal family, Aurelonians do not take eunuch lovers. Boys are cloned before they reach maturity so their clones can provide acceptable outlets for their sexual urges. The clones are always submissive, and they are sterile but whole."

When Garnet smiled at him, Romulus couldn't help smiling back and reassuring her. "I can't vouch for all Aurelonians, but given the choice, I would take my mate over any eunuch I've ever seen. Even over my clone."

"I had heard rumors you kept a clone. Since we are related now, I will ignore that rumor. I suggest, however, that you present him as a brother... and that he do or say nothing to make people question the story." Arik paused, as though considering his words carefully. "It is not my intent to shut down the Streets of Pleasure, or to pauper any of my subjects. However I cannot condone mutilation. My edict will stand. Your eunuchs may go or stay in your employ, as they choose, for I insist you offer them their freedom. If you have treated them well, I wager many of them will want to stay."

Romulus stood and faced his prince. He couldn't argue with Arik's logic, or with the rightness of the new rule. Though he couldn't be certain, he imagined the majority of his eunuch sex slaves would opt to stay -- particularly since he was even now considering what enticements he would offer to keep them on. It might not be as bad a rule as it had seemed on the surface.

His only real concern was in Arik's timing. Why had he decided to issue his edict now? Though the prince could not have known it, Romulus was well on the way to falling in love with Garnet. And Garnet had accepted him sight unseen, but only because he was a wealthy man.

"It's all right," Garnet whispered as they wound their way down the tower steps and to the transporter Romulus soon might not be able to afford. "If your business suffers, we can always sell our jewels."

He couldn't have been more surprised, or happier, when his mate caught his cock ring between her teeth and licked the sensitive flesh beneath it. "It's true, I married you for your wealth, but I love you for the way you make my cunt weep for this. Come, take me home and fuck me until we're too tired to fuck anymore. Then fuck me some more."

"Gladly, my jewel." Romulus gunned the engine of the transporter and sped them home.

Chapter Five

"If you wish you may have your freedom," Remus told the comely eunuch he'd selected from the dozens on display in the showroom and brought with him to his new quarters. "If not, you will become my life companion."

"I will be your companion. Gladly." The tall, blond eunuch knelt and took Remus's cock between his teeth. "Mmmm," he said when Remus arched his hips and seated himself within his lover's throat. His balls drew up, tickled deliciously by the warm, damp breath that bathed them in heat... affection.

For years now Remus had been the willing recipient of Romulus's seed. Now he wanted to give some of his own. "Cease or you'll make me come, and when I do that I want my cock to be buried deep in your hot, tight ass."

The eunuch rolled over on his back, raising and spreading his muscular legs to reveal a long but slender half-hard cock and an inviting asshole stretched taut around a good-size butt plug. "Take me, master. Put your hard cock in my ass and fuck me."

"I'd know the man I'm about to fuck. What's your name?" Remus realized he had much to learn about interpersonal relationships, now that he no longer was confined to his master's rooms.

"Darrell. Of Earth's Federation until I ran afoul of the law there. I can tell by your coloring you hail from Aurelion."

"Yes." Remus laid Darrell's legs over his shoulders, bending as he did to tongue-fuck his mouth and run his tongue over the eunuch's full, reddened lips. His cock swelled with anticipation when he removed the butt plug, lubricated his cock and his partner's quivering ass, and positioned himself against the other's stretched-out sphincter. "Relax. I'm going to fuck you now. Mmmm."

Remus sank his cock into the tight, hot passage, imagining that he was doing this while Romulus plumbed his own ass, the way he had the other night. Oh gods, it felt good. Darrell moaned, opening himself further as though begging silently for more... for everything Remus had to offer.

When he shot his cum deep in his lover's ass, Remus knew he'd come home. With his cock still lodged within Darrell's tight asshole, he turned them on their sides, slept... and dreamed.

* * *

They must be dreaming. Garnet peered into the darkened sleeping chamber, listening to the slow, steady breathing of Remus and the sex slave he'd chosen. The two seemed well matched, as matched as she was with Romulus. He stood behind her now, his rigid cock nudging the jewel-encrusted plug in her ass.

"Bedtime," he whispered, and she breathlessly agreed.

"You don't mind if I can't always give you the beautiful things you wanted so much? If I'm not always known as the man of gold?" Romulus divested her of the fabulous jewels he'd put on her earlier, leaving her naked but for the rings that dangled from her nipples -- and the brand-new clit ring he'd had placed there before they'd gone to plead his case to Prince Arik.

"I doubt you need to fear the poorhouse. By all reports, your emporiums are the finest in the Streets of Pleasure. And sex sells. With or without the eunuchs, business should continue to thrive."

Romulus smiled. "I hope you are right, for I want to give you everything you've ever dreamed about. I want to fulfill your every fantasy."

His skin glowed golden in the twilight, alien but so beautiful she wanted nothing at the moment but to touch it, feel its warm smoothness against her own heated body. "You can give me of yourself, master mine, for that is what I want most. I wish you would do it now."

She loved the way his eyes glowed when he became aroused. His rigid cock beckoned her eyes... her hands... her mouth. "Go ahead," he said, his voice hoarse with need, "take me as you will."

"Oh, yes. I will take you... consume you." Dropping to her knees, Garnet stroked his long, narrow feet, his muscular calves and thighs. Everywhere she touched him, she felt his heat, his barely leashed lust. When she cupped his sac, he let out an anguished groan. "Hush. Let me mate with you as you mated with me."

She had none of the fragrant incense that had perfumed the altar where she'd lain, a passive gift to her master, king of the Streets of Pleasure. She didn't need it, not now, as she made slow, sweet love to Romulus, her beloved mate.

The perfume came from him and her, and from the fragrant garden outside their open window. Gods in the heavens, but he made her hot, hotter than she'd ever dreamed she'd be. She licked and stroked his magnificent cock, sampling the pre-cum that glistened around the ring at its tip. Salty -- slightly bitter -- yet part of him she yearned to take and nourish within her body not just now but forever.

She cupped his tight ass cheeks. "Have you ever taken your clone this way?"

"No. You can use a strap-on, though, if it would give you pleasure..."

Would it? Garnet ringed his asshole with one finger, remembering the pain and the pleasure when Romulus had claimed her tight rear passage. "What I want to know is whether it would give *you* pleasure."

He clutched her shoulders, brought her up until their hot bodies meshed, male to female, lover to lover. "I fear you've taken yourself a sexual dominant. I want to give pleasure to my partner by taking, not by being taken. Will you go willingly or must I restrain you on the platform to show you how I want to love you?"

Garnet's cunt clenched, for she'd found her own pleasure came by pleasuring her mate. "I go willingly, master. Not only now but always."

Romulus bent, using his tongue to caress her scalp, to find and stimulate the erogenous places on her bared skull. "You know, it's incredibly arousing when you touch me this way."

"For me, too." He lifted her as though she weighed no more than a feather in the wind. "Wrap your legs around me and let me in." Slowly, slickly, he impaled her on his cock. His pelvic bone ground deliciously into her swollen clit. The scent of flowers from the garden swirled around them as they fucked, two souls made one days earlier by law, now by their mutual desire.

Heat began in her cunt where he claimed her, spreading cell by cell through her body until she caught fire. Uncontrollable fire that consumed her, made her clamp down on his invading cock as though she could keep it inside her forever. Nothing else mattered. Not wealth or power. Nothing but the sensation of coming... of joining... of being one with her mate now and forever more.

"Gods yesss," she said when she felt his hot cum bathing her cunt in powerful spurts that seemed to go on forever. "This is the wealth of yours that I claim. Only this. Only your love."

"And yours for me."

At that moment Garnet knew, her mate had given her the wealth she sought. Wealth that would last a lifetime, whether they be rich or poor.

As she cradled her life mate in her arms, the words of an old Earthling vow she'd heards kept repeating itself in her head. *For richer, for poorer... as long as we both shall live...*

Epilogue

"I wish Prince Arik would take off that fearsome mask."

"Yes. His face is no longer so bad it frightens small children. Just the other day I saw him in the Streets of Pleasure, and he was not wearing the mask."

Garnet smiled at the two old women who, despite their complaining, seemed happy enough to be drinking Arik's wine and stuffing their wizened faces at the christening of his baby boy.

"I asked him to wear the mask today," Emerald whispered in Garnet's ear. "Once this is over, he will claim the part of me that so far has remained my own."

Her ass, Garnet assumed, for she'd heard her sister complaining for months now that Arik wouldn't take her that way while she carried his child. "If he is gentle, you will like it," she said, glancing at her own golden lover while he conversed with another of the businessmen who purveyed their wares on the Streets of Pleasure.

Business hadn't slowed as much as Romulus had feared it would. Though there had been grumbling from the tourists about the shortage of eunuch sex slaves, those same tourists had for the most part chosen from the emporium's available alternatives: beautiful women and whole but sterile males. Remus and his eunuch lover ran day-to-day operations, leaving Romulus free to pleasure Garnet.

"You seem happy, little sister," Emerald said, her gaze on Pearl, who would take her own mate about the same time Garnet hoped to present her master with their first child. "I hope Pearl will find as much contentment with Pak Lin."

"I hope so, too." Garnet would take Romulus's hot cock any day over that of a sexbot, even one of Pak Song's best. She imagined Emerald preferred Prince Arik to any 'bot, as well.

Pearl, though, seemed to be anticipating a lifetime with her future mate's inventory of sex toys more than she looked forward to mating with the cyborg-maker's son himself.

That could provide for some discord, but only time would tell. Needing her mate, Garnet looked his way and smiled. As always, Romulus responded quickly, meeting her gaze with a heated one of his own. "Let's go home," he said, clasping her hand and nodding his good-byes to the royal assembly.

Yes, Romulus always knew what Garnet wanted, for she always wanted him. In the transporter, he suckled her newly tender nipples while she stroked his golden cock. Soon they'd be home, hearing the sounds that told her Remus was as happy with his lover as Garnet was with Romulus... stripping off the celebratory garments they'd donned for the christening... and making slow, hot love.

The reality of that love beat her wildest fantasies. "You know I love you, master mine."

"Yes, but I love you more. More than wealth. More than life itself."

Obsidion: Pearl of Passion

Ann Jacobs

Prologue

His girls were priceless. More precious than the most costly jewels in his inventory. Eli of Obsidion, jeweler to kings and rulers throughout the galaxy, had negotiated matches for his three beloved daughters, the last of which was about to be celebrated.

"Eli, how do you feel, knowing that in just a few minutes the last of your beautiful daughters will take a mate?" Meredith the matchmaker wore a satisfied smile as she stood at Eli's side, her sparkling sapphire-blue gown shimmering in the light of Obsidion's three moons.

He looked down at Meredith. Several times before he'd felt a strong attraction to her, but today that feeling was stronger than ever. Though his heart would always belong to his Sadie, Meredith had a way of making his ancient cock stiffen, his pulse race. Perhaps...

But now was not the time for considering his own future. Pearl, his youngest daughter, waited by a jewel-bedecked altar in the central courtyard of his home, flanked by her eldest sister, Emerald, and her own prince, Arik of Obsidion. Garnet stood at Pearl's other side, her arm casually looped through that of her mate, Romulus, the sex slave king. If the gods were smiling on them all today, Pearl's match with Pak Lin, son of the famed cyborg-maker, would make her as happy as her sisters.

Eli frowned when he glanced at Pearl's future mate and noticed the implacable expression on his face. From the beginning, Lin's credentials hadn't particularly impressed Eli. The boy was much too young, only a year older than the headstrong, beautiful Pearl, and unlike Arik and Romulus, he'd demonstrated none of the traits of a master when Meredith had brought him around two years ago for an initial interview.

Not that he could fault the boy's appearance. Tall, with golden skin and only a hint of the Oriental Earthling features so prominent on his father, Lin had a regal look about him, surrounded as he was by his six equally detached looking attendants. His apparent aloofness troubled Eli, but he shoved aside his concern. The boy might seem distant now, but as soon as the consummation began, his passion would surely take over and he'd become the eager bridegroom.

Pearl wouldn't tolerate aloof. Not at all. Eli turned to Meredith. "Tell me you made no mistake in choosing this boy. He seems -- detached. Not eager as I'd expect a bridegroom to be. Pearl has a healthy libido she'll insist on having satisfied."

"A typical understatement from a loving father, considering you told me from the outset your daughter kills off one of her sexbots every few months. Relax, Eli. I chose Pak Lin precisely because he is ideally qualified to feed Pearl's voracious appetite for sex."

Eli wasn't entirely reassured, but the ceremony was about to begin. The time was long past when he could call a halt to the proceedings on the basis of nothing more than an uneasy feeling about the match. As the assembled guests watched, Garnet and Emerald stripped away their sister's pearl-encrusted robe, leaving her naked but for the choker of pearls and moonstones her bridegroom had selected last week from Eli's stock.

Pearl's sable curls surrounded her head when she lay on the ceremonial altar. Against age-old tradition, Lin had insisted her hair not be cut, but bound atop her head as one of the priestesses was doing now.

"All will be well, my friend," Meredith said, giving Eli's hand a reassuring squeeze. "There go the attendants now. The bridegroom will soon follow. Let us go closer to the altar, witness Pearl's joining with Pak Lin."

Chapter One

Pak Lin's cock swelled. His pulse raced. His gaze locked onto the woman on the altar, on the age-old mating ritual unfolding before him -- an ancient tradition of groomsmen preparing a bride, to which he had added his own modern twist.

For his attendants were not men but 'bots. Sexbots of his creation, indistinguishable from living beings to all but the most discerning. Lin watched, blood pounding in his cock, as his 'bots set his intended bride to writhing on the altar, breathing hard, anticipating the mating that was about to take place.

Fucking his beautiful mate would prove no hardship. Keeping his feelings under control didn't promise to be as easy as it had before he'd seen her, felt the sensual promise that had him salivating as he watched the 'bots bring her to the edge of orgasm. But he would be strong. He'd defeat the urge that tried to snare him in its grip. He was master of his emotions, and no mere woman was going to entangle them, make him a mindless slave to his cock's demands.

Lin stood, waiting for his cue, reminding himself he'd long ago sworn off emotional attachments... that by avoiding them he could avoid the pain and anguish of losing loved ones, pain that visited him in dreams, after nearly twenty years had passed.

He schooled his features into a mask of passivity, bared one shoulder from the black velvet cloak that masked his nakedness, and began the long walk to the altar. With every step he told himself the woman he took as his mate was no different from another high-tech sexbot -- except that she could provide him with the means of perpetuating his line.

Every time his gaze strayed to her laid out on the altar for his pleasure, he was struck by her beauty, her vitality. It was going to require his best efforts to think of her as fuck-mate and consort, but never anything more.

* * *

Gods help her, she was going to disgrace herself if the six gorgeous males charged with preparing her for her mating didn't signal Pak Lin to join them soon. Pearl gasped for breath, clamped down on her cunt muscles. She couldn't come yet, before her bridegroom even showed up. But she wasn't going to be able to hold back much longer if these guys kept up their sensual onslaught.

Her clit swelled and hardened under one talented tongue. Her breasts tingled from the wet, warm stimulation from two others. The other three sucked her fingers and toes, and she found their attentions almost as stimulating as what the others were doing to her more erogenous zones.

Fragrant smoke from incense swirled about, enveloped them in a haze, obscured her vision and made her focus on touch alone, a milieu of hands and mouths driving her to a fever pitch of sexual need.

"The bridegroom cometh."

The words of the head priestess echoed through the courtyard. Oohs and ahs rang out as guests admired her mate's broad, lean chest... his muscled abs... Pearl closed her eyes, imagined...

... his long, thick cock, his hands in her hair, his lips on hers. Their tongues would tangle, mate as his companions continued the delicious assault on her senses, bringing her passion to a crescendo before he'd wave them away, slide his cock into her sopping cunt and fuck her until she passed out from the incredible pleasure of the mating.

If he accepted her.

Pearl's breath caught in her throat. Her pulse raced as the man chosen to be her mate looked down on her, his handsome face impassive. His expression inscrutable, he inspected her from head to toe, lingering nowhere, not even on her lush, full breasts most men ogled.

Was his cock hard and ready? Did looking at her send blood slamming out of his brain? By the gods, she couldn't tell. His expression was unreadable, as though he were one of his famous father's cyborgs, complete with all the necessary functioning parts except for feelings. "Has someone struck you dumb?" she asked before she could hold back the words.

"Silence." Just one word, no more, accompanied by a fierce scowl. Pearl trembled on the altar of submission, worried now. Would he reject her, make her the object of pity to all on Obsidion?

Lin swept her with an appraising gaze, his eyes intent, lips drawn tight as though deep in thought. His attendants continued stimulating her as if he were not there, warming her flesh, readying her. For what? she wondered.

Then he tossed off his cloak, stood naked before her. "I accept this woman as my mate," he said, his voice as devoid of emotion as his forbidding expression. For long moments he stood above her saying nothing further, making no move to claim her. Lin's attendants continued their sensual assault, forcing her body to grow hotter, wetter. Making her want her mate though she read his lack of action as lack of desire to make her his own.

Meredith the matchmaker had talked up this man's virility, his stamina as well as his lusty appetite for women, and his father's desire for him to take a mate. His father's desire but not his own, Pearl surmised as he stood there watching his attendants titillating her, shoving her inexorably toward the climax she was supposed to have here on the altar, but only when he claimed her.

Why wouldn't he fuck her? She squirmed, embarrassed at the copious cream flowing from her cunt. It drenched her ass and probably had pooled on the altar between her widespread thighs. She bit her own tongue so hard she saw stars, just to keep from screaming for Lin to take her *now*. Her nipples hardened painfully and her clit swelled even more.

Still Lin did nothing. Nothing but look down at her as she writhed in unwilling ecstasy from his attendants' ministrations. Pearl wanted to fucking kill him even as wave after wave of luscious sensation coursed through her. Even as...

Finally! He strode around her, moved the attendant who still was tweaking her clit, stood between her legs and… resumed staring down at her. Attendants' hands, seeming as though disembodied now, began a sensual stroking of her calves and knees, her arms. More hands lifted her head, giving her a bird's-eye view of his cock which seemed to lengthen and thicken before her eyes, its plum like head nudging her glistening cunt lips.

By the gods he was huge. And naked. None of the traditional adornments pierced his flesh. Pearl's mouth watered at the thought of feasting on his massive tool, of taking it into her cunt and ass and…

Oh gods. Now he was strapping on another cock. The dildo looked eerily like his own flesh, only smaller. At his silent nod, his attendants untied her, flipped her onto her belly, and secured her ass-up on the transparent altar, her breasts hanging free when the upper part of the altar retracted. An attendant held her by the hair while another clamped her master's collar to metal rings in the altar. The mirrors positioned beneath the altar allowed her to inspect her mate's dark, tight scrotum, his throbbing cock poised to sink into her needy cunt -- and the strap-on he now was oiling with one big, capable looking hand.

Two of the attendants knelt beneath the altar. Two mouths clamped onto her nipples, suckling like twin babes. Their tongues flailed the sensitive nubs. Their teeth grazed her flesh, seemingly in unison. Pearl felt her stomach muscles tighten yet again as her cunt grew impossibly hotter and wetter. The heavily greased finger her mate had just worked into her asshole set off waves of need -- need more intense than any she'd experienced.

Lin withdrew his finger, positioned himself, sank into her cunt and ass at the same time, filling her, stretching her. Claiming her. He steadied her with hot hands as he pushed deeper, harder until his cock head rested at the entrance to her womb and the strap-on completely filled her anus. For a moment he stilled, letting her grow accustomed to his dual invasion. The two attendants who suckled her breasts stopped, too, in an eerily coordinated choreography of motion, the wet heat of their mouths containing her even as her master contained himself within her. His heavy balls rested against her clit.

Gods but she'd never been quite so hot. Pressure built up, spread its searing heat from her cunt, her ass with every pulsing of Lin's cock inside her. Her nipples tingled. "Yesss," she hissed as waves of pleasure began to overtake her. "Fuck me hard."

He began to move, his hips pistoning, the dildo sliding in and out of her ass, his long, thick cock slipping in the wetness of her cunt. Slurping sounds of sex echoed in her ears, a symphony of sorts. Loud burps from her cunt and ass as her body tried to hold onto his withdrawing cocks, the softer sounds of suckling mouths on her nipples, the noises she couldn't help emitting from deep in her throat as another, stronger climax threatened to take her.

The mouths sucked harder. The cocks slammed into her cunt and ass faster, deeper. Lin's balls tightened, hardened against her clit. Teeth grazed her nipples. Her mate's cock swelled inside her, twitched, then erupted, sending burst after burst of searing liquid heat straight into her womb. Pearl didn't think she could come any more, but Lin's orgasm sent more waves of pleasure through her body, leaving her limp, practically unconscious...

Well and truly mated, she thought as her eyelids drooped and closed.

Chapter Two

The ritual mating was done, and finally the celebratory gathering had broken up as well. Lin's jaw ached from smiling. His eyes felt as though they'd been crossed and uncrossed a hundred times. Damn, but he'd have to figure another unobtrusive way besides eye signals to orchestrate the activities of his sexbots -- or resolve never again to use as many as six of them at once, no matter the occasion.

His cock twitched when he thought about how good it had felt, lodged inside the wet, swollen cunt of a real live woman. Perhaps... No, his father most likely had been right. Pak Song usually was, Lin admitted. The old cyborg-maker had always insisted until the day he died that no sexbot could compare with a living female, no matter how carefully it was designed.

But the scientist in Lin wanted to try. After all, he'd managed to create the attendants who'd taken part in his own mating ceremony, and no one had guessed they were anything but six of his closest friends, taking part in the age-old ritual of claiming a bride. Not even Pearl.

She'd know soon enough, when he told her the six would be their constant companions in the mating chamber. Even now two of them bathed and perfumed her, and they'd soon be chaining her to the bed so he could fuck her again. This time he'd try out the new cock he'd recently perfected, see if she could tell the organ wasn't precisely real when she took it in her pretty mouth. Alpha Two was the 'bot in which he'd installed the experimental phallus and its drivers. He must remember. Perhaps he should order the other sexbots from the room so as not to get confused about which of them had the equipment he wanted to test.

Stupid, to have created them all to look like more or less generic Earthlings, varied only by subtle differences in skin tone and height. Lin made a mental note to make some alterations to the 'bots so they would be easier to distinguish. As it was, he sometimes couldn't tell which 'bot was which, when they all wore the same biogenetically engineered muscles and skin that made them look like living beings. Still, Lin was proud of the progress he'd accomplished, taking the sexbots for which his father had become famous throughout the galaxy and making them look and feel so real no casual observer -- or horny female for that matter -- could tell the difference between them and the real thing.

Lin dropped his robe carelessly to the floor and regarded his own half-hard cock. This time he'd fuck her in the ass, and try out the experimental cock he'd built into Alpha Two. His cock twitched as if it understood his thought, approved heartily, looked forward to invading its mate's dark, tight hole.

Two cocks on one man. Lin considered the possibility of creating one 'bot that could take care of all three of a woman's holes at the same time. He laughed at the fanciful mental picture he drew, of a cock growing out of the mouth of a sexbot, ready to deep-throat its owner while the 'bot used its other two cocks to fuck her cunt and ass.

He looked down at himself after positioning the "smart" cock in the harness. The pair of cocks in the 'bot's groin would have to be arranged like this -- equal sized cocks positioned so they could invade a cunt and ass.

Lin immediately recognized the triple-hole 'bot he'd conjured up in his mind would have at least one major disadvantage. The woman and the 'bot would have to face each other, which would prohibit her ordering it to try many arousing positions. Rear entry, for instance. His cock swelled further when he recalled having clutched Pearl's plump ass cheeks while he fucked her, having watched the 'bots suck her tits and wishing at the time they hadn't been there so he could have tugged at her puckered nipples with his fingers.

He would not succumb to maudlin emotion, would not become a master who was in truth submissive to his own slave-mate. He'd seen countless men come to his father's shop, looking for sexbots to provide what their women would not. He'd even witnessed the phenomenon in the crown prince -- a fierce looking man who nonetheless turned to jelly in the hands of his princess. In the sex slave king, Romulus, who if rumor could be believed had all but deserted his cloned lover in favor of his own mate. Lin was stronger than either of them. He would satisfy his father and keep their line going.

It wasn't that he didn't intend to enjoy fucking the beautiful Pearl. He simply wouldn't let his feelings become involved.

"No. I refuse to be chained like an animal. Leave me," Pearl screeched loud enough to damage Lin's eardrums, even through the closed door to the mating chamber. Alarmed that one of his 'bots might have malfunctioned and done something to hurt her, Lin charged in to find her sitting up in the middle of the fucking bed, staring down Alpha Four, who was trying in vain to get her to lie down so he could fasten the chains to the metal eyelets in the collar around her neck.

Lin sighed. Beautiful his mate might be, but she was obviously no biddable creature. This might mean trouble. "Go. I will tether her myself," he said, relieved to see Alpha Two still waiting quietly by the door to the bathing room.

"Yes, Master," Alpha Four croaked as it made its way out. Damn it, Lin should have remembered to mute the 'bot's speaking mechanism. No way would any living being listen to it talk and not know, because the sexbot's voice sounded mechanical. Tinny, nowhere near the way a normal male spoke. Lin obviously had spent too much time on perfecting their looks and ability to follow commands, and not enough on making their computer-generated voices sound real. Of course, he rationalized, the 'bots didn't often have the occasion to speak.

Quick action would forestall Pearl's questions -- and the vocalization of her outrage. Lin pushed his mate onto her back and deftly tethered her collar to the neck and headrest portion of the bed. "Come," he ordered Alpha Two. "Fuck her mouth."

"Damn you! I -- oompf." Her words cut off around Alpha Two's rigid cock, but Pearl lashed out with both feet, caught Lin in the right thigh, inches from his balls.

"Do not. It is my will. Suck his cock." Lin grabbed one flailing limb at a time, securing her arms at her sides, her gorgeous legs in stirrups so she would be helpless, open for his possession. "I intend to claim your ass, the same way I claimed your tight wet cunt at our mating."

Despite having schooled himself to ignore all but her most essential parts, he couldn't help noticing her creamy skin felt softer, more supple than what he'd bioengineered for his 'bots. Looking at her full breasts with their rosy nipples pebbled now with apparent arousal got him hotter than he'd ever been when fucking any 'bot, even the Omega female he was in the process of perfecting.

Damn it, mating was purely a biological function. The giving over of one body to another. The sharing of bodily fluids that might join to produce a new generation. He didn't need Pearl for more than that. Didn't want her for more.

Of course he didn't. Lin reminded himself again he needed no living companions, wanted no entanglements that eventually would cause him pain. He tore his gaze from his mate, concentrated instead on remembered sounds and sensations of impending release.

With every indrawn breath Lin grew harder, hotter as the heady smell of woman surrounded them. Lubrication oozed from the tip of his cock, captured inside the condom he put on. He tried not to wish Pearl was the one preparing him, smearing the cool gel lubricant over his sheathed male flesh and the smart dildo in its sturdy harness. When he felt her grip his finger with her inner muscles as he pushed the gel up her ass, he tried not to consider anything but the coming pleasure -- and failed.

As he sank his fingers slowly into her ass and cunt, preparing her, her whimpers around the Alpha Two's high-tech cock turned slowly to moans of pleasure. The enthusiastic sounds of her cock sucking made Lin want to order the 'bot away and shove his own throbbing organ down her throat. *He* would appreciate feeling her lips and tongue on his cock, the swallowing motions of her throat, the warm damp caresses of her breath on his balls.

The sexbot didn't. Couldn't. Lin had programmed the 'bots to do exactly as ordered. He hadn't imbued even the most advanced of the Alphas with feelings of their own, hadn't transformed them into living things. Alpha Two was cheating Pearl, giving her pleasure without enjoying the joy she selflessly gave back.

Lin had a sudden compulsion to throw Alpha Two against the wall. That gave him a moment's pause. It seemed he was doing something he'd sworn never to do, becoming possessive of his mate, considering her as more than a vessel for his seed.

He played his fingers along her swollen, damp slit, finding her cunt again and inserting two fingers before moving back, playing with her asshole until he felt the flesh contract and expand as though needing to be filled. His own cock throbbed, and his balls tightened with anticipation. Whoever had convinced him fucking a 'bot gave the same sort of satisfaction as fucking a mate was wrong. Dead wrong.

'Bots didn't tremble under his touch. They didn't moan when he slid the lower part of the bed aside and stepped between their legs. They didn't lift their asses in invitation when he positioned his cock. Lin told himself it didn't matter, that Pearl's feelings meant nothing. What he felt now had to be unvarnished lust, no more and no less than he'd eventually experience with the Omega sexbot that was his current project.

Accepting that rationalization, Lin began to fuck her ass, gently pressing forward until his sheathed, lubricated cock head popped past her anal sphincter. When she tugged against her bonds, he fed the smart-cock into her cunt and began to inch forward.

Gods but she was tight. Her ass gripped his cock almost painfully. The smart-cock stretched her cunt, provided arousing sensations to his own flesh through the thin wall of flesh separating the two channels. The sight of Alpha Two methodically fucking her mouth aroused yet infuriated him, but he couldn't tear his gaze from the slender column of her throat, the motions of the sexbot's cock within it, of her swallowing reflexively… of the glistening sheen of sweat on her brow, between her breasts, on her flushed satiny cheeks as they rose and sank while she sucked the 'bot.

The orgasmic clenching of her cunt around the dildo stimulated his cock, made the tight passage even tighter, an erotic spot between intense pleasure and excruciating pain. His balls drew up. If he didn't come soon, he'd explode.

There. The first spurts of come drenched his cock, filled the tip of the condom. His thigh muscles contracted, strained as burst after burst of his hot seed shot out, leaked onto him and her. Her own wild contractions kept him coming until he was gasping for breath and struggling to stay on his feet. "Cease. Leave us," he managed to rasp out to Alpha Two before collapsing over his mate in a stupor of supreme satisfaction.

Chapter Three

Pearl woke pleasantly sore -- and majorly pissed. Lin knew how to use his long, thick cock, all right. But from all the emotion her mate had expressed while they fucked, he might as well have been one of his father's famed sexbots.

The attendants, she understood. They had one purpose, to arouse her for Pak Lin's pleasure. They'd done a damn good job of driving her almost to the edge of orgasm, even though she'd gotten the distinct idea the attendant Lin had called Alpha Two would have been equally engaged if he'd had his cock sucked by a 'bot. He hadn't come, and he hadn't let out a sound -- not even a howl of frustration when Lin had ordered him to stop and get out.

Something funny was going on, and she intended to find out what.

Crawling out of the wide, soft bed Lin had deposited her on after the last very impersonal fucking session, Pearl slipped into a creamy satin robe, flipped her long high ponytail over her shoulder, and went off in search of her brand-new mate.

Why hadn't Lin stayed in bed after they'd made love? The answer was obvious -- he hadn't made love, he'd had sex with her, same way he would have with a 'bot. That fucking pissed her off. She bet neither Emerald nor Garnet's mates had left them to awaken alone and lonely -- although on second thought Prince Arik might have. Emerald had mentioned he'd been reluctant at first to let her see his scars. Still, Lin had no excuse, no disfigurement to justify his deciding to abandon her on their first whole day as mates, nor a cloned lover he needed to placate, as Romulus had after he'd taken Garnet as his bonded mate.

The first door Pearl opened led to an airy room with tiled floor and comfortable looking mats arranged around a low table. Grayish green draperies of slick, soft looking material matched the covers on plump cushions stacked neatly in front of floor-to-ceiling windows. Her nostrils flared at the flower-like aroma of steam coming from an antique lacquered teapot -- probably was a relic from Lin's family's time on Earth -- in the center of the table. The room was perfectly appointed yet as devoid of emotion as Lin himself. Suddenly hungry, Pearl sank cross-legged onto one of the mats, landing pretty close to the spot she'd aimed for, and filled a thimble-sized cup with the fragrant brew.

No sooner had she sat down than a silent servant appeared, bowed, and set a plate of almond encrusted pastries before her. "Welcome to Pak Lin's home," he said, his voice mechanical, much like the inflectionless voice of the attendant Lin had summarily dismissed last night.

Mechanical. Not real. Temporarily rendered speechless, Pearl stared at the servant as he walked away. A 'bot? He didn't look like one. As a matter of fact, he looked a great deal like one of Lin's attendants at the mating ceremony yesterday. She took a bite of the pastry, savored the crunchy almonds. The creamy frosting contrasted with flaky layers, reminding her of the *rugala* her mother used to make. Pearl set down the pastry and lifted the dainty teacup.

"Jasmine tea. I hope you enjoy the taste."

When she turned toward the normal, low-pitched male voice, she saw Lin. "It's excellent. So are the pastries. I had hoped to wake and find you still in our bed," she said, not able to squelch the tone of disappointment that crept into her last comment.

"I rise early. You are welcome to sleep as late as you like. If I want you, I will awaken you." He sat much more gracefully than she had, but then Pearl reminded herself he'd probably been sitting on the floor to eat for most of his life, and she'd made her first attempt this morning.

With unusual grace for one so large, Lin lifted the teapot and poured himself some of the tea. His expression was inscrutable. Emotionless. Maddening. Pearl could barely restrain herself from slapping that infuriating lack of feeling off his face. "I hope I pleased you," she said, not really caring a whole lot but figuring conversing about it would open a dialogue between them. She had to know what he expected of her. She suspected his expectations might be completely different from hers.

Sex and lots of it, mind-blowing sex. That's what she'd come into this mating expecting -- sex that would surpass every whispered story she'd heard from Emerald and Garnet about life with their respective mates. But she also anticipated a certain amount of affection. Damn it, even the pets in her father's household rated a pat on the head, a cuddle, a romp outside on a nice day.

"I have no complaints." Lin finished his tea, rose as gracefully as he'd sat, and glanced at the timepiece on his wrist. "I do, however, have much work to do. I will require your company later. You may await me in my bedchamber after the evening meal. I will send one of my attendants to show you around the house. I will instruct him to see to your *other* needs until I return."

By the gods! Lin had just taken her expectations and blown them clear out of the galaxy. She expected affection from her mate. Both her sisters had told her that by loving their masters, they'd tamed them. But to do that with Lin, Pearl needed to make some emotional connection with him. That wasn't likely to be easy, since it seemed she'd taken a master with no more feelings than the marble statues in the street of sex slaves. Pearl bit her lip until it hurt. If she hadn't, she'd have lashed out at Lin -- at his back, since having issued his highhanded fucking order he was on his way out -- with words that would have made her father wash her mouth out with the stuff he used to soak the dirt off uncut gemstones.

She'd see about this! Somewhere hidden beneath his stoic exterior, Lin had to possess the qualities she wanted in a lover. Pearl trusted Meredith wouldn't have deliberately paired her up with a statue. After all, the matchmaker had picked ideal mates for her sisters, who'd asked for qualities much harder to find than a huge libido and the imagination to match. In addition to the fact Meredith had a soft spot for their father, she had to protect an unblemished record for matching all her clients with their perfect mates.

So far, the only admirable features Pearl had noticed about her mate were his massive cock and balls, and a mindless, almost 'bot-like skill at wielding them within her cunt and ass.

She scrambled up from the floor, her mind made up. Maybe she'd missed something about Lin that she ought to have noticed. She'd call on the matchmaker. But before she could appeal to Meredith, Alpha Two appeared. In skin-tight pants and shirt that clung lovingly to his every well-developed muscle, he might as well have been naked. As naked as he'd been last night when she'd sucked his clean-shaven cock and balls. Unlike Lin, who wore his black hair cut short and shaggy, Alpha's nicely shaped head was shaved in the style most Obsidion males preferred. Like Lin, Alpha's expression was blank, as though he had not the ability to register pain, joy... anything.

His cock, however, drew and held her gaze, hardening and thickening before her eyes. If Lin didn't want to fuck her, maybe Alpha did. Pearl's juices began to flow. Her nipples turned hard and ached for attention. Her clit swelled and ached.

Hmmm. Lin had alluded to her *other* needs When she looked at Alpha and saw his visible state of arousal, she surmised he was well equipped to take care of those needs, whatever they might be. "I don't need a tour of my master's house. What I need is for you to fuck me."

"Your -- wish -- is -- my -- command."

The words sounded good. The fact they were uttered slowly and distinctly, in a voice free of any inflection, disturbed Pearl -- not enough, however, to make her send Alpha away. "Then show me to your fucking chamber." She thought it seemed, well, unseemly, to have Alpha do her in her master's bed.

* * *

"These -- are -- my -- quarters." Alpha opened a door at the end of a narrow hallway off the room where Pearl had taken the tea and pastry, and stood back for Pearl to enter. What she saw made her mouth drop open.

There were the other five of the attendants who'd readied her for the mating yesterday, lined up against one wall. If she hadn't known better, she'd have said they were mannequins like the ones merchants used to display clothing in their stores, for she detected no motion. Not the first rise or fall of a muscular chest, not even a twitch of an eyelid among the lot of them. No, these guys weren't merely sleeping. They showed not one single sign of life. "What the fuck?"

"I -- do -- not -- compute -- Mistress -- Pearl."

"What are your pals doing in here, lined up against the wall like cordwood?"

Alpha hesitated so long Pearl imagined his mind whirring away like a computer. "Are you a fucking robot?"

"I -- am -- processing -- your -- question -- mistress. One -- moment -- please."

The guy she was about to fuck even sounded like a fucking robot. Maybe -- the idea came to her like a light bulb bursting in and illuminating the darkness -- maybe her mate had an army of very special sexbots. After all, his father was renowned for building the best that could be had.

Nah, couldn't be. These guys didn't look like 'bots. They hadn't felt like mechanical toys -- no matter how cleverly made. Pearl lifted an eyebrow toward Alpha Two, as if an exasperated look might hurry him in his thoughts.

"Yes. We -- are -- sexbots. Specifically -- programmed -- to -- meet -- your -- needs."

"I knew it!" Pearl didn't know whether to laugh or hit something. She imagined Lin bent over a mainframe, orchestrating every move, playing the 'bots like violins and her like a fucking fool. Or a hot mate he thought he needed help to satisfy.

Alpha Two grasped her hand, practically dragging her to the big bed in the center of the room. Pearl didn't like this, not one bit, living in a house full of 'bots that could pass for people -- with a mate who exhibited no more feelings than the sexbot she was about to fuck.

Alpha's cock had tasted real enough last night, though. Very real. The slightly salty taste of him lingered even now in her memory. Her cunt twitched. By the gods, her mate had invited this super-sexbot to fuck her, so who was she to disobey? Shooting a come-hither smile, realizing as she did that the 'bot needed no encouragement, she slipped off her robe and stretched out on the bed. "I command you to make me come."

Methodically, Alpha Two stripped off his clothes, first the soft-soled boots which he toed off and set by the bed. Then, with efficiency of motion, he drew his shirt over his head, paused a moment, and tackled the closure of the skin-tight breeches. Pearl had trouble remembering he wasn't alive -- hard to believe the hard muscles and throbbing cock were products of some genius's imagination, and the handsome face had been conjured up by that same fiend. Lin?

Could be, she decided. Or Lin's father might have made these creatures. In any case this one made her pulse race and her mouth water when he lay beside her and... nothing.

"You -- need -- to -- instruct -- me -- mistress."

Instruct? Oh, yeah. Alpha could talk, in a manner of speaking, but apparently he had no imagination. Since listening to his halting speech turned her off, she reached over and grabbed his hands. "Touch me. Taste me. Fuck me. Oh, and don't speak." Surely he could process such a simple order.

Obviously he got the "touch me" part, because he rolled over on his side, sat up, and stroked her cheek, tracing around her lips with a finger before moving on to her throat and shoulders. When he reached her breasts he gently kneaded them, paying special attention to her nipples by rolling them between thumbs and forefingers.

What Alpha was doing to her felt good, yet impersonal. Pearl felt as though disembodied hands explored her, paying as much attention to her prominent hipbones as they did to her clit and pussy lips. She was discovering erogenous zones she hadn't realized before were sensitive, such as -- "Oh gods yes, do that some more!" -- matching spots behind each knee that nearly made her jump out of her skin when he caressed her there. "Stop." The sexual tension suddenly was too much.

He did. Stop. Completely. When she opened her eyes he'd sat up and was staring down at her, arms folded across his chest as though awaiting further instructions. Pearl wanted a fucking *man*, not a fucking sexbot! She wanted one who'd take the initiative, make her come until she couldn't come anymore...

Where the fuck was Lin? How dare he leave her to this... this automaton. If he'd looked like a sexbot, she'd have expected to tell him exactly what to do and when to do it. But by the gods, he looked like a man. A drop-dead gorgeous, beautifully endowed male animal with a computer for a brain. Literally.

Pearl's cunt contracted, as though telling her she needed satisfaction. "Get down between my legs and lick my pussy," she snapped, the way she had done to her own metal and plastic 'bot before her mating.

"Not -- understanding -- mistress."

One of the 'bots against the wall -- this one tall, blue-eyed, and buff -- suddenly came to life and strode purposefully to the bed. Silently he stretched out between Pearl's legs and began to lick the length of her slit, using his tongue to pierce her cunt and lap the juices there. He covered her clit with his lips, sucked, nibbled...

"Oh gods, yes." The waves of pleasure coursed through her, left her drained -- yet needing more. Pearl needed a man, and she was about to go find one. A real man, with a real brain and real feelings.

Chapter Four

What was going on with Alpha Two and his mate? As hard as Lin fought to hold his concentration, he couldn't keep Pearl off his mind. He plotted adjustments he needed to make to the Alpha series of sexbots in order to ready them for the marketplace, but none of the models he tried were working.

"Cannot build the sorts of 'bots you're working on, my son. If sexbots look and act like people, our customers will expect them to have real feelings. They will be sorely disappointed." Pak Song's words rang in Lin's ears, but he wasn't yet ready to accept them. He'd been perfectly satisfied with the Omega female prototype he'd been using in his bed for close to six months. After one night with Pearl, he was beginning to realize how a customer might find himself dissatisfied with an Omega.

Especially a customer who'd experienced sex with a real, living woman. Lin's cock swelled, but he was thinking about Pearl's soft mouth, her tight wet cunt. Not the Omega Pocket Pussy he usually used to take the edge off his lust while he continued with his work.

Fuck. Lin wanted nothing and no one to intrude in his neat, ordered life, or distract him from his quest to make the galaxy's finest sexbots -- better even than the ones his esteemed father sold. He didn't need his mate invading his mind, keeping him from accomplishing what he'd set out to do. What he definitely didn't need at the moment was a raging hard-on, which came up the moment he pictured her joining him here, kneeling before him, taking his cock in her mouth the way she had last night for Alpha Two.

Damn it. She might be sucking him off again right now.

And he shouldn't care. Didn't care. Alpha Two was only a 'bot, and it was only doing what Lin had programmed it to do.

All the gods be damned, he did care. Rolling his chair back from the computer console, he got up, made for the door. Sat back down. He wouldn't give in to his emotions. He mustn't.

Determined to take care of the inconvenient problem expediently, Lin unfastened his pants, took the Omega Pocket Pussy out of the drawer, and sighed when it encircled his cock in a tight, rhythmically undulating grip, moving up and down on him, wiggling from side to side. He closed his eyes, let the sensations take him...

Until he reached out to hold his mate and there was no one there. By the gods, he no longer wanted simple satisfaction, though he felt his climax coming on. He wanted a woman. His woman.

No! He would fuck his mate, but he would not allow his emotions to become involved with her. Never. He forced himself to concentrate on his cock, on the tightness in his balls... on the release he realized would bring physical satisfaction.

But not contentment.

* * *

Restless, Pearl paced through her new home, looking for something -- any hints as to what might have shaped her new mate. Nothing. No expense had been spared in building and furnishing his home. The sparse but elegant furniture, construction details like this curved glass window spanning two stories and looking out on a courtyard planted in various exotics from around the galaxy, all pointed to the fact Lin appreciated the finer things life offered.

But there was no color. No vibrant affirmation of life.

Even the plantings in the courtyard featured specimens in almost monochromatic shades of gray-green. No whites, no brightly colored flowers like the ones in her father's garden dotted precisely manicured beds bordered by stone walkways. The reddish brown stones along the walkways lent the nearest thing to warmth to the scene.

Lin's house, like Lin himself, displayed no emotion... no heat. Pearl couldn't help thinking he must have made himself into a living, breathing creature much like the cyborgs his father was famed for having produced.

Was Lin a cyborg, too? Or, gods forbid, a sexbot? Pearl shuddered. If she had to spend a lifetime with someone who never smiled, never exhibited joy or pain, she knew she'd die. She'd asked for a man who would satisfy her craving for wild, imaginative sex. Meredith had found her one -- and at the time Pearl had been thrilled at the idea of mating with a man whose sexual arsenal included high-tech sexbots and toys beyond what most men could amass, and whose personal prowess was known throughout Obsidion.

But Pearl had wanted more than that. She'd wanted a man, not a super sexbot without a heart. She hadn't realized how sex without emotion would leave her feeling empty, unsatisfied. Of course she hadn't even considered until she met Lin yesterday at the ceremony that she might be mating with a man without feelings. She hadn't had a clue men like him existed.

Pearl turned away from the garden that so reminded her of its owner. If she was to stay here -- and she wasn't at all sure she was -- there would be a lot of changes made. She couldn't live without color, without variety in textures, in sound, in shapes. Most of all, she couldn't live without laughter -- or tears.

Alpha Two walked along beside her, saying nothing. The 'bot hadn't uttered anything in its halting monotone since she'd ordered it to be silent hours earlier. If Alpha had been a living thing, she'd have accused it of sulking because she'd put a halt to their fuck session before he'd had a chance to come.

I'm losing my fucking mind! Everybody knew sexbots didn't come. Or have feelings to be hurt. Alpha's silence was beginning to grate on her nerves. "You. Where is my mate?"

Nothing.

Alpha probably was keeping its mouth shut because she'd ordered it to, so Pearl figured if she wanted an answer, she'd best rescind that command. "You may speak. Answer my question."

"Works -- office -- upstairs."

"Take me to him." Pearl intended to have words with Lin, and she didn't plan on waiting for the opportunity until he had her bound to the fucking bed in his bedroom.

Alpha shook his head. "Cannot -- disturb -- Master."

The 'bot might be afraid of disturbing Lin, but Pearl wasn't. "Leave me, then. I will find him for myself."

"Find whom?"

Pearl turned to see Lin approaching, his expression as inscrutable as the 'bot's. "You, damn it."

"Is that the proper way to speak to your master?" He turned to Alpha. "Leave us."

Alpha bowed, then strode away. Pearl parked her hands on her hips and looked up at Lin. "That's the way I speak to my sexbots. Are you one of them?"

A tiny hint of a smile played on Lin's lips. "I fear not even my esteemed father is capable of building a sexbot who lives and breathes and can build other 'bots. No, I am very much alive."

"Then you're a cyborg?"

"I'm afraid not. I am a living being, unaltered, just as you are. A being who at this moment wants to ease his lust within his mate's tight, wet cunt." Lin clasped Pearl's hand and dragged her down the hallway to his bedchamber.

Pearl balked at the door. "Just a minute here. Are you bringing in your sexbot army?"

"Do you want me to?"

"No!" She'd had enough of fucking 'bots. If she was going to fuck, she wanted to fuck with a living, breathing, *feeling* creature. She wanted her mate to -- she struggled a minute for the term Garnet had used the other day when she talked about having sex with Romulus -- make love to her. She liked the sound of lovemaking, as if there was something involved beside cocks and cunts and screaming orgasms. "I want to give you pleasure, and by the gods, I want that pleasure to show."

Lin looked bewildered, but he pulled her inside, shut the door, and proceeded to take off his clothes in much the same manner as Alpha had done hours earlier. Come to think of it, Lin even looked like Alpha once Pearl lowered her gaze below his rather unique face.

"Undress," he ordered tersely.

"I understand more than a few words, unlike the sexbots you're obviously used to fucking. If you want me undressed, I suggest you undress me."

There. A small spark showed in his chocolate brown eyes -- anger, she guessed, since she was supposed to be obeying him without question. Instead of saying anything, however, he jerked her robe off and tossed it to the floor, then drew her down onto the bed where she'd awakened alone several hours earlier.

He ground his hips against hers, the action smacking of barely controlled violence. "Does this feel as though I'm unaffected? Does it?" As quickly as he'd taken on the almost desperate tone, he seemed to regain the robot-like control she was coming to hate. "Spread your legs," he ordered, his tone matter-of-fact.

"No."

"Yes." His motion smooth, controlled, he nudged her legs apart and knelt between them, his rigid cock throbbing against her swollen outer lips. "Wrap them around my waist. Do not make me bind you."

His dark eyes glittered. Sweat beaded on his brow. Maybe he wasn't as unaffected as he appeared. Who was she kidding? He obviously wanted to fuck her. He had all the physical signs of arousal. Was she trying to read them as emotion? When he drew back, found her cunt, and thrust home, she forgot she wanted more.

He gave her all she'd ever wanted, all the power of a man intent on taking her with him, driving them both over the edge on a wild ride to ecstasy. Her muscles contracted around him, holding his searing heat inside her. With every move he made, pressure built, spilling over, sapping her strength to resist. All she could do was focus on the delicious friction of his cock driving into her cunt, the sucking sounds when he withdrew, the slapping of his balls against her swollen flesh when he thrust deep. Over and over.

He was unrelenting, gathering her up and taking her for the ride, until she couldn't think... couldn't move... could feel his hot flesh searing her, driving her over the edge to a place where there was only his pulsating cock, her throbbing cunt... and hot sensations draining her, sapping her yet carrying her along the most erotic journey she'd ever experienced.

She came and came and came, over and over, barely recovering before he swept her up again. Drained, certain she could come no more, she screamed out her pleasure once again when he let go and came inside her, the long, hot bursts triggering a mutual climax that left them both barely hanging on to consciousness.

* * *

Once again, when Pearl awakened, she found herself alone and lonely in the big, soft bed, surrounded by the lingering smell of Lin... of musk and sandalwood cologne and sex.

He'd felt it, too, the raw emotion that had fueled the searing sex they'd shared. She'd seen fire in his dark eyes, watched his expression change from bland to intense when he'd sunk into her cunt and begun to move. When he'd finally come, she'd seen tears in those eyes... and a real smile on his lips.

She didn't understand. Why was he trying to deny he had feelings? It didn't make sense. Maybe Meredith... Pearl had intended to go see her earlier, before Lin had found her in the courtyard. If anybody could tell her how to reach into her mate's soul, it would be the matchmaker.

She'd go now, before Lin or one of the 'bots came back. At the very least, she would have a few choice words for the matchmaker, for having picked her a man who seemed as devoid of feelings as any sexbot. Most of the time, anyhow.

Chapter Five

A visit from Pearl on the day after her mating? This didn't bode well, Meredith thought as she rose to greet her guest. "What brings you here, my darling?"

"Pak Lin has no feelings. I might as well have mated with my sexbot. Speaking of 'bots, did you realize he used them yesterday as his attendants? I refuse to be nothing more than a living 'bot to be ordered about at his whim and set back on a shelf until he wants me again."

"Now, now. One thing at a time, please." Uh-oh. Meredith had wondered about Pak Song's stoic young son, but the father had assured her he was a lusty boy, more than capable of satisfying Pearl's sexual demands. "Sit down, dear, and tell me what is wrong. Surely you are mistaken. The young men who attended you at your mating certainly were not robots. Do you mean they are cyborgs?"

"No. They're sexbots. Lin admitted as much. He created them. I saw them today, in the room where he keeps them propped up against a wall like so many pieces of furniture. The only way I knew they're 'bots was they -- well, anyway, Alpha Two, it was the only one of them that spoke -- sounded funny, as though it was waiting for a computer to calculate what it should say."

"My, my." Either Pearl had a healthy imagination or Lin had managed to go one step farther down the road toward making Meredith's profession obsolete than his father had done a decade earlier by inventing 'bots like the one now recharging in her bedroom. "From what you tell me, I'd say you're feeling overwhelmed, my darling. I'd think, loving sex the way you said you do, having a vast choice of 'bots like these you describe -- as well as a virile mate like Lin -- would make you ecstatic."

"It would. Except Lin might as well be another of them. He has no feelings. No emotion. He fucks me, very well I might add -- " Pearl's fair cheeks turned a pretty pink, as though the memory of the fucking was so vivid it embarrassed her. "-- but he doesn't want me for anything else except sex."

Words bubbled out from Pearl's lips, about Lin's blank expressions, the sterile and colorless environment in which he chose to live. She went on about the fact that he closed himself in his workroom, emerging only to have sex with her and returning immediately afterward. "Meredith, he never sleeps. He says he's not, but he might as well be just another one of the sexbots he's created. I can't live with a man who doesn't have a heart."

Meredith could easily see Pearl's point, but she wasn't sure what advice she should give the poor girl. "Hmmm. I'd say the young man needs some stimulation. Not in bed, for from what you tell me it seems he has the sex part down quite well. You say he became angry when you defied him... Yes, dear, I know you said the anger lasted only for a moment, but the mere fact he became that way at all tells me Lin is not emotionally void."

"If not void, then certainly he's emotionally deprived."

"Yes, he is." Meredith recalled the occasions over the years when she'd had social contact with Pak Song and his only son. Lin had been a quiet, studious boy, encouraged by his father to pursue his interest in robotics rather than interact with other children of his class. She remembered his mother had died young, which might have had much to do with Lin's inability to communicate with members of the opposite sex.

"I believe Lin is afraid of caring for you -- he's probably afraid to care much for anything with a will of his or her own. You must teach him it's all right to use all his senses -- to feel rather than think, to see beyond the obvious, hear the message beneath the words.

"Now he tastes and smells only the sweet, sour, and bitter basics -- you want to show him how to revel in the nuances of life's infinitely varied experiences." From all Pearl had said, Meredith deduced the best -- possibly the only -- way Lin could be taught was through sex. "Use his clever submission devices on him. Restrain him. Show him before he can be your master, he must submit, accept the feelings your touch evokes in him. Teach him he can afford to show his anger, his joy -- by letting his feelings out he can bring pleasure not only to you but to himself."

"But how? Lin is hardly likely to lie down and let me strap him onto a fucking platform or tie him to the bed."

"Darling, use his sexbots. From what you say, it seems he has programmed at least some of them to follow your every command. Command they restrain him. Then do to him what he did to you in the ceremony. Use them to arouse him as they aroused you. Drive Lin to the point where he can do nothing but give in to the emotions he has kept inside him all his life."

Pearl smiled. Meredith detected a devilish gleam in her eyes and imagined the young robotics expert was in for a night unlike any he'd ever experienced.

After Pearl left, Meredith went to her room and eyed her eleven-year-old sexbot. Her pussy creamed, thinking of the hot sex and hotter 'bots her young client had described. Perhaps the time had come to trade her sexbot in for a new and improved model... but then she considered how much nicer having a living man would be. They could share so much, all the joys and sorrows of living. A man like Eli the jeweler, who now was as alone as she.

Just maybe Meredith would quit letting Pearl's still very desirable father mourn for his lost Sadie and make a living match for herself. Yes, that was exactly what she'd do!

Chapter Six

On the way home, Pearl detoured by the Street of Slaves, but she ignored her favorite sex toy stores in favor of the merchants hawking exotic imports from all over the galaxy. Her enthusiasm building with each purchase, she picked out a bright cushion here, a colorful bolt of fabric there. She selected several flats of vibrantly colored flowers to add some zing to the courtyard, a brilliant-hued coverlet for Lin's bed. At this point she didn't care whether or not he'd like the changes she intended to make in his house -- or in him.

Back home with her purchases, Pearl set about putting her mark on Lin's sterile house. While he holed up in his workroom, she transformed the dining area with colorful cushions, bright dishes, and a huge bouquet of multicolored straw flowers she'd found in the import store across the street from Pak Song's Sexbot Emporium. Once everything was arranged to her satisfaction, she ordered a meal rich in color and textures -- one she and Lin could eat with their fingers.

Testing Meredith's assumption that she could order at least some of the lifelike sexbots to do her will, she commanded Alpha Two and the 'bot who'd licked her pussy so well to plant the red, purple, and white flowers she'd bought among all the greenery already growing in the courtyard. Finally she stripped away the gray duvet cover on the bed where she and Lin had slept and replaced it with a cut-velvet coverlet in a hundred tones of rose and red. She could hardly wait to see him laid out on it, as bound and helpless as she'd been last night.

The idea of tying down her mate and having her way with him made Pearl chuckle. The matchmaker might have given her the idea, but she was well on the way to making it her own. Just as she was turning his house into their home, she'd turn Lin into a lover. Hers.

* * *

As night descended on Obsidion, Lin roused himself from the calculations that had perplexed him all afternoon. Perhaps after dining he could solve the problem of the sexbots' halting speech. He'd have resorted to using a more powerful thought synthesizer, except doing so would give the 'bots a dangerous level of independence. Lin shuddered at the frightening possibility that he might inadvertently create a robot with a will of its own.

An interesting combination of smells assaulted his nose as he made his way downstairs. Not unpleasant. Just different from the aroma of his usual fare of roast fowl, rice, and vegetables.

Pearl's doing, he imagined. If switching around their diet kept her occupied, she could change the menu any way she wanted. Food was food, fuel for his body and his mind. If his mate wanted variety, he didn't mind. Turning the corner into the dining room, he couldn't help noticing the blaze of riotous colors she'd mixed in with the unobtrusive beiges and grays he'd chosen.

He started to comment but did not. Color, after all, was a minor issue unworthy of his concern. Sitting at the head of the table, he waited for a 'bot to serve him.

Not a 'bot. Pearl. Garbed in something see-through that flowed around her like a cloud, she came bearing a tray filled with something steaming. Whatever it was, it smelled delicious, made his mouth water. The outline through the gauzy material of her naked thighs and her full, firm breasts had his cock standing at attention, ready for action. When she set the tray before him, he had difficulty restraining himself from dragging her onto his lap and fucking her then and there.

"Let me feed you." Her voice sounded smooth, sweet, not unlike the pool of amber honey he'd noticed in a small oval bowl beside a bowl of fruit. Moving gracefully, she picked up a spear of fresh pineapple and dipped it, then brought the dripping fruit to his lips. When he took a bite, she leaned over and licked a stray drop of honey off his lower lip and chin. "Good?" she asked.

"Yes." Too good. She was too disturbing to his tightly controlled emotions. He was too tempted to let go, to give in and let his beautiful mate worm her way into his mind. But he must not. "I could program a 'bot to feed me. I do not need you for this," he said, schooling his expression to one of supreme indifference.

"Indulge me." Her voice poured over him, as soft and sweet and smooth as the honey. "I added some colors here and there. The place needed cheering up."

"I noticed." She obviously wanted praise, but Lin wasn't about to tell her how much the bright colors reminded him of her -- or admit he was beginning to see her as a ray of light in what had been his dull but predictable world. "Since you seem determined to feed me, I will try one of those prawns."

He couldn't resist the urge to suck her soft fingertip into his mouth, savor the sweet aftertaste of honey mingled with some piquant sauce from the fat, succulent piece of shellfish she'd just dropped into his mouth. His hunger for food was only exceeded by the need -- something beyond the ache in his groin, he feared -- to take her, master her before she had him turned to a quivering mass of out-of-control emotions tumbling end over end to fulfill her every whim.

It was all he could do to resist taking her, to endure the sensual onslaught of all her colors, flavors, and textures on his ordered world.

Finally. The tray was empty but for a few drops of glistening honey and the tails from a dozen or more of the prawns. "I have eaten enough," he said, rising and pulling her to her feet. "Come, I have a very different hunger."

* * *

Pearl held her breath, praying to all the gods Lin would not see the 'bots until it was too late. Good. Alpha Two grabbed his arms, and Alpha Four -- the magic tongue was how she thought of that one -- had his legs in what looked like a death grip. Lin struggled mightily but could not break free.

"I command you to put me down," he said, his voice as calm as his actions were frenzied.

"Mistress -- commands -- we -- restrain -- you."

The look on Lin's face was priceless. Consternation, confusion -- and yes, even a bit of righteous fury, Pearl thought with satisfaction. She watched the sexbots wrestle her mate onto the brightly covered bed and restrain him there, spread-eagled and ready for whatever sensual tortures she might devise. She picked up a dagger and brandished it before Lin's eyes.

"What...?"

"This." In one deft motion she split his shirt and pants from neck to crotch, ripping the fabric away, baring him for her pleasure. Then she set the dagger down and captured his lips with her mouth, tongue-fucking them, preventing him from protesting as the portion of the bed beneath his hips gave way. Alpha Four took Lin's hard cock in its mouth while Alpha Two crawled under his legs, pulled away the remnants of Lin's pants, and got into position on the lowered mattress to fuck his naked ass. At first Lin struggled, but soon he was tangling his tongue with hers, moaning into her mouth as he bucked against his bonds.

He was ready. Ready to learn she was more than a 'bot, more than the Omega pussies the Alphas had told her about -- her rivals for Lin's affection. Pearl dismissed Four with a wave of her hand. Moving gracefully over Lin, never losing contact with his mouth, she sank her swollen, wet cunt onto his straining cock.

Gods but Lin was huge. His massive cock stretched her beyond anything she'd known from the 'bots she'd enjoyed. When Four fit its cock into her ass, she thought she'd explode. Her clit brushed Lin's smooth groin with every downward stroke. Two's energetic pummeling of its master's ass reverberated into his cock, her cunt, her ass.

Lin wrenched his head away, made a masterful effort to buck free. "Damn you all, I don't want this." His fingers curled into tight fists, and his biceps bulged as he fought to free himself. Sweat ran down his chin, settled in his Adam's apple as he struggled. Suddenly he went still. "Gods no, I'm coming. I don't want to... Fuck me. Fuck me harder. Don't. Don't -- stop!"

He came and came and came, each hot burst triggering another wave of ecstasy through Pearl's body. "Leave us, Alphas," she ordered between gasps of pleasure, certain that if they didn't, she and Lin would both die from the incredible sensations.

Afterward, once they'd both begun to breathe normally, Pearl loosened Lin's restraints, placing soft kisses on the red marks they'd made on his wrists and ankles before pushing the button to reposition the missing section of bed. "Why don't you want to love me?" she asked quietly, her head resting on Lin's broad chest. "How can you expect to be my master if you can't submit to your own feelings?"

He shot her a nonplussed look. "I submitted to you just now, didn't I?"

"Well, yes, you did. But you had no choice. I want you to make love with me because you want to."

He sat up, rearranging her so she lay across his lap. "I don't want to care. When I've cared, I've lost whatever I care for." While his tone was bland, the look in his eyes hinted at heartrending loss.

"What have you cared for?" Pearl kept her voice calm, though she made no move to smooth the lines of strain from around his thin but sensual lips.

"Elvira." The word came out cracked, broken. As though it pained him even to say it.

It pained her, too, to see her stoic mate so distraught. Wanting to soothe him, she reached up and caressed his cheek. "Who was Elvira?" she asked more sharply than she'd intended.

"Not a woman, my jealous mate. Elvira was my Earth-cat. Pak Song brought her back to Obsidion from the last trip he made to take sexbots to the rulers of the Federation. I was only eight years old." His voice broke, just barely, yet enough for Pearl to notice and give him a soothing hug. "Every night Elvira would curl up beside me, and her purring would put me to sleep. One cold day one of the 'bots let her outside. She curled up inside the warm motor of a customer's transporter. When he started the engines to prepare for blastoff, Elvira was a goner."

That hurt, just to picture how Lin had lost his pet, but Pearl attempted to redirect his memories. "But while you had her, you loved her. Surely you didn't use up all your love on her." She was beginning to understand how Lin might want to guard his emotions -- but loving and losing one childhood pet couldn't be the whole reason he'd decided to climb into a protective shell of self-absorption. "Tell me the rest. Please. I want to understand."

"When my mother died not too much later, I had nobody who cared. Nobody but my father, who told me I must be strong, listen to my mind and ignore my heart. He encouraged me to put all my energies into learning my trade -- building better, more lifelike 'bots, using them as my companions, instead of living beings."

"Because they couldn't die and leave you?"

"Yes." He paused, as though in deep thought. "I never thought of why I did it exactly that way, but it's true. I build better and more lifelike robots to be my friends -- friends and lovers who will never leave me."

Pearl reached up, framed Lin's stubbled cheeks between her hands. "You don't want to care for me because you're afraid... afraid something will happen to me?"

Lin nodded. "I couldn't take losing someone else."

"You survived losing your mother and your pet. I wager if you had to, you could survive losing a beloved mate as well. I could if I had to." Pearl took his cheeks between her palms, drew him down for a long, deep kiss. "I'd rather love you now and lose you later than never have the joy of loving you at all."

"I must think..." Lin moved to get up, but Pearl refused to be pushed out of his arms.

"Do your thinking right here. Think about how good this feels." She stroked his chest, paying special attention to the flat bronze nipples when they began to harden under her seeking fingers. "Think about how warm I feel in your arms, how incredible our matings make you feel. Most of all, consider how wonderful it is to share your thoughts and dreams with someone who can understand, react. Someone who lives and breathes and loves and wants, same as you."

"I don't want to care --"

"But you do. Hard as you try not to, you care. I'm not going to let you crawl back in your shell. I'm going to make you see the world in all its colors, experience the joys and pleasures as well as the pain. Damn it, Lin, I want to fall in love with you, and I'm going to make you love me back."

* * *

Lin wanted to love her, too, almost as much as he feared the pain of caring and then losing her. Still Pearl edged her way into his heart, with smiles, with small gestures of affection, with thoughtful touches like the aromatic tea she'd brought him this morning while he was working.

He found himself needing her, and not just for the orgasms that beat anything he'd been able to achieve with his Omega woman. He found himself craving the warmth of her slender body, the softness of her that no bioengineered skin could duplicate... her willingness to share not only her body but her soul.

Fuck, he might as well shut down the computer for tonight, because he was getting nothing done for thinking about his mate. Half angry at himself, half resentful of her, he tracked her down, found her in the marble bathing room, her raven hair piled atop her head, beckoning his hands.

"You know, I can get no work done for thinking of you. Of these." Bending over the tub, Lin cupped Pearl's pale breasts, caressing the rosy nipples with his thumbs. "I believe I will have to join you."

"Be my guest." Smiling, she held up her arms, a welcoming gesture like so many others she'd made these past few days.

Her smile warmed his heart as much as it fueled his lust. A glow of contentment spread through him as he shed his clothes and stepped over the rim of the marble tub. When she took his hands, he couldn't resist gathering her in his arms, holding her. Her heart beat in time with his as she drew his head down, joined their lips.

Steaming water swirled around them, a surreal setting that encompassed them like a cocoon, held out everything but him and her and their desire. His cock hardened painfully, yet he was in no hurry for relief, not when it felt so good just to hold her, to nestle his sex with hers, anticipating without the kind of desperation that characterized his matings with his 'bots.

Because Pearl wanted him, as much as he wanted her. Her tiny moans, the arching of her hips toward him, the giving way she opened her lips to his tongue -- no 'bot could do that. Lin wasn't even sure he wanted to create such a 'bot, because Pearl was teaching him quickly the value of a living female as opposed to the Omega woman that sat, unused, in the workroom while Lin made love with his mate.

"Fuck me, please," Pearl whispered against his lips, and Lin was happy to oblige. When he sank once again into her wet heat, she cried out his name. And when he joined her in an earth-shaking climax of his own, he realized he'd gone past the point of no return.

He loved her. He dared not say it yet, but he did. "I thank you, my beauty," he said into the fragrant mass of her hair. "Come, let us dry off and go to bed."

Epilogue

"Meredith looks beautiful, don't you think?" Pearl looped her arm through Lin's as they watched the simple ceremony that marked the matchmaker's mating with Pearl's father.

"Yes, she does. Eli looks as though he's thrilled to be mating with her." Lin reached over, tilted Pearl's chin up, and placed a long, deep kiss on her lips.

In three short months he'd come a long way toward breaking out of his emotional shell. Just this morning he'd wakened her, told her he was glad she'd become his mate. Before long, she figured he'd be saying he loved her, though he'd do it in his own good time. She could wait for the words, as long as he made progress every day -- which he was.

Her oldest sister, Emerald, looked on while Prince Arik held their year-old son in the crook of his damaged arm. She was pregnant again, unafraid of producing another boy now that Arik had outlawed the making of eunuchs on Obsidion, even royal ones his father had ordered mutilated because he'd feared they might otherwise seek to usurp the position of the rightful heir.

The new prince or princess and Garnet's first baby would be born within days of each other -- playmates, Pearl thought as she watched the children of two of Eli's servants frolicking near a jeweled fountain. She waved at Romulus's clone Remus and his newest partner who seemed intent on watching the ceremony, then shifted her gaze to Romulus and Garnet, who held hands like newlyweds even now, after more than a year had passed since their mating.

Pearl was content, pleased her father had found happiness again after so many years alone. She looked forward to having Meredith in the family -- after all, they'd all become fond of the matchmaker during the time she'd negotiated the three sisters' matings.

When Lin laid his hand on the curve of her hip, the gesture warmed her, for things like that -- small signs of affection to most -- were milestones for the man who three short months ago had vowed never to care for his mate. He grew more loving, more affectionate, each day, in public as well as when they were alone in bed. Each touch, every fleeting caress, even the heated looks they exchanged told Pearl as loudly as any words how Lin valued her, not just as a convenient sex partner but as a woman.

For her part, she'd come to accept Lin's very special 'bots. They added another, sensual dimension to lovemaking, like the imaginatively made dildos, Omega pussies, and other toys Lin had created to enhance their pleasure -- yet more. There was something incredibly erotic about having a half-dozen males seeing to her satisfaction. When she considered the fact that the Alpha males, unlike living beings, were created by her mate to bring her pleasure, her heart overflowed. Besides that, she liked feeling she was helping Lin by creating a marketing plan to capitalize on his incredible talent.

Pearl covered Lin's hand on her hip, squeezed it, and drew his attention to the six Alphas who even now were looking at them, as though anticipating their next assignment. Pearl could hardly wait to get him back into their bedroom -- a place now filled with color, light -- and pleasure beyond anything she'd fantasized about before her mating. Going up on tiptoes, she found his lips, took them, loved it when he wrapped her in his arms and mimicked the rhythm of lovemaking with his tongue, the rocking of his hard cock against the softness of her belly.

"I love you, my Pearl of Passion," Lin whispered as they watched her father claim the matchmaker as his mate. "Let us go home."

Ann Jacobs

Ann Jacobs has lost track of how many books she's published. At least thirty at last count. That count includes several awards, including Eppies, Golden Quill awards, More Than Magic awards, and two Lories. Ann has multiple personalities -- she also writes as Sara Jarrod, Ann Josephson, and Shana Nichols.

Ann loves to hear from readers. You may contact her through her website, www.annjacobs.us

Changeling Press E-Books
Quality Erotic Adventures Designed For Today's Media

More Sci-Fi, Fantasy, Paranormal, and BDSM adventures available in E-Book format for immediate download at www.ChangelingPress.com -- Werewolves, Vampires, Dragons, Shapeshifters and more -- Erotic Tales from the edge of your imagination.

What are E-Books?

E-Books, or Electronic Books, are books designed to be read in digital format -- on your computer or PDA device.

What do I need to read an E-Book?

If you've got a computer and Internet access, you've got it already!

Your web browser, such as Internet Explorer, Foxfire, or Netscape, will read any HTML E-Book. You can also read E-Books in Adobe Acrobat format and Microsoft Reader, either on your computer or on most PDAs. Visit our Web site to learn about other options.

What reviewers are saying about Changeling Press E-Books

Romancing the Banshee -- Alecia Monaco

"Five Angels! Alecia Monaco has done a tremendous job creating a heart-warming yet passionate story…"
-- *Jessica, Fallen Angel Reviews*

Dragon's Egg -- Lena Austin

"This story moves at a fast pace with a plot filled with surprising revelations about Jack's past. Dragon lore and magic fill the pages, topped with some tender m/m erotica for extra spice."
-- *Kelley, Coffee Time Romance Reviews*

Pink -- Stephanie Burke

"Five flags! If I've ever read anything funnier, I can't remember it. From the first page to the last, I was thoroughly entertained. Not only does Ms. Burke create likeable characters, she makes it fun getting to know them while keeping the sexual heat sizzling!"
-- *Kerin, Euro Reviews*

Feral Magnetism -- Lacey Savage

"Four hearts! Open the windows, because Feral Magnetism is hot, hot, hot!! Lacey Savage has written a story that is sexy, erotic, exciting, and oh so pleasurable."
-- *Stacey Landers, Just Erotic Romance Reviews*

Sundown, Inc: Baby Sham Faery Love
Cat Marsters

"Four cups! Ms. Masters has written a hot, and often times funny, sexual romp of a story. I loved these characters and found Ell to be quite endearing. The sex scenes are hot and plenty. So make sure to buy this book now and read it quickly."
-- *Candy Cay, Coffee Time Romance Reviews*

Changeling Press, LLC

www.ChangelingPress.com

Printed in the United States
102610LV00003B/134/A